P9-AOD-664

Viking Library System
915 Fir Avenue West
Fergus Falls, MN 56537

Withdrawn

2
SECONDS
LATE

Center Point
Large Print

Also by Eric Wilson and available from
Center Point Large Print:

By the Numbers Series:
  1 Step Away

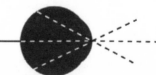

**This Large Print Book carries the
Seal of Approval of N.A.V.H.**

— Book Two —
By the Numbers Series

2 SECONDS LATE

— For Such a Time as This —

Eric Wilson

CENTER POINT LARGE PRINT
THORNDIKE, MAINE

This Center Point Large Print edition is published in the year 2014 by arrangement with Kingstone Publishing, an imprint of Kingstone Media Group.

Copyright © 2013 by Eric Wilson.

All rights reserved.

The text of this Large Print edition is unabridged.
In other aspects, this book may vary
from the original edition.
Printed in the United States of America
on permanent paper.
Set in 16-point Times New Roman type.

ISBN: 978-1-62899-023-2

Library of Congress Cataloging-in-Publication Data

Wilson, Eric (Eric P.)
2 seconds late : for such a time as this / Eric Wilson. — Center Point Large Print edition.
pages cm. — (By the Numbers series ; book 2)
ISBN 978-1-62899-023-2 (Library binding : alk. paper)
1. Large type books. I. Title. II. Title: Two seconds late.
PS3623.I583A613 2014
813'.6—dc23
2013046966

To my family on the Daniels side:

Mary Ann,
an adorable mother-in-law
and a true friend of Jesus;

Elizabeth,
a sister-in-law with a sharp mind
and a big heart for children;

Andrew,
an intelligent young man and brother-in-law;

Ross,
an uncle, who has a generous spirit
and a winning smile;

Mary,
an aunt, who cares deeply for the downtrodden.

And in loving memory of
Ron Daniels,
an uncle who lived and died on his own terms.
My wife and I will always remember
our meal together in Paris.

For if you remain completely silent . . .
you and your father's house will perish.
Yet who knows whether you have come to the
kingdom for such a time as this?

—Esther 4:13&14 (NKJV)

2
SECONDS
LATE

In Her Eyes

"From the time she was born, Natalie's been a live wire. 'Course, no need to tell you that. Some days I wasn't sure I knew how to look after her, especially without her momma 'round to help."

"That was rough on us all."

"There was that time when I was with her at the playground. Not a day over five years old, she's swinging back and forth, thick brown hair falling across her face and then blowing back like the tail on a horse. It was her giggling that almost did it, almost made me forget what I was doing."

"I love her laugh."

"All of a sudden, she comes out of that seat and expects she's gonna be caught. Well, sure, she was fine and dandy, but lemme tell you, it was close. I wished I could just wrap her from head to toe in pillows."

"Sometimes a child has to learn the hard way."

"Oh, I thought she'd never learn. Down on the river, my girl was fearless, not a smidgen of worry. She'd paddle around in the rubber raft like it weren't no big thing, working those thin arms, huffing, puffing, determined to reach the island in the middle. Said she was gonna make her own fire and cook s'mores and camp out with her little sister beneath the full yellow moon. Imagine that."

"She's always had a thing for the outdoors."

"Runs in the family, I s'pose. Even so, I wasn't letting her go on over there alone. Nosiree, not on my watch. You taught me better than that."

"I certainly hope so."

"Now she's all grown, pretty as can be. Till recently, she still had that look in her eyes, like she could handle anything on her own, anything at all. Then this September came along. And that, well, that shook me and her up something fierce."

Chapter One

September 2010

Natalie Flynn cowered in the darkness.

By her count, this was her second day in the abandoned Quonset hut, hands chained behind her back to the interior metal ribbing. The moonlight that poked through dusty windows failed to reach her. Tiger mosquitoes buzzed nearby. Her tongue was dry, and she worked her jaw against the cotton gag that cut across her lips.

She felt weak, having had nothing to eat or drink in over thirty-six hours. At least that meant she had little need for the five-gallon bucket she had been provided as a toilet. She'd used it only once, and that was to pee.

Were the police looking for her? Where would they even start?

Nowadays, millions of pets were microchipped so as to keep track of them, but she'd been stripped of any technology that might lead authorities to her. Her cell phone. Even her iPod.

By now, her manager at the café must be furious, and her roommate frantic. It was Monday, and Natalie should have been in night class at Trevecca Nazarene University, where she was in her final year at the School of Education. She hoped that by next fall she would be teaching elementary school, a lifelong dream that might never come true now.

What, she wondered, did her captor want from her?

He was a stocky man, one of her customers from Sip Café. Magnus, he called himself, as if he were some sort of Greek god. He came on smooth, friendly, even got her feeling sorry for him when he talked about his traumatic boyhood.

And I fell for it. Way to go, estupida.

The previous morning, Magnus had pulled up behind the shop in his black Dodge Charger and flirted with her. Yeah, OK, and maybe she flirted back. She told him to give her two secs and she'd get him a free cup of coffee once she had set up everything for business.

She had pushed through the back door to do her job, never even heard him come in after her. She was running the grinder, inhaling that rich coffee aroma, when she glimpsed him over her shoulder.

Then everything went blacker than the French Roast.

She awoke much later in this sweltering hut. She was alone. Her teeth and her jaw throbbed on the right side, as though she'd been clobbered with a bat. Her gums were tender. Her back was sore. She heard bugs skittering across the floor and the sounds of a river not far away.

The Cumberland? Was she still in Nashville?

The structure's rusty walls flexed and groaned in the late-summer heat. Something fluttered overhead. At the far end of the hut, the door screeched open, and the beam of a flashlight cut toward her. She lowered her eyes and caught a glimpse of a large slump-shouldered figure.

It was him. Magnus.

He opened a bottle of water and dribbled it over her lips. "My little coffee bean," he said, "how're you doing this evening?"

Though she choked at first, the sweet moisture washed the chalky taste from her mouth. He jabbered on, but she wasn't listening to him. This man who had deceived and abducted her and left her in the dark with a paint-bucket porta-potty.

Momentarily rejuvenated, she strained against her shackles, got to her feet, and kicked at him.

"Well, well, you still have some fight in you, Natalie."

He assured her that he didn't mean to break her, only to make her stronger so that she could infiltrate the Vreeland family, her friends from the café.

"They know you. Trust you," he said. "Once you are free and show your wounds, no one will doubt your traumatic circumstances."

Wounds? Oh no. What is he planning?

Magnus offered her one more drink, which she rejected out of anger. She hoped defiance would make her seem less vulnerable, less desirable, but he only shrugged, as though to say it was her loss and not his. Which was true enough.

"Pain," he said, "has its benefits."

Please, don't let him go through with this.

He brought out a retractable antenna, extended it, and a moonbeam slid down its silvery surface. "Now sit yourself down, all the way down."

She felt more alone now than at any time in her life. "And stretch out those pretty legs of yours."

Are You there, God? Hello?

For the first thirty seconds, she cried out against the gag for her dad's help, for the Lord's help, for anyone's help at all. After that, if the pain had any benefit at all, it made her forget her sore jaw and her night classes and her empty stomach. For a while, it made her forget everything.

Crouched in foliage that skirted the overgrown airfield, the Russian heard Natalie's cries. She was in a metal hut, the only one out of five that contained more than rusty oil cans and single-prop engine parts. Each muffled scream stirred memories from his motherland, and he dragged his knuckles across his lips as though to wipe away the taste of rotten meat.

He heard the young woman again, and he shrank farther into the shadows.

"Leave her alone," he whispered.

Orphaned at age seven, Serpionov was thirty-two now, five foot ten weighing 212 pounds of gym-hardened muscle. He avoided steroids and ate farm-grown foods, like his grandmother had raised him to do.

In early 2000 in Moscow, he had applied to be an officer with OMON, the Russian acronym for a special-purpose police unit that handled hostage situations and terrorist threats. After four months of intense training, his final test for admittance pitted him simultaneously against three of the unit's top-notch members. Less than 20 percent of the applicants made it through this, but he was determined to succeed.

The confrontation lasted eight minutes. He snapped the first man's forearm with a kick. Felled the second with a vicious combo of body blow, uppercut, and right hook. Grappled the third to a draw. When they accepted him into their ranks, he wore his broken nose and split eyebrow with pride.

In the years that followed, he did nothing but serve and obey orders.

He also did things he would regret for the rest of his life.

In 2008, Serpionov made a clean break and moved to America. His skill set earned him a living here, and his current assignment included weapons development, asset management, and surveillance. Though he and Magnus were both under contract with a man named Alex Page, Serpionov's job was to monitor Magnus's movements in case he pursued goals of his own.

Already, Magnus had gone off-course. As proof of that, Natalie's screams continued issuing from the hut.

"*Pozhaluista*," Serpionov said in his mother tongue. *Please.*

He had first met Natalie a few weeks ago, at Sip Café in East Nashville. He sat in a corner with his hot tea, scratched the frizzy beard that was then part of his disguise, and observed her over his laptop as she worked. She was attractive, with her tiny nose stud and thick brown hair that high-lighted remarkable hazel eyes. Moscow's Metro stations contained their share of long-legged beauties, but this Tennessean girl had a shorter shapeliness worth admiring.

Serpionov also watched her on the days Magnus came into the café. Neither Magnus nor Natalie took much notice of the bearded man in the corner, but Serpionov didn't mind. He had no trouble getting attention when he wanted it.

Natalie's moans came in intervals now. They crept through the grass, curled past fence posts and oak trunks, and reached through the leaves to the Russian's ears. They tugged at the loose threads in his skull, unraveling the tapestry meant to conceal the memories of his own misdeeds.

What man didn't have secrets to hide? In the battle against evildoers, did anyone from the side of good ever really walk away clean?

Of course not. Such a thing was impossible.

He gazed through the binoculars, wishing he could crush Magnus with his bare hands and carry the captive to safety. He'd been trained in such maneuvers, but it was too late to act now. Whether or not by accident, Magnus had given the unsuspecting girl a role in the events to come.

Serpionov frowned.

This is not my choice, Natalie. You must now play your part.

Chapter Two

October

Exhaustion dragged Natalie down into darkness. She burst back to the surface after sundown, wild-eyed, gasping for breath, hair matted with sweat. Insects flitted along the walls. In the moonlight, she saw wolf spiders prowling the area—nocturnal hunters, aggressive and large. She drew her arms and legs close to her body, hoping the blood on her shins didn't interest them.

The metal hut groaned. She was a tiny morsel, and the hut was the creature trying to digest her and grind her down, hour by hour, minute by minute.

Was that Magnus at the door? She let out a whimper at the thought.

No, chica. *How pathetic. Pathetic and unacceptable.*

She decided that the next time he came to feed her, she would meet his gaze without fear.

Her fears were relentless, though.

Would she die in this place? By the time they found her, would there be any fingerprints left, any facial features to match with a photo? What if they found nothing but bones? With her college expenses, she had not been able to visit a dentist in ages, but surely there were records on file that could confirm her identity.

She told herself death would be all right, if only she knew that her family would be able to bury and remember her. How horrible it would be if they never found her, unaware that she'd been left in some hovel to rot. She hadn't talked to her dad in months. Her younger sis, well, she'd just been released from prison.

As for Natalie's mother, Janet Flynn, she had disappeared when Natalie was three and her sister a year old. She hadn't left any note. There was no evidence of foul play.

Mardy Flynn raised his girls on his own, did the best he could, with occasional help from widowed Grams. After Natalie graduated from Oak Ridge High in East Tennessee, she worked two years to save money for Trevecca. The day she left for Nashville was the first time she ever saw tears in her father's eyes. Having already lost a wife made it that much harder for him to let his daughters go.

Would they ever learn what had happened to Janet?

Had she deserted them? Or had she been stolen away, left to perish in some shack just like the one where Natalie was now held captive?

Despite the barriers of their shared past, Natalie knew that if she died here, her father would be crushed.

Absolutely crushed.

She worked her hands behind her back, found a rock, and scratched out a message on the wall:

Always your girl, Dad—Duckie

On the tenth day, Magnus told her she was free to go. No fanfare. No apologies. He had beaten, starved, and terrified her, but never violated her in any intimate manner. He'd implied that he would keep such delights for later, for the day when she too acknowledged the chemical reaction between them.

The chemical *what?*

FYI, she was not some experiment, and such results could not be manipulated in the lab of his diseased mind.

He stood over her, waiting for her to move. The shackles were loose, and so was the gag. She rose on stiff, scabbed legs. She massaged her jaw,

19

opened and closed her mouth, felt her dry lips crack at the corners.

Magnus nodded toward the exit. "If you want, Natalie, you can take a walk to the nearest neighbor's house and call the police. But don't forget the—"

She charged headfirst, driving her skull into his belly, clawing at his limbs. He laughed and threw her aside. She landed on her knees, her back to him, and grabbed clods of dirt in both hands. Spinning, she flung the dirt into his eyes. He dodged, chuckled, and drove her to the ground with a foot to her ribs.

She groaned, curling into a fetal position.

He told her again she could leave and dropped her cell phone at her side.

"But don't forget our agreement. You keep that phone of yours handy. When I call for help, you will give it without question."

As he rambled on, she blinked back tears and rose to one knee.

"What is our word?" Magnus said. "Just so you'll know that it's me."

"Antenna," she whispered.

"Easy for you to remember, I should think."

She watched him move toward the door. She stood, shuddering. She suspected her legs would be scarred for life, but reminded herself she was still pure and unblemished on the inside. He had not taken that away. At twenty-four years of age, she'd done a bit of coed partying but managed to ward off the grimy paws of her guy friends. Did saving herself for the right man make her America's oldest living virgin? Except for Tim Tebow, maybe so. Her roommate, a chubby blonde, seemed to think nothing of sharing her bed.

Natalie tottered outside, working the tightness from her limbs. She blinked in the moonlight. Gulps of fresh air filled her with sudden emotion.

"Don't do this." She shoved a palm across her cheek. "Don't crumble."

Her thoughts turned from the kids she tutored—Kevin and Katie Vreeland, safe with their parents—to all of the suffering boys and girls out there. Even at this moment, there were kidnapped children who might not live long enough to get another meal or a hug from someone who cared.

Did they know they were loved? Know how very precious they were? Not one of them deserved the horrors of helplessness and abuse.

From across the field, Magnus waved at her. "Keep those antennae up."

Natalie jutted her chin in the other direction, refusing to wave back.

As he walked off into the night, she hesitated. Why had Magnus released her, even urged her to call the police? Sure, he wanted her to "infiltrate" the Vreelands, but did he intend to watch her every step once she was free?

To her right, the waters of the Cumberland lapped at the limestone cliffs on the far side. She couldn't be far from home, and yet for a week and a half she'd been cut off from humanity.

Unheeded cries. Bruised bones. Torn skin dripping beads of blood.

For now, her abductor was gone, and that was all that mattered.

Natalie turned and saw a house up the slope, light glowing in its windows. She had been spared, and she told herself there must be a reason for her survival, some purpose she had yet to fulfill.

Spurred by this conviction, she stumbled on tender legs toward the light.

Chapter Three

December

Serpionov stood on the CSX train trestles that bridged the icy Cumberland River and surveyed the carnage along the banks below.

A late-night showdown had occurred. Two dead bodies lay sprawled on the lot of the dilapidated Storinka Defense Systems warehouse, and a third man, Bret Vreeland, had survived with a bullet-torn thigh. Bret's family huddled nearby, while a detective knelt beside him and gestured an ambulance into position.

Serpionov eyed Magnus, the larger of the dead men. "Arrogant American, you failed," he mumbled. "But this, it is of no concern to me."

Serpionov took note of three things:

1. His subject of surveillance, Magnus, was now a corpse.
2. Their employer, Alex Page, was the second corpse.
3. Natalie, the Vreelands' tutor, was still alive.

As the ambulance pulled away from the warehouse lot, he shifted his focus to the young woman who stood shivering by the police car. Natalie's role in this drama was only beginning, and he did not envy her that.

The iron trestle was cold. He pushed away, flipped open his phone, heard it come to life with the classic Police song "Every Breath You Take." In addition to this cell's ability to perform its normal functions, it was a nod to old-school KGB spyware. By tapping in the correct combination, he could arm it with four $5.45 \times 18mm$ cartridges. As a former OMON officer, he preferred a PP-19 Bizon submachine gun, but if he fired even one of these smaller rounds through an ear canal or an eyeball, it would scramble the brain.

Already the cell phone had claimed five victims.

Five dropped calls.

Serpionov dialed the encryption-protected line

to his employer, headquartered in Seattle, and heard the familiar telltale click.

"Make this worthwhile," Darcy answered. "You're on my private line."

"Your husband, Alex, is dead," he told her. "I do not know, but I think he and Magnus killed each other in the moments before I arrived."

"Dead? Why does that not surprise me?"

"This, it doesn't make you upset?"

"I'm deeply traumatized," Darcy said. "What about the prototype?"

"It's in Magnus's car, in long-term parking at Nashville International."

"Well, go fetch it. There are millions of dollars at stake here. U.S. dollars, not that stuff you Russians call currency."

"*Nyet.* I no longer work for you. You forget this, I think."

"I'm still your boss, and I'm giving you a raise, effective immediately."

"I want double," he said. "Twelve thousand a month."

"Eight. Plus the lease on your condo."

He grinned. "When I see it in my account, yes, I go back to work."

"You're still my employee, as I said at the start. Serpent? Scorpion? Whatever your name means, sink your teeth in and don't you let go."

Serpionov vowed to do so, ended the call, and returned his gaze to Natalie in the lot below. She probably thought things were over now and she was safe, but tonight was simply the end of a chapter.

This was his story now, his plot to twist and tell.

Far below, the streets of Seattle bustled. Darcy Page strutted from the window to her desk of exotic coconut wood, and folded her limbs into the padded chair. Serpionov was hers to use. Magnus, on the other hand, had been a fool. Nevertheless, his errors had provided her an opportunity to test the company's most promising technology.

"You've left me in a tight spot," she said to the photo of her ex-husband.

Propped on the desk even after the divorce, the picture reassured stockholders that personal differences would never undermine the company's strength. Now, with Alex's demise, she must produce quick results before investors started jumping ship.

Darcy tapped the picture frame with a fingernail and watched the image of a dead man tumble into the wire trashcan.

Chapter Four

Natalie couldn't stop shaking. Her teeth chattered. The lights of the departing ambulance lashed at tree limbs and busted-out warehouse windows, before darkness settled back over the lot.

Katie Vreeland, an adorable second grader, darted over and threw both arms around Natalie's legs. "I'm scared. Is my daddy gonna be OK?"

"I don't know," Natalie said. As an aspiring teacher, she believed children needed honesty, not platitudes. She looked down into Katie's round blue eyes. "He's pretty banged up, but we'll go see him in the hospital and tell him to get better."

"My ears still hurt. I don't like guns."

"Me neither."

"He was brave, huh? And Kevin too."

"*Si, muchacha*," Natalie said in her stilted Spanish. "You better believe it."

As she spoke the words, guilt gripped her throat. Where was her own bravery in all this? The entire fiasco stemmed from her days chained in that hot metal hut, from ten long nights fending off bugs from her open wounds. After Magnus released her in early October, he had manipulated those fears and used her to keep tabs on the

Vreelands right up until tonight. He vowed that any refusal to cooperate would result in little Katie suffering bodily harm.

Not like Natalie had any good alternatives. She couldn't run, couldn't hide. He seemed to anticipate every move that she and the Vreelands made.

It had all culminated earlier today. Magnus ordered her to lead the family to a specific limo at the airport, and then he steered them to this deserted section of town. Although Magnus's schemes backfired and cost him his life, Bret's blown-out thigh would require months, even years, of healing and rehabilitation.

And I'm to blame. Magnus fired the gun, but I led them right to him.

"You're still gonna be our tutor, aren't you?" Katie said.

"I, uh . . ."

"You have to, Natalie. Pleeease."

"Only if your parents still want me."

"Of course, we want you," Sara Vreeland said, moving closer. "Listen, Detective Meade's arranging for someone to drive us to Vanderbilt Medical."

"Where Daddy went?"

"They'll take good care of him," Sara assured her daughter. "I'm sure he'll be back on his feet in no time."

She was wrong, though.

Within hours, fragments of the same bullet that had shattered Bret's femur and severed an artery also triggered an infection. Seated in the hospital waiting room, Sara grabbed Natalie's hand as the surgeon delivered the news. Later, the doctors decided there was no other option but to amputate the leg.

Cell phone in hand, Serpionov sat on his Honda Interceptor beneath an overpass by Nashville International Airport. Like most modern Russians, he was a good capitalist who not only held on to certain stubborn ideals but also understood that practicalities preempted everything. Even idealists needed cash flow.

Minutes after midnight, he checked his cell again and learned that a deposit had been posted to his bank account.

Five figures from Darcy Page. Routed through an offshore account.

While he was pleased to know that the death of one of the company's founders had little effect on its solvency, he wondered how Shield Technologies would perform with Ms. Page in sole control. She was a conniver. The fact that she'd increased his pay with hardly a fight meant she had much to gain from his success.

Serpionov left his motorcycle beneath the overpass and strolled toward the airport's long-term parking area, gaze locked on a 2010 Dodge

Charger in the northeast corner. He wasn't too concerned with the security cameras recording his presence from nearby poles. American football baffled him, but the NFL team jacket and cap he wore would blur his form, shade his face, and make nighttime identification difficult.

Go, Titans.

If all went as planned, he would bypass the car's alarm, locate and acquire the desired object, and vanish minutes later on his crotch rocket.

This English language. He was still trying to master its slang.

Three rows over, a young lady with pink boots and a guitar case slung across her back came to a stop beside a Prius. Two rows over, two men climbed into a silver Yukon. On his left, a man with a shaved head paralleled Serpionov's course.

Serpionov stayed alert yet focused on his target.

Only sixty yards to go.

The Charger's registered owner was Magnus, the corpse now headed for a slab in the county morgue. Authorities would not look for his vehicle for another day or two, not while still deciphering the mess outside the old Storinka warehouse. A crime scene chronology had to be established. Blood spatter patterns analyzed. Gunshot angles calculated.

During his time with OMON, Serpionov had worked worse scenes, mopping up the handiwork of rapists, terrorists, and murderers.

Only forty yards.

OMON was founded in 1979. With Moscow hosting the Olympic Games the following year, the unit's initial job was to prevent a massacre such as the one that took place at the '72 Munich Games. The unit grew and multiplied, composed of males between the ages twenty-two and thirty, mostly ex-military, experts in hand-to-hand combat and small arms. To this day, units across Russia dealt head-on with threats from within and without.

His most gruesome memories with OMON involved an incident at Beslan in '04. Chechens in green fatigues, with explosives strapped to their bodies, had challenged Moscow's authority by threatening the lives of hundreds of school kids. "Freedom fighters," they called themselves. In his mind, they were nothing more than terror-mongers and baby-killers.

He could accept that death visited the homes of grown men and women, but he believed it an abomination when death kicked down the doors of the young.

Serpionov shook off the memories. Blocked out the shrieks.

Fifteen yards.

The man paralleling him suddenly veered between the vehicles and reached the Charger first. He was a wedge-shaped fellow, his neck thick, his skull bluish white in the cold.

"Please," Serpionov said, "step away from my car."

"Your car? Oh, that's rich, pal."

"Who do you work for? I'll pay you to leave."

"How 'bout you walk away, and I forget I ever saw your face?"

"You work for the government, I think. Is this true?"

"Me. The government. You're a real card, aren't you? That accent. What are you, Russian?" Though a bulge showed beneath the man's coat, his hands still hung at his sides. "Probably tough as nails, but I've got thirty pounds on you."

Tick-tick-tick . . .

The clock was running in Serpionov's mind, and he knew the only way to his objective was through this buffoon.

"I don't see you moving," the bald man said. "Scram."

"There are security cameras, yes? A fight will draw attention."

"Then I'll make sure to end it quickly."

"Stop." Serpionov lifted his cell, tapped in the code, watched *R-E-A-D-Y* scroll across the screen in luminous green. "Or I will send this call."

"Whatever bloats your diaper, pal."

Serpionov's mercy reached its end. He took two calm steps, aimed the cell, and fired twice into his foe's chest. The small-caliber rounds barely nudged the man back, but his large head dropped as though to stare at the damage, his smooth crown glistened hard and smooth beneath the sodium lights, and he crumpled face-first onto the pavement.

Six dropped calls now. Six people sacrificed for the greater good.

And it is you, I think, who needs his diaper changed.

Serpionov picked up the spent cartridges and searched the man. He found a card from Storinka Defense Systems. *Nyet*, this he didn't expect. Corporate espionage? It seemed he wasn't the only one who knew of this item in the car.

Tick-tick-tick . . .

He rolled the body into the lee of a neighboring SUV, checked the time, and allotted himself three minutes to complete his task. Should security come to investigate, he had two bullets left in his cell. He suspected, though, that these overhead cameras fed into an entire bank of monitors where stored images were checked mostly after the fact, in cases of theft or a fender bender.

Fender bender? Another bit of odd-sounding slang.

He turned his attention to the black Charger, where a blinking dash light warned him of an antitheft system. His training told him that most latest-model automobiles were preprogrammed to interact with cellular networks. While each vehicle's secret number allowed GPS units and roadside assistance to function, it also left the system vulnerable to specially crafted text messages that could disengage an alarm, unlock doors, and even start an engine in some models.

All a matter of pinpointing that unique number.

On his cell, Serpionov used a hacked network administration program to do just that. Ninety seconds later, he grinned and sent a text.

The alarm light winked off.

Locks clicked open.

Tick-tick-tick . . .

He pulled on surgical gloves and started exploring. He found the sturdy yet slender case in the back, cradled by a spare tire beneath the carpet. He ran his fingertips over the letters pressed into the case's black matte finish: SHIELD.

He strapped the item to his shoulders, closed the trunk, and strode past the last row of cars and over a berm of frosty grass. He watched an airport police vehicle loop by and then continued to his Interceptor and let it propel him toward his condo in Nashville's Gulch, a once-forgotten area of train tracks and eroded buildings that now counted as one of the city's trendiest neighborhoods.

Serpionov reached his building at 12:28 a.m. He changed into shorts and a T-shirt and settled onto the couch by the window. Below him, headlights streamed in multiple directions at the interchange between I-40 and I-65.

He opened the Shield case on his lap and basked in its warm amber glow.

Chapter Five

New Year's Eve. This entire situation just didn't seem right.

With purse in hand, Natalie negotiated the maze at Vanderbilt Medical Center and wondered how she should react when she saw Bret Vreeland in his hospital room. Should she avoid looking at his missing leg? Apologize? Or should she ask matter-of-fact questions about the procedure and his options for the future?

She detoured into a women's restroom, locked the stall door behind her, and propped herself on the lowered seat cover.

God, I don't want to face him. I feel so helpless.

Phantom pains stabbed through her legs, and she hiked the cuffs of her jeans to examine the uneven lines on her shins. She fished a small tube from her purse and rubbed lanolin cream into the stretched, shiny ridges of scar tissue.

He was still there, at the edges of her mind.

Magnus. Her abductor.

She saw him standing over her twelve weeks earlier, whipping her bare flesh with that thin metal rod. She had tried so hard not to cry, tried her best, but the tears had come anyway and burned trails down her cheeks.

Stop this. Don't let him live for even a second in your head.

She dabbed more cream onto her skin and thought of a passage the Vreelands had read to her from Isaiah 53: "He was whipped, and we were healed!" It was a reference to the beating Jesus would endure on His way to the Cross, to His sacrifice that brought about healing for those who acknowledged their sin and accepted His gift of salvation.

She had accepted that gift for herself, and now she hoped that her own meager sufferings would remind her to do good for others.

Especially for the neglected children of the world.

The bullied boys.

The abused little girls.

The very thought of someone hurting Kevin or Katie Vreeland infuriated her. She would spend another ten days in that hut, another ten days of hell, if it meant keeping them from the hands of some demented freak.

As for herself, she deserved these scars. No doubt about it. It was her cowardice that had let Magnus lure the Vreelands into his limousine and to the warehouse lot. If not for her, Bret would still have both his legs, and Kevin and Katie would still have a dad who could ride bikes with them and play baseball in the park and teach them how to waterski at nearby Percy Priest Lake.

OK, Natalie, enough with the pity party. 'Least you can still walk.

And that's what she did. She marched back into the hospital corridors and followed the signs to the right. She knocked softly, heard a muffled response, and entered a room with pastel walls and muted lighting. Sara was at the bedside, both arms around her children. They turned and smiled at her.

"Am I interrupting?" Natalie asked.

"Not at all," Sara said. "The kids've been asking about you."

Bret gestured to her to join them. "C'mon in."

Usually strong and broad-chested, he looked small in the bed. His cheeks were drawn, his skin pale. The smell of antiseptics filled the air, and an IV ran from a bag on a portable stand to the needle in his arm. He wore a smile, no doubt to ease his family's worries, but the depths of his loss showed in his eyes.

"Hey," he said. "Join in, if you want. We're just listing all the things I can still do, such as play my guitar."

"And write music," Sara said.

"And give us kisses," Katie added.

Kevin frowned. "Can we still kick around the soccer ball?"

"Sure, buddy. I'll work up to it."

Natalie's mouth felt dry, her tongue swollen

and useless. She hoped Bret didn't notice her gaze as it wandered to the sagging sheet below his torso. How did doctors dispose of amputated limbs? Were they used for medical purposes? Her mind replayed the showdown outside the warehouse, and she wondered what steps she could have taken to stop the gunfire.

"Your turn," Bret said, looking at her. "Let's hear you name one thing."

"You can, uh . . ."

"C'mon."

"Honey," Sara cut in, resting a hand on her husband's shoulder. "You're still a man, fully my man. Don't force her to—"

"You have big arms," Natalie said. "You can still hug your family."

Bret spread his arms wide, stretching the IV tubing to its limits. "You got that right," he said. "Get in here, everyone. Group hug."

"How much longer?" Katie asked, tugging on Natalie's sleeve.

"Only an hour till the ball drops." Kevin pointed at the wall-mounted TV across from his father's hospital bed, where Ryan Seacrest schmoozed with a female pop star and the lights of Times Square blazed at their backs. "What?" he said to his sister. "You gonna fall asleep?"

"I'm not even tired, Kev."

"Then why'd you ask?"

"That's enough," Sara said. "Let's try to keep it down for your dad."

"Here." Natalie pulled Katie onto her lap. "Sit with me for a while. I'm cold."

In the days since her captivity, Natalie had chosen residence with the Vreelands over a university dorm room. She loved her new life, despite the recent calamities, but wished to be closer to her dad and sister this time of year.

Her thoughts flitted back to 1999. She was thirteen, her sister eleven. Ready to ring in the new millennium, they rode with Dad to Gatlinburg, where the three of them huddled beneath a Tennessee Vols blanket, drank hot chocolate from a plaid Thermos, and cheered as fireworks exploded over the Smokies.

Seemed like a lifetime ago. For Natalie, time didn't fly so much as it flapped its wings over the years gone by and cast elusive shadows.

With bottle rockets screaming in the crisp air outside, she failed to hear the hospital room door open behind her. She jolted when a hand touched her shoulder and shot tingling warmth down her arms.

"OMG." She turned. "Eli, when'd you get here?"

"Been here all along." He was wearing Wranglers and a quilted shirt, and his salt-and-pepper hair was combed back from his lively gray eyes. He winked. "Just taking notice now, are ya?"

Natalie had met Eli Shaffokey soon after her

move to Nashville, even before she had befriended the Vreelands. He was a regular at Sip Café. He did janitorial work at the Vreelands' church and had recently moved his camper-pickup next to their house at Groves Park Road in East Nashville. He pruned the bushes, mowed the lawn, and repaired the chain-link fence that contained two dogs and separated their backyard from a steep drop-off onto train tracks below.

Bret hitched himself up in his bed. "Join the party, Eli."

"Only fifty-nine minutes to go," Kevin said.

On TV, the pop star took the stage and launched into her latest hit single. Teens in 2011 glasses and party hats bobbed their heads to the beat.

"Let's turn that off," Bret said. "Whaddya say we share some favorite memories of the last year and pray for what lies ahead?"

"But, Dad, what about our tradition?"

"We'll turn it on just before midnight. Don't worry. You'll see the ball drop."

Ten minutes later, the entire family was chuckling as Bret told of how he got a speeding ticket a few months back. Just then, Natalie's cell vibrated in her pocket. She lowered Katie from her lap and checked the screen.

"It's Abby, my old college roomie," she informed the others. "I'll just make sure she's all right." She stepped out into the corridor and took the call.

"Nattie? That you?" Abby's voice sounded high-pitched and giggly. She was probably two or three drinks into an all-night binge.

"Hi, Abby."

"Where the heck *are* you? Why're you whispering?"

"Long story. I'm with the Vreelands in the hospital."

"De*press*ing. We're hanging at Trey's condo, and everyone's asking about you. It's been, what, a week or two since we talked? Lotsa free booze and Jell-O shots. And the guys in this place? I'm talking some serious hotties. Who to *choose* from? Get yourself over here, and that is not a request."

"Can't make it, Abby. Sorry."

"Ahh, don't tell me you've gone all Goody Two-Shoes on me again."

"I'm looking ahead," Natalie said. "Trying to graduate and—"

"Boooring."

"Thinking about my future and teaching."

"The future? Who said anything about *that?* I'm talking right now, baby."

"You're such a dingbat. Just remember, I won't be there to bail you out."

"Don't worry about me, Nattie. You and the Vees enjoy your sparkling cider."

"Actually, Sara snuck in a bottle of champagne for us adults."

"Sipping the bubs? Sounds *wild*. Ugh, it tires me out just hearing you talk like this. You know me," Abby said. "I do volunteer work and all that, but a girl's gotta have a little fun. You, you're letting your peak years go to waste. Tonight, some guy'll be eating his heart out while you cling to your precious virtue."

Natalie bristled. "One day, I bet the right guy won't complain."

"The right guy? What*ever*. You come first. Always, always."

She wasn't so sure. As a young girl, she had made meals for her dad and helped raise her sister. Thinking solely of herself was out of the question.

"Gotta jet," Abby said. "They're calling for me downstairs."

Natalie urged Abby to stay safe and ended the call. Back pressed against the wall, she lowered her eyes to avoid the attention of a passing nurse.

Was it true she was wasting her peak years?

Was she saving herself, or was she just afraid of getting close to and trusting someone again?

Natalie went online on her cell and visited her dad's Facebook profile page. Social networking baffled him, yet Mardy Flynn had managed to upload a high school yearbook photo, and to respond to comments from old classmates.

She typed a quick message and hoped he would see it.

Her sister's profile showed more recent

interactions. Her posts were hard-edged and raw, but she won people over with her honesty. Instead of posting a photo with the soft edges and bright smile of her youth, she had a more current one in which her hair was short, the corners of her eyes and lips weighted down by eighteen months spent behind bars at Tennessee Prison for Women.

Natalie typed: Happy New Year, Tuf. Love ya tons.

Tina Flynn's initials had earned her that nickname years ago.

Natalie wished Dad and Tuf were here now. She wondered how they would get along with the Vreelands, and then decided that bringing the two groups together would only blur the lines between the separate parts of her life. Right now, those distinctions were clear, providing parameters for her desires.

She wanted to graduate.

Wanted to find a good job.

Wanted to teach and protect hurting children.

More than anything, she wanted a man by her side.

There. In an age of post-feminism, she was liberated enough to admit that. Longing for a boyfriend didn't make her weak, did it? It made her human. She knew that one day her commitment to a husband and children would win out over personal ambitions, but who said both couldn't share space in her heart? Wouldn't a good spouse encourage her to blossom rather than wither and die?

Yes, she desired a man who would look her in the eyes and shut out the world as she spoke, who would give her gentle kisses and wrap her in his arms.

Knowing her, though, she'd probably botch it from the very start.

"Natalie, how're you this evening?"

She turned toward a tall black man in the hallway. His voice was steady, his eyes large and dark, his leather jacket open over a charcoal gray shirt. Detective Reggie Meade. After helping her and the Vreelands during their ordeal with Magnus, Meade, a trusted public servant, had become a family friend.

"*¿Que paso?*" she asked. "You off-duty, or is this a professional visit?"

"Little of both. Is Bret still awake in there?"

"They're waiting up for New Year's." She pushed off from the wall, eyes locked onto the detective's. "What's wrong? They've already been through a lot."

"And you have been too, Natalie. After your abduction, I went to bat for you so that you could work with the Vreelands. It was the right move. I don't regret that. But as I looked at your records, I came across a few things that concern me. First off, answer me this: Why did you lie to me?"

Chapter Six

The Ice Queen. It was the name most people called Darcy Page behind her back. Although she didn't mind on a personal level, she despised their cowardice. The ones who said it to her face were those who were daring, thought for themselves, and deserved places of power within her courts.

And naturally, they were right.

She was an ice queen.

Last year, a *Forbes* interview quoted her as saying, "An aggressive man gets called 'top dog,' while a strong woman, especially an attractive one, gets labeled with the derogatory term for a female dog." The *Wall Street Journal* featured her in a subsequent article titled "Hot Dog," which she framed and hung in her seventeenth-floor office, next to her diploma from UCLA.

This morning, she gazed through floor-to-ceiling windows at the Seattle Space Needle, snow-white hands folded across a dress suit with burgundy pinstripes.

Without turning, she said, "Did I tell you to come in, Bigz?"

" 'My door's always open.' Your words."

"Did you find it open?"

"Hey, if you didn't mean what you said, then lock the stinkin' thing."

She heard him close the door and plop onto her settee, and she nodded as though he had passed a test. Swiveling on low heels, she nudged the day-old copies of the *Tennessean* and the *Post-Intelligencer* on her desk. "Have you read the latest? It seems Serpionov was telling the truth."

"I read it. Your husband's dead."

"I don't have a husband."

"Your ex."

"That's correct. What am I supposed to call a dead ex? An ex-ex?"

Bigz chuckled. His real name was Darius Hammond, and in actuality, he was a short black man who wore tailored clothes and silk ties and refused to be overlooked. He was Darcy's personal assistant, and even with proud thick hair, he reached no higher than her earlobes.

"Ex-ex," he said. "I like that. But it's completely inappropriate anywhere outside this office. You hear what I'm saying, Darce?"

"What would I do without you to filter my words?"

"You'd set yourself on fire, then burn out somewhere in the stratosphere."

"So I have you to thank, do I, for keeping me in orbit?"

Bigz arched an eyebrow. "I put you into orbit."

"Well, in six years of marriage, that's something Alex could never do."

Darcy and Alex Page had cofounded Shield Technologies, wedding her love of money and marketing with his desire to destroy Storinka Defense Systems, a rival company that belonged to his estranged father. Soon, Shield's researchers developed a savvy product line, she launched a national ad campaign, and the Pentagon showed interest.

My, did stockholders respond.

Which meant a fortune for Darcy. And for Alex, sweet revenge.

The Pages were combatants in their marriage, but rock stars in terms of business. When they split in 2009, each retained stock and position in the company, and Shield Technologies continued its rise. Now Darcy alone held the reins, well aware that others would try to wrench them from her grasp at the first opportunity.

"How's the news affected our numbers?" she asked.

Bigz glanced at his BlackBerry. "Dropping like a rock."

"I should issue a statement reflecting our resilience and strength."

"Whoa, Darce. First, you need to express a touch of sadness. I'll hold a press conference and address the reporters, while you stand behind me dressed in all black, as befits a woman in mourning."

"I'll drink to that."

She slipped to the corner refrigeration unit—chest high, brushed silver, and powered by RFID components straight from Shield's labs. Although mostly hidden from human eyes, radio frequency ID was everywhere these days—flattened metallic coils that functioned as antennae within heat-resistant tags.

The chips in some of these tags were the size of postage stamps, others as small as pepper flakes. They were hidden in clothing, books, store loyalty cards, even in passports and driver's licenses. Handheld and doorway scanners read and translated their encoded info, aiding in everything from airport security to mall theft prevention to inventory control of hotel robes and linens. Consumers remained largely oblivious, "frisked" daily going in and out of retailers and offices.

"We're short on Coke Zero," Darcy said. "And turkey provolone subs."

The refrigerator not only displayed its inventory on the door's digital pad, but posted an up-to-the-minute shopping list of items absent from its usual stock.

"I'll have Hospitality take care of it. Any Red Bull in there?"

"You get the last one." She tossed the can to her assistant, then wiped the condensation from her hand. "I'm not sure how you even stomach that stuff."

On the door pad, red digital letters blinked: *"Recall . . . Recall . . ."*

"You see that?" Bigz said.

"I'd wager it's the spinach, which spells doom for my leafy lunch plans."

"Macon's Farm Spinach, 12 oz. bag . . . Recall."

She pointed. "Like I said."

"It's been all over the news, woman. Not much of a wager."

"Woman?" Her cell vibrated on the desk, but she didn't answer right away. She popped the tab on her Coke Zero, sipped at it, and wiped her lips. "I do have a name. Don't get too casual."

"You know you couldn't do this without me."

"I'll remember that," she said, "when I'm done grieving over my ex-ex."

The phone rattled again.

She checked caller ID. "It's Representative King." She propped her backside against her desk, crossed snow-white legs in front of her, and answered the call. "Good morning, and how's our favorite state representative? If I haven't said it already, congrats on your second term . . . Oh, thank you. I . . . yes, it's awful. A tragedy. Alex and I had lived apart for over a year, but I . . ."

Bigz put on a droopy-eyed look.

"But of course, I still cared for him . . . No, let's stick with our original schedule. The memorial won't interfere . . . Listen, I won't pretend I'm not

48

interested in the millions in potential profit for Shield, because I am. Unabashedly so. But this country was built on free enterprise, and truly, Shield is the right company at the right time. We're thrilled to have your ear on this issue, and once proper legislation is in place, you'll . . . Yes, my mistake. *If* legislation is approved, you'll be in position to offer your constituents safer, happier lives."

When the call was over, she slid the phone onto the desk and clacked her nails together. "He's a man of conviction. It's his type that worries me."

"You'll win him over, Darce."

"My initial homework led me to believe he was our man, being one of the younger state legislators and from a rural area. Now I'm having doubts. I want a complete profile on him—what he loves, hates, hides, all of it. Should we need to apply more pressure? I want to know what'll make him break."

Bigz folded his arms behind his head and clicked his tongue. "And for a moment there, you sounded almost human."

"I *am* human."

"I know that's right. Your pupils dilated when you talked about the money."

"And not mere millions, Bigz. Billions. If this swings in our favor, I'll not only make a fortune and save my job, but we'll change the world as we know it. Imagine every man, woman, and child implanted with a microchip, and every one of those chips bearing the logo of Shield Technologies."

Since acquiring the Shield case, Serpionov had left it open and "live." He now studied the hi-res satellite view of Davidson County, moved his fingers on the touch screen, and zoomed in on a quadrant of Metro Nashville. Amber lines formed a grid over Vanderbilt Medical, where a blood-red circle pulsed with life.

He phoned Ms. Page. "It's still working."

"Good," Darcy said. "I'll have my production manager ship the components you requested. Our potential investors'll need to see a live demonstration."

"This I can arrange. But we have problem."

"How so?"

"At the airport, a man came to steal your secrets. He was sent by your rival."

Chapter Seven

"Lie to you?" Natalie lowered her voice as a pair of orderlies squeezed by and turned the corner of the hospital corridor. "When did I ever—?"

"You told me your father lived in Idaho."

Natalie took a step back. She studied Detective

Meade's face, tried to recall those first few hours stumbling toward the house on the slope, calling the police, telling her story. So much of it was blurred by her terror and relief.

"Not true, was it?"

She shook her head. "He, uh . . . that's where he grew up."

"He now lives in Oak Ridge, is that correct? Works at a high-security government facility."

"His work was always private. We weren't supposed to talk about it."

"And your parents," Meade said. "They're not divorced, are they?"

"Not exactly. My mom's been out of the picture since I can remember."

"Since you were three years old."

"She disappeared." Natalie snapped her fingers. "Gone, just like that. OK, so I mixed a few of my facts around. *Perdóneme.* After all that happened with Magnus, the Vreelands seemed like the perfect family to me, the type I'd always wanted, someplace safe. Seriously, I owe you for that."

"Mm-hmm." The detective's leather jacket squeaked as he put his hands on his hips. "Next time, don't use lies to get what you want."

"I was scared, Detective. Shouldn't have done that."

"Fear'll push you to do strange things, both good and bad." He glanced down the hall. "Your mom. She's still a cold case, I hear."

"Guess so. They stopped looking for her years ago."

"Well, I know some people over in that general vicinity, used to take classes at UT. I'll call the Anderson County Sheriff's Department and try to stir up some interest, maybe get the case reopened."

"OK." Natalie nodded. "Sweet."

"You sound ambivalent."

"I, uh, yeah, I wonder about her often, but I'm not sure what to expect. Like maybe she's still alive out there, remarried, enjoying a happy little existence in the Florida Keys and hoping she's never found."

"And that'd hurt worse than not knowing, huh?"

Natalie shrugged.

Detective Meade said, "I've lost loved ones of my own." He dragged a coal-black hand across the back of his neck, and his nostrils flared. "You ask me, it hurts no matter which way."

"Listen, I appreciate the offer. I do."

"Enough of that, though." His official tone was back. "I came to give you and the Vreelands a heads-up. Last night, a man wearing a Titans coat and hat targeted Magnus's vehicle over in airport parking. The plates match up. Surveillance cameras caught him in the act as he shot another man, left him for dead, and walked off with an unidentified item."

"A random theft?"

"With all that's gone on, I can't afford to make that assumption."

"So what're you saying?" Natalie asked.

"Things might not be over, not the way that we'd hoped."

In the hospital room, Detective Meade voiced his concerns to Natalie, Eli, and the Vreelands. He assured them Magnus was no longer a threat from his place among the dead, but that this possible rival or partner of his had killed a man at the airport and was still on the loose.

"If this guy was out by the car that late at night," Bret said, "he must've known something about what was in it."

"I'm not free to divulge any of those details," Meade said.

"Can you tell us what this thief, this murderer, would want from us?"

"That I don't know. Maybe nothing at all."

"Dad," Kevin said. "The TV. The ball's s'posed to drop in four minutes."

"Sure, bud, you can turn it back on." Bret looked to Sara. "And let's start pouring those drinks. I doubt Meade here's gonna nail us for our contraband."

The detective raised an eyebrow.

Smiling, Sara reached into her husband's night bag and pulled out a bottle of Martinelli's sparkling cider and another of Korbel champagne.

Natalie stepped forward to help. Sara peeled back the plastic from a sleeve of fluted plastic cups and shot the detective a glance.

"There's even one for you," she said. "You're not on duty, are you?"

"On the clock, no. But my wife says I'm always on duty."

"And thank God for that. Otherwise, the rest of us might not be alive."

"I should've been there sooner," Meade said, his gaze sliding toward Bret's missing leg. "Should've been on the scene before any shots were fired."

A knock at the door stopped Sara's hand as she was peeling the gold foil from the champagne bottle's neck. Natalie peered out and found a stout middle-aged couple bearing flowers and a card. She had met Pastor Teman and Rhonda Teman through the Vreelands, and although she didn't see eye to eye with them on certain points, she respected their years of service and their care for others. Rhonda had counseled and consoled her in the months following the abduction.

"Come on in." Natalie held the door open for them. "You're, like, just in time."

"Only two more minutes," Katie said.

Kevin pointed to the clock. "Hundred and fifteen seconds, to be exact."

"How about a quick prayer?" Bret suggested. "Anyone?"

Pastor Teman took up the cause and stepped to the foot of the bed. His eyes scanned the room from beneath bushy eyebrows, waiting for every head to bow.

Not like it was a prerequisite for talking to God. In fact, Natalie's silent chatter went on throughout the day—thanking, petitioning, questioning, and praising Him. He was real, right? He knew her thoughts and saw her deeds?

"All yours, Pastor," she said, dropping her chin.

"Father God," he began, "we thank You for Your provision and protection during this past year. Your angels have stood watch over the Vreelands, and even in their loss of an inheritance and a limb, You spared their lives. Your Word tells us You have purposes for each one of us, and like Queen Esther, we dedicate ourselves to serving in the arenas of influence in which You've placed us. We pray these things in Your Son's holy name. Amen."

"Amen," the gathering responded.

"Eighteen seconds," Kevin said. "Seventeen, sixteen . . ."

Serpionov cradled the case on his knees. Going into a new year, he had a chance with this technology to make a difference for the children of the world.

The world was a dangerous place. Who would argue otherwise? As a result, fear spread daily like

55

a virus through the Internet, TV, and live feeds to millions of laptops, tablets, and cell phones. It delivered speeches to Congress. It pounded pulpits. It juggled numbers on Wall Street and raked its fingers through the hair of Hollywood's brightest stars.

And now, I think, it is time to fight back.

"A safer future, that is all I want," he had told his grandmother a decade earlier, the day he left to work for OMON. "While others hide behind words and walls, I want to fight for something better."

"And violence will end violence? You think this is true?"

"It stopped Adolf Hitler, yes."

His grandmother's Ukrainian roots were steeped in religion, and she mumbled prayers at the ceiling and kissed an icon with pruned lips. "If you give fear power over you, peace will never be possible," she said, then quoted from the Scriptures: " 'O Death, where is thy sting?' "

"I want only to make a difference. Doesn't that deserve your approval?"

"Of you, I approve. But of this decision? No."

"Bah," Serpionov said. "You're an old *babushka* who hides behind the outdated rituals of Rasputin and the tsars. Religion holds you down."

"Even if you don't believe, Stepan, you cannot escape that which is true. Your very name comes from the first martyr in the New Testament. You know, he lifted his eyes to the heavens instead of fighting back."

"I hate his name. I will use it no longer."

"But your name is already inscribed upon the palm of God's hand."

"And does He still see it when He makes a fist?"

"You mock," she said. "You wish to fight against your Maker?"

Serpionov leaned toward her over the wooden table, his voice low.

"I wish to put a stop to the madness. It's not right that terrorists kill children, sometimes even their own countrymen. What sort of God allows this?"

"And you think it is He who builds their explosives?"

"He does nothing to prevent them. He's either deaf or dead."

"Tell me, then, who carved this sense of justice into your heart? Standards shift if left in the hands of villagers, priests, or Putin. There is only one standard, don't you see?" She gave a rattling cough. "You've been to Lake Baikal, yes?"

"A weekend, while in the army. We traveled there by train."

"It was beautiful, you said." She coughed again, thumped her chest. Her eyes turned watery, but she pressed on. "Even though you'd heard how large it was, the largest freshwater lake in the world, didn't its size surprise you? Wasn't it vaster than you imagined? You only learned this by seeing it for yourself, I think."

"Seeing is believing. Of course. So then, let this Maker show Himself."

"First, Stepan, you must have eyes to see."

"Bah. You twist your words like a country priest." He shoved away from the table, pulse throbbing in his neck. He wanted to slam down his fists and make plates and utensils jump, but he refused to let her get the best of him.

"Do not forget," she said, "that you're in my prayers. You do not believe? This doesn't matter. God hears, and He whispers your name back to me."

Serpionov stopped by her village only once after that, eight years later, to gather his belongings for the move to America. He was done with OMON. He would miss some of his comrades, but never the terrible deeds done in the name of the law, deeds that had little to do with public safety and everything to do with power and oppression.

"You will call, yes?" said his grandmother. "These days, I'm not so well."

Although she knew of his work with OMON, there was no judgment in her eyes or scolding from her tongue. She simply embraced him with frail arms, kissed his cheek with thin, dry lips.

"*Do svidanya*," she said as he climbed into his car. She waved, her face chiseled by years of tobacco use, her back hunched by a fit of coughs.

Seated now at his condo window in Nashville, Serpionov adjusted the case on his knees, poured himself a shot of Zyr vodka—his one indulgence—and watched the fireworks bloom over the nearby Adventure Science Center. He would send her more money soon.

"To my *babushka*," he said. "And to a safer future."

Natalie cast a sideways glance at the others in the Vanderbilt hospital room, found joy and excitement lighting their faces. Sure, much had been lost. But they were alive, they had each other, and as Bret liked to quote from Romans 8, "God causes everything to work together for the good of those who love God and are called according to His purpose for them."

She wanted to believe this was true, but if God was kind and God was strong, why hadn't He helped the authorities find her mother? Why hadn't He warned her somehow before Magnus ambushed her in the café? Why hadn't He stepped in two seconds earlier and stopped the gunshot that ruined Bret's leg?

Seemed like fair-enough questions.

The clock on the TV showed there were only seconds left till the stroke of midnight, and everyone had age-appropriate beverages in hand, save the Temans, who chose to sip Martinelli's with Kevin and Katie.

"Five," Kevin counted, "four, three . . ."

"Two, one . . . ," the others joined in. In New York City, the ball descended, and its lights burst into brilliant colors amidt raucous cheers. "Happy New Year!"

In the crowded hospital room, toasts were raised, glasses clinked, hugs exchanged, and kisses given. A chorus of hope resounded, and Natalie shoved aside her melancholy long enough to embrace this joint optimism. She had so much to be thankful for, so much to look forward to in the coming months.

Why, then, this sense of fear? Was she being paranoid?

The detective's warning lingered—like a migraine, like the ache of a tooth—and she couldn't shake the sense that, somehow, she was still being targeted.

Chapter Eight

The glowing screen gave Serpionov a voyeuristic thrill. The dot was still there, hovering over Vanderbilt Medical, winking off and on as though the life it represented was already fading.

Fading? Yes. Such was the bittersweet cost of victory.

Truth be told, Serpionov would've completed

the previous night's airport assignment for a free steak dinner. Money was only a tool. It paid the bills and enabled his endeavors. It did not, however, erase the horrors in his head.

What sort of man would that make him if it did?

He poured himself another shot and considered some recent milestones:

1. In 2004, the Food and Drug Administration approved a microchip that could be implanted into human beings for medical purposes.
2. In 2005, Homeland Security gained the power to insert chips into ID cards, opening the way for tracking citizens.
3. In 2006, U.S. passports were issued with embedded RFID tags, as a protection, it was said, against counterfeit documents.
4. Now in 2010, cellular service providers fulfilled millions of requests from police departments across the country, who, under the Patriot Act, wanted GPS data that could help them triangulate signals and keep track of suspected criminals and terrorists.

Yes, these technologies frightened consumers and concerned the courts, but the truth was that microchips could be read only at close quarters, ID cards could be stolen, and phones could be used by someone else.

By joining GPS and RFID technology, this prototype changed all that.

Good-bye to past limitations. *Do svidanya.*

Staring at the blinking red circle on the screen, Serpionov raised his glass for a final toast. "And to you, Ms. Natalie Flynn."

In Her Bones

"I still feel responsible. Natalie's mine to take care of, no matter how big she gets, and I shoulda never let Magnus come and just snatch her up."

"You can't protect her from everything."

"I know, I know. I s'pose her mother's a case in point. Natalie's all grown and got choices of her own to make. That's her right, and I can't get in the way of that, I understand. But what I'm asking is, how am I s'posed to watch after her if she goes wandering straight into a trap? What then?"

"You point out the warning signs. Sometimes it's all you can do."

"That leaves me feeling so helpless."

"At least the man who took her is dead and gone."

"And thank goodness for it. She's tried her best to move on, getting back on her feet and going back to college. Some of them wounds're still there, but she puts on a smile and plugs through each day as if things're just the way they used to be. Sometimes she lifts her chin and puts on that fearless look, and I think, Well, there she is. There's my girl, back from the jaws of death."

"I'm glad to hear she's becoming herself again."

"I dunno, though. She's not the carefree young'un anymore."

"She'll always be to me."

"Well, true as that may be, dontcha think she's gotta see her own self that way? There's bad in this world, much as I wish it were otherwise, and she now knows that deep down in her bones. Believes it for an absolute fact."

"Believing is half the battle."

"It's the other half that's got me concerned. Oh, I'll do my best to steer her right, but she has got it in her mind that she's gonna do this a particular way. She's got me worried, no two ways about it. Like I said, I think it's a trap."

"A trap, sure. But for whom?"

Chapter Nine

February 2011

This was it, the most crucial step yet in a race that started years ago.

Darcy stood with her assistant and faced the Ionic portico on the southern end of the Tennessee State Capitol. Today's results would impact not only Shield's sustained viability but her personal fortune and future as well.

Her eyes climbed the massive stone walls and cupola to the state flag fluttering high over Nashville. She knew that Davy Crockett once served this legislature, and portraits of former U.S. presidents Andrew Jackson, James K. Polk, and Andrew Johnson guarded these marble halls. The building even served as a Union fortress during the Civil War.

All that history is behind us, she thought. *The future is today.*

The House of Representatives had been called to order, and once the prayer and the pledge were out of the way, the bills would be up for consideration.

"This is it," she said. "I won't let any rival or representative hinder me."

"I know that's true," Bigz said, staring up from

beneath a fedora. "For now, though, we watch and wait. Not much else we can do."

"My, how small-minded. There's always more that I can do."

Darcy led him through security into the building's marble corridors and beneath the frescoed ceilings. On the second floor, they passed the sergeant-at-arms, climbed narrow stairs to the visitors' gallery, and joined other observers in red-cushioned seats. They gazed between limestone columns at the House chamber below, where politicians represented Tennessee's ninety-nine districts.

In this year's policy-making, these districts were racehorses jockeying for position, and House Bill 6336 was next on the day's agenda.

Here we go. Darcy crossed her legs. *Let the races begin.*

"As enacted," the clerk read for all to hear, "HB 6336 authorizes hospitals and health care facilities to implant children and patients with FDA-approved microchip technology, for their safeguarding, upon the notarized request of a parent, legal guardian, caregiver, and/or licensed medical practitioner."

An abstract summary followed, detailing how a bioglass implant containing an encrypted chip could be injected under the skin, without stitches, at a cost of under $200. In terms of documentation, it wasn't much more complicated than getting a library card, and the state had little financial liability since private clinics and health care facilities would meet consumer demands.

The House floor was now open for debate. Despite the bill's far-reaching ramifications, a collective yawn seemed to stretch throughout the chamber.

So some mom with sole custody wanted to ensure that her ex didn't run off to Mexico undetected with their child.

Why not? A kid's safety was priority.

OK, so some old woman wanted to be certain her addle-minded spouse didn't wander off without any ID or medical instructions for those who found him.

Go ahead. Tag the old fellow.

A number of representatives slipped from their desks and headed out through the back doors, some for toilet breaks, others for coffee and pecan rolls in the antechambers. Without a horse in this particular race, it was time to take a breather before weighing in with a final "aye" or "nay."

"This might go easier than expected," Darcy whispered.

"Did you really expect trouble?" Bigz said. "Once a bill survives committee, most of the suits figure it's good to go. All we need now is a majority vote."

"Sounds easy enough, coming from the sharpest-dressed man I know."

"You realize these threads're paid for by that pittance you call my salary? How am I supposed to eat, Darce? Answer me that."

"Not my concern. You know, if the ACLU catches wind of this bill, they'll enter a horse of their own in the race. And if the religious Right makes even one mention of the 'Mark of the Beast,' it could be disastrous for us. Completely disastrous. Every loony with a cardboard placard would show up in force."

"Bill 6336. Hmm. Add those middle digits and—"

"You have 666. Now you sound like some fundamentalist wacko."

"Hey, you can dial back the worry," Bigz said, smoothing his pant leg. "The wording in this legislation leans in favor of parental and medical concerns. Who can vote against that? No politician worth a donkey's fart—"

"Or elephant's," Darcy noted. "To keep things party neutral."

"No politician's going to deny the people of this fine state the right to look after their own children as they see fit."

"You were born here, weren't you?"

"Streets of Memphis, baby. But now the Ice Queen watches over me."

Darcy met his gaze and squelched any desire kindled by his striking green eyes and creamy dark skin. She had hired him for his physical appeal as much as for his professional résumé, but her passion at this moment was for the bill.

HB 6336 had been cosponsored last September by a Democrat and a Republican. When it was first filed, it was nary a blip on the political radar, but her people had picked up on it from Shield's headquarters in Seattle.

The bill was soon numbered, introduced to the House, and assigned to the Health and Human Resources Committee, where Representative King served as chairman. After passing through committee, it was added to the consent calendar, and, if approved today by the House and later by the Senate, it would be enrolled, signed by both speakers, and sent to the governor's desk, where a signature would turn it into law.

Although Shield's recent advances still required real-world testing, Darcy knew her company could be in mass production within weeks, thanks to contracts with a Belgian copper coil manufacturer and a German bioglass facility. The ultimate goal was to tag all who called themselves U.S. citizens.

It was a hard sell, of course. No use ignoring that fact.

In independent surveys, individuals responded negatively to tagging. Consumer advocacy groups raised red flags, and the Internet gave a platform to every left-wing fruitcake and right-wing fearmonger who wanted to stir the paranoia.

Even in open-minded California, Governor Schwarzenegger had signed a bill banning companies from using human implantation as a requirement for employees to get their paychecks or benefits.

But RFID could not be swept away.

For years, companies such as Abercrombie & Fitch, IBM, Kodak, Pepsi, and Walmart had invested in related technologies, citing countless advantages in theft prevention, inventory control, and data mining. With hundreds of millions of dollars at stake, they went to great lengths to soften the public's reception.

RFID had a bad name? Well then, call it an "improved barcode," a "green tag," a "contactless smart card," or an "intelligent label."

And the strategy paid off.

Millions of Americans now used RFID daily, gladly, willingly.

With nearly every wallet, purse, or keychain infiltrated, the next frontier was the human body. And Darcy knew that only a careful strategy would be successful in this race for market dominance.

Darcy Page was no slouch. She had not only tested high on IQ tests since childhood and earned her master's in communications strategy through hard work, but she also used good looks to blackmail professors and keep classroom rivals from edging her out as summa cum laude. She settled for nothing less than the top position. Second place? In her estimation, it was for first-place losers.

Blending her head knowledge and street smarts, she knew tagging would never go national if it didn't gain trust on a state level first.

Tennessee looked to be that launch state.

And Representative King was her jockey of choice.

She sat up in her gallery seat as King asked for permission to address the assembly.

"What does he think he's doing?" she mouthed to Bigz. "This thing's a shoe-in."

"Damage control."

"What for? There's barely been a word of dissent. 'Assume that victory is yours, and don't stoop to defend that fact.' Those were my instructions to him."

"Imagine." Bigz flashed a wry grin. "A politician who thinks for himself."

"I never gave him permission to think. He's a representative, a title he retained with no small thanks to my campaign contributions. So then, let him 'represent,' " Darcy said, hooking the air with her fingers.

"Let's hear what he has to say."

All heads turned to Reuben King. He was a tall man, stately, boasting a head of black hair. Even to Darcy in the balcony, his eyes looked blue and alert, touched by a hint of playfulness. At only twenty-eight years old, he spoke with the authority that came from now serving a second term in District 33.

"I stand by 6336," he said in a warm baritone, "and our committee brings this bill to you knowing it could save lives. We've all heard reports of Alzheimer's patients who wandered off in the night and froze in snowdrifts, and Elizabeth Smart could've been found earlier with some sort of implanted device.

"In committee, we discussed the bill's benefits for health care officials, law enforcement, and private citizens. We also discussed the negatives. With satellites circling overhead and Google mapping and taking pictures of our homes, the rights to privacy are under attack. There are companies already tracking our vehicles through toll booths and highways. Social networking invites us to check in at the places we work and eat. Cell phone companies monitor our whereabouts. Clearly, this could give corporations and government an edge."

His gaze swept the chamber. "The more I think about it, the more I worry that a bill of this nature could open the door to others, not only in this state but across the land. It has military and security implications. Numerous issues lurk at the edges of this legislation. While I appreciate the hard work of our committee members, I think we'd be wise to go back and insert some precautionary language. I propose further investigation before 6336 is engrossed."

"Further investigation?" Darcy hissed, loud enough to turn a few heads in the gallery. "He's sending us back to square one. This is a debacle."

"Apparently," Bigz said, "the man is a man."

"And what exactly is that supposed to mean?"

"A man even you can't control." He leaned back, arms folded high on his chest. "Hmm. Who knew?"

Below, representatives punched in votes at their paneled mahogany desks, and large electronic screens displayed the first setback for HB 6336.

Ayes: 41. *Nays:* 58.

Chapter Ten

Natalie dreaded this time of year. She dragged herself out of bed, already late for class, but there was no escaping the romance in the air—the balloons, the roses, the cards and heart chocolates.

"Any plans for this evening?" Sara asked her at breakfast.

She shrugged, downing a glass of red grapefruit juice.

"You like it?" Sara said. "Red for—"

"Valentine's Day. Yeah, I got it."

"Don't worry. A beautiful girl like you, I'm sure there's some guy out there with his eye on you."

"Sounds creepy."

Sara laughed. "You know what I mean."

"A guy from church did ask me out last Sunday."

"Oh?"

"One of the youth leaders," Natalie said.

"Really?" Sara turned from the stove, spatula in hand. "Was it Tommy?"

"No, the other guy."

"Ohhh."

"Guess they're showing romantic comedies out at the old Stardust Drive-in, in Watertown, but I told him I couldn't skip my night class."

"He's not your type, huh?"

Natalie shook her head. Living at the Vreelands' place on Groves Park, she was a daily witness to loving gestures. Bret and Sara gave her hope for her own relational future, but today only loneliness gnawed at her chest.

She washed her glass, set it on the drain board, and grabbed car keys from the cluttered computer desk. She had been without a vehicle since Magnus dumped her Vespa in the river, but she shared gas and insurance costs for the Vreelands' old Subaru, and most days, she was free to use it as needed.

Sara stopped her. "This morning Eli's going to run you to Trevecca. He's already out at the curb warming the engine. You know how he loves to help."

"He's great. It's just, well, the fumes get pretty thick in his pickup."

"You'd be free to take our car," Sara said, "but I'm meeting Bret over at the studio in an hour. Some execs from Desperado Artist Development are worried that he won't be able to fulfill his touring commitments, what with travel logistics and required wheelchair access."

"Are they *loco*? He can still sing and play his guitar."

"And we'll convince them of that. If anything, he has an even deeper passion for touching lives through his music."

"His music's been epic in my own spiritual growth."

"I'll tell him you said so. You go on. Eli's waiting."

Backpack slung over her shoulder, Natalie trudged out the front door. Eli Shaffokey was behind the wheel of his Caribou camper-pickup, gray eyes watchful as always, elbow hanging out the window.

"Morning to ya." He lifted his fingers from the sill in greeting. "You got all of whatcha need?"

How about an air mask? And ASAP.

She kept the words to herself, climbed into the cab, and rolled down her window. "Thanks for helping out. I can always count on you."

75

"Surely hope so. What good's a friend other-wise?"

He dropped her off at the Trevecca Nazarene campus, told her to call him on his cell as soon as she was ready for a ride home, and then drove off in a cloud of exhaust. Natalie headed to class, where she received good news from her professor. He had signed off on her "Funda-mentals in Alternative Learning" syllabus and approved her final credits for the live-in tutoring with the Vreeland kids.

"You're three short months from earning your degree," he said.

A bachelor of arts in early education.

"*Gracias.*" She beamed. "You have no idea. I just don't want to get tripped up here at the end. I mean, I've been dreaming of this since I was ten years old."

"You're a sharp young lady. I'd say there's nothing to stand in your way."

Chapter Eleven

The vote was over, and legislators scurried off for the afternoon.

Darcy Page waited in the sun-drenched State Library, at the base of a nineteenth-century spiral staircase. She knew this room well from previous meetings. Scrolled iron steps rose to narrow balconies and to bookshelves that catalogued thousands of public acts and state resolutions dating back two hundred years. Portrait medallions adorned the rails, featuring men such as George Washington, Patrick Henry, and Thomas Jefferson. Famous individuals who stood for radical ideas.

Unlike Representative King.

"He had better watch his back," she murmured.

"Beware your surroundings," Bigz said. "Try to remain diplomatic."

"Diplomacy's only good for so long, and then I give the Russian a call."

"You make it sound so ominous. 'De Russian, he vil fix dis.' "

"He's no joke."

"Whoa, Darce." Bigz patted at the air, suggesting she lower her volume.

Whereas some people let rage tremble in their fingers or quiver in their voices, Darcy felt it tighten her abs and hips and trickle like glacial water down her shapely calves. She had been told her legs looked best when she was ready to kick some tail, which was the reason she never hid her strength in men's attire.

"You realize," she said, "that King and I stood in this very spot last week as he spoke glowingly about the bill. It was a 'victory for the infirmed,' he claimed. 'A blow to those twisted souls who prey upon our children.' "

"I was there."

"Did he, or didn't he, say those things?"

"He did. He also expressed some concerns about—"

"Go to your hotel, Bigz. Your day's over."

"And the Infiniti?"

"I'll need it to drive back to my place. You're a big boy. Grab a cab."

"I'm out," he said. "But remember, this vote was only a setback. Handle this carefully, Darce, and you'll be able to nudge the ball back into play."

"Go."

She watched him leave, his pressed slacks hugging his firm quads.

What a day. She pinched the bridge of her nose and longed for the antidepressants tucked away in her nightstand, something to file down the prickly spots in her skull. Although her permanent residence stood along the shores of Seattle's Lake Washington, a $2 million prize from the divorce settlement, she also kept a Nashville suite. Shield had local holdings here, a necessity, with Music City being close to many military contractors and only a half day's journey from more than 50 percent of the nation's population.

"Ms. Page." Reuben King was padding toward her on the patterned carpet. "Thanks for coming this morning. How are you?"

"Cranky and confused. Explain to me what happened in there."

"Did you see yesterday's paper?"

"I take the *New York Times*, the *Wall Street Journal*, and the *Post-Intelligencer.* The local news less regularly. Skip the guessing games and get to your point."

"You're upset. I understand that, and I—"

"Your point."

He fixed her in his gaze. "This technology worries me."

"And you waited until today to inform me of this?"

"Did you know that Nashville schools are thinking of switching to RFID student cards? Parents and teachers will be able to know where their kids are, what they're ringing up in the cafeteria line, and so on. In another district, hundreds of private citizens signed up to be tracked for a month, in order to establish traffic patterns in their area. It'll save the state a lot of money in deciding which roadways need widening and which intersections need stoplights."

She shrugged. "Taxpayer dollars put to good use."

"From a strictly financial perspective, yes."

"Is there any another perspective?"

"Many people seem fine with it, unaware of how far this stuff could go."

"Unaware." Darcy folded her arms. "In this day and age?"

"*Conditioned* might be a better word. Or maybe just *numb*."

"This bill pertains to people's health and safety. Don't you see that, Mr. King? Each new technology stirs fear, as usual, and each generation overcomes their mental hurdles to make the world a better place. You're young—"

"No younger than you," he said, touching her shoulder.

She stiffened. "Let's just say I'm a student of human behavior. During my time at UCLA, we studied how mirrors were once viewed as witchcraft, how microwave ovens were supposed to cause outbreaks of cancer, and how people a hundred years ago thought of cars as rolling death traps."

"Cars do kill people, every minute of every day."

"And yet you still buckle in and turn the key, don't you?"

"Which brings me back to my point, Ms. Page. We've regulated the way cars're made and driven so as to mitigate some of those risks. In the same way, I think we should weigh this bill a bit longer before opening wide the floodgates."

"You mystify me. You chaired the very committee that sent this through."

King nodded. "I did, but most of our discussions dealt with the implant's health effects. We didn't want some three-year-old getting microchipped only to have it slip out of place and require corrective surgery. Or even worse, think of some elderly woman getting an MRI and having the implant torn from her arm by those powerful magnets in the machine."

"Please. These are common fear tactics, almost crass. The chip is no larger than a grain of rice, and an anti-migration coating holds it in place."

"Well, we had to be certain." He glanced at his watch, a hefty metallic thing with a face that matched his blue eyes. "Even with those concerns put to rest, I spoke up today because I don't want these advances running amok. I'm grateful for the donations you've made, but I have a duty to all of my constituents, not only those with deep pockets. No one person will dictate my vote."

"So be it." Darcy patted his chest. "I was afraid you might say that."

A mile east of Capitol Hill, nine men and women ambled toward the entryway of a stodgy gray building. They had been selected from the city's homeless population and delivered here by van to receive free medical care, as well as hot food and drink donated by a nearby Chick-fil-A. A local doctor was on hand, as were a nurse practitioner, a dentist, and a volunteer greeter.

Only one of them knew of Serpionov's plans.

None of the homeless did.

While Nashville attracted music hopefuls from

around the country, it also drew many of the less fortunate to its moderate climate and Southern hospitality.

Of late, that hospitality had lost some of its luster. A few years back, thugs had targeted one down-and-out woman named Tara Coles and rolled her into the Cumberland River, where she drowned. Vigils were held in her honor, but now in 2011, Nashville politicians and law enforcement seemed more apathetic than ever. One Metro police official famously offered free one-way bus tickets to get the bums out of his town.

Serpionov watched them as they entered the lobby. Such easy targets.

"Don't be shy," a chubby volunteer greeted them. She had blonde hair, a disarming smile, and attended nearby Trevecca Nazarene. "I'm Abby. Step on in, and I'll get each of ya taken care of."

"Where's the food?" asked the man at the front of the line.

"On its way, hot and fresh. I need each of you to tell me your name, then sign this waiver, and I'll direct you where you need to go."

"I'm not puttin' my name on nothing."

"It's for your protection, sir."

"To protect the doctor, more like. Whadda you know, hmm?"

"Sir, I'm just a college kid trying to help. Either way," Abby said, "I need you to sign before coming in."

"I bet Daddy's payin' your way. Well, that don't make you smarter'n me."

"Leave her be," said a bearded man in a cavernous wool coat. "Me, I got a bad tooth needs pulled, so if you won't cooperate, least let the rest of us by."

"You just hold your horses, Freddy C."

"I'm not picking no fights, just asking you to choose."

"OK, guys." Abby stood, hands lifted in surrender. "I'm not getting paid to be here, not *even*. I came to help, not referee."

"Help, hmm? More like do your good deed to pay off some sins."

"We're all in need of forgiveness," Freddy C cut in again. " 'Specially me if you don't let this girl do her job. You are getting on my last nerve."

Others in the line voiced their agreement.

"Think what you will, but I ain't puttin' my name on no paper."

Abby shifted her feet, looked back over her shoulder at Serpionov. "Are you *hearing* this? Aren't you supposed to be the bouncer or what-*ever*?"

He stepped forward. His arms bulged against the cheap tailoring of his Eastern European suit, and his thick neck strained the top button of his shirt. Though he preferred to be a silent observer during these events, he couldn't allow a disruption from these rebel-rousers. Or was that *rabble-*rousers?

"You two." He pointed at the men in the front of the line. "You go."

"I'm still not givin' nobody my name," the first man said.

"Good-bye, yes. You go now."

"Say, what'd I do wrong?" Freddy C objected. "I tried to be nice."

"It is decided. Good-bye."

"Sir, one of my fillings fell out, and my tooth's hurting something awful."

Serpionov drilled cold eyes into the older man and found only quiet pleading. He shrugged. "It is OK. You stay. This, it's good for you, I think."

"Thank you," Freddy said. "Thank you kindly."

Serpionov's cell buzzed in his pocket. Still focused on the line, he returned to his place behind Abby and answered the call. Darcy's tone warned of trouble, and she explained that her man in the House had derailed HB 6336.

"King's an idealist," she said. "He claims to be a man of the people."

"Such a man, bah. I do not think he exists."

"Agreed. Someone else must be footing his bills. I need you to find King's pressure points and squeeze him. If he still won't respond, squeeze harder."

Chapter Twelve

April

As predicted, Natalie was on her way. Four weeks from now, she would take her diploma in hand, turn the tassel on her cap, cheer and holler with hundreds of others, and then get shoved out the doors of higher learning with expectations strapped to her back and $32,000 in student loans cemented to her feet.

No guarantees of a teaching position.

No vehicle. No place of her own.

And absolutely no excuses to be made, not on her part.

Was anything more pathetic than one whiny soul in a sea of already-floundering families and shuttered businesses? She had seen the hardships the Vreelands went through, losing almost everything, and she decided to keep her complaints to herself.

First things first. Starting with a place to live.

Seated in Eli's pickup, Natalie brushed her hair away from her face and examined the small rental house hugged by overgrown magnolias and a lawn dotted with dandelions. The neighborhood was older but well kept, not too expensive. "Well, I like it. What about you, Eli?"

"You sure you wanna do this?" he asked from behind the wheel. "You, you're on your way up and ready to sprout wings. Last thing you need's some old codger holding you back."

"Don't be silly."

"This decision, it's up to you. Your choice."

"Seriously," she said, "where could I find a better housemate?"

"A match made in heaven, huh? Dunno if I'd go saying that too loud."

"We don't have to move in till after I graduate. The two of us, we could pay the deposit now and still have a month to save for rent and utilities."

"Nothin' doing. But an old guy like me, and you being just a young'un . . ."

"You think people at church're going to talk?"

"You know how it is. Don't wanna give the appearance of evil."

" 'To the pure, all things are pure,' " she said. "Isn't that in the Bible too? I say we go for it. I just agreed to working part-time hours at Roast, that little coffee place around the corner on Trousdale, and I can walk to work from here. Sweet, huh? And in June, I interview with Metro, which means I could be teaching soon."

"I'm mighty proud of you, Natalie. Hope you don't mind me sayin' so."

"Thanks. So we agree this is the place?"

"Reckon so. Landlord said he judges more by

the person than by their past. Said he'd be by 'round nine to go over things, if'n we were still interested."

"We're still interested."

Eli grinned. They meandered from the pickup to the front door. Cicadas buzzed in the trees, and a monarch butterfly floated past.

With graduation concerns still crowding her head, Natalie found herself needing to talk this through one more time. "I'm not being hasty, am I? I mean, this is the right thing, isn't it? It's not fair to mooch off the Vreelands forever, and space is even more crowded now that Bret's in a wheelchair. Forgive me if that sounds bad, but it's the truth."

"It's the right time," Eli agreed. A wistful look clouded his eyes. "One day, though, we'll be done with these ole bodies, eh? One fine day."

"In heaven, you mean? You ever wonder what it'll be like?"

"Boy, do I."

"You think we'll still look the same but, hopefully, be in our primes? What about this hole from my nose stud? And what about our scars? I wonder if they'll still be visible, or just fade away as if they never happened."

"We'll have glorified bodies, says so in the Scriptures."

"Yeah? Well, I have no idea what that actually means."

"Jesus, He walked through walls after His resurrection. Still ate food and broke bread, same as before. But they hardly recognized Him till they saw where those nails went in and that spear done pierced His side."

"So our scars won't go away?"

"I dunno. Could be that He just kept 'em as proof of His love."

She straightened the cuffs of her jeans. "Personally, I'd rather not remember the bad stuff that's happened down here."

"Don't blame ya there, not one bit. Some things I reckon we'll just hafta wait and see, but me, I got this feeling deep down in my knower that we won't be disappointed when that day finally comes."

"You and the Vreelands, I guess you have more faith than I do."

"Tiny bit goes a long way."

Natalie wanted to believe that. Yes, she wanted to trust that she would never be abandoned by a parent, never suffer unheard in the darkness, never feel blood seeping down into her socks as insects crawled over her wounds.

Too bad, though, about this little thing called life.

Hard to shake that off.

Shading her eyes, she watched an older Mercedes ease into the driveway. Out stepped a squat Persian-looking man in navy blue slacks and a matching tie. He adjusted his glasses and came up the walkway.

She balled her hands in her Trevecca hoodie, scolding herself for not removing her nose stud and wearing nicer attire. This decision to move into a new place was a step of faith, and she was going to botch it on first impressions.

The landlord shook Eli's hand. "You are Mr. Shaffokey?" he said with a heavy accent. "I'm Mr. Faranzmehr, owner of this house."

"Good to meet ya, sir."

"And you, you are Ms. Flynn?"

"Good morning. *Natalie*'s fine." She clasped the man's warm, fleshy hand. "Sorry, I would've dressed a little nicer, but I—"

"Trevecca?" Still holding her hand, he nodded at her hoodie. "Good, good. I took classes there after I escape from Iran with my family. For Christians, things are difficult in my country, you see. When we come to USA, my English is not so good and my grades are so-so, but now I am manager of five properties. So, Natalie, this is true you want to move in next month? Good, very good." He released her hand and made a grand gesture. "Please. Welcome to your new home."

"For real? *Bueno*," she gushed. "I mean, this is great. Thank you."

Chapter Thirteen

Serpionov spread out the court documents received through the mail for a small fee. Bathed in late-afternoon sunshine near his condo's windows, he browsed through the papers and selected one in particular.

Very interesting.

No person was without secrets, as any good Russian knew. He would use these facts like ropes to tug Representative King's limbs in opposite directions. Tug hard enough, and the man would cooperate.

Back in Serpionov's motherland, the government didn't release damaging information about public officials. The Romanovs had ruled a hundred years ago from gilded halls and palaces. They fell to Lenin, who ruled with a heavy hand, followed by Stalin, who was a ruthless tyrant. Nowadays, Putin was the puppet master, resorting to the tactics of his former KGB comrades.

Freedom for a Russian was an illusion. For a Ukrainian grandmother too.

Here in the United States, it was different. Citizens viewed personal freedom as a God-given right, and this could be used against them.

In God We Trust.

Let them trust, yes, in something that did not exist.

As if to counter this thought, his grandmother's words echoed through his head: *But your name is already inscribed upon the palm of God's hand.*

The teakettle whistled from the condo's stove. The weather was cool despite the clear skies, and Serpionov poured himself a glass of tea, which he cradled in a nickel-plated *podstakannik*, a traditional tea-glass holder. Americans were always amazed that such thin glass could hold such hot liquid, but molecules in thicker glass expanded too slowly and resulted in breakage.

No, bigger was not always better. Thick-headed was not always safer.

On the kitchen's tiled bar, the black Shield case was plugged into the wall socket, recharging. He removed its handheld monitor, no larger than a phone.

Last December, only one red drop had been splashed upon this screen.

Hazel-eyed Natalie.

Now, thanks to the recent free clinic for the homeless, other colors brightened the display. Medical and dental care had been given to the group of eight men and women, including Freddy C. They had received not only tetanus shots but also injections that lodged minuscule Shield devices in their triceps. Despite signing the waivers, none were aware of this violation.

On the monitor in Serpionov's palm, five yellow circles sat stationary at the Nashville Rescue Mission, most likely getting their meal for the evening. The mission staff did good work, unaware of his designs.

A sixth circle was at a shelter in Louisville, Kentucky.

A seventh on a train moving southeast toward Georgia.

The eighth in an espresso shop on nearby Elliston Place.

As Serpionov sipped his tea through a sugar cube between his teeth, he panned the cursor over that last circle. Up popped an oblong window that told him the bearer's basic info and tag number:

Frederick Chipps, male, age 62
ST-1-08-1799-2254

1. The letters identified Shield Technologies as the manufacturer.
2. The single digit categorized the tagged object: human, animal, vehicle, machinery, salable goods, and so on.
3. The two-digit number narrowed down the region of origin.
4. The remaining numbers specified the individual tag bearer.

Whether placed in an infant's arm, a waitress's uniform, or the cardboard lining of a cereal box, most RFID tags were passive, unable to power a long-term battery and broadcast data. Limited-ranged scanners unlocked the information in the encoded chips and supplied links to more details online and/or on proprietary computer systems.

The components within this case went a step further.

Shield had integrated satellite systems and radio frequencies to work with implanted microchips. In much the same way XM could play radio tunes in a car, special GPS scanners could triangulate and pinpoint individual RFID tags anywhere on the planet.

A child with an implant would never be lost.

A tagged terrorist could no longer hide.

Such thoughts warmed Serpionov even more than his tea. He had seen the atrocities visited by evildoers upon the young, and, to his eternal shame, found his own hands and face splattered with innocent blood.

He touched the screen again, noting the address.

Black's Espresso
2216 Elliston Place, Nashville, TN.

He pulled on his jacket and took the elevator down to the subterranean parking. He rode his motorcycle to Church Avenue, which took him to West End. He wanted one peek at Freddy C, to assure himself that the implant had been encoded properly and matched the correct person.

At the espresso shop, he spotted an unmarked vehicle with government plates. A tall black detective stood at the curb, hands on his hips. Beside him was a man with handsome Mediterranean features, a dark brown apron, and scroll-entwined swords tattooed on his forearms. His apron read, "Black's Espresso—The best. It's just the truth." Surely, this was the shop owner.

Serpionov edged his bike behind a Camry, able to observe without being obvious. He kept his helmet on, his visor down, and watched the aproned man beckon to someone in his shop. Out walked an individual in a bulky wool coat.

Was it . . . ? Yes, it was Frederick Chipps. Freddy C.

Disheveled and in need of a haircut, Freddy launched into a tirade. He waved frantic hands as he spoke, and the detective suggested he take it easy. Growing wild-eyed, he turned to the shop owner.

"Aramis, whaddaya think? Tell me, you think I got some screws loose?"

"Not at all, Freddy."

"They mighta been trying to help, but I'm telling ya, them doctors did something to us. I just know something wrong's been done."

Not good, Serpionov decided. He must report this to Ms. Page.

Chapter Fourteen

Natalie's workplace was tucked into the corner of a strip mall on Trousdale Drive. Roast Inc. had started as a wholesaler, then turned to the retail side of things when locals came knocking, drawn by the aroma of roasting coffee beans.

"You know," said a customer, "you're one of Nashville's best-kept secrets."

"How'd you hear about us?" she asked from behind the counter.

"My colleagues threatened to drag me here in chains if I didn't try it for myself."

"Secret must be getting out, huh?"

"The smell alone, wow."

The entry bell rang behind this man in business attire. Natalie tilted her chin, trying to peek around him as he flipped his tie over his shoulder, signed the debit card slip, and added a tip to the receipt.

He looked back up. "You have beautiful eyes."

"Thanks."

"Are they green?"

Least it's only my eyes he's checking out.

"Hazel," she said. "That's what I've always been told anyway."

"Hazel, wow."

"Here you go." She set down a to-go cup of fragrant Costa Rican.

He reached for it, fingertips grazing hers. "You're really beautiful."

"Uh . . ." She took a step back, trying to return to her cleaning.

"Hey! Yeah, you."

The raspy voice brought both Natalie and the businessman to attention. It came from a short young woman with full hips, thick shoulders, and a thorny tattoo crawling from beneath the collar of her My Chemical Romance T-shirt. Her platinum hair was dark at the roots, her eyes the same shape as Natalie's.

"Tuf?"

"Guess who?" said Tina Flynn. Her gaze remained on the man with the tie. "Door's that direction, creep. My sis, she's not interested."

"I'm sure she can decide that for herself," the man said.

"Sis?"

Natalie dealt with unwanted attention on a daily basis, all part of serving suited alpha males and bearded bohemians with guitars. Though most guys backed off when the interest wasn't reciprocated, she still wrestled with the old fears. It had been a big step forward to start working once again with the public.

"Tell him," Tuf said.

"He didn't mean nothing by—"

"Tell. Him."

"She's right," Natalie said. "Not really interested."

Tuf twisted her lips into a smirk, gave the man a slow wave good-bye.

"One good reason to take my business elsewhere," he said, elbowing his way out the door, tie flapping over his shoulder.

"What would you do without me?" Tuf said.

"You're going to get me in trouble." Natalie glanced around the shop, but at this late-morning hour, she had only one customer in the corner, a man bouncing his head to the music in his earbuds.

"Men, they're creeps. Every last one of them."

"How can you say that, Tuf?"

"How can you say otherwise? You spent, what, ten flippin' days as some whack job's prisoner? You think a suit and tie makes 'em any less sleazy? Not where I come from. Not even close."

"And to think we grew up in the same home."

"Well, sure, Dad's OK. When he's not drinking with his buddies."

"Dad's a good guy. Don't make it out like he's an alcoholic."

"He's like most guys on the weekend, coupla beers during the game. Never gets mean or nothing. Just wasn't 'round much after you left, that's all."

"Oh, and now somehow your mistakes are his

fault? Don't even blame your garbage on him," Natalie snapped. Arguments from years earlier ran through her head, and she felt that same rush of hot emotion followed by a familiar chill. "Sorry, Tuf. I take that back. Can we just, like, put this on rewind and start over? Why don't you tell me what you're doing here?"

"Do I need a reason to drop in on my big sis?"

"It's good to see you."

"Really?"

Natalie beckoned. "Get over here."

Tuf rolled her neck, flashing three rings in her ear cartilage. "I don't wanna, you know, like you said, get you in trouble or anything."

"Don't be silly." Natalie rushed around the counter.

They met in a hard embrace. Tuf's arms were solid from her days in the pen, but she had put some weight on her hips, an issue Natalie had also battled. They had talked about this before. Since their dad possessed barely enough derriere to hold up his pants, they complained that it must have been their mother's parting gift—this genetically sabotaged trouble spot.

"You're looking good, sis," Tuf said. "How long's it been?"

"Two Christmases ago. Remember?"

"Yeah, yeah, you came during visiting hours."

"You know, I think about you, like, every day. I do."

"Sheesh, the whole thing makes me sound like such a cruddy sister. Well, I'm done with all that, just so's you know. And that loser boyfriend of mine, the one from Knoxville? He's history."

"He was bad news."

"Yeah, but when things were good between us, they were—whew! They were flippin' intense. Now, c'mon, don't gimme that look. It is definitely over."

"I hope so," Natalie said. "You deserve better."

"Anyways, he's in for ten."

"Years? What for?"

"I told him, done said it right to his face. And did he listen?"

"He was dealing?"

"Meth. Even I'm smart 'nuff to know that that's some *bad* stuff."

Natalie's shift supervisor, a lady with strawberry blonde hair and a whimsical grin, came through the back door toting a five-pound bag of coffee beans and bottles of organic juice. She set down the supplies. "Everything OK?"

"Things're slow," Natalie said.

"That time of day. Take your break if you want. I've got it covered."

"Thanks, Erin. I'll, uh, be outside if you need me." Natalie led Tuf out to a pair of metal chairs. "I should've asked. Do you want anything to drink?"

"Nah, I'm fine."

Natalie leaned back. "Are you clean? Be straight with me."

"Clean? The answer's a solid yes. Straight? The jury's still out."

"What?"

"Well, I've sworn off men for the time being. That's a fact."

"And you're not using?"

"Said it already. I'm clean."

"Look me in the eye, and tell me you're not using."

Tuf blew air from the side of her mouth and crossed her legs the way a man would. "Like that'd mean jack. I could flippin' lie to Mother Teresa, and she'd never suspect a thing."

"She's not even alive."

"You're kidding? Did this go down while I was still inside? There's stuff I never heard about, you know. Stuff everyone else just takes for granted."

"This happened ages ago. She died the same week as Princess Di."

"Di's gone too?" Tuf punched Natalie. "Just kidding. That much I knew."

Natalie leaned back in her chair. "So, what're you doing in Nashville? How long're you going to be here?"

"Well, that's what I gotta talk to you about."

"Here it comes," she said. "I should've known."

"Why you gotta assume the worst, huh? That's not fair. I've been out for, I don't know, six, seven months, and I just need a place to crash till I can scrape up some cash for a place of my own." Tuf shrugged. "Plus, I thought you'd wanna know. They think they found Mom. Or at least what's left of her."

Chapter Fifteen

Darcy was back in Seattle, at her home on Lake Washington, where the ceaseless rain darkened her mood and the dampness settled into her bones. As a native of this state, she could understand the seasonal suicide rates, but her own tendency in such weather was to lash out at others.

Fair warning to her board members, whom she would address tomorrow morning with her update on HB 6336.

First, her laundry.

She upended her clothes basket over the open washer. Fitted with Shield's latest scanners, the machine "sniffed" the RFID tag in each piece that dropped into the basin, gathered data about types of material, and selected the optimal temperature and spin cycle settings.

She trusted her company's products and wasn't worried one iota when her rayon-blend skirt landed atop the pile, still smelling of smoke from the last night she went clubbing with Bigz in Nashville.

What a disastrous evening.

Though Darcy would never admit it, she had already felt vulnerable at the time, coping at last with the reality of her ex-husband's death. When Bigz left her at the club, complaining that he was tired and the DJ was a joke, her thoughts of Alex rushed in to fill the void.

Darcy hadn't loved Alex in years. Perhaps she never had. They were two driven people, pushed together and then pulled apart by their ambitions. Even the lowliest of Shield's board members realized that every decision Alex made was aimed at undermining his father's company, Storinka Defense—and not all of these decisions were profitable. In the end, that vengeful nature was the undoing of Alex Page.

So be it. Such was life.

She couldn't deny, however, that the two of them had an initial bond. And yes, on some level, she missed him.

After Bigz fled the club, she returned to her own place in Nashville and found her bottle of anti-depressants empty on the nightstand. It was too late to refill the prescription, and a stark loneliness settled upon her shoulders, a vulture leering over her, biding its time for her death and the scraps left behind.

Here now, in Seattle, Darcy's phone rang. It was "de Russian."

She closed the lid on her washing machine and

answered. "Serpionov, give me some good news."

Instead, he detailed a potential problem and awaited her decision.

"Take some initiative," she told him, "and make sure this doesn't come back to bite us. Do I need to remind you of the regular deposits I make into your account?"

"But this, it is extra work, yes? A bonus would be nice."

"Where's all this money of yours go, I wonder? What is it you want?"

"World peace," he said.

She huffed at that. Who knew these Russians had a sense of humor? "Well then, sounds as though we're both after the same thing."

Behind her, the washer purred into action, engineered to make things more efficient, make life easier. She hoped to capitalize on this soon. In America, even the lazy masses had the right to purchase and pursue happiness, didn't they?

"It is dangerous, this work," he said.

"An extra ten. I'll grant you that. Do it quickly and discreetly."

Detective Meade received the message on his phone while propped in a corner chair along the front window of Black's Espresso.

He frequented some great coffee places around town, from Roast to Fido's to Portland Brew, but this remained his favorite. From this spot, he could observe the customers in line and at the tables, as well as the passersby on Elliston Place. The variety ranged from Vanderbilt coeds in pajama bottoms and tank tops to doctors from nearby Baptist Medical.

However, it was his friendship with the owner that put this place at the top of his list. Aramis Black was a transplant from the Pacific Northwest, a man who had overcome a checkered past, endured various trials, and become a man of good repute here in the buckle of the Bible Belt. Meade wished there were more like him. In fact, it was due to this camaraderie that Meade responded two nights ago when Aramis called about the mumblings of Freddy C, delusional talk about microchips and toothaches and sore arms and medical quacks.

"Here ya go." Aramis came around from the espresso bar in his dark brown apron, both sleeves rolled up, tattoos exposed. He plopped down a drink in front of Meade. "Your infamous Hair Curler."

"With extra juice, like I asked?"

"Dude. You're a very sick man. No offense."

"Well, Aramis, you never have been a good judge of character."

"Made my share of mistakes. Listen, gotta get back to the bar."

Meade thanked him and took a swig from the ceramic cup. Based on an Italian concoction, the drink included shots of espresso topped with squeezes of fresh lime juice. "Hair Curler" was an understatement.

Having served Metro Nashville for fourteen years, the detective had witnessed things that dulled the glow in his eyes and carved lines in his brow. He no longer looked in the mirror except to shave, and he shaved only so that his wife would let him get close on the nights that the job didn't keep him away. Regular espresso drinks were his legal way of maintaining his edge.

Ready now for his message, he lifted his phone. He hoped for Natalie's sake that it was word from his longtime acquaintance, the sheriff in Anderson County. Perhaps there had been a break in the long-forgotten case of Janet Flynn.

Instead, the call came from Ballistics.

Meade had already learned that the man gunned down in airport parking last December worked for Storinka Defense Systems, a military contractor that had fallen from grace after con-tract disputes with the Pentagon. According to this new message, the rounds recovered from the deceased were a rare caliber and bore riflings more con-sistent with certain foreign handguns than with any U.S. brands.

Chapter Sixteen

Freddy C didn't feel any premonition of death as he left Thursday night's dinner at the Rescue Mission. He needed space, just as simple as that.

"And a gulp of fresh air," he muttered. "Fresh air from the river."

He veered east through Sobro, Nashville's south-of-Broadway district. Still under construction, a multimillion-dollar convention center towered over the area. He walked through an alleyway, caught tantalizing whiffs from Joe's Crab Shack, and cut north toward Fort Nashborough on the bluff over the Cumberland.

Long ago, a stockade much like this replica had protected Nashville's founding families from Native American warriors. A few years back, Aramis Black, owner of Black's Espresso, had saved his mother's life at this very location. Now the structure huddled in the neon glow of nearby Hard Rock Café and Coyote Ugly while tourists, lovers, and panhandlers plied the walkway.

"Lordy, I'm feeling tired," Freddy prayed under his breath.

He stopped at the fence along the bluff, and a breeze tugged at his beard. Below, the huge paddle wheel of the *General Jackson* pushed the riverboat beneath the downtown bridges while the water reflected its rows of lights. On the far bank stood LP Field, where the Tennessee Titans played.

"This world," he said, "it's got its share of pain and sorry, but me, I'm trying to be grateful. Yessir, mighty grateful."

He was glad to be away from the crowd at the Rescue Mission. The staff was hardworking and dedicated, but he was too weak for the pushing and chattering in the halls, too old for the few who cursed and showed disrespect.

To boot, he had been feeling crabby these past few weeks.

Ever since that visit to the free clinic.

Sure enough, they'd fixed him up and sent him on his way, but he wasn't the only one who felt wobbly and upset after that strange injection. They also helped him with his tooth so that there was no pain at all for the next few weeks. Recently, though, it'd started bothering him again, and he worried there might be an infection that the dentist had simply covered with enamel.

"Mr. Chipps?"

Freddy C turned, pulling his wool coat tight, and saw a man approaching. It made Freddy antsy that this person knew his last name, until he realized it was the Russian from the clinic, the guy with the big arms and the barrel chest.

"It's you," he said. "Just the man I gotta talk to. Just the man."

"This river." The Russian stopped. "At night, the lights are beautiful."

"Yep, them lights. Uh-huh. You know, sir, I ain't feeling my best. Not since those doctors looked at the group of us. Was free, but sometimes free's not so free. Sometimes it costs ya in other ways. You ask me, I think they done some sorta experiments on us. My friend, Mr. Aramis Black, he thought the whole thing sounded fishy, called the cops, and they asked me a whole lotta questions. Haven't heard nothing. Maybe I oughta call 'em back."

"It is not good you talk to everybody."

"Eventually, someone's bound to listen. Dontcha think?"

"Come." The Russian pulled a cell from his pocket. When he flipped it open, it played a bar from "Every Breath You Take," which was kind of creepy. He said, "Reception here is not so good. Let's walk, and this time, I make call for you."

"To 'em doctors from the clinic? No, thank you."

"I promise, you'll feel no more pain when call is over."

Freddy C followed the man along the bluff that paralleled the thick foliage and the river's murky currents. He watched the muscular fellow punch numbers into the cell phone, and the screen glimmered in the trees' deepening shadows.

"You want, I can tell 'em what I'm feeling," Freddy said.

"No." The Russian pivoted and pointed the cell at Freddy's ear, his gaze hardening in the green glow. "You wanted help for tooth, and I let you stay. Now, I think you talk too much."

"Well then, you tell 'em. Either way's fine by me."

"I did you this favor—"

"And I'm mighty grateful, sir."

"Because it gave me a chance to conduct an experiment. This phone is a gun, Mr. Chipps. Yes, this is true. I want you to walk with me farther along river, and if you run, I will kill you."

"You'd shoot me?"

"In this city, who'll care if you disappear?"

A burst of fear overrode Freddy's indignation and dull toothache. He thought of a friend, found dead beneath a Nashville overpass a few weeks ago. No witnesses, no suspects, no public outcry. One less bum to feed.

"The guys at the mission, they'll know something's wrong."

"Bah. They will think you go to another city."

"No, sir, I been here for years. And my friend, Aramis, he'll know something's not right. He'll come a-lookin'."

"Walk ahead of me," the Russian commanded. "Not too fast."

Freddy started moving forward, considering his

options. It had been four decades since his days in 'Nam, hunkered down in the heat, peeling off leeches and avoiding Viet Cong trip wires. He never talked about that time in his life. Most people didn't know of his past. Back then, he had cursed the skies and believed only in Dylan and LSD. These days, he was slow and stiff, but he praised the heavens anyway and believed in someone greater than himself.

"You're wrong," he told the Russian. He slowed his pace, figuring he might be able to drop, spin, and tackle the man with the gun.

"Keep walking."

"Somebody's gonna know, yessir. Somebody's always watchin'."

"Me." The Russian chuckled. "This is the purpose of my experiment."

"No, God's the one watchin'."

"Religious talk? You sound like my grand-mother."

"He sees, yes, He does. And He knows your name," said Freddy C. He tensed, ready to defend himself against this younger, stronger man. Then he felt a thin object press against the base of his neck and heard the beep of a button.

The Russian jeered. "This call, it's from Him. Maybe He wants to talk."

The evening's second call came as Darcy slipped into her wrinkle-free rayon-blend skirt. Not a whiff of stale smoke. She took the call, expecting Serpionov again, but this time, it came from a less-frequent contact. "Pastor Teman," she said. "Good to hear from a man of the cloth."

"How're you? If I'm not mistaken, we haven't seen you in our pews for a good month or two."

"Only when in town, and only when my schedule allows."

"Well, you'll be pleased to know I have an appointment this Friday, a chance to minister, if you will, to an influential young Republican. My hands're tied to some extent by nonprofit laws, but there's nothing that bars me from offering strong pastoral words of advice."

"My, there's an opportunity. I'm sure your guidance will be appreciated."

"That's my prayer, yes."

Although such religious sentiments nauseated Darcy, she had learned long ago how to play along. Raised on the north end of Seattle by parents who were well-to-do social minglers, employees at Boeing, and staunch atheists, she reacted during her high school years by attending various church youth groups with a friend. Whatever they were selling, she wasn't buying.

"Mine too," she purred. "I'm pleased to have you backing me on this, Pastor, but what about End Times prophecies and such? Don't you worry that you'll come under fire from conservatives and the fundamentalist crowd?"

"Now, let's be kind. I dip my toes into those same waters, Ms. Page. In the case of HB 6336, however, I don't see that there's any connection. After all, we have our elderly and our young ones to think of."

"Agreed. Next time I'm in Nashville on a Sunday, I'll be sure to pay a visit. I did enjoy that one fellow's music. Bret Vreeland, I believe it was?"

"He's fantastic, isn't he? He'll be touring soon for his debut album. And Rhonda and I, we'd be thrilled, of course, to have you worship with us again."

"I'm sure you would," Darcy said, knowing how much he coveted her donations. "A minister is worth his wages, isn't that right?"

Chapter Seventeen

Natalie could barely breathe. Since hearing the news yesterday, she had said nothing of it to her Roast coworkers, but her knees wobbled this morning as she made customers' drinks. Cold fingers pried at her ribs, threatening to seize and silence her heart.

OK, so an Anderson County sheriff had found skeletal remains in the woods northeast of her childhood home.

OK, so the shape of the pelvic bones suggested a female.

OK, so they might, might, *might* be those of her mother.

Natalie knew Detective Meade had urged the sheriff to reopen the case, but never expected results this fast. She called her dad moments after Tuf delivered the news. "Is any of this true?" she demanded. "If Tuf's feeding me a line here, I swear, I'll—"

"They think it's her, Duckie."

"Mom, you mean."

"Yes." Mardy's voice sounded thin. "Some college kids, they's messing 'round in the Oak Ridge Forest, some educational hike or whatnot on them nature trails. One goes trudging off. Next thing, he's lost in all that acreage, and, well, he comes 'cross some old bleached bones and a half-buried shoe. All rotted, but the size, well, it's the same as your mother wore. Size 8."

"That's, like, the same size I wear. That doesn't prove anything."

"You know, she always did love walking in 'em woods. Said it calmed her. Reckon we'll know better in a coupla weeks. They'll run tests, forensics, and whatnot. This might put to rest some of them things been said 'bout me."

"Dad, I know it's been tough for you. I understand that. I heard the sort of stuff kids said when I was in school, all the rumors and speculation."

"Cops questioned me 'least three or four times."

"And you were cleared."

"Woke up for months, Duckie, thinking they was coming to take you and your sis from me. That was my greatest fear."

Natalie dragged her lower lip through her teeth, drawing blood.

"I kept my chin up," he continued. "Never flinched. All the while, I was missing my wife and wondering what I coulda done that made her up and leave."

"We don't even know that's what happened," Natalie said.

"If she was taken, dontcha think there'd have been somebody out there who seen something fishy? A person don't just disappear without a trace. 'Less, of course, they want to. That there's a different matter. Fact is, I had to let go of it all years ago. What else could I do? Woulda died otherwise."

"Listen, Dad. These bones, I don't believe it's her."

"You don't wanna believe."

"What if I'm right, though? What if she's still alive?"

"Croutons in a bucket! Don't ya see it? If that's so, she's made it mighty clear she don't want nothing to do with us. Nah, I say we wait to hear from 'em investigators, then give her the burial she deserves and move on. Tuf agrees."

"Tuf. Right. Why'd you tell her before me?"

"Called you first, actually. Couldn't get through and didn't wanna leave it on no message. My next step was to call your sis. Caught her on a Greyhound, headed out to Nashville of all places. I asked her to keep it quiet and lemme tell you myself, but seems she took it upon her to share it anyways."

"Why am I not surprised? How'd she even find me?"

"Your new job, well, ya got it posted right there on Facebook."

Natalie nodded. "You're right. I'm sorry, Dad."

"I done the best I could with you girls, and thank the good Lord I had Grams to help out. Would I change what happened if given the chance? You bet I would. And in the flick of a lamb's tail. But what's done is done, and no matter where this leads, we've got lives to live. Am I right? Maybe this is just what Tuf needs to get herself turned around. As for you, Duckie, you keep doing what you're doing. Best thing we can do is to honor your momma's memory."

After a busy morning shift, Natalie made the ten-minute walk to the rental house, where Mr. Faranzmehr waited in his Mercedes. He'd agreed to meet so that she could explain her situation.

Her situation.

Like it was an everyday sort of thing.

She approached the house, heart pounding. How could starlings chirp in the overhead branches while her entire world teetered on the edge? She felt moisture streak her cheek, and she shoved her hand across her skin. *No mas.* Time to pull it together. Nearly two decades after Janet Flynn's disappearance, no one cared to see Natalie turn on the waterworks. Especially a landlord.

"Good day, Natalie," he said.

She shook his hand. "Thanks for coming, Mr. Faranzmehr."

He led the way into the rental and took off his shoes at the entryway. Natalie did so as well, hoping her socks didn't reek from hours of sweat, splashed milk, and coffee grinds.

"Removing the shoes, this is habit for me." He pushed his glasses up his nose. "Very Persian. But please, when you move in, you do not have to do this. Only that you wipe your feet. I wish for you to feel at home here. That's important, no?"

"We'll treat it with respect. Absolutely."

They moved into the unfurnished living room, where sunlight splashed through the large window and massaged Natalie's feet with its warmth on the hardwood floor. Despite Eli's approval of Natalie coming to speak with their landlord, she didn't want to entangle him in this mess with her sis.

Mr. Faranzmehr's voice softened. "So, is there problem, Natalie?"

"I hope not. Here's the thing, I'm wondering if we can move in, like, a little sooner than planned. It's my sister. She just showed up in town and doesn't have her own place yet. We're all stuffed into a house in East Nashville—the Vreelands and their kids, Eli, my sister, two adopted Doberman pinschers, and me."

"This also sounds Persian." He grinned. "But maybe not so American."

"The problem's our first month's rent. Eli's pastor is paying him next week, and I'm saving every bit I can, but we won't have it all till the end of April."

"My handyman, he must make small repairs. Then it is allowed for you to come. I did a check, Natalie, and Mr. Eli Shaffokey has no credit history. I like him, so this is not big problem, but it falls on you. I insist, full rent is requirement before I give you the keys. I learn this from my rental properties, you see."

"Anyway, could we do half now, half later? *Por favor?* I hate even asking. This is not my style, but I had no idea that my sis would . . . Never mind."

Mr. Faranzmehr hitched his slacks over a rounded belly. "How old?"

"Tina? She's twenty-two."

"She would stay here with you?"

"Only till she can work out something else. I mean, I don't want to impose on you or anything."

"She's family, no? This is important."

Natalie gave a quick nod, looked out through the window. Her whole life, she had felt obligated to watch after Tuf. While she embraced that duty, it always stirred the pain of their mother's absence. Whatever. She saw no reason to dump her personal business on her landlord, and surely, he had his own family issues to deal with.

Mr. Faranzmehr said, "It is not good business when I make exceptions."

"I know. Listen, I shouldn't have even—"

"But as Christians, it is good we listen and show grace. You will promise me your sister is responsible? She honors your family name?"

"Honestly? She's, uh, had some problems in the past."

He peered over his glasses.

"She's trying to turn a new page, though."

"Sometimes," he pointed out, "the next page is more problems."

"For her sake, I hope that's not the case."

"I hope for you too, Natalie. Pay half now, and I give you the keys. But if we have trouble, I hold you accountable. This is best I can do, no?"

Serpionov didn't know the exact meaning of his family name, but last night, he had seemed to live up to it. He was the scorpion who delivered one fatal sting, the serpent who slithered up the riverbank, leaving a dead man to the whims of the deep, flowing waters.

A sacrifice. Hadn't even the God of the Bible offered up one life in hopes that many others would be spared?

Freddy C's final words rang in his ears: *He knows your name.*

Serpionov had heard such talk before from his grandmother.

As he climbed the bank in the darkness, branches slapped at his angular face, and thorns snagged his bloodstained shirt. Keeping to the shadows, he stole over a stone barrier tagged by local graffiti artists and found his motorcycle a block farther north. He rode beneath the Woodland Street Bridge, turned near the Criminal Justice Center, and passed a pair of patrol cars heading out for the evening shift. Neither showed any interest in the man on the Honda Interceptor.

There, my babushka. *There was your God's chance, and He did nothing.*

This meant one of three things:

1. God was nonexistent or too far away to care.
2. God was powerless to intervene.
3. God approved of Serpionov's work.

The former OMON officer considered it his personal assignment to rid this world of terror. In

Russia, he'd been trained to uphold the law, then been used as a political pawn. His hands had been dirtied in the name of justice.

Nyet. No longer.

He burned his shirt in his condo fireplace, determined that any work he did from this point on must fit his greater purpose. Take Ms. Page, for example. She believed he was acting on her orders, but this remained true only so long as those orders matched his own goals.

Seven dropped calls now. Seven sacrificed.

How many more before this was over?

Although he couldn't predict the answer, he knew all of it would end with Natalie. She would be the final sacrifice.

Chapter Eighteen

With the Space Needle visible through the boardroom windows, ten men and two women sat around the massive rosewood table. Darcy's hold on the company was tenuous, and she knew that each of them coveted her position. They had already delivered their departmental updates, and now her own pet technology was up for discussion.

"The House vote was a speed bump," she explained. "Nothing more."

Someone coughed. Thunder rumbled in the east.

"What went wrong?" the chief operating officer asked. Jack Norwood was a capable COO, even if his imagination was as limited as his skills on the golf course. "I thought you'd hired one of the best lobbying firms in Tennessee."

"And it paid off. The bill did make it through committee."

"But failed to get a majority vote."

"Only because of a last-minute stumble by our representative. The House will be out of session in another month. Then the bill returns to committee for further review. They'll poll constituents, float variations on the wording, hold public hearings, and we'll have this legislation back on the agenda in early 2012."

Norwood rubbed his chin. "You think this Reuben King fellow is slow-playing us, trying to get more money on the table before he shows his cards? We've already invested in his campaign, haven't we?"

"And he got reelected. He has concerns, though, about RFID."

"For that matter, so do I."

Darcy arched an eyebrow. "RFID applications are our bread and butter."

"That's not in question. Even now, we're closing in on that deal to integrate General Electric's line of next-gen household appliances. Could be huge."

"Tell me something I don't know, Jack. I initiated that conversation."

"It's this foray into human tagging that concerns, well, not just me."

"Who else?"

"I don't think specifics are necessary."

Darcy stood. "Show of hands. Who questions me on this?"

Norwood's eyes moved to the slit in her skirt. He moistened his lips, closed the cover on his tablet. "We're not questioning you. This isn't even about your management style over your husband's, God rest his soul. It's—"

"I own Shield outright. Do you think I stay awake at night worrying whether you like the way I do things? I am worried, though, that one of you is selling secrets to Storinka Defense, my husband's bitter rival."

"Preposterous," Norwood said. "We want this company to succeed. Like you, we'd all love to become obscenely rich." A few grunts from around the table encouraged him to go on. "I'm tired of hearing our Microsoft pals talk about their glory days. The past is the past, and we're on the brink of a brave new world."

"Agreed. So then," she said, "what's got you wetting yourself with worry?"

Norwood flashed a thin smile. "The Ice Queen is back."

Others flinched, while Darcy simply chuckled.

"I would be remiss," he pressed on, "if I didn't point out that we're rushing into a field of social and legal landmines. Consumers don't want us looking over their shoulders, peeking into their purses and wallets. They'd like to think they still have some privacy left in this day and age."

"How blissfully ignorant of them."

"It's all about perception. You know this better than I do, with your degree in communications strategy."

"Nice bit of flattery, Jack."

"It's a valid concern. The average person fears intrusion."

Darcy extended her palms. "Then we package intrusion as protection. Give them options, a sense of empowerment and control. Take Facebook. Most users never spend a dime advertising there, but rarely stop to question how billions of dollars have been made. They think they have some control over who sees their information, and so they're pacified. Those in this room know better. Personal preferences are the new currency, and data mining goes on 24-7."

A few faces turned her way.

"That's right," she said. "Did you think we'd bet everything on the sales of microchips alone? True, that could make us rich, but the deeper treasure here will be the data we're able to collect and offer to the highest bidders."

"If your bill passes," Norwood pointed out.

"It'll happen."

"Even so, Tennessee's only one state. A small step in a long race."

"One of the final steps. Once precedence is set, other states will follow."

The head of marketing, redheaded Lindsey Sims, leaned forward at the table. "It could backfire, Darcy. Remember the rumors that leaked in the eighties about those stars in the Procter & Gamble logo? Connect the stars and you saw the number 666? Christians spoke out. The media ran with it. Boycotts nearly ruined them until they dropped the logo and started fresh as simply P&G."

"One of our biggest competitors in RFID development."

"We don't want to repeat their mistakes. Early test groups have already brought up the Mark of the Beast and the Antichrist, and it's not only conservatives we're worried about. Even the most liberal college students could start blogging about Orwellian control and Big Brother."

"The public is fickle," Darcy said. "P&G overcame that bad press, and *Fortune* now lists them as one of the most trusted companies in the world."

"Sure, but we can avoid those initial troubles altogether if we're wise."

"Tell me your plan."

"My ad team scours the news every day," Sims said, "for stories that shed a positive light on tagging. Dogs returned to their owners. Escaped convicts tracked down within hours. Sex offenders found peeking through school fences. We've been disseminating this stuff far and wide, softening public perception."

"Protection is the perception."

"In so many words."

"No. In those exact words," Darcy said. "Write it down. I'm flying back to Nashville next week for more meetings, but that's the mantra I want to hear chanted through these halls the next time I come into this building."

"It's good. It's concise."

"You and your team, you brainstorm, come up with a marketable name for this device, one that oozes trustworthiness. I need promos ready to go."

"Yes, Ms. Page."

"Let's shift the dialogue about microchips from the paranoid fringe into the mainstream. Believe me, I'm not deaf to public fears. Nor to the whispers of those in this very room who are clawing their way up the ladder. Hear me now, hear me clearly. I'm at the top of your particular ladder, and if you want to kiss my heels, feel free to do so. But the view from the top is mine. Solely mine."

Rain drummed against the windows, obscuring the panorama of the harbor and Puget Sound.

Darcy turned to Norwood. "Speak up. Any more questions?"

The COO tapped his pen on the table. "We only want to be sure that your political rabbit chasing doesn't, well, distract from our more stable partnerships."

"Rabbit chasing."

"If you'll pardon the metaphor."

"On Friday, I'm meeting with investors to demonstrate our technology and secure more funds. But let's run with that metaphor," she said. "Yes, I'll hunt down the needed political votes, and we'll make a killing with our implantation devices. There's no shortage of ways to get Representative King's attention, and there's also no better place for our launch. Nashville is a health care mecca that brings in $70 billion annually. The support from their local clinics will be strong. Forget the bread and butter, Jack. We'll be eating rabbit stew."

"And if your rabbit darts off in some unexpected direction?"

"He won't."

"I'm sorry," Sims interjected, "but can you give us any guarantees?"

"I'm applying financial, personal, and political pressure. There's even a neighborhood pastor willing to offer 'spiritual direction' to our stubborn representative." Darcy wanted to mention physical threats at her disposal as well, but thought it best to maintain plausible deniability. She gazed around the table and said, "The next time Mr. King goes into the pot, he will not be hopping out."

Chapter Nineteen

Natalie heard the idling motorcycle and thought nothing of it. Not at first. She pulled the strings of her hoodie tighter, hunched her shoulders, and strode through purple shadows toward Roast.

The walk wasn't bad, only seven blocks up Trousdale Drive. As a band of tangerine clouds hinted at one *fabulosa* sunrise, she breathed in the cool air, thanked God for this job and for news that Bret Vreeland would be headed out on tour soon. She prayed for Tuf. For Dad. For some answers about her mother.

She picked up her pace, not wanting to be late. This was one sweet job, and she needed every penny, particularly while staring down the barrel of rent, utilities, and student loans that could linger into her forties.

Behind her, the sound of the motorcycle grew louder, and she wondered why it hadn't passed her already. She hugged the roadside, just as her phone rang.

"Grams," she answered. "You're up early."

"Oh, it's this arthritis, dear. I'm lucky to sleep more than two or three hours at a stretch, and my mind's been racing, wondering about your mother."

"Still no word? I thought they'd know something by now."

"It's not for lack of trying. Sheriff showed us the bits of clothing excavated near the body, but there were only tatters, nothing your father or I recognized. Fact is, we may never know. And after all these years, will it make a difference either way? Sometimes it's best to look forward and let the past work its own wrinkles out. I do hope I caught you before work. It's an hour earlier here, eastern time, and I've been meaning to call ever since I heard of your situation."

"With Tuf?"

"I feel partly responsible."

"What? How? She's a grown woman."

"I know that. Of course, I do, dear. But you two are like daughters to me, and it pains me to see either of you fall upon hard times."

"I'm fine, Grams. We're fine."

"Would you tell me otherwise? You've never been much for complaining."

Natalie weighed her current realities. While Eli wouldn't move into the rental for a few more weeks, she and her sis were settling in amid boxes, backpacks, and sleeping bags rolled out atop air mattresses from the Kmart down Harding Road. The cupboards were almost bare, and their primary cooking appliance was a microwave that they had picked up at a yard sale for fifteen bucks.

Not like either of them had learned any culinary arts from Dad.

"I'll admit," she told her grandmother, "things're a bit tight, but Tuf's put in some applications and it seems she's really trying to turn a corner. What else am I supposed to do? Toss her out on the street?"

"You know, I did offer for her to stay at my place once she was let out."

"That was nice of you. Really, Grams. Your house is special to us—all those Thanksgivings, Christmases, and Easters. Tuckaleechee Cove is a cozy town, but you have to admit it's not, like, the hot spot for a single, up-and-coming woman."

"Do tell. And have you found a dashing young beau in Nashville?"

"Uh, not yet. Still trying to graduate and start my career."

"Which, incidentally, is the other reason I called."

Ahead, the junction between Blackman Road and Trousdale signaled to Natalie that she was near her workplace. The exercise and the cool air had reawakened her brain after last night's cramming for finals, and her thoughts were flooded with Jung's and Freud's contrasting views. When she had students of her own, she would try to remember the stress of taking tests.

"You've been so diligent," Grams said, "and I couldn't be more proud of you, Natalie. I called to discuss your gift. I intended to deliver a check to you in person, the day of your ceremony, but an early present might do you more good."

"No. No, you don't have to—"

"Oh, of course I do. Now give me your new address, will you?"

"I still have finals to take. Who knows? I might not even graduate."

"Nonsense. I'd send more if I had the means, but I do hope twenty-five hundred dollars will be enough for you to find a dependable little car."

"Grams, I . . ." Natalie's voice gave out.

"It'll go out with this morning's mail. You have a blessed day, dear."

Natalie's eyes blurred as the call ended. Could it be true? She would have wheels of her own ASAP? This was epic, since she could no longer count on driving the Vreelands' Subaru, or even Eli's pickup. She would need reliable transportation if she was hired at one of the nearby schools—Granberry, Crieve Hall, or Tusculum.

Should she shop for another moped? Or should she go for one of those old Honda Civics that could go forever on a tank of gas and tuck into tight spots downtown?

Blinking, she looked back over her shoulder and prepared to cross the street. She thought she saw Eli on the sidewalk, which seemed strange. Then the motorcycle diverted her attention.

It was still there, idling close by.

What the heck? He's following me.

At the controls of the sporty bike sat a stout figure in boots, black leather pants, and a jacket with streaks of red and white along the sleeves. As Natalie jerked back from the road, he coasted by and his helmet-clad head turned her way, his eyes hidden behind the darkened visor, a gloved hand raised in greeting.

She watched him turn the corner onto Blackman, then she trotted across the street, slipped into the shop, and disarmed the alarm. She locked the door again and squeezed into a corner with the lights still off, eyes scanning the parking lot through the wide front window. Her mind replayed that moment eight months earlier when Magnus followed her into Sip Café and attacked her from behind.

She swallowed. No, that was over and done. As for this new zip code, it was supposed to be safer. At least that was what Mr. Faranzmehr had told her when she signed the lease.

I'm losing it here. Lord, help me.

The joy from Grams's news gave way to apprehension. So who was the guy following her on the motorcycle? Was she reading too much into it, assigning guilt to some innocent commuter who had been polite enough to offer her a wave?

Either way, she should have noted the license tag.

A little late now for that, dingbat.

Chapter Twenty

Seattle. Friday morning. Time for a demonstration.

In the Shield Technologies boardroom, Darcy munched on organic snacks from a caterer's cart against the panoramic window and watched her assistant distribute iPad 2s around the table. Bigz was outfitted in a fedora angled low over his head, a gold tie, and a green suit that matched his eyes. He hummed, tapped his fingers on the chairs, and circled back to her.

"Doesn't this all seem a trifle childish?" she said.

"The iPads? Are you crazy, woman?"

She shot him a look. By way of apology, Bigz nudged closer to straighten the collar of her blouse, and she offered him a slice of Golden Delicious apple.

"Forgive me for spouting off like that." He took a bite. "But if there's one thing you can count on, it's that even rich boys and girls like their toys."

"Don't poke fun at me again."

"I hope I'm more than just a toy to you."

"Keep hoping."

He shrugged that off. "The iPads are a welcome gift, Darce, a way of letting them know you value their time. I've preloaded each unit with user-specific data, as well as with the Shield Yourself promo that Lindsey Sims put together."

"Secured Human Identification, Encrypted Lifetime Device."

"SHIELD," he stated. "It's a mouthful, but Mrs. Sims and her team plan to feed this concept into the public consciousness and make it a way of life. By this time next year, when the man on the street says 'It's time to Shield myself,' he'll be thinking lifelong security and protection."

"And he'll be correct. Believe me, Shield's going to save lives."

"Sign me up."

She fed him another bite. "Consider it done."

"Your audience is gathered in the hospitality suite. You ready to do this?"

"Bring them in," she said. "I'll get the Russian on the line."

"De Russian, de Russian. I vunder, do you haf crush on dis mahn?"

"I'm all about profit margins, Bigz. You ought to know that. If de Russian convinces our guests to invest, you better believe I'll be head over heels for him."

"So predictable, my queen."

"Go. We don't have all morning."

Once Bigz was gone, Darcy logged on to her laptop and connected via Skype with Serpionov at his condo in Nashville's Gulch. She'd been to his place a few months earlier, knew it to be more than adequate accommodations for a bachelor, and didn't mind covering the costs so long as he carried out his assignments with discretion.

"Good morning, Ms. Page."

The Russian's voice was altered to mask his identity, and his features were shaded on her screen so that only an angular chin and thin lips showed.

She skipped the niceties. "My investors'll be patched in for your demonstration in a matter of minutes. You have nine tagged individuals that we'll be able to monitor in real time, is that correct?"

"Eight," he said. "This includes Natalie."

"I take it, then, that you handled the other situation for us?"

"He wanted to make trouble. I had no choice."

"If it raises suspicions, you do realize you're on your own."

"It's no longer problem."

Behind Darcy, the boardroom doors opened. "Hold on," she told him.

She spun in her chair and rose to greet her hand-picked guests—business tycoons, media moguls, surgeons, and venture capitalists. They were well financed and well connected. Their single common denominator, one Darcy shared, was an insatiable drive for more profit, more power.

She gestured them to the goodies on the cart, then to their places at the table. Bigz served as the oil in the machinery, smoothing introductions, offering a bit of off-center class that put those in attendance at ease.

These were visionaries and thought shapers.

Shifters of the paradigm.

They understood that positive results often required drastic measures. Take for instance the brave physicians of yesteryear, those who dissected cadavers to mine the body's secrets and pioneer new methods of treatment. They were demonized in their day. Called sorcerers and necromancers.

No, these here in this room were smarter than that.

"The iPads," she told them, "are yours, no strings attached. That said, each of you knows why you've been invited, so I won't pretend I want anything less than your generous resources and wholehearted commitment. Far be it from me to twist arms, but this'll be your one and only opportunity to join our march into the future. I won't wait around for stragglers."

"It'll take more than a simple gift to convince me," said a stockbroker.

Others nodded their agreement.

"Then let's turn on said gifts and let the convincing begin." Each networked iPad flashed to life. "We'll start with a thirty-second video, something I had my marketing department put together."

Vivid black-and-white stripes filled the screen

with an uneven yet beautiful pattern, as a soothing male voice asked, "Do you ever feel like a number? Ever feel lost in the crowd?"

The view broadened to reveal a group of zebras on a sun-soaked savannah. A nearby lioness stalked forward, and the zebras shifted but held their ground, a formidable front, protected by nature's design.

"Six billion people now inhabit our planet, and each one is precious."

A single animal broke into a run, and the lioness isolated it from the pack.

"Not one child should be ignored. Not one elderly soul should be forgotten."

The creature was chased and dragged down behind a curtain of waving honey-colored grass.

"When even one is lost, we all lose. Be known," the voice urged. "Be recognized."

The view zoomed in again on the stripes. Zoomed closer to unveil a tapestry of overlapping hairs. Zoomed even closer to show that the hairs were actually thousands of individual RFID tags bearing the company logo.

"It's time to stand strong in community. Time to Shield yourself."

Questions were posed around the boardroom table. Objections were raised. If millions were to be poured into this technology, it needed to bear up under intense scrutiny.

So far, so good.

"We already have favorable legislation under consideration," Darcy told her guests, "and I'm confident of its passage into public law."

A media mogul eyed her with a sly grin. "You're in bed with a politician?"

"I trust that you mean that figuratively." She pointed to the iPads. "Now for your real-time demonstration. At your fingertips, you have an app that allows you to track the movements of eight encrypted tags. These particular tags have been injected into individuals who will remain anonymous. As you will see, most of them are thousands of miles away at this moment. Nashville, Atlanta, Louisville."

"This is live? Impossible."

"We've bought into private satellite usage, piggybacking with a prominent cell service provider, and this allows us to pinpoint each microscopic antenna to activate and decode the enclosed chips and simultaneously update the info in our database. If a tag passes through the antitheft readers at a mall, a time stamp is electronically noted in that individual's file. If someone drives onto a E-Z Pass toll road, that is also noted. If you're in Outer Mongolia, nowhere near a reader, you'll still be visible to the circling satellites."

"Sounds invasive."

"You've read the story of Admiral Shackleton's ship and crew, lost in Antarctica and counted for dead? That happened nearly a century ago, during the First World War, but this technology would've led rescuers straight to them."

"Do these eight subjects know they're being monitored?"

"In this case," Darcy said, "we've done a good deed for some of Music City's transient population. They're helping with our research while we make sure they don't go missing, which has been a problem in that particular area."

Oh, the irony, she thought. *Considering what's been done.*

"Are they aware of this?" the mogul asked. "Was it consensual?"

"They signed waivers," she said. "Though I doubt they read the details."

"How do we know this isn't an elaborate hoax? These could be cars or—"

"Look there. Did a car just enter Hard Rock Café in downtown Nashville?"

"We'd like some proof," a banker said. "That's all we're asking."

"And our friend is now exiting Hard Rock. Probably not by choice."

"Proof, Ms. Page."

"Bigz, you know where I'm parked. Go fetch my bag from the trunk."

"The Gucci?"

"Now." She handed him her keyless remote. "People are waiting."

Once he was gone, she smiled. "Watch your screens, and you'll see we now have a ninth tag to follow." She tapped the display and brought up the new addition, a pulsing green dot that descended in the elevator in the Shield headquarters. "There. You can read his name for yourselves."

Darius Hammond, male, age 29
ST-1-85-2223-4332

"Darius," the banker said. "That's his real name?"

"Now you know."

"Does he realize he's being tracked?"

"His device is temporary. He ingested it earlier in a slice of apple."

"What if he'd bitten into the tag? You mean to say it's in his stomach?"

"For no more than a half day or so. Now let's stop talking about the poor man. He'll never know, and I'm sure it'll, uh, work itself out in the end."

"This is your assistant you're talking about."

"Sometimes," Darcy said, "he assists without even knowing."

"You're cold."

"All we need now," an investor quipped, "is his shoe size."

She clacked her nails on the table. "Consider it done. Such details'll be readily available in the database, once the proper legislation is in place. If a person picks up a pair of Nikes at their local outlet store, the product's encoded info will be linked through the credit card transaction to the consumer."

"What about cash buyers?"

"If they use any loyalty card or store membership, it'll still be linked."

"And all of this data will be for sale?"

"A virtual gold mine," Darcy said. "What is he up to now?"

On their screens, the green dot detoured to the first-floor lobby.

"Probably taking a leak," the investor suggested. "What business is it of ours? How do we know that you haven't fed each of us a similar device?"

"It's your money I'm after. Your personal habits and movements are of no interest to me." She leaned forward, pale arms braced on the rosewood table, cleavage on subtle display. "I'm sure some of you are wondering, why go to all the trouble of tagging homeless individuals when Bigz serves as an example of the microchip's effectiveness? I wanted to prove to you that distance is no factor, and the live subjects help us confirm this tech-nology's longevity and durability."

"These other subjects, their chips are permanent?"

"Encrypted Lifetime Device, precisely as the name suggests."

Oblivious to his part in their discussion, Bigz walked through the boardroom doors and handed Darcy her bag.

Darcy dropped it on the carpet. "You took longer than I expected."

He stood there like a scolded child. "The Gucci, right? I did as you said."

"Look at him. He's indispensable, isn't he?" She winked at those around the table. "Such a fine assistant can't be let out of my sight."

"What about this bright red dot?" A rotund man at the table's far end brought their attention back to the iPads. "Looks like a drop of blood, at some place called Roast Inc. The numbering sequence is different than the others."

"That was the prototype. Its application varied slightly, but it'll prove to you the durability and longevity of these tags. Take a look." She touched her iPad, bringing up fresh parameters. "Each tag also bears an AD, activation date, which is stamped electronically within five minutes of reaching between ninety-seven and one hundred degrees. In other words, we know when each is implanted."

"The red dot shows September 30, 2010. Nearly seven months ago."

"That's correct. And the green one?" she said. "Note that it's stamped with today's date. Seems the jaunt downstairs was slightly over five minutes."

Chapter Twenty-one

May

Natalie Flynn, college graduate. She liked the sound of that.

She flung her mortarboard cap into the air, screamed, and hiked her gown to reveal knee-high green stockings. Joined by three girlfriends and Abby, her former roommate, she broke into a surprise Riverdance upon the platform. Fellow students cheered while the dean of students fumed, but no one could take their diplomas from them. Not now. Not today.

Seated together in the crowd, Mardy beamed, Tuf whooped and hollered, Grams applauded, and the Vreelands and the Temans joined in the celebration. Natalie spotted Eli in their midst and gave him a nod. He nodded back in approval.

Wherever you are, Mom, I hope you're proud too.

They all converged later that evening in Hillsboro Village for dinner and drinks at Boscos. It was a loud, rowdy time, and Natalie's sense of accomplishment was equaled only by her appreciation for family and friends.

Her dad and Grams were right, she decided. It was best not to worry over a set of old bones, best to look to the future and turn to God for direction.

But if You're so trustworthy, where were You when—

Her grandma tugged on her arm. "Tell me, what're your plans now?"

"Right now? To, uh, savor every yummy bite of this dessert."

"Isn't it wonderful? By all means, dear, you do that. I hope you realize, though, that jobs aren't so easy to come by these days."

"I'll find something." Natalie leaned closer to be heard over the din, and a wisp of Gram's hair tickled her cheek. "I've already passed the state exam, and now all I need's my certification. Thanks to you, least I have a car to get around."

"Oh, and I'm so glad. Is it giving you good gas mileage?"

"An old Civic? Heck, a single tank could take me to Seattle and back."

"You won't be moving out of state, will you?"

"No, no. I was just, like, saying that as an example. Seattle'd be sweet to visit, but I want to stay here in Nashville."

"Close enough that you can still come to your Grams's for Christmas?"

"Better believe it." Natalie nibbled at her dessert, letting the shavings of dark chocolate melt on her tongue. "OMG."

"Believe what?" Tuf asked, leaning across the table.

"That you'll always be my little girls," Grams said.

"For dang sure." Mardy joined the conversation, stiff in his outdated suit. "The two of you, sure, you're all grown and ready to take on the world, but don't think for one minute that's gonna stop your ole man from worryin' about ya."

Tuf elbowed him. "When've I ever given you reason to worry?"

Natalie saw pain flash in her dad's eyes, but then he pasted on a smile.

"I'm just glad," he added, "that you've got sis to look after you now."

"Excuse me?" Tuf leveled her gaze at her father. As though ashamed of her attitude, her tattoo seemed to have slipped down beneath her collar. "I'm not freeloading, if that's what you think. I've got applications out there, and I'll get a job, you just watch. Is it easy? No, but I'm not gonna let my flippin' record stand in the way."

"I'm glad Tuf's around," Natalie said. "We'll make it work."

"You see? You hear that, Dad?"

"He meant no harm." Grams reached forward, but Tuf yanked away and nearly toppled a water glass. "We care about you. That's all we're trying to say."

"I've got my faults," Mardy said, "but I'm doin' the best I can. You know, Tuf, you don't . . . well, you don't always make it easy."

"Easy? Ahh, that's right. My job's to make it easy for y'all."

"I'd like to think we're all here to help each other. A two-way street."

"Whew." Tuf pushed back in her chair, arms crossed. "Now that's a relief."

"Such sarcasm is unbecoming," Grams mumbled.

Mardy pressed on. "What I'm sayin', Tina, is your sister's done time of her own. She's put in four years of college, and she doesn't need anything dragging her down just now."

"Yeah, I got that. Don't be a weight. Don't be a burden. Got it."

Though Natalie had been offered work only as a substitute teacher in Davidson County, it was a start and meant some income in the months ahead. Eight days ago, Eli had also moved into the house per their original agreement, and his church janitor's income would help them make ends meet.

So far, the arrangement with Tuf was going better than expected. As sisters, Natalie and Tina shouldered together the questions regarding their mother's possible demise, and this drew them closer than they had been in years.

Least that was the case until a few hours ago.

Kitchen-bound, Natalie crept past her sis, who was asleep on the living room couch, face scrunched against a pillow, fingers dangling on the rug beside an empty bag of M&M's. Natalie found Eli at the stove, stirring a pot of grits.

"When'd she drag herself in?"

Eli shrugged. "Can't rightly say. Musta been late."

"She's alive anyway. That's a good thing."

"Shoulda heard her five minutes ago. She was snoring something fierce."

"Even louder than Kevin?"

"Vreeland, you mean? Poor lil' guy."

"It's his sleep apnea. Without his mouth guard in, he can rattle the walls." She peered back into the living room. "Tuf, she's always been a deep sleeper, but my guess is she's sleeping off a few drinks. She's dead to the world."

"If'n only that were true."

"Excuse me?" Natalie frowned. "What's that supposed to mean?"

"We're s'posed to die to the old nature, isn't that so? Die to sin, to our worldly desires? Best for everyone if we could be 'dead to the world.' "

"OK, I see what you're getting at."

"Came out wrong at first."

"*No hay problema.* Listen, I don't want her to outwear her welcome. I'll talk to her, see what she's thinking. Last night was just plain rude of her." Natalie plopped into a chair at the small table. "I don't know where it all went wrong, Eli.

She used to be a sensitive little girl, even with our mom gone. Then, about the time she hit her teens, something snapped. She turned sullen and sarcastic, stayed away hours at a time. Dad and I tried getting answers out of her, but—"

"Answers 'bout what?" Tuf called out. Springs creaked as she sat up on the couch. "Is that stove-cooked grits I smell?"

"You want some, you're welcome to 'em."

"Thanks, Eli." She strolled barefoot into the kitchen, three blonde hairs stuck to her cheek, her tattoo poking out of the neckline of the Braves baseball jersey that swished about her knees. "Little cheese and paprika, that's how I eat mine. Natalie, she likes 'em with milk and sugar. She always was the sweet one. Sweet smile. Sweet voice. Just all-around sweet as can be."

"I have my bad days."

"Well, look out. Ms. Prim and Proper's 'bout to do something naughty."

Natalie settled onto a fold-up metal chair by the card table they used for their meals. "Where were you last night, Tuf? We called, left messages."

"I'm twenty-two. Not like I need a flippin' baby-sitter."

"You have a key to this place, and you don't pay a cent for that privilege. Eli and I don't mind helping, but you could show some common courtesy and let us know when you'll be home. I drove around the neighborhood a couple of times myself. I was up past two, wondering if I should gather a search party."

Tuf laughed. "That is so typical. You know, you're not my mom anymore."

"Never was. Never wanted to be."

"Could've fooled me."

Eli handed them bowls of grits, one tangy, one creamy and sweet.

"Thanks," Natalie said.

"Mmmm," Tina purred. She jarred the table as she slid into a seat.

"I'm just glad you're home and alive. I had Detective Meade on speed dial, ready to wake him up, like, three or four times."

"And here I stand, sober as can be. Would you chillax already?"

"You weren't out drinking?"

"Nope. Got a job, if you must know."

"Congratulations," Eli said. "Reckon that's some good news."

"Really?" Natalie tilted her head, pursed her lips. "Where?"

"Look at you, sis, all stressed out and thinking the worst. What, you don't think there's any respectable jobs that late at night? I got me a monthly bus pass, and I'm loading dock at a warehouse. Yeah, believe it or not, they don't discriminate, and the pay's better than anything I ever got in East Tennessee."

"So, you'll be able to save up for your own place. That's good."

"Or," Tuf said, "I figure I can stay and help y'all out."

"Whatcha got in mind?" Eli asked.

"With rent, I mean. Throw me into the mix, and we've got, what, four hundred a piece, instead of six hundred with just the two of you?"

"Where would you sleep? On the couch?"

"A palace compared to a prison cell."

Natalie glanced at Eli, who shrugged as if to say this one was her call.

"Really?" she said to him. "Don't you want to—"

"Far be it from me to come between. You and me, Natalie, we'll always be friends. But life takes its turns, and ya never know which way the wind's gonna blow. The two of you, you're family —and that goes a long way, dontcha think?"

Tuf downed a spoonful of grits. "I don't just like the way this man cooks, I like the way he thinks." She jabbed him with an elbow. "And that's high praise, coming from me."

"Coming from anyone."

"Wait," Natalie said. "You're not thinking of bailing on me, are you?"

"Me?" Eli rested a hand on the shoulder. "Signed a lease, didn't we?"

"Fine." She turned to her younger sister. "You keep clean, keep the job, and we'll see how this goes. FYI, though. With the lease being in our names, you'll have to respect whatever decisions we have to make down the road."

"Of course. Would I do anything to jeopardize that? No, not me."

"There ya have it." Eli clapped his hands. "All settled then."

"Well, sheesh, sis, you don't look too happy about it."

"*Cautious,* that's the word," Natalie said. "I love you, Tuf. Please, please, *please* don't give me reason to feel anything otherwise."

Chapter Twenty-two

The night wind buffeted Serpionov's body and riding gear, roaring about his helmet with all the fury of hell's legions released from their fiery gates. He hugged the motorcycle with his thighs, lowered his head, and twisted the throttle. The Interceptor shot into a higher gear, reducing trees and guardrails to a blur.

Cradled by speed, he felt everything slow and grow quiet. He loved this moment.

The zone.

The rattle and hum of the road dissolved into a steady, comforting purr, and objects racing by at ninety-eight miles per hour faded into a past reality where time had no more meaning and danger had no claws.

But he couldn't outdistance the cries.

The children.

Beslan.

Ahead, dusk's shadows pried at the pavement and made it difficult to judge a bend on the Oak Ridge Turnpike.

He downshifted, let the engine do the braking, and leaned the bike into the curve as his body tipped in the other direction for balance. Adrenaline bathed him in momentary exhilaration and flushed the cries from his mind. With a leather-padded knee mere inches from the ground, he tore around the banked section and onto a straightaway.

A green sign stated *Oak Ridge, 9 Miles.*

This wasn't his first visit to the area, nor would it be his last. Located in District 33, Oak Ridge was Natalie's hometown, and her father still lived and worked there. As did Representative King, when he wasn't in session.

Serpionov slid into town, parked his bike on a side street a block and a half from his destination, and set out on foot with a small pack over his shoulder. When he reached a certain cul-de-sac, he circled clockwise through the shadows. He eyed a sleek white Audi belonging to the first of this evening's targets and visualized himself as the coils of a snake, squeezing, tightening, cutting off oxygen, and crushing bones for easier digestion.

This car, he knew, was registered here in Anderson County to Reuben King. It was his primary vehicle. He probably wrote off the mileage on his taxes, in addition to collecting his allotted per diem for each legislative day. Most Tennessean politicians didn't make fortunes serving their state, and many worked regular jobs when they were not in session.

This, of course, made them easier prey to monetary temptations.

Their session generally ran from January through May, and King was now back in his hometown. He and two other insurance agents shared a small downtown office, where he tried to keep up with customer claims and stay involved in community events. Nonetheless, occasional committees, meetings, and lobbyist fund-raisers drew him west to the capitol in Davidson County.

From Oak Ridge to Nashville.

From the Secret City to Music City.

Over the past months, Serpionov had learned quite a bit about this town nestled in the Appalachian foothills. Though no longer secret, it still bore its nickname from World War II. Built as a military project in response to the attack on Pearl Harbor, Oak Ridge mushroomed into a small city, a site for developing the world's first atomic bomb. It played host to uranium diffusion facilities, to the Y-12 National Security Complex, and to scientists such as Oppenheimer and Fermi. In 1945, the Manhattan Project produced the weapon that ended the war.

These days, Oak Ridge was smaller, but still home to thousands of scientists, government personnel, and civilians.

People like Target #1: Representative King.

Like Target #2: Mardy Flynn.

Still circling on foot, Serpionov disturbed a dog behind the fence to his left. The barks grew loud, shrill, so he picked up his pace. He reached King's car, slipped a small pack from his shoulder, and ducked into the darkness at the front passenger side, where a Michelin tire showed deep new treads.

The dog kept yapping. A porch light came on.

The neighborhood was nice, the yards tidy, and moderate vigilance was to be expected. Who, though, could imagine his true intentions here by the tire? Even if they caught him and he confessed, they would do nothing but laugh.

Peeking over the hood, Serpionov saw a curtain being pulled aside and a woman looking out. The dog quieted, apparently satisfied that reinforcements had been roused. Once the curtain fell back, Serpionov continued his work.

Coiling.

Squeezing.

Within sixty seconds, he was strolling back to

his motorcycle a block and a half away. He kept the throttle low, eased through the side streets until he reached Lafayette Drive. From there it was a short ride to Mardy Flynn's home, where Mardy had lived the past three decades, lost a wife, and raised both daughters. All of this was public information, not hard to find.

Mardy worked as a security guard with a private contractor, and for many years, they'd assigned him to a booth at Y-12. By all accounts, from corner market to local mechanic, he was a good guy.

As a former special-purpose police officer, Serpionov liked good guys. They were usually trusting, concerned about others, and predictable.

The Russian turned at a checkered orange-and-white mailbox and coasted between tulip poplars down the gravel drive. He turned off the engine, toed the kickstand, removed his helmet, and strode up the front steps into the pale yellow glow of an antibug lamp. The house needed a new coat of paint, but the grounds were clean, save for a rusty tractor near the garage.

The screen door squeaked open.

"C'mon in," Mardy said. "I was gettin' to wondering if you'd make it."

Serpionov stepped inside. "We made a plan, yes? I am man of my word."

"I appreciate that. Sit. Go on, go ahead. I

reckon you're cold after that ride. Me, I'm a Folgers guy, plain and simple, but I'll let you fix up your tea just the way you like it. Once we're all settled, we can talk."

Yes. A good guy.

Serpionov sipped his tea, thanked his host, and pulled a packet of papers from an inner coat pocket. He had copies of old newspaper articles, some regarding the disappearance of Janet Flynn, others the abduction of Natalie Flynn, and one that mentioned Mardy as the recipient of a company service award.

"You've done your homework, looks like," Mardy said.

"I need your help. In return, I'll help you also, yes?"

"You mentioned something already 'bout a finder's fee."

"Of course. But it is good, I think, if I prove how this works. You worry about your daughter Natalie. You are good father, so it is natural. Here," Serpionov said, opening the black Shield case, "you can follow her movements. Never again do you worry that you lose her. No, she is here for you to see."

Mardy's eyes widened. "This is the prototype?"

"This red circle, it is Natalie."

"Or could be any ole person in Nashville. Someone's pet even." When Serpionov wiggled the cursor over the circle, it produced Natalie's data and location. "She is at church in East Nashville. Call and see if this is true."

"That there's the place the Vreelands go. Don't know if it's proper to call, her being in a house of God and all."

Serpionov took another sip of tea. "But you want proof, yes?"

Mardy dialed his cell, got a hushed response. "Sorry, Natalie," he said. "Yep, I'll call back when the service is over." He ended the call.

"It is her?"

"Yessir," Mardy said. "Alrighty, I'm impressed."

"You will help me, then? This is good."

"I'm a man who loves my country, but first, I need to know that you're on the right side of things, if you know what I mean. Me, in my position, I can't just go 'round trusting any ole person, you know? Best to be careful."

"Things in my country, they are tense, Mr. Flynn. You watch news? You see how Putin tries to control the people, and Russians, they are upset and want change. I want also, but evil men will kill to cover secrets and keep control."

"What's this gotta do with me? Or with this case here?"

"I'm a former police officer, in unit called OMON. I know of sleeper agent here in America, a man who plans to kill a politician of yours. It is weeks from now, but he will do this. Assassina-

156

tion, it is very Russian, I think—a traditional way to deal with trouble. I'll give you information so you can stop his plans."

"Your way of proving you're on the right side, huh?"

"I want peace for our children."

"Well, gotta admit, you talk a good game."

Mardy furrowed his eyebrows, compressed his lips, and examined the open case on the table. The luminescent grid cast amber lines across Mardy's nose and cheekbones, as though his face were a topographical map. In his training, Serpionov had learned to read all sorts of maps, and he discerned by Mardy's expression that his ridges of resistance were crumbling.

"You will help me?" he pressed.

Mardy folded his arms. "First, you gimme that info."

"Of course." He handed over a note. "This is date, time, and place."

Mardy read it. "You're sure 'bout this?"

"His life's in your hands."

"Something like this, I reckon the authorities oughta know."

"Bah. They will laugh." Serpionov's finger traced the rim of his tea mug. "No, you do this alone. I can deliver the technology only if you agree to help."

"Wait up." Mardy tapped the Shield grid. "There's something not right with this thing.

She's gone. Or the dot is, anyhow. My girl, she just up and vanished."

"Nashville has many hills and dips. Dead spots, you see. Perhaps also satellite trouble or weather. I thought last week that I lost her, but when I ride motorcycle to check and be sure, the light came back on, and yes, there she was."

"Oh, and here she is now." The red circle swelled to life again on the screen, moving along Eastland Avenue. "Had me worried there for a sec."

"She's safe, Mr. Flynn. Safe and shielded."

"Shield." Mardy tapped the letters on the case. "Yep, I get it. OK then, I've decided to help ya, but it's gotta be on one condition."

Chapter Twenty-three

June

Natalie kicked shut the bathroom door and leaned over the sink, lower back aching, insides feeling crampy. This wasn't the way she envisioned the evening. Her first trip to Oak Ridge in over a year was supposed to be a homecoming of sorts, after her graduation last month.

"What's keeping ya, Duckie? C'mon, we're running late."

"Give me two seconds," Natalie said.

"One thousand one. One thousand two."

"Dad, puh-lease." She wasn't about to explain to her father that her monthly cycle had started. Although Mardy did his best and always treated her like a lady, it would probably be too much information. TMI.

"Was just ribbing ya," he said.

"Seriously, two secs. I'll be right out."

His keys jingled. "Be waiting in the Bronco."

She saw to her feminine needs, and wished again that she and Tuf could have had a mother to walk them through their early teens. Enough of that, though. Time to look to the future. Least they had Grams—long-suffering Grams—which was more than some girls ever got.

She sighed, popped ibuprofen into her mouth, and washed the pills down with water from the tap. She pursed her lips and made a face.

This water tasted strange. Or was she imagining things? She still recalled her juvenile fears of contamination after nearby East Fork Poplar Creek tested for toxic mercury levels, residue from the military's nearby production of hydrogen bombs. Yep, this place was called the Secret City for a reason.

She flipped her hair from her face and caught the sparkle of her tiny nose stud. In the mirror that still bore butterfly stickers in the lower corner, she noted her own wary eyes.

Stick with the plan, she told herself. *You can do this.*

Natalie shuffled out to her father's vintage red Bronco and climbed in. "Sorry I took so long," she barked over the twang of a country tune.

"S'OK." Mardy adjusted the volume. "Had ole Hank to keep me company."

"Hank Williams?"

"Junior," he corrected.

"Not exactly my thing, but I'll take your word."

"You alright?" He stopped at the end of the driveway, at a mailbox checkered orange and white for the Vols football team. "You know, Duckie, we really don't got to do this tonight."

"What? No, you've been looking forward to this. I mean, it's Ricky Skaggs on the festival stage, right?"

"Oh boy, is it." Mardy thumped his palm on the steering wheel. "And I'm a big fan. Not to mention he's got a fella from Nashville opening for him, a young star named Johnny Ray Black. You must've heard him on the radio."

"I'm, like, more of an iPod girl. Let's go. We're already running late."

"And whose fault is that?" He gave her a sideways look, winked, then edged onto Lafayette Drive. "Well, we're on our way now, and ain't nothing like the Secret City Festival to stir the ole juices."

Natalie wondered if he was anticipating the

musical acts, the hot funnel cakes, the World War II reenactments, or the clusters of women strolling in the summer evening breeze. At times she worried about him—in his fifties and still on his own. Despite a few shots at dating, he hadn't remarried. On occasion, she saw his eyes cloud over and his jaw muscles knot under cropped, pointed sideburns.

The Bronco found a pothole, and Natalie winced in the passenger seat.

Oh, isn't it lovely being a girl, with all the issues that go along with that?

During Natalie's last visit to the doctor, she had been told that her menstrual cycle would regulate once she was sexually active, and that the greater concern would be her ability to get pregnant. That fear stuck in her throat. She yearned to have kids of her own one day, to brush out their hair, make their school lunches, and impart to them all the things she was forced to learn and do on her own.

That old schoolyard jingle ran through her head:

First comes love, then comes marriage,
Then comes Nattie and the baby carriage.

Well, if love came first, she had a long way to go. She knew some decent guys in her graduating class, but no one who ignited any real sparks in her. Sparks were important, weren't they? And while she'd been intrigued by a few of her customers at Roast, her past encounters with Magnus had soured all that.

How had she been so blind? How could she give herself to someone new when she hadn't even spotted those old deceptions that stared her in the face?

Forget the sparks. Best if she stayed in control.

Si, chica, *and we'll see how that works for you.*

"You're awfully quiet over there," Mardy said.

"Saving up my energy for the festival."

"Good thing, 'cause there's someone I been meaning for you to meet tonight. One of our own, grew up right here in our backyard."

"A guy?"

"A guy."

"Dad, no. I'm fully capable of planning my own love life." Traffic was thicker here on the turn-pike, corralled by festival pylons and streamers. "No, this is not cool. Like, you don't even ask, and now he's coming just to meet me?"

"Natalie, what kinda teacher goes 'round saying 'like'?"

"I'm talking to you, not to a classroom full of kids."

"Hey now, why're ya sounding so upset?"

"You want to know? Really? OK, well, it's that time of the month."

"That time? You mean, your womanly . . ." Mardy's cheeks reddened.

"Yes. It doesn't exactly put me in the mood to

162

meet some weirdo who's been sipping from these nuclear waters since birth."

"He ain't here just for you. Ain't nothing special like that."

That deflated her a bit. "Hello?" She crossed her arms and shifted the focus. "And you wonder where I learned to talk."

"The man's got himself a booth, if you must know."

"Sweet. He can comp me a caramel apple."

"Not that kinda booth."

Natalie drew her arms tighter, hugging her tummy. The warmth was nice, but she felt bloated and two sizes larger than normal and the very idea of meeting a guy while in this condition made her want to dunk her head in a tub of ice water. Maybe she should call the whole night off.

"He's single," her dad added.

"Well, that's a start."

"A handsome fella."

"Remains to be seen."

"And a politician. State Representative Reuben King."

"Tell me you're kidding."

"A Republican," Mardy added in a satisfied tone.

She stared between the roadside maples at picnic tables dressed in red, white, and blue tablecloths. Crowds were gathered, and teens roamed in groups. The festival was in high gear.

"I don't care which party he is." She sniffed. Her neck felt hot. "Tell me honestly, do I look like the type to catch a politician's eye?"

"Got the looks, sure, but you're more than that. I've always said so." He downshifted, scanned the curb for a parking space. He pointed out a flyer on a tree. "There, that's him."

Natalie searched the paper. No photo.

"Don't take my word 'bout his good looks. That's just what the ladies 'round town been saying."

"You go, Dad. So you've been talking with the ladies."

He shrugged and tried to hide a grin. "Not me, no. But there's quite a pack of 'em trying to hunt down Mr. King."

"A womanizer? He sounds like loads of fun."

"Didn't say nothing, did I, 'bout him hunting them? Way I hear it, he's been hurt before and don't seem much interested in all that. He's interested in the lady-folk, sure, but he's got his eyes on his work and all that comes with it."

Natalie first chuckled at her dad's assessment, then almost burst into tears. What a wreck. Biting down on her lip, she scooted closer to him on the seat. "Sorry I snapped at you."

"Ahh, I know you're not feeling full up." He checked his mirror, clasped his hands again at ten and two on the wheel. "You, you're one of the good ones."

She kissed his cheek. "*Gracias.*"

"Still pains me just thinking of you chained up in that hut. Shoulda been there for you. Woulda been if I'd known where ya were."

"Stop. That's all in the past, and I'm here now, aren't I?" She had yet to show him her bare legs, knowing he would blame himself for every ridged scar.

"Who you trying to fool? I see that worry all churned up in your eyes."

"My mind's just going over what's ahead, working as a sub, trying to cover expenses. And you know how it is with Tuf sometimes. We're barely scraping by. If it weren't for Eli's part of the rent, we'd be in trouble."

"Eli. Don't know that I approve."

"Oh, don't act shocked. You met him at my graduation, the older guy with the salt-and-pepper eyebrows. Eli Shaffokey."

"He's still a he, no matter his age. And what kinda name's *Shaffokey?*"

"Polish. Russian. I don't know. The Vreelands can vouch for him. He stayed in his camper next to their house for months, so this is a good change for him. And after what happened to me last fall, I wasn't ready to live by myself."

"What about Grams? She's got a nice place, full of good memories."

Natalie snuggled up with those memories. She heard her sister's squeaky six-year-old voice calling out, "Ready or not, here I come," saw the blue mist in the valley and the black bear that wandered down from the Great Smoky Mountains to scavenge from the garbage can. Tuf wanted to shoot the thing with Grams's double-barreled shotgun, while Natalie wanted to take a picture.

"I love Grams," she said, "but I wouldn't exactly call Tuckaleechee Cove the happening place for prospective schoolteachers."

"Well, my door's always open. You can move back in with your ole man."

"Back to Oak Ridge? Believe me, Dad. Not even an option."

His jaw tightened, the muscles clenching.

"No." She regretted her words and rushed to clarify. "I mean, it's not a bad option, but I don't want to be in your way should the right woman come along."

Mardy waved that off. "Not happening, not till I know my daughter's squared away. Plus, the sheriff hopes to gimme some answers 'bout them remains soon as he can. Says it can take a while, what with how things is backed up at the labs, and 'em bones being so old and all."

"Do you have to . . . can we talk about something else?"

"Oh," he assured her, "I've let it go, and you oughta do the same. But it's still baggage on a date—all them unanswered questions and suspicions. Time we set it to rest."

"Dad, I don't see any baggage."

He edged into a parking spot. "So then, do me this one favor, huh? Talk nice to Mr. King. Least give him a chance and see if there's anything there."

"Every girl dreams of being a princess or a queen, right?"

"You surely did, yessir. That's a fact."

"OK, I'll talk to him. I'll be on my best behavior and smile through any cramps. Heck, I might even try to impress him with my infamous rain dance."

As they climbed out, Mardy groaned. "Nah, let's not go that far. Was cute when you were three, but I think it's best you let it be."

"Dad?"

"Uh-huh?"

"You realize it's inevitable, don't you? Somewhere, someday, the right guy is going to see that dance."

Even as her father groaned a second time, Natalie wondered whether that day would ever come. She would give this harebrained scheme a shot, run with it as far as it would take her, and see if she could make something happen. Maybe it would work out. Maybe things would change.

With regard to love, though, perhaps there was no right guy for her.

And even if he *was* out there somewhere? With her track record, she'd walk right past him and lock lips with the lone killer in the crowd.

Chapter Twenty-four

In a NASCAR cap and sunglasses, Serpionov meandered through Bissell Park and nibbled at hot corn on the cob. Just ahead, Mardy and Natalie Flynn were part of the throng.

Officials estimated that thirty thousand people would attend this year's Secret City Festival, nearly doubling the town's population for one weekend. The place was smaller now, but during the days of World War II, this isolated valley had housed over seventy-five thousand men and women who worked to ensure an end to Hitler's madness.

Signs paraded the festival slogan: "From the '40s to the Future."

This slogan, Serpionov liked it. Too many people stayed mired in the past, afraid to march onward, whereas he focused on a bright and better future.

And on Natalie, of course.

He finished his food, tossed the cob into a trashcan, and wiped his mouth. Children darted past him, their balloons bouncing on strings. A bright yellow one broke free and wobbled skyward. He hopped up and nabbed the escapee.

"Mine," a boy said, tugging on his pant leg.

He crouched down. "You should be careful, yes? If you want something, do not let it out of your sight." He returned the balloon, and the child dashed off.

The Russian smiled. These youth inspired him, gave him reason to continue his work. But his happiness faded as phantom gunfire and youngsters' shrieks filled his thoughts. He saw their tears. Smelled the charred remains of—

Nyet, *do not do this. Eyes on the future.*

He steeled himself, fixing his gaze on the Flynns once more.

Craft booths and a food court crowded one section of the park, while BMX riders did stunts across the way. On the lawn, men in army helmets and uniforms guarded a tank. A band tore down their gear on the main stage as an announcer teased concertgoers with facts about the next artist, Johnny Ray Black:

"Johnny Ray burst onto the country scene five years ago. Since then, he's been a radio darling with seven Top Ten hits, and he's still golden-haired and single. Don't you go anywhere, folks. He'll be taking the stage any minute now."

Ahead, the Flynns detoured toward a booth fitted with flags and patriotic flair. Such pride these Americans displayed. Serpionov remembered times in Moscow when his own countrymen were ashamed to sing their party anthem.

He saw a banner that bore a familiar name: Representative Reuben King.

But the booth was empty.

Serpionov moved closer, searching the premises for the public servant. Tonight was an opportunity that couldn't be missed. Caught up in his search, Serpionov bumped into a tall man wearing charcoal- gray slacks, a dark blue tie, and a pinstriped shirt. The man's wide shoulders flexed against the material. His sleeves were rolled up to the elbows, indicating a politician willing to work.

"Mr. King? It is you."

A cautious smile. "Hello."

"You cannot leave," Serpionov said.

"Excuse me?"

"Someone is waiting at your booth, I think."

King's black eyebrows lifted, and his eyes swiveled toward Mardy and Natalie. "Why, there is, isn't there? Thank you. A couple of seconds later, and I would've missed them altogether."

"This woman, she is beautiful. Perhaps you can win her vote."

"Now, that'll be entirely up to her."

Serpionov rested a hand against King's lower back. "But you will try, yes? I know you will try." He nudged him in the right direction.

Natalie thought she had dodged a bullet. The booth was unmanned, its flags fluttering in the breeze, its brochures anchored to the table by an obsidian paperweight that bore the words "This King Listens. 2012."

"Now where'd he run off to?" her dad muttered. "Public servant, my foot. What's he think, he can come and go whenever he darn well pleases?"

"Don't worry," she said, second-guessing her own intentions. "Maybe this just wasn't part of the plan. Look, the sun's setting, and Johnny Ray's about to play. Let's enjoy a gorgeous evening together and forget this other stuff."

Mardy frowned, sweeping the area with shaded eyes.

"Dad, seriously."

"I'm telling ya, what if this here's part of the plan and you're missing it?"

His urgency stopped her. Fine. She would give this a shot.

Under the paperweight, the edges of King's photo peered from a handout. Was he as handsome as she had been told? Even if he was, she had no guarantee he'd be attracted to her. And there were practical considerations. King represented this district, whereas she lived nearly three hours away. And what if he served on, say, the House Committee on Education? In her career as a teacher, that would present a conflict of interest.

Whatever. With one peek, she'd know what she was dealing with.

She lifted the paperweight.

OMG.

In the photo, Reuben King was sharply dressed yet relaxed, with a boyish grin beneath bright eyes. He gave off none of that insincere, butt-kissing, smile-even-if-it-hurts attitude that seemed standard for most politicos. In fact, if this was the new look on Nashville's Capitol Hill, it was time she took more interest in the shenanigans that passed for bipartisan leader-ship.

"Not one of my better pictures," said a mellow baritone voice.

She turned. "Mr. King?"

And, with the meeting of their eyes, the sparks flew.

She knew that a fire couldn't last long on sparks alone, that it needed fuel and oxygen, needed commitment and care. But she couldn't deny that even a bonfire required that initial moment of ignition.

Those undeniable, unreliable sparks.

Two hours later, Reuben and Natalie were seated at Big Ed's and sharing childhood stories over pizza. The next morning, they biked around Melton Hill Lake. Sunday night, Natalie returned to Nashville and wondered just what she had done.

Chapter Twenty-five

July

What Natalie had done was start a fire.

And fire scared her.

With offices in the shadow of Capitol Hill, Reuben King came often to Music City for political functions and fund-raisers, and the two of them had texted regularly and gone out twice since their introduction a few weeks earlier.

One Thursday, he asked her to join him for coffee at Drinkhaus, a small establishment in Nashville's Germantown.

The following weekend, he took her to Pancake Pantry, where they waited forty minutes just to be seated. A patron whispered that Scott Hamilton, the former Olympic ice skater, was only a few spots farther ahead in line, but they were lost in conversation and barely registered this tidbit.

Today, he was back and asking for a third get-together.

"Get-together?" Natalie giggled. "Is that what we're calling it?"

"Calling it a date sounds a bit aggressive."

She giggled again. Pathetic. Like a schoolgirl with a crush.

An hour later, they met at Centennial Park. They

walked the paths, kicked around her soccer ball, took pics with their phones at the Parthenon building, and did cartwheels near the small lake where ducks squawked for food. The humidity was doing crazy things to Natalie's hair, and she pulled it back in a ponytail. Despite the sweltering heat, she was wearing full-length black exercise pants that showed off her curves and hid her shins.

She wasn't about to flash her scars.

To see those, he'll have to wait.

Reuben led her to the shade of a magnolia tree, where he sprawled beside her in his Nike shorts and T-shirt. "Am I rushing all this? Does it seem like too much too soon?"

"Just friends," she said. "Right?"

"Oh boy. The dreaded word."

"And what's wrong with it, *amigo*? It's a good starting point."

"I'm nudging closer to my thirties."

"Yeah? Well, I'm almost a quarter of a century."

"Birthday coming up?" He lifted a hand. "Let me guess. July 22nd."

"Nope, I'm an October baby."

He chuckled. "Why, that's three months away."

"*Si.* And I'm counting down the days. By the way, if you're actually conversant in Spanish, take it easy on me. I always thought it'd be sweet knowing how to speak another language, but my vocabulary is puh-retty limited."

"Full disclosure? This boy over here is sadly monolingual."

"What?" she gasped. "Well, in that case, it's *adios, señor*."

Reuben looked up at her, his blue eyes vibrant in the sunlight spilling through the magnolia branches. "You know, it feels to me as though we've known each other for years. Probably the fact we grew up in the same place. Did you know that Tolkien believed in a sort of collective local history?"

"I love J. R. R. You know they're now filming *The Hobbit*?"

"I'll be there opening day."

"Really?" Natalie raised an eyebrow.

"In some of his writings, he describes a family working the land, dying and being buried, then enriching that same soil as nourishment for their own kids and grandkids. The circle of life at its most down-to-earth."

"At its most Middle-earth," she joked. "No, that's interesting. You think those of us who grew up in Oak Ridge have a common bond? Some, I don't know, some visceral connection?"

"Let's hope not from the water or the air."

Her lips twisted. "Can you spell 'nuclear waste'?"

"It was only a theory of his, but you see it in his depictions of the Shire."

"Never knew a politician could be a Tolkien geek."

"Geek. Ouch."

"The good kind of geek."

"Sure," he said. "Now who sounds like the politician?"

She gestured. "Bring it on. Hit me with one of your most difficult bills or measures or whatever. Representative Flynn here, offering free advice."

"You're mocking the process."

"Hey, don't be so serious." She leaned back on one arm, batting her eyelashes at him. "Or is it that you don't think a woman's up to the task?"

You shouldn't be doing this, Natalie. You're a bad person.

"Actually," he said, "a very qualified woman happens to be our Speaker of the House. So you want a tough one? You know anything about 6336? It was on the agenda last assembly, but we postponed it after I expressed some concerns."

"Uh, 6336." She tilted her head. "Tell me more."

"In a nutshell, it opens the door for private citizens to be implanted with encoded tags. It's a tiny device. Imagine a grain of rice inserted into the back of your arm."

"Sounds painful."

"Not much worse than a flu shot, or so I'm told."

"Like those microchips they put in pets."

"Exactly." He sat up and flicked back the lock of black hair that swept his brow. "It has plenty of positive applications. In fact, some prisons use it to keep track of their inmates and prevent escapes. The military's even looked into it for combat scenarios, where it's hard to pinpoint all troop locations and sometimes even harder to identify those killed in action."

"Makes sense to me. It could also help in, uh . . ."

He glanced at her.

She swallowed. "In, you know, cases of abduction."

"That's one of 6336's strongest selling points."

"Well then, I, Representative Flynn, give it my unapologetic support."

Reuben smiled. "I wish it were that easy. The bill brings up issues regarding the invasion of privacy, and on one side, I have consumer watchdog groups flooding my inbox with e-mails. On the other, there're more lobbyists than holes in Swiss cheese, hired by medical firms and large corporations to lay out their arguments. Even church leaders want to toss in their two bits."

"Let me guess. Fears about the Mark of the Beast."

"Revelation 13 speaks of a mark that everyone—rich or poor, large or small—takes upon their hands or their foreheads, something that allows them to buy and sell goods. The Bible's adamant that this shouldn't be allowed."

"The implant sounds different, though."

"I've spoken with Pastor Teman about it. He points out that these implants are put into the upper arm instead of the hand. And they wouldn't be for commerce, not initially anyway. But that technology is only waiting to be linked. They've already developed grocery carts that scan each item you put inside, then charge you for them as you slide your card on the way out the door. The next step would be scanners that simply read your implant as you pass by."

"Have to admit, it sounds pretty convenient."

"Convenience cards. There's a reason they're called that."

"These lobbyists," she said, "do they get paid to hound you?"

Hounding, he explained, was too strong a word. The good ones gathered valuable data regarding upcoming bills. Yes, they had agendas, but with lobbyists fighting on both sides of an issue, legislators received solid information they wouldn't otherwise have the time or the resources to gather on their own.

"Sounds like you both use each other."

"I suppose there's some truth in that. Then again, Natalie, isn't every relationship built on a bit of give-and-take?"

She recoiled from the question. While she didn't want to manipulate this man's emotions, she was still working through her own issues, her own doubts.

Their gazes held, and her heart thumped in her throat. Reuben brushed his fingers across her open palm on the grass, his skin smooth and dry, the way her father's used to feel after he had cleaned up from chopping firewood or rotating the tires.

Better think this through, chica. *You play with fire, and somebody's going to get burned.*

Natalie dropped her gaze. She saw Reuben's ring from UT, where he'd earned his bachelor of science degree. He had shared with her his love for his country, his home state in particular. He had leveraged his experience on the Oak Ridge Chamber of Commerce and City Council to win his district's seat in the House. And in two years, he would be old enough for a run at the State Senate.

I'm fine, she assured herself. *A-OK. It's all under control.*

She rolled onto her back, hand still splayed beneath his touch. Sighing, she closed her eyes, basked in the sun's warmth, let it ooze through her skin.

"Amazing day, huh?" Reuben said.

"Uh-huh."

During her time with the Vreelands, she had rediscovered an interest in the Scriptures, as well as a realization that God's Word still offered timely advice even in today's world. What was that verse they'd taught her, from the seventeenth chapter of Jeremiah?

"The human heart is most deceitful . . . Who really knows how bad it is?"

Good question.

She liked him. After three "get-togethers," she knew that much. Having been hurt before, though, she didn't want anyone else to go through that pain. How far should she push to have him cooperate with her unspoken desires?

"Natalie? I need to ask you something."

Her eyelids fluttered open.

Reuben squeezed her hand as a breeze swirled across the park and ruffled the nearby lake. "When I said relationship earlier, I wasn't referring to just friendship. Years ago, I . . . Please, I need to know now if I'm wasting my time. I'm a big boy. If I'm not what you're looking for, I can handle the truth."

"You're not," she said.

His mouth stretched into a grim line.

"No, wait." She squeezed his hand back. "What I mean, Reuben, is that you're not wasting your time. Not at all."

He leaned closer, his eyes searching hers, and then his hand cupped her face, and his lips met hers beneath the blossoms of the grand magnolia.

Chapter Twenty-six

Serpionov leaned back on his Honda Interceptor, parked close to the lake at Centennial Park. Though his sunglasses provided meager concealment, he'd rested his helmet on the gas tank. Across the water, Mr. King and young Natalie seemed too distracted to take note of his presence anyway.

This fire between them, it was a good thing.

All part of his twisted tale.

They weren't going anywhere soon, and he decided it was a good time to phone his grandmother. In honor of her parting request, he called each year on her birthday in mid-July. And each year, instead of chiding him for his infrequent contact, she addressed him as though he had been gone only a day or two.

"Hello," she said this time. "I'm so pleased you called."

"Happy birthday, *babushka*."

"*Spasibo*," she thanked him. "It's good to hear your voice."

Her voice didn't sound good. Her rattling coughs grated on his ears, and he heard the sickness there. Yes, he could accept that life and death formed a never-ending cycle, but it angered him to hear her being caught in their gears. This was her God's beautiful plan? This was His reward for those who groveled at His feet?

She coughed again. "I didn't want to leave, not before we talked again."

"Leave?" The moment he asked, he knew the answer.

"Yes, Stepan. I'm—"

"I don't answer to that name."

"I'm dying," she confessed. "Both of us, I think we know this."

"Don't talk of it."

"Death's sting is short, yes? I am not afraid. Each day, I long to see Him face-to-face."

"This God of yours, why doesn't He heal you?"

"Earth is only training ground." She coughed. "A small step before I leap into eternity. No more pain, no dying, and no tears."

"Training for what? Explain this foolishness."

"The Scripture says—"

"Bah. Always this talk of Scripture."

"In the army, and in OMON, you got a training manual, yes?" A muffled rattle punctuated her words. "This was your guide, and you held on to it. As young girl in Kiev, I became a follower of God. I must know my manual too, or I won't know my mission." She hacked until he thought she would die on the spot. "The Bible tells me

I'll rule and reign with Christ. My training's over. My body's old. Now, at last, I'm ready to go rule and reign."

Serpionov envied such childlike confidence, even if he doubted its source. Talking sense into her was futile. She was old and stubborn, and he knew she wouldn't listen. Nothing he could do would restore her health, and he could only hope she was right about her God.

"Rule what?" he asked. "A galaxy of super-novas and black holes?"

"This I don't know. Perhaps." Her voice swelled with renewed hope and strength. "Whatever it means, it will be heaven."

Five days later, he got word that she was gone. Serpionov straddled his motorcycle and tore eastward on the interstate, eyes flat, chin set. By the time he reached Mardy Flynn's place, the sun was setting at his back.

Since his grandmother's God was powerless, he had work to do.

"You wanted proof that I'm on right side?" He slid a note across the table to Mardy. "On Wednesday, you'll see this proof and know danger is close."

"Me, I'll do anything for my country. I bleed red, white, and blue."

"There is the name, time, and place. Now you can be patriot, yes? You'll call and give warning, or sleeper will make sure that Representative King dies."

"You're sure 'bout this?" Mardy took a deep breath. "If I'm wrong, could cost me my job. Don't wanna sound like the one crying wolf."

"Bah. This agent, he is not wolf. He is a snake, ready to strike."

Chapter Twenty-seven

"Honey, what's there to be scared of?" said Rhonda Teman. "He's a respectable politician, a true gem. My husband himself vouches for the man."

Natalie shifted on the floral-patterned sofa in the office of the pastor's wife. Mrs. Teman was a sturdy Germanic woman who once a month invited Natalie to unload her burdens and fears. She was not only familiar with last year's circumstances involving Magnus and the Vreelands, but seemed to speak from a place of real concern.

"I'm starting to second-guess myself," Natalie said. "I don't know. Maybe it's moving too fast."

"But you've only been going steady a month or so."

"Steady? I'm . . . No, that's not what we're doing, whatever that means. We've chatted and texted a lot, and Reuben took me to Centennial

Park last week while he was here in town."

"Isn't the Parthenon impressive? A faithful replica, down to the half inch."

"It's big, all right."

"Why do you feel it's moving too fast?"

"I'm not sure I should be getting this close. It's nice, sure, but I wonder if it's right. I mean, how does a girl really know when it's right? It's scaring me."

"Is he pushing you to . . ." Mrs. Teman waited.

"What?" Natalie said.

"To compromise your values."

"Reuben? He's a gentleman. It's more like I'm scaring myself. He's done nothing I haven't allowed. But it's been a long time since I've had a serious relationship, and he's just so . . . so *there*. Does that sound strange? We sat out on the grass by the lake, and we talked for, like, at least two or three hours. He was looking right at me and hearing every word I said. Really hearing."

The pastor's wife rested her elbows on the desk and steepled jewelry-encrusted fingers beneath her chin. "An attentive man can be quite bedeviling."

"Tell me about it. I look into those eyes and feel myself melting away—not a care in the world, not an ounce of resistance. Can I be honest with you, Mrs. Teman?"

"I'd expect nothing less."

"I've only known the guy barely five weeks,

and I'm stretched out on the grass watching the way his lips move while he talks, the way his thick eyelashes move over deep blue eyes, and the thought pops into my head: *I want to have this man's babies*."

Mrs. Teman put a hand to her ample bosom. "Natalie."

"Just being honest."

"Oh, honey."

"Yeah. You see why I'm scared?"

"Has he expressed a similar attraction to you?"

"We kissed. And, just to be clear, he was the one who started it."

"By the color in your cheeks, I assume you weren't quick to finish it."

"We get along so well. He likes hanging out with me, sharing many of the same hometown memories and stuff. But what if that's all it is to him? A nice diversion. The girl next door whom he'd never seriously consider."

"Natalie, don't underestimate yourself. You're charming, educated, and wholesome. And those childbearing hips are sure to catch any man's eye. It's the way God intended."

"*¿Que?*"

"Let me qualify. Any single man's eye."

"Sure, I want children. Guess I made that pretty clear a second ago." Natalie tilted her head, pushed back a strand of hair. "But please tell me that's not the only thing that makes me worth-while as a woman."

"Oh, no, not at all. Don't misunderstand. Your truest beauty, though, shines forth in motherhood. A husband, wife, and a quiver full of babies. I have three grown children of my own, and who could want anything more?"

Natalie crossed her arms, looked away.

Given that she had no example, she wondered what sort of mom she would be. Her own mother couldn't hack it, and left them to do with life on their own. Would she be as irresponsible?

She noted the *Guideposts* on the end table, its cover showing a mother with four, five, six children gathered under her arms. Six? That was three times more than Natalie wanted. Assuming she could even conceive. While she respected such sacrificial, maternal love and hoped to give it someday, she didn't want it to be her sole measure of success.

The number of kids she could pop out.

The amount of food she could grow in her own backyard.

The speed with which she could change a diaper, while texting with all the gluten-free-and-proud-of-it moms on the block.

"You know," she said, "I'm not as innocent as you might think."

"Whatever do you mean? You've remained pure, have you not?"

"Technically speaking. But it's not like I haven't done stuff I regret."

"You must leave those things behind," Mrs. Teman said. "You've a bright future ahead of you. You're a teacher now—"

"A sub."

"I was under the impression that your interviews—"

"Went well," she said. "But without tenure, I have to take what I can get."

"Well, you've not been slothful. These things'll fall into place, and I hear you're working as part-time barista at Roast—a safer location than the café here in East Nashville. It would seem you have a knack for making good coffee."

"*Gracias, señora.*"

The older woman came around the desk, wafting lilac perfume. She smoothed her dress, sat on the sofa, and took Natalie's hand. "You are precious in God's sight. Don't allow what was done to you at some coed party or in some abandoned hut last year color your view of yourself."

"I won't wallow, if that's what you mean."

Mrs. Teman squeezed her hand.

"I do want to be beautiful in God's eyes," Natalie said. "But I hope He's basing it on more than the number of times I can conceive. Heck, the doctors told me I might never get pregnant. Having kids scares me, scares me just thinking of raising kids in today's world with all the weirdos out there. I think back to my own childhood and all the trouble my little sister and I got into."

"This is Tina, the one who's boarding with you?"

"It's a temporary thing."

"Please, go on."

Natalie shifted into the corner of the sofa, slipped free of Mrs. Teman's jeweled fingers. "Underneath it all, Tuf's the sweetest thing, but she never got over not having a mother around. Maybe I didn't either. Doesn't matter. I swore I wouldn't put Dad through all the garbage Tuf put him through."

"We each answer for our own actions, don't we?"

"She'd get these ideas in her head and disappear for days at a time. She'd call from some unknown number, act like things were A-OK, and . . . No, wait. I don't want to bad-mouth her. It's not like I'm Ms. Innocent here. My first year of college, I was a complete dingbat, with my share of social drinking and late-night antics. The thing that spared me? I'd think about Tuf, the situations she ended up in, and I'd remember that I was saving myself for something better."

"Let me express," Mrs. Teman said, "how proud Pastor and I are that you have stood by that decision. In this day and age, it's not easy."

"That's the problem. It's, you know, *too* easy."

"In light of your integrity, I had no qualms when I heard that you and Eli would share a rental. He's been a dear here at the church, and—"

"Wait a sec." Natalie pursed her lips.

"What is it?"

"How does Pastor Teman know about my 'decision'? I thought the things you and I discussed were confidential."

The pastor's wife picked a loose thread from the sofa's arm. "Perhaps I overstepped. If ever I do share, honey, it's only so that the staff and prayer team might better understand the needs of our members."

"Technically, I'm not even a member. I'm usually here just to be with the Vreelands when Bret leads worship."

"Be that as it may, your needs are held in confidence."

"So how many people are on the prayer team? And how many of their friends did they call? This is my personal life here."

"And it remains so."

Natalie snorted. She wondered what other doubts and longings of hers had been divulged. What gossip had been passed along under the guise of a prayer request? "Listen, I know I'm practically just a kid to you, but the stuff I've told you is close to my heart."

"I overstepped. My deepest apologies, truly."

"Since I was three years old, I've fought not to

be hardhearted and distrusting. Always afraid of having those closest to me torn away. Afraid of trusting God. Somehow I let Magnus slip right past those defenses, and now, once again, I realize how stupid I've been in believing, actually believing, I could entrust my secrets to another person."

"Those secrets are still safe."

"No," Natalie said. "No, they're not. You and Pastor Teman mean well, but I really thought you'd changed after all you watched the Vreelands go through. It's not right to go around judging others by . . . by their words or their things."

"Don't be naïve. Words and possessions do reflect on a person."

"If I have money in the bank, that means I'm a good person? What about the Vreelands who chose to let go of most of their earthly trinkets? Oh, right. Since Bret's now a sought-after musician, you judge him on that basis instead. Or is it because he lost a leg, which puts him one step away from sainthood?"

"That hardly seems fair."

"My point exactly."

With Mrs. Teman's perfume wafting through, the office turned suddenly claustrophobic.

Natalie brushed a strand of hair over her ear. "What Bret suffered for his family, I admire that. They all mean a lot to me. Far as I'm concerned, you and your husband gave them some shaky advice from the very start, especially about their money, as though they'd somehow earned God's blessings. Now I question how you've handled my own situation."

"Honey, please. You misunderstand my intentions."

Sure. Just one big misunderstanding.

Having already voiced more than what was necessary, Natalie decided to take the high road. "Let me say I appreciate the hours you've spent walking me through some rough memories. Your time is precious, I recognize that. And I do believe you care for those you counsel. Please, though, from now on, don't pass along to others the details that people share with you in confidence."

"I meant no harm."

"*No hay problema.*" She opened the door.

"Next month?" Mrs. Teman asked. "Should I pencil you in, as usual?"

"Seriously?"

"I have some openings."

"Sorry," Natalie said. "August and September are looking pretty busy. After all, I'm now dating the esteemed Mr. King."

"Oh?"

"No need to be scared, right? Isn't that what you told me?"

"Feel free to walk out that door, honey. Far be it

from me to stop you. Speaking from experience, though, these sorts of decisions and relationships will be put to the test. Often, directly so. If that occurs, I'll be here should you be in need of wise counsel."

"Good to know."

In the church parking lot, Natalie climbed into her faded blue Civic and plugged her phone charger into the lighter. She had a new text message, and despite her show of bravado only minutes earlier, it roused conflicting emotions. If she responded, would she get hurt? Or would she do the hurting?

Maybe it was best to bow out now.

Stop your second-guessing, chica. *You're doing the right thing.*

She filled her lungs, brushed the screen with her thumb. And texted back.

Serpionov worked by moonlight. Cars and trucks roared past, their headlights carving the shadows along this wooded portion of Oak Ridge Turnpike while he wedged a plastic spike into the dirt less than ten strides from the roadside.

Forest-green paint camouflaged the spike, which featured a small protrusion near its top, a battery-powered radio transmitter. This antenna emitted a signal that would activate a number-specific RFID tag, one that for weeks had lain dormant in a Michelin tire.

The tag itself was passive. Completely harmless.

But it would amplify the incoming burst of power from the transmitter and trigger a detonator. This detonator, inserted into an off-white plug of C4, was shaped around the rim of Mr. King's tire and hidden beneath the hubcap.

He had jerry-rigged it weeks in advance.

Or was that *jury*-rigged?

In his motherland, Serpionov had seen the damage wrought by explosives such as Semtex and C4. Compound 4 looked like molding clay, but it was no child's toy. Military forces around the world used it to great effect, as did freedom fighters and agents of al-Qaeda. It could be stretched, dropped, and pounded without consequence. When confined and detonated, though, the pressure of its explosion intensified a hundred-fold.

Serpionov directed the antenna northeast, toward the mouth of Novus Drive a half mile away, giving the signal a wider swath in which to catch the passenger side of all southbound vehicles.

He trusted that Mardy's call would not only convince Mr. King to continue his cooperation, but would also alter the representative's plans and divert him from danger.

It was to be a violent warning, yes.

A way to make King rethink his stance on HB 6336.

If, however, the politician still climbed into his luxury sedan and passed by here tomorrow morning, he would pay for his stubbornness. Once that RFID tag entered the antenna's electro-magnetic zone, it would receive its orders and deliver a deadly blast.

Chapter Twenty-eight

Threats. They came with the territory. In an age when average citizens felt powerless to effect change, when protesters gathered but had little to show for their efforts, was it any wonder that certain individuals barked out warnings, sent powder-coated letters, and left ominous messages on politicians' phones? Despite being more prevalent when the assembly was in session, threats came from nutcases all year round.

Reuben King slid into the driver's seat, smoothed the wheel with both hands, and familiarized himself with the gauges on the dash.

8:12 a.m.

In moments, he'd be traveling to Nashville via the Oak Ridge Turnpike and I-40. On this last Wednesday of July, he had two meetings in the state's capitol—one as chairman of the Health and Human Resources Committee, another with local and influential Pastor Teman. They'd met before for prayer.

First, however, Reuben planned to take Natalie out for brunch. Assuming, of course, he didn't die en route.

He could still hear the call from two nights ago, from an unknown number. Most threats came laced with angry curses, but this was muted and calm:

"Mr. King? I reckon this'll sound like a prank, but please don't mark this down as the work of some loony. Thing is, sir, I've been given a message to pass on a heads-up that somebody's out to kill ya. He says it ain't right that you stop kids and old folks from being watched after and helped. Says your vote can help change that. I dunno the fella's name, or I'd give it, but I'm told this deed'll get done Wednesday morning, somewhere 'round quarter to nine."

The caller's number was blocked. No surprise. How hard, though, would it be to trace its origin and subpoena the phone company for user details?

Was one cryptic call going to change his schedule?

Not a chance.

Yesterday, Reuben had explained the situation to the county sheriff, who suggested some precautionary measures and assigned undercover deputies to escort him today to the county line.

Reuben also alerted the Capitol Police in Nashville, hoping to prevent harm from befalling any other state legislators.

As he now clicked his seat belt into place, he wondered how the caller knew of his plans. Apparently, the man supported HB 6336's tagging of children and the elderly, and had taken note of today's committee meeting.

"Lord, I'm a bit worried," Reuben prayed. "I admit, there's probably nothing to this, but please surround this vehicle with Your angels and guide my steps."

"D'ya say something?" asked the man standing at the driver's door.

He shook his head. "Just asking for a smooth trip."

"Car checks out, Mr. King, so you oughta be in good shape."

"Much appreciated."

"You drive safely, sir."

8:16 a.m.

Reuben waited, then nosed the car into traffic between an Audi A4 and a Chrysler sedan. He headed southwest through town, along East Fork Poplar Creek, and past Bissell Park, where he'd met Natalie six weeks ago. Brunch would be their chance to celebrate the milestone, minor as it seemed.

For Reuben, no relationship was minor. He had dated only three girls since high school, the first of whom went to London on an exchange program and fell for her British professor. He got over that. The second fizzled out for a variety of reasons. The third? He thought he'd found the one, thought it was for life. She tore out his heart the day he caught her with his best friend. Those feelings of betrayal still lingered, despite the energies he poured into his political work.

Perhaps it was best to call things off with Natalie.

That would spare them both the inevitable.

Not to mention Reuben had other responsibilities, obligations, and deadlines. He owed it to his fellow legislators and to the citizens of Tennessee to vote wisely on the issues, such as 6336.

8:27 a.m.

Serpionov had confidence in the technology. After completing last night's work, he had raced westward on the interstate and slept six hours in his condo.

At 6:45 a.m. central, 7:45 eastern, he awoke to his alarm, made a glass of traditional smoky-flavored tea, and propped himself on a kitchen bar stool. He opened the Shield case, cradled its remote unit in his palm, and tracked Mr. King's car from downtown Oak Ridge toward the waiting transmitter.

8:29 a.m.

• • •

The car's tires hummed over the pavement. Reuben checked his mirrors and let the gap grow between him and the nearest vehicle. Behind, a deputy followed in an unmarked vehicle, a professional courtesy from Anderson County's finest. The escort would hold this position until ten o'clock, then peel off to patrol the north-bound lanes of the turnpike.

Looking in his rearview mirror, Reuben tugged at a few black strands. His hair was trimmed, held in place by a dab of mousse, but he liked to sport a dark, carefree wave across his forehead. A good forehead, his mother liked to tell him as she pinched his chin. Strong and wide like his father's.

He could hear her voice now.

Why so serious, Reuben? Why this look of one carrying the weight of the world? You really ought to smile more.

I smile.

You grimace.

I grin.

I want my boy to be happy, that's all.

Why wouldn't I be, with a mom like you?

He checked his reflection, wondered if these were worry lines at the corners of his mouth or simply the first signs of aging. Wrinkles at age twenty-eight? Not a chance. He spread his lips and flashed his straight white teeth. Perhaps by sheer repetition, he could turn the worry lines into smile lines.

Speaking of worry, he was only ten minutes, maybe fifteen, from discovering whether last night's phone call was a prank or prophecy.

The tea burned Serpionov's fingers, and he propped the thin glass in his *podstakannik*. He pushed it back from the Shield case, and trained his eyes on the screen where Mr. King's vehicle inched nearer to the death zone.

Did the politician think last night's call was a joke?

Serpionov had set this trap to serve as a warning only, but he would adjust his plans. Like the molecules in his tea glass, he relied on flexibility.

8:35 a.m.

Despite efforts to remain calm, Reuben couldn't block out the caller's words that echoed between his ears: *"Somebody's out to kill ya . . . Wednesday morning, somewhere 'round quarter to nine."*

As threats went, this one had been delivered secondhand.

Nothing but leftover news.

8:42 a.m.

If, however, the threat was real, what method would the assassin use? A sniper's rifle fired from a hillside? A barricaded ambush? A severed brake line?

Give it a few more minutes, and you'll find out.

His grip tightened on the steering wheel, and his foot nudged the gas pedal toward the floor. A stew of adrenaline roiled in his stomach. His let his car creep closer to the one ahead of him, and the unmarked vehicle was still following in his wake. Eyeing the speedometer, he eased off the accelerator. It would be ludicrous to get a ticket from the very deputy sent to keep watch on him.

Reuben turned his thoughts once more to Natalie. He envisioned her thick hair framing her face, her pink bottom lip drawn between her teeth, and her warm hazel eyes. She was a strong, independent woman, yet she harbored some secret, some unexplained vulnerability.

Was there any reason to tell her about the phone threat?

No. She had worries of her own.

He would continue on his usual route to Nashville, watch the clock tick past the hour without incident, and meet her before noon at Capitol Grille, within walking distance of his office. He would give her a tour of the office another day. Taking her there would kick-start the rumor machine, and that was to be avoided this early in their relationship.

A month and a half in? Yes, much too early.

And yet it seemed that he had known her for years. Already, he could feel himself falling for her.

Perhaps it was the fact that they'd both grown up in Oak Ridge, a small and unique city. Not only had they frequented the same burger joints and pizza places, they had graduated four years apart from the same high school. He played football, as a wide receiver. She played soccer and took honors English. They had attended many of the same festivals and community events.

Now they were college grads, self-reliant, career-minded, and focused on helping those around them.

Were they ready for this next step?

Was Natalie willing to deal with his baggage, to handle his life in the limelight, to put up with the newshounds, gossip rags, and prank callers? Was Reuben prepared to add domestic duties to his civic ones?

'Round quarter to nine.

According to the dash clock, the time was at hand.

His gaze flickered between his mirrors and the sedan ahead of him. He saw no evidence of a lone gunman in the woods, or barricades in the road, or fast-approaching cars with mobsters standing on the runners and spraying bullets from Tommy guns braced against their hips.

8:48 a.m.

The whole thing was a hoax.

Just as suspected.

Zipping past a sign for Novus Drive, he noted

the blur of the roadside trees, the curve of the turnpike, and the shimmer of sunlight on distant waters. Then, in one cataclysmic moment, the searing white flash of an explosion scorched his retinas, walloped his eardrums, and shattered the car's windshield in a skull-rattling shockwave.

Chapter Twenty-nine

Natalie waited. She sent texts and left messages. Ten minutes before eleven, and still no word from Reuben King.

Standing in the lobby of Capitol Grille, she thudded a fist against the massive wood railing. The aroma of Belgian waffles and applewood-smoked bacon wafted over her, and the hostess shot her another questioning glance. She shook her head. Nothing yet. Over an hour past their reservation, and her date still hadn't showed.

It just wasn't like Reuben to ignore her calls. She had a noon meeting for Metro's substitute teachers, which meant that if this brunch didn't work, her next best chance to get together with him wouldn't be until later this afternoon.

Had she been stood up? Would he do something that cruel?

Nope, something was wrong.

God, if anything's happened to him . . . Please. Por favor.

Natalie climbed the stairs and exited through the doors of the historic Hermitage Hotel. Most state senators and representatives worked around the corner at the War Memorial Auditorium and Legislative Plaza. Would it be presumptuous of her to show up there and look for Reuben's office?

Si, señorita. *Now you're just seeming desperate.*

Maybe she was overreacting to this whole thing. Maybe he'd been called in earlier than scheduled. Too bad if that were the case, because she had hoped to have some time with him before he got caught up in committee discussions.

She swiveled and marched toward her car at a meter two blocks away. With the day's humidity on the rise, perspiration dotted her cheeks as she lifted her phone to her ear and waited for her old Trevecca roomie to respond.

"Nattie? What is *up,* girl?"

"Hey, Abby." She fumbled with the Civic's lock. "You have a minute?"

"You don't sound too happy."

"If you're in the middle of something, I don't want to—"

"Spill," Abby said. "Hold nothing back."

"I think he stood me up."

"This new guy? The one you said was *muy caliente*? OK, I'm just gonna put this out there.

For the record, I never really imagined you going for a suit."

"He's not a—well, he's not like that." Natalie steered her car toward the interstate and headed for her teachers' meeting. Best to be early, since tardiness was a cardinal sin in this profession. "I mean, yes," she continued, "Reuben comes across poised and polished for his job, in complete control, but—"

"*Yummy.* A girl's gotta like that."

"Abby."

"My bad. Finish."

"Haven't even started." Natalie turned through an intersection and coasted down the on-ramp onto I-40. As she picked up speed, the words poured forth in a rush. "Thing is, we had plans for brunch. And there I am, and he's nowhere in sight, and he's not answering his phone, and he doesn't even call or text. Nothing. Nada. I know it sounds *loco*, but I was starting to open my heart to him. And believe me, that was not part of the plan. When I met him at the festival in June, I never thought I'd have any connection with him—never, never—and yet there I am three hours later, jabbering away with him like some giddy eighth grader."

"Guys like a little enthusiasm."

"He's four years older than me, though. He has a master's degree. He's worked in city and state government. Really? He's, like, way out of my league. I should've known better, but I was gullible enough to think it was possible."

"Until his no-show this morning."

"That's what I get, right?"

Abby sighed. "You're gonna make me say it, aren't you?"

"Say what?"

"He's a politician."

"So?"

"So when's the last time a politician kept his word? And why's a man with that sorta résumé still single anyway? Hel-*looo*. He's either playing the field, zeroed in on his career, or still stuck in the closet."

Natalie hated the fact that she couldn't find holes in that logic.

"Just keeping it real," Abby added. "OK, probably *not* what you wanted to hear, but this *is* my area of expertise. Men. Can't trust them. That's the dealio."

"My sis says the same thing."

The words rang in Natalie's ears as she considered her relationship with God. Another male. He had let her down too, hadn't He? In her childhood, in that hut, and in the warehouse lot. Seemed horrible to even think it, yet that was sure how it looked from where she sat.

"Thanks for talking, Abby."

"Hey, why don't you come volunteer with me at the mission? I'm trying to arrange a benefit concert. I know, right? Abigail the humanitarian? There's something about it, though. Keeps me from stressing over my own drama. They have over eight hundred beds. Eight *hundred*. Couple weeks ago, one of the older guys there just disappeared into thin air, and all his friends—they're big-time convinced that he was murdered."

"And that's supposed to encourage me how?"

"He was a good guy, Nattie. Kinda puts everything in per*spective,* that's all I'm saying. As for the cops, they've yawned and rolled their eyes about the whole thing, all except for this one detective. A black guy, reserved and real smart."

"Detective Meade?"

"How'd you . . . you know him?"

"Yeah, he's helped me and the Vreelands. Listen," she said, "I have a teachers' meeting, and my exit's coming up. Gotta go. TTYL."

Natalie parked, then combed a hand through her hair. A few of her peers, most of them older, entered the building through a set of gym doors. She followed, hoping this was the start of a long career in education. Teaching was her focus, absolutely. For now, she would give Reuben a pass and extend a little forgiveness, but if he wanted this relationship to continue, he would have to make the next move.

There was no movement. There was nothing at all.

Sipping tea, Serpionov had monitored the event from his kitchen stool a few hours earlier, while the politician's car, a glowing circle on the grid, cruised along Oak Ridge Turnpike in apparent defiance of Mardy Flynn's warning. It paralleled East Fork Poplar Creek, curved south of town, and entered the electromagnetic zone where the RFID tag's flattened copper coil reacted to the nearby transmitter with a brief surge of energy.

Serpionov had to imagine the detonation, but its results were evident on his screen.

The tag was obliterated.

The glowing circle had vanished.

Mr. King's Audi A4 was no more.

The event had occurred at 8:49 a.m. Within an hour, the local TV channels were airing still photos of the demolished vehicle, a mangled wreck amid orange-red tongues of flame and sparkling shards of metal and glass.

How would he explain this to Ms. Page? She was his source of income, and even though she gave him much leeway in his work, an assassination was never part of their discussion.

On the kitchen bar, his cell vibrated. Serpionov picked up.

"You watching this?" Mardy Flynn blurted. "It's all over the doggone TV."

"Now you know, yes? This sleeper agent, he is real. I want to protect your country from this danger, but you know people that can help me, and you must make them listen. You can do that?"

"I dunno. I called him just like you said, and he didn't heed a word. Not one word. He was seeing my daughter, and she's gonna be tore up something awful. The cops, they're gonna come after me, that's what's gonna happen."

"*Nyet*. You called from library? From the public phone?"

Mardy's tone hardened. "C'mon, I'm not stupid. I'm a security guard, and me, I want no part in nobody getting hurt." A long pause. "Croutons! And here it is, just like I figured. Deputy's pulling up my drive this very minute."

Chapter Thirty

Detective Meade first got word of the fatal explosion while at his desk in Metro's Investigative Services.

Yet one more tragedy.

This time, in distant Anderson County.

He leaned back in his office chair and savored the to-go double shot he had picked up from Black's Espresso on his way to work. Too bad about the latest news, but he couldn't worry about matters beyond his own county lines, unless they overlapped with one of his ongoing investigations.

He still wondered what had happened to

Frederick Chipps. Over the years, Meade had encountered Freddy C pushing a wobbly grocery cart through parks and along the downtown riverfront. He was a harmless old soul who rarely caused trouble. He'd even offered the cops assistance a time or two, when his eyes and ears on the street turned up helpful evidence.

Missing three months now.

And still counting.

Then there was Natalie's mother and the discovery of human remains in the woods outside Oak Ridge.

Had there been a positive ID yet?

Meade gulped down the last of his double shot, ran a hand over his cropped hair, and called the Anderson County sheriff. He would make a few polite inquiries about today's incident and then segue into the issue of Janet Flynn.

"Detective Meade," the sheriff answered.

"Good morning, Sheriff. How're you?"

"Been better. What about you?" The man sounded weary. "You might've heard that we're having a rough day of it here."

"A car bomb, that's the word around Metro."

"Heckuva thing. Keep it under your hat, if you will."

"Of course."

"Can't go into details just yet, but we lost one of our own this morning—a respected public servant."

Meade balled his fist on his desk. "Hate to hear that. I'm sorry."

"Feds're already sending a team this way, which means a larger mess just waiting to happen. Comes, of course, in the midst of our own grieving. Speaking of . . ." The sounds of a computer and clacking keys came through the phone. "I thought you'd like to know, since you're the one that pushed us to revisit the Flynn case. We got visual confirmation from the husband on an item of jewelry from the site. We also heard from Forensics yesterday about the skeletonized remains. Using Jantz's formula, they figured that the femur matches up with a woman of her height, and the smoothness of the pubic symphysis lines up with her age at the time she went missing. An 85 percent probability."

"No fairy-tale endings this time around, huh?"

"Usually aren't."

"Any signs of violence?" Meade said. "Blunt-force or sharp-force trauma?"

"Cause of death's still uncertain."

"Have they run marrow tests yet?"

"Twenty-one years after the fact, it's hard pinning anything down. The deterioration's extensive, and results vary widely under such conditions."

"That a yes or a no?"

"I've viewed the remains myself, and this wasn't a homicide, if that's what you're asking."

The sheriff sighed. "Sad to think that she was right there all along, two or three miles out of town. Seems she wandered off and got lost. We're closing the case."

"Just like that?"

"After all these years, maybe the family can get some closure as well."

"Have they been notified?"

"Mr. Flynn lives close by. Sent over a deputy an hour ago."

"Appreciate that, Sheriff. You hang in there."

Darcy Page narrowed her eyes, clutching her phone to her ear. "You're certain it was his car, Pastor?"

"We were supposed to meet today. I'd tried his phone earlier without success, but it was my wife who brought the situation to my attention, breaking news about a fireball on the Oak Ridge Turnpike." Pastor Teman cleared his throat. "The car, they say, belonged to Representative Reuben King. The sheriff's confirmed that the driver died at the scene, but won't release the identity."

"Someone could've borrowed his car."

"It's possible, yes."

"Do they know what caused the explosion?"

"They're not saying. Engines've been known to catch fire and blow, but by the looks of it, I'd guess it was one of those IEDs our troops've faced in Iraq."

"A bomb." Darcy's thoughts turned to Serpionov. "I'm well aware, Ms. Page, that the representative set your company back by delaying 6336. You must've lost millions of dollars. With that in mind, it seems that his demise could benefit you."

"Whatever it is you're trying to say, just say it."

"Did you have any advance knowledge of . . . of a . . ."

"What? An attempt on Mr. King's life?"

"Let's say an attempt to sway his vote. I too use my position to sway opinions, as part of my God-given job, but I object strongly to methods that exceed the scope of the law."

"No," she said. "Unequivocally, no. I had nothing to do with this."

"Glad to hear that. Truly, I am."

"Accuse me again, and I'll take my financial support elsewhere."

Pastor Teman's tone softened. "That won't be necessary. Now look, I have Mardy Flynn on my other line, calling from Oak Ridge of all places."

"Natalie's father?" Darcy grew even more suspicious of Serpionov's involvement in this matter. "Go on, take the call," she told the pastor. "Call me back the moment you learn anything new."

Chapter Thirty-one

"He's dead? You're certain of it?"

"Happened in a split second." The Anderson County sheriff stood grim-faced at the hospital bedside. "He died instantaneously."

Supported by pillows, Reuben King hefted himself into a sitting position. His breaths were shallow, shot through with lances of pain. He was in a room at Methodist Medical Center of Oak Ridge. A thin blanket was twisted around his waist, restricting his ability to move, while guilt and relief and confusion swirled through his head and pricked at his eyes. A droplet ran down his cheek, burning in the treated lacerations.

"It's my fault," Reuben mumbled.

"No, it was my decision," the sheriff said. "My responsibility."

"Because of one threatening call?"

"You're a public servant, and we had to protect you, sir. We can't take these threats lightly, and that's why I had Deputy Browne tail your rental car. Deputy Sevier led the way in your Audi, also well aware of the potential danger."

"I should've canceled the whole trip."

"It's not your fault, sir. He died doing his duty."

Reuben looked away, trying to comprehend

what had happened. His recollections were hazy. Earlier, a doctor had explained that it wasn't uncommon to experience short-term memory loss in an accident, particularly one this violent.

He was told that an explosive device had gone off in the Audi's front passenger-side, destroying the struts and axle, and triggering an eruption of gasoline. Although the deputy at the wheel had been rendered unrecognizable, a charred corpse, the doctor said he would've died the moment the bomb's superheated oxygen tore through his esophagus and lungs and boiled the blood pumping through the ventricles of his heart. The same shockwave bubbled the tar in the pavement, scorched grass and tree trunks along the turnpike, peeled paint from Reuben's rented Ford Focus, and blew out its front windscreen.

He had multiple abrasions on his face, chest, and arms. He'd broken a rib from contact with the steering wheel, and his neck was sore from both the whiplash of the initial blast and from the driver's airbag that deployed as the car veered into a berm of dirt and stone.

"He took my place," Reuben said. "That should've been me, Sheriff."

"Deputy Sevier was a great admirer of yours."

"I wasn't aware of that."

"He thought you were a heckuva politician, one who stuck to his guns."

As Reuben furrowed his eyebrows and tried

to piece together recent events, the cuts on his forehead made their presence known, a dozen tiny bee stings. He recalled the rippling air, the heat, and the roar.

He said, "Do we know who did this? Was it a remote-controlled device?"

"Still looking into it, sir, but our investigators discovered a radio transmitter up the slope, only eighty yards from the scene. Components? Standard stuff you could put together from Radio Shack. Clearly, that phone call was no prank. One of our own has fallen, and our entire department mourns his loss. We'll do our best to identify the perpetrator and bring justice to bear on him."

Reuben lifted his chin. "Do you think this person'll try again?"

"We're operating on that assumption, Representative."

"What am I supposed to do? Where do I go from here?"

"I've briefed TBI and the Capitol Police, and Homeland Security's already sent a team to the scene, on the suspicion this was an act of terrorism. Doctor says it's a miracle you're alive, considering the speed you were traveling when the car left the turnpike. That broken rib almost punctured your lung."

"Which explains why it hurts to breathe."

"You also suffered a concussion, and he expects you to be a bit tired and disoriented. He

216

ran a CT scan and MRI, says things look good, but wants to monitor you through the night to be sure there's no intercranial hemorrhaging."

"Sounds like I'm in good hands."

The sheriff nodded.

"The deputy," Reuben said softly. "What was his first name?"

"Christopher. Just Chris to us, sir."

"Did he have . . ." Reuben steadied his voice. "Was he married?"

"Divorced. That's why he transferred to us last year, came over from Knox County. Deputy Sevier was thirty-two years old." The sheriff's chest expanded, and he fixed his eyes on the far wall of the hospital room. "I see your age listed at twenty-eight, Representative."

"I feel twice that at the moment."

"Well, let's hope you have many more years ahead."

Reuben could hardly fathom tomorrow. Life felt suddenly short, and he took stock of his situation. Despite being educated, relatively healthy, and on a career path many envied, he was still on this journey alone.

Oh no. My brunch with Natalie.

Did she know what had happened? Did she know he was safe?

The sheriff broke into his thoughts. "Make the most of those years," he said. "Make each one of them count."

Reuben finished off his serving of hospital food. The soup was hearty and warm, the mashed potatoes seasoned with herbs and garlic. He handed the tray to a nurse, told her he felt fine, then surrendered himself to her poking and prodding.

On my best behavior, he decided. *She's simply doing her job.*

The nurse was also a constituent of District 33, one who might have voted for him in the last election, and he knew his actions were under constant scrutiny.

When the newspapers weren't commenting on his policy-making, the smaller independent rags were looking to take potshots. As a Republican, he was open game for the liberal columnists. Heaven forbid any of them would write about his actual decisions. It was much easier to attack what they perceived as his biases.

Such was politics.

He was either too conservative or too liberal, too softhearted or too hard-nosed. And if he walked a path somewhere in the middle, both sides opened fire.

"Reuben?"

Mindful of his rib, he angled his torso toward the opening door. He watched the entrance of someone wearing low black heels with white cotton leggings, a tan skirt just above the knees, and a soft sweater brushed by a wave of thick brown hair.

Boy, oh boy. Well, let the gossipers gossip.

"Hey there," he said. "Thanks for coming all this way, Natalie."

She took slow steps toward the bed. "You're alive."

"So they tell me."

"I waited over an hour for you at Capitol Grille. I thought you'd—"

"I was en route." He took hold of her right hand. "It was going to be my treat, and I was thoroughly looking forward to it. Then, all of this happened."

She squeezed. He saw her hazel eyes swim with tears.

She swiped them away with her shoulder and gave him a light kiss. "I didn't even know. My dad says he heard sirens all morning long on the turnpike, and then found out you'd been in an accident. He thought you were dead, was afraid to even turn on the news. Then he heard you'd been brought here and called me right away."

"It wasn't an accident, Natalie. I should tell you that up front."

"A bomb. Yeah, that's what they're saying. On the way here, I heard the radio DJs spinning conspiracy theories like you wouldn't believe."

"I can imagine."

"Look at you. Your face. Does it hurt?"

"That bad, huh? A vision of horror?"

"Not at all." She moved her left hand toward his cheek. "Is it OK to touch?"

He nodded, forced himself not to flinch.

"Do they know who did this to you? They better make sure that you're safe from here on out. OK, so there's a guard at the door, but is that enough? Some freak goes after you and tries to blow you to smithereens. What for? Why you? I mean, it's not like you're the president of the United States."

"Why, thanks. I feel duly humbled."

"You're better by far. You know what I mean, though."

He blinked. Adjusted himself in the bed. The concussion was still jumbling his thoughts, and the fluorescent lighting seemed harsh.

"Think about it, Reuben. When's the last time someone tried killing a politician? That's so 1960s. So JFK and KGB and Cold War. It's like something the Russians would do to one of their outspoken journalists or authors. Poison-tipped umbrellas. Mercury poisoning. Banishment to the gulags."

"I got a phone call," he said.

"*¿Que?*"

"I remember that. A man warned me."

"What'd he say? Did you find where the call came from?"

"Sheriff tracked it to a payphone at the town library. Not much help."

220

"What'd this guy sound like?"

"I didn't get the impression he was the bomber, simply someone relaying a message. With his voice muffled, he could've been anyone. Didn't sound particularly educated, but I know some pretty smart people who never finished high school and some clueless ones with college degrees."

Natalie put a hand on her hip. "Well, *gracias* to you too, *amigo*."

His grin turned into a grimace.

"Hurts to smile?" she said.

He nodded. He was sure there was more the caller had told him, though it was just beyond his grasp at the moment.

"You think another kiss would help?" Natalie said. "I mean, I'm willing to do my part for a wounded servant of the people."

Another grin. "Why, I'm a proponent of natural medicines. Let's try it."

Her lips were soft, brushing his forehead, his nose, his mouth. He closed his eyes and felt a slight tremble pass through him. After today's events, he knew this was what he wanted. She was who he wanted. Life was too fickle, and he'd waste it all away if he let fear stand in his path.

Across the room, the door whooshed open.

A male voice said, "Duckie, you in here? Don't mean to interrupt, but the nurse said you were still around, and I gotta talk to ya. It's about your momma."

Chapter Thirty-two

Certain that Serpionov was to blame, Darcy weighed the ramifications of this morning's attack while flying direct from Seattle to Nashville.

Was it a fiasco? Yes. Unforgivably so.

It did present, however, an opportunity to rally and regale her forces.

She finished her glass of Riesling and glanced at Bigz snoozing in the adjacent first-class seat. She had kept him up late last night, and now was a good time to make a call. She preferred talking over texting. So much could be communicated through subtle pauses and tone of voice, and even with the encrypted line, she worried that some techno geek in a national security office might sniff out trigger words in her texts and alert a supervisor.

Darcy called three times, with no response. Very well then.

She chose her words with care: You see now, too much pressure could ruin everything. Do as I say and don't deviate. Be firm, but don't rush.

The screen on Serpionov's cell showed that Ms. Page was calling from her secure line, no doubt anxious for an explanation. He couldn't tell her about his deal with Mardy Flynn, though he would love to see her reaction. Neither could he reveal his larger scheme, because she would try to twist it for her own benefit.

Bah. This was his story to tell.

Months earlier, Alex Page had tried weaving a tale of revenge aimed at his father's company, even used Magnus as his pawn. Now both men were dead. Subplots in a previous story. Corpses in a warehouse lot.

Darcy Page wanted to shape her own tale of riches and corporate manipulation using Serpionov as her pawn, but she made the mistake—the very American mistake—of believing larger paychecks would buy his obedience.

"Ms. Page," he replied in a drowsy tone. "I was sleeping."

"Explain to me what happened."

"The accident?"

"That was no accident. Yes, the method was rather impressive, if not ostentatious, but it's the timing I take issue with. A homeless man is one thing. No one cares. You stepped beyond your bounds, though, with this attack. And in so doing, you've drawn the attention of federal authorities."

Good, Serpionov thought. *This was my hope.*

He said, "You want him to cooperate? Today was warning to him."

"I want *you* to do as I ask, and only as I ask. Since you chose to act on your own initiative, you'll feel my fury in your bank account. Nothing next month, not one sparkling U.S. dime. If anything, I ought to make withdrawals for the damage you've done to my cause."

"*Pozhaluista*," he pleaded. "This money, it's important."

"Money speaks loudly in any language, doesn't it?"

"My *babushka*, she is sick. She needs this for hospital."

"So that's your big secret. Your grandma's in poor health. Well, truthfully, I don't care if it's for your *babushka* or your red-rumped baboon. You work for me, and you'll follow my rules instead of making them up as you go."

Serpionov smirked. "Yes, Ms. Page."

So easy to deceive. With apologies to my grandmother.

"You do understand," she said, "that we're nearing the final hour? It all culminates September 30, a Friday morning, when the Health and Human Resources Committee decides whether to submit HB 6336 for another vote in the House. If we cannot convince their chairman, Mr. King, to do his part, Shield Technologies will suffer a major setback, and all our efforts'll be for naught."

"My work, it's not done yet."

"I hope not. As things stand, there are already board members, investors, and stockholders shouting 'Off with her head,' and I suspect Jack Norwood, my COO, is heading the mob. Does he actually believe I'll melt beneath the pressure? No, I'm the Ice Queen. You had better have no part in their betrayals. I refuse to bow a knee to King, or to Norwood, or to anyone else who dares oppose me on this."

Chapter Thirty-three

Once the identity of the deceased was made official, the local TV station featured the deputy in a five o'clock news segment, and the newspaper ran an article about his shortened career. The public responded with an outpouring of sympathy, but their questions weren't far behind.

Was the explosion caused by a roadside mine similar to those encountered by soldiers in Iraq? How safe was it to drive these streets?

Had there been any arrests? Was there a killer on the loose?

Would it happen again?

Deputy Sevier's memorial was held on Saturday, a closed-casket affair. The time and the chapel's location were kept private for purposes of security, and the majority of those present were family members or employees of the sheriff's department.

Natalie attended with Reuben. Though she had never met the deputy whose framed photo stood on an easel beside the coffin, his courage stirred in her a deep gratitude. If not for his actions, she would be mourning her boyfriend.

And heaven help her. Considering the recent news of her mother, could she have absorbed the loss of Reuben as well?

Absorbed? Sure.

Like a sponge soaking up battery acid.

Pastor Teman had called yesterday to offer his condolences. He'd heard the news from her father, and said he didn't want her feeling alone in her grief. Really? Well, hello, she did feel alone. And annoyed. And confused.

"Welcome, friends and family," the minister greeted from the podium. "Thank you for gathering on this solemn occasion, when we remember and celebrate the life of a man taken from us sooner than any of us expected." He gave a short eulogy and prayer, then introduced Representative King.

Reuben stepped to the podium in a black suit with a dark green tie.

"I'm alive today," he said, "because of the bravery of one man, a man who fell while in the line of duty." He squared his shoulders, eyes panning the crowd. Thin lacerations marked his cheeks and brow. "The first and last time I spoke with Deputy Christopher Sevier was on the morning he died. He shook my hand, took my car keys, and sat in my place behind the wheel. I had received a threat, and his aim—the aim also of Deputy Browne and the entire sheriff's depart-ment—was to shield me from any danger. 'You'll be fine,' Chris said to me. 'It's probably nothing, and if there is any trouble I'll be here. It's what I signed on for.' I thanked him, and he said, 'Nice Audi. I'll be sure to treat her gently.' "

Natalie heard a few sobs, felt her own throat tighten.

"It's people such as Deputy Sevier who make Tennessee such a great state to live in. If not for our fine men and women who protect and serve, we'd all be victims of violence and lawlessness."

Heads nodded along the wooden pews.

"I look to the Bible for some way of making sense of this, and I find in John 15:13 that 'the greatest love is shown when people lay down their lives for their friends.' In Jesus, we see the ultimate example of this, and Deputy Sevier emulated that on Thursday morning when . . ."

Reuben stopped, clenched his jaw.

You're good. You got this, Natalie urged him on.

He checked his notes and lifted his chin. "On Thursday, 8:49 a.m., Deputy Sevier laid down his own life and, in so doing, saved mine."

With grave expressions, mourners clapped Reuben on the back. They moved into a small hall, where one table held a punch bowl, a coffee percolator, vegetable trays, and desserts. The next table bore photos, plaques, and medals honoring the deputy.

"You did great," Natalie told him. "I was proud of you up there."

"This wasn't about me," he snapped.

"What's wrong?"

He shook his head once. "It just infuriates me," he whispered. "Whoever did this is walking free. Why, for all we know, he or she could be in this room."

Chapter Thirty-four

Natalie had one more memorial to attend. The evening was pleasant, the air balmy as it came through the windows of the old Ford Bronco. Natalie and Tuf squeezed together in the passenger seat, cradling a decorative urn of ashes, while their dad drove the few miles southeast of town to Oak Ridge Forest.

This forest, it seemed, was the site of Janet Flynn's passing.

The place that always calmed her.

So close to home, yet so far.

Public access to these thousands of acres ended at sunset. Already, the sky was bleeding gold and violet over the western ridge. Mardy led the way on foot from the parking area, taking them to the spot where he was first called to identify tattered rags and a rotted shoe. The urn felt heavy in Natalie's hands.

"Thing is," he said, swatting at an overhanging beech leaf, "I think 'em cops first brought me here wanting to see my reaction, still wondering if I done it."

"It's over, Dad," Natalie said. "No more accusations."

"If they know what killed her, they're still not saying."

"Sheriff made it clear there weren't any signs of foul play. He says there're records showing she was on medication for depression and high anxiety, that she might've wandered this way on foot during one of her bouts and got disoriented amongst the trees and the darkness."

"Nope," Tuf said. "She still woulda survived long 'nuff to be found."

"Maybe she needed her meds. You remember what she was on, Dad?"

Mardy marched toward a group of black oaks.

"Dad?"

"She was sick, OK? That what you wanna hear? Your mom, she couldn't get no rest, no peace. Was all she could do to feed you girls breakfast in the morning and get me out the door. That 'bout took it outta her."

Natalie and her sis exchanged glances, and

followed in their father's tracks. While this was more than he had shared before, it didn't excuse a mother's act of abandonment. A homicide might be easier for them to come to terms with.

"Wish Grams were here," Tuf said.

"It's for the best. She loves you girls like her own, and she never could forgive your momma for leaving things the way she did."

"What if it'd been murder? What then?"

"Either way, Grams put it behind her years ago."

Natalie infused her voice with warmth. "Least you're done carrying it around now, Dad. You can move forward. Start dating again. Whatever."

"First off, we pay our respects. It's only proper."

"What's it flippin' matter?" Tuf lifted a shoulder. "Me and sis, we didn't ever know her. She just popped us out, left us to fend for ourselves. However things went down, it's a tragedy. Let's get this over with, boo-hoo, and move on."

Mardy swiveled around. "There's no call for that, Tina."

"Do we even know if it's her? Know it for a certainty? What about DNA testing?" she called to his back as he resumed his march. "While I was doing my time, that's all anyone talked about, how they got DNA these days that can prove you didn't do the things they said. Get you off free and clear. Well, y'all shoulda tested the bones, huh? Woulda knowed it for certain then."

"The bone analysis put it at 85 percent," Natalie said.

"Which leaves fifteen that coulda gone the other way."

"She makes a valid point, Dad."

He shook his head, called over his shoulder. "Some stuff's not worth picking over. It's her, and that's all that matters."

"What, and it's a crime for us to know it for ourselves?"

"Sis, it's OK," Natalie said.

"It's cruddy of him, that's what it is. We're part of this too."

Their dad stopped in the deepening shadows, examined the lay of the ground and the surrounding trees. He made a quarter-turn, stepped forward, and squatted near a fallen trunk. "This here's it," he said in a hushed tone.

Tuf folded her arms. Natalie shifted the urn, draped her free hand over her sis's shoulder.

By their weight, the contents of the urn seemed drawn back to the ground from which they had come, and Natalie remembered Tolkien's concept of a link between the soil and those who worked it. Ashes to ashes, and dust to dust. With only portions of Janet Flynn's bones recovered, cremation had been the simplest option, but how did that work in terms of the final resurrection?

Natalie recalled words she had read in First Thessalonians 4:16&17: "First, all the Christians who have died will rise from their graves. Then, together with them, we who are still alive and remain on the earth will be caught up in the clouds to meet the Lord in the air and remain with Him forever."

She decided it would be up to God to draw her mother to Himself on that final day, same as He would draw all those who had perished in house fires, in napalm attacks, as well as those who died as martyrs burned at the stake.

Jesus had conquered death on the cross, hadn't He?

She believed that, absolutely.

Why, then, did she still have such a hard time accepting how certain things played out in her life? Maybe after God had done His part and sent His Son, He'd gone on to other galactic projects, leaving this globe to deal with its own self-induced pain. He would have every right, wouldn't He? She would do the same in His shoes.

"Tina, Natalie," their dad said, standing. "I'm proud of you. Not saying any of us is perfect, but here we stand—the three of us, still together. As your father, I done the best I could all these years, but there's things a daughter needs that a man can't teach. Been times I wasn't sure what I's s'posed to say and what I was s'posed to keep quiet. Your momma? You gotta believe that she loved ya too. She just didn't always know what was what."

"Getting dark out here," Tuf said.

"You wanna know it's her, know it for certain? Well, the sheriff showed me an amethyst ring they dug up near the remains. I didn't wanna tell you girls about it till the cops got them tests back. But me, I already knew. That ring, it was a gift to her from Grams. Christmas of '89. Duckie was, what, two, three years old? And you, Tuf, you were still in diapers. Cutest doggone bug on the block."

"Now look at me, huh? Inked up and flippin' porcupined."

"Don't ya knock yourself," he said. "You're still cute, piercings and all."

"Got Mom to thank for that, at least."

Mardy stared off into the distance.

The sun was sinking below the ridge, stretching a cloak of burnt red and russet brown over the Appalachian foothills. Here in their wooded alcove, Natalie felt the evening's first shiver touch her neck, and she almost dropped the urn.

"Careful, Duckie. Here, hand 'er on over."

She surrendered the item to her father.

Her dad pried at the lid. "We each of us take a handful," he said, being the first to do so. "We say our good-byes, scatter 'em ashes where we will, and keep her close in our hearts. God rest her soul. Your momma deserves that much."

"Why not?" Tuf shrugged and grabbed her portion.

"Janet, I loved ya," Mardy muttered. "Always did."

Hand cupped, Natalie reached into the urn. She planned to say a quick prayer, dribble the ashes between her fingers, and be done with this.

She jolted instead at the first touch. Tingles ran up her arm and crawled across her neck. Her mother's ashes were gritty against her skin, weighty in her grasp, and while they didn't contain her mom's essence or personality or spirit, they were the closest she would ever be to her mother this side of eternity.

Oh God, no. No, NO, NOOO!

A heaving sob rose in Natalie's chest, and she didn't care who heard her out here in the darkness as the pain rushed up from her lungs like a creature unleashed at last from its prison. "Why'd you leave us?" she screamed. "Why would you *do* that? We needed you! You hear me? God, are *You* listening? WHERE *WERE* YOU?"

The sobs took over, wringing her insides until she had no tears left. Lost in a grief all his own, her father paced along the fallen trunk. Her sister pressed in beside her, and together they spread the ashes across the coarse, dark soil.

In Her Pain

"She's got her share of anger, that's a plain-as-the-nose-on-your-face fact."

"Anger, you say."

"Covers it best she can, but it's there, all right. Been simmering inside since she was a lil' thing, coming and going, never quite making up its mind."

"You're sure that it's anger?"

"It's . . . Well, I reckon it's pain, down deep at its core."

"Agreed. Yes, that's usually the case."

"Call it whatcha will, hurts me to see my girl hurting. And now she's got this thing with Reuben, good guy'n all, but it makes ya wonder who's gonna be doing the hurting next. Do they ever learn?"

"People who are in pain either inflict it upon others or—"

"She doesn't, though. Least not too much."

"Or they inflict it on themselves."

"Sure 'nuff, but that's better than lashing out and hurting everyone around ya, dontcha think? Hmm? Why aren't ya saying nothing?"

"Look around. Even self-inflicted pain hurts others. When one part of the body's wounded, the entire body is affected. In one way or another, that anger spreads its poison, and the wounded souls multiply."

"Way you tell of it sounds hopeless."

"I'm only telling the truth, and the truth is never hopeless. In Natalie's case, her anger's birthed in her pain, and her pain in her loss. Her hope, her one real hope, lies in finding a love large enough to fill that hole."

"I dunno. What about this thing with Reuben, think it's got any shot at helping? You seem to know what's what when it comes to that stuff."

"It's a bright spot, certainly, but there's bound to be more hurt along the way. You and I both know that the entire truth's not yet out in the open."

Chapter Thirty-five

August

For a time, Natalie felt purged of her anger and grief. She had let it out beneath the black oaks, with a shriek that raked her throat and stung in both her tear ducts. On an intellectual level, she believed in God's power and love, though her heart still wrestled for assurances and understanding. She loved the Psalms. In them she found expressions of fierce emotion from David as he bemoaned the very day of his birth and hurled questions at the heavens.

See there, it was good to be honest with the Lord, wasn't it? Didn't He know her thoughts anyway? Know her deceitful little heart?

She preferred not to dwell on that fact.

Nine weeks had passed since their introduction at Secret City Festival, and the fire between Natalie and Reuben burned even hotter, fanned by the bombing incident and its reminder that life was short. He was healing quickly. They talked and texted often. There wasn't time to stay huddled in isolated dread.

With Eli ever present, like a kindly old uncle, Natalie and Tuf had settled into routines at their place off Trousdale Drive. Natalie worked first shift at Roast, whereas Tuf worked third shift five nights a week at her warehouse job, and often arrived home at the time Natalie was hitting her snooze button.

And now, Metro Nashville Public Schools was back in session.

OK, Ms. Flynn, time to give this a whirl.

She found the online employee portal, entered her username and password. If a teacher was sick or there were openings for any other reason, they would be here, and she could respond through the automated system by clicking Approve or Deny.

Available: Tuesday, August 23, 7:40 a.m., Shayne Elementary.

With over seventy elementary schools in the system, she wasn't certain of the location of this one, but she hit Approve and received a confirmation e-mail within seconds. This was it. In a few days, she would stand as a certified teacher before her first full classroom, sign a time sheet, and collect her per diem and hourly rate. Her years at Trevecca and the thousands in student loans were about to pay off.

"I'm a schoolteacher," she said aloud. "This is the real deal."

Serpionov's plot was soon to take an unexpected twist.

Seated at his kitchen bar with the black case, he noted Natalie's location at her rental off

Trousdale. The blood-red circle moved. Settled at Roast only blocks away. She was at her workplace, and all was well.

He nudged the case aside and cleaned the barrels of his modified cell phone with Q-tips and mineral spirits. He had no intention of making any more "dropped calls," but he loaded his last four shells anyway. This ammo was hard to find in the United States, and he hoped it would see him through to the end of the story.

His story. His sprawling, bittersweet plot.

With its primary cast of characters:

1. Bitter yet helpful Mardy Flynn
2. Stubborn yet vital Reuben King
3. And, of course, hazel-eyed Natalie

The threads were coming together now, intertwining. Though he had never intended for Mr. King to die along the Oak Ridge Turnpike, even that could've been worked into the plot.

Yes, like the great writers of his motherland, Serpionov was blending a sense of destiny with earthy agony. While he was no Tolstoy, Solzhenitsyn, or Dostoevsky, he would spin a tale worth remembering, one that would bring about a greater measure of safety for future generations.

You'll see, babushka. *Yes, bloodshed can bring peace.*

He pocketed his weapon and downed a shot

of Zyr to numb the pain of his grandmother's absence. Who, he wondered, would he call next July for birthday wishes? What family, what home did he have left without her? He knew next to nothing of the Scriptures she revered, yet he wished for a moment that there was some truth to her belief in a God of ages past, to her hope in an afterlife.

"Aggh." He gritted his teeth as another vodka shot scorched his throat.

The drink betrayed its purpose, easing open the doors in his mind. He didn't want this, didn't want to feel or hear or see the things in there. It was senseless, the stuff that had happened in a school full of children, hostage to masked gunmen, surrounded by OMON troops.

Beslan.

Screams and blood and—

Knock-a-knock-knock.

Serpionov was startled. A visitor at his door? Only Darcy Page and Bigz had visited his condo since he moved in.

He eased the house slippers from his feet, armed his cell with a few taps on the keypad, and glided from the kitchen to the entryway in his socks. Through the spyhole, he saw that it was the chubby blonde he had recruited months ago as a volunteer for the free clinic.

"Abby?" he said, cracking the door. "How is this you find me?"

"You remembered." She flashed a coy grin. "Truth? I didn't even *know* you lived here, but gotta say, I'm liking the place. There I was around the corner, what, like a half hour ago, having drinks at Yazoo with a friend, and I see you ride by. Your visor was up, so I knew it was you. Did I mention how much I *love* a man on a motorcycle? If that's too forward, well, fine then, shoot me."

"Why're you here? Does anyone else know?"

"Hey, don't be mad. I told a guy coming in at the front, one of your neighbors, I guess, that my friend lived here, didn't know what floor or anything, but said you had a Russian accent. He thought about that, said yeah maybe he knew, and pointed me in this direction." She smiled wide. "So here I am."

"I need reason, Abby." The loaded phone was in his hand.

"So serious. Sheesh. If you *must* know, I'm pulling together a benefit concert for the Rescue Mission. When I saw you, I figured, hey, let's maybe set up a medical tent to help the homeless again. You seem to be hooked *up* when it comes to all that. Whaddya say? Can I mark ya down?"

He stepped back. "Please. Come inside."

Detective Meade exited the Nashville Rescue Mission, stood beneath its cross-within-a-heart logo. This was the last place anyone had seen Freddy C alive. He felt responsible. Back in April, he had interviewed Freddy at Black's Espresso, dutifully jotted down comments, told the bearded fellow to take it easy.

And Freddy was still nowhere to be found.

Was his disappearance linked to his rambling suspicions?

With the late-August sun high overhead, the humidity wrung sweat from the detective's dark skin. Of the men and women languishing in the building's shade, none gave any notice of his presence. They knew he was here. Oh, they knew. Deserving or not, most of them were familiar with cops, patrol cars, and holding cells. Even in plain clothes, he seemed to repel them.

He wanted to tell them that he was here to protect them, that he cared about their welfare.

Empty words, now that their comrade was missing.

When the homeless man's disappearance was first reported, Meade had taken statements from longtime staff members who said it was tragic, "Freddy being such a nice guy and all." A few recalled that he was "wigged out" the days prior to his disappearance, but Meade knew Freddy wasn't the first or last to come through here with a "head crammed full of conspiracy theories."

Meade also interviewed Abby, a senior at Trevecca who had volunteered at a free clinic for the homeless, where she helped Freddy and seven others sign waivers to receive medical assistance.

Those others, if they were even still in town, weren't coming forward to tell their stories. Maybe there was nothing to it. Maybe they thought the police were involved in some conspiracy.

If, however, there was merit to the story, he needed to hear from them.

Abby. Now she might be able to help. That girl had spunk.

Minutes earlier, the mission director had told Meade that she was putting together a benefit concert for the city's homeless. Such an event would give a face to the hungry and downtrodden. It might also draw out the seven others.

Meade called the number he had for her, but there was no reply.

Chapter Thirty-six

Reuben's tone sounded playful through the phone. "Are you willing to give me another chance, Natalie? A nice brunch, just the two of us? Have to admit, I had a fairly valid excuse last time, but I think I still owe you."

"You do," she said. "When?"

"I'm in town again for committee. How's nine forty-five work? We're hammering out a few upcoming measures, and later, I have a photo op with some bigwigs at St. Thomas Hospital. I could use a good meal in advance."

"Are you still ignoring security measures and taking the machoman approach to all this?"

"I'm not going to cower in a corner until trouble tracks me down, if that's what you mean. I'm wearing a Kevlar vest, which does double duty protecting my rib while it mends, but I refuse to put any more law officers in harm's way."

"That's their job."

"Once was enough," he said.

"You were this close to dying yourself, Reuben."

"And so now I should ride around in the pope's bulletproof bubble?"

She sighed. "See you there, *corazon*."

During the last month, they had explored the Frist Center for the Visual Arts, toured Belle Meade Plantation's famed stables and mansion, and hit blues clubs in Printers Alley and honky-tonks along Broadway. Now, it was brunch at swanky Capitol Grille.

She arrived at 9:50 a.m. Five minutes late.

OK, maybe there was some passive-aggressiveness in that.

"Hello, gorgeous." Reuben never once glanced at his watch in some veiled countermove. Instead, he slipped an arm around her waist, the Kevlar pressed between them, and guided her down the steps into the restaurant.

Natalie chose Belgian waffles with huckleberry compote, served with coffee and cream. Reuben ordered a smoked-salmon omelet with mush-rooms and Brie to accompany his glass of cran-berry juice.

"Are you sure about this?" she said after their server left. "Any place that spells *grill* with an *e* is beyond my budget. And have you seen the restrooms?"

He grinned. "Only the men's."

"Well, believe me, they could sell tickets for tours of the women's."

"I'd buy one, except the tabloids might have a field day with it."

"How do you handle it? The whole watch-your-*p*'s-and-*q*'s, always-in-the-public-eye thing. I'm not sure I could deal with that."

"A teacher's held to a similar standard, don't you think?"

She shrugged. "FYI, I'm just a sub."

"You shouldn't downplay that, Natalie."

"I taught my first class on Tuesday."

"Why, that's great. How'd it go? Were you nervous?"

"I, uh . . ." Natalie saw a short black man slip into the booth at Reuben's back. She noticed his green eyes, the fine lines of his slate-gray suit, and thought he looked vaguely familiar. She said, "I messed up my time sheet on, like, the very first try, but at least I'll still get paid. Overall, I'd say it went pretty well. No major disasters. Didn't lose anyone's children or anything."

"I never doubted you."

She smiled.

"Those kids need you," he added. "You realize you might be the only person who gives them that beautiful smile or takes the time to listen."

"Spoken like a true politician."

"The best ones mean every word."

"You know, I first pictured you as some stodgy, balding good ole boy."

"With a backwoods drawl?"

"Maybe," she admitted.

"And a belly out to here?"

"Definitely."

Reuben patted his black hair. "All I'm missing is the bald spot, then."

She chuckled.

"But don't ya worry, ma'am," he said, eyes crossed and lips scrunched up, " 'cause I is smarter than the day is long."

Businessmen at a neighboring table shot him a look.

"Tha's right." He turned their way, poured on the accent even thicker. "Than the day is long. Y'all heard me right the first time."

Natalie's laughter caught in her throat and came out as a snort.

Eyes still crossed, Reuben snapped upright. "Boy howdy, what was that?"

"I can't . . ." She placed a hand on her chest. "I can't breathe."

He turned serious. "You need some water?"

"I'm . . . nope, I'm fine."

"You want to stand up and walk around?"

"I'm fine, really."

"I shouldn't have carried on like that," he said. "Why, look at the effect you have on this stodgy ole politician. Forgive me, Natalie. I simply wanted you to know that beneath the suit and tie, I'm still a regular, fun-loving guy."

"I believe. I believe."

Their meals arrived, and the first taste had Natalie moaning in appreciation. Reuben tried his omelet and declared that it wasn't half bad.

"You're kidding." She took another bite. "Is stuff this delicious even legal?"

"Barely. I introduced the bill myself and got it passed last assembly."

"Well then," she played along, "you get my vote."

His eyes found hers. "I certainly hope so."

She sipped her orange juice. Dabbed her napkin at her lips. She cared for him more with each passing day, and despised herself for the continued inner conflict that held her at arm's length from his affections. Of course, that was for his own good, wasn't it? She didn't want him to get hurt again.

Natalie decided now was the right time to change the subject. "So you and the committee are hammering out some bills, huh?"

He nodded. "House Bill 6336, to be specific."

"The one about putting tracking devices in people."

"Yes." His eyes brightened at the subject. "It's a divisive issue, no doubt about it. We hold the majority in the House, which you'd think would help. But the reality is we can't even come to a consensus within our own party. The ACLU's shown some opposition to 6336, based on privacy concerns. That fact alone has stirred some of my fellow Republicans to support the bill. At times, we're more focused on our perceived enemies than on the actual facts at hand."

"Doesn't that seem, you know, sort of childish?"

"Welcome to the sandbox."

"Sounds more like a . . ."

"Go on," he said.

"Litterbox."

The corner of his mouth twisted. "You have no idea."

"But hey, what do I know, being fresh out of college?"

"Enough with the low self-image," he said. "Your opinions matter."

Natalie put down her fork. "The whole thing just seems like a no-brainer. I mean, we use technology at work, school, home. It's in our phones, our cars, our TVs. Either we hide away like hermits, or we figure out how to use this stuff in the best way and how to protect those who can't protect themselves."

"It's a bit more complicated than that."

"Really? And a side order of condescension, *por favor*."

"You make valid points, Natalie. It has many great uses, yes." He rested an arm on the table, his hand near hers. "But it's the abuses that worry me."

She sniffed. "And so we're back in fifth grade? One kid abuses a privilege, and snap, just like that, it's yanked away and everyone else has to suffer."

"I'm trying to weigh both sides of this issue. It has long-term ramifications for private citizens, as well as for antiterrorism, crime prevention, and—"

"Right there. Why should any kidnapped child be left helpless?"

"You have some strong emotions about this."

She looked away.

"I know you care deeply about children. I admire that."

"It's not just kids," she said, thinking of herself as a captive.

"There's no question, Natalie. This would aid police in their jobs, as their officials mentioned in a recent public hearing. So far, the committee's opposition is soft. As chairman, I'll carry the deciding vote. Our deadline's September 30th, the day of reckoning. We either agree to push it through the House in its next session, with our full support, or we kill it now."

She winced at the wording.

She was in that hut. Chained and on her own.

She pulled her legs close against the restaurant seat, the fiery throb of each antenna blow whipping at her thoughts. She imagined Magnus's matter-of-fact demeanor, his hands speckled with her blood.

"Natalie?"

Her abductor's voice drowned out the sounds in Capitol Grille. *"What is our word? . . . Easy enough to remember, I should think . . ."*

Her shoulders caved forward, and her breath caught in her throat.

"Keep those antennae up . . ."

"Hello?" A warm baritone. "Honey, what's wrong?"

She lifted her gaze across the table. From the next booth, the sharp-dressed black gentleman angled his face back at her. She narrowed her focus to include only her concerned boyfriend. "Reuben."

"I lost you there."

"Yeah. I was just . . . Did you call me 'honey'?"

He swung around to her side, rested a hand on her shoulder. The smell of his cologne was faint, woodsy with a hint of spice. "Tell me what's wrong."

Natalie planted an elbow on the table, set her chin on her palm, and turned toward the windows, where sunlight fanned across leather, wood, and brass. She did not want to be that girl, the one men tiptoed around and fretted over. She was stronger than that.

"Eleven months ago, I was . . ."

Stop now, she told herself. *You shouldn't be doing this.*

Reuben waited, gave her shoulder a squeeze.

"I was kidnapped. Well, I mean, the correct word's *abducted* for an adult."

He sat up. "By either name, sounds horrible."

"Pretty much."

"This was last October? I wasn't here in town then, but I'm sure they ran something about it on the news in Oak Ridge."

"I was working at a café over in East Nashville, and one of my customers met me as I arrived that morning. I never, you know, never even suspected a thing." She lifted her chin. "He held me captive for ten days before letting me go."

"He let you go? Just like that?"

"He wanted me to spy on the Vreelands, the family I tutored for. Heck, I might do more of it for them this fall, since Bret's a musician playing shows all over the country. Thing is, this guy was after the Vreelands, and I lived the next few months dreading every day, worried he'd hurt them and it'd all be my fault."

"They're safe now, though, aren't they?"

She nodded. "They're fine. I'm fine."

"Honey, ten days is a long time. Did he hurt

251

you?" Reuben lifted a hand. "Wait, no. No, I don't have any right to pry into such a thing."

"It's all right. I'm not going to claim I came through it completely unscathed, but he never violated me in any way. Is that what you wanted to know? If the cops could've tracked me somehow, one of these microchips or something, he might not've had time to beat me the way he did. Every night, like he was trying to toughen me up. Whatever. He's dead now, so it's all over." She stretched her lips into a smile. "All in the past, right? Almost a full year gone by."

"With your mom and all, it's been a rough year, huh? I wish none of that'd happened to you." He touched her chin, turned it toward him. "And he did violate you. He had no right to steal your peace of mind. Even now you're doubting your self-worth and questioning yourself, and you deserve much better, Natalie Flynn."

She pulled back, shaking her head.

You're the one who deserves better. I mean, look at you.

The man in the slate-gray suit from the other booth stood up, cast a wink and a nod at Natalie, then placed a fedora on his head and strutted away.

Chapter Thirty-seven

Serpionov hugged the Honda Interceptor with his thighs, kept his helmet low, his feet braced against the pegs. How long, he wondered, until they found the body? Wishing to avoid any encounters with the police, he maintained a speed of 70 mph as he traveled south of Nashville along I-65 to the Cool Springs exit.

He was checked in at the Hyatt Place. It was a nod to his grandmother, since this hotel chain had been started years ago by a Ukrainian immigrant.

Babushka, *why'd I speak so harshly to you?*

Nearly a week ago, he had left the Gulch condo empty. Though it was leased through Ms. Page, perhaps under another name, he thought it too risky to stay. Within twenty minutes, he had cleared out the closets, refrigerator, and cabinets. He had lived a Spartan existence here, and it wouldn't take long to replenish his wardrobe with a visit to Kohl's, his groceries with a trip to Publix.

It took him only one trip to the Dumpster, with three black garbage bags, to be done with the task.

Abby was not in the bags.

Nyet, that strategy would have drawn too much trouble.

He piled all letters, junk mail, and receipts showing his information in the fireplace. While utilities were handled by Ms. Page, his cell was personal. He added the service provider's bills to the pile. With less than four weeks until the final sacrifice, he wanted nothing pointing back to him.

He sprinkled the last drops from his bottle of Zyr onto the pile.

One strike of a match.

Whooosh!

Abby hadn't left any clothing or belongings in his room, but he vacuumed all carpets and bedding in case a blonde hair remained as evidence. He flushed the dust and dirt down the toilet, flushed again, scrubbed with bleach and water.

Curving along the cloverleaf off-ramp, he coasted toward the Hyatt. Cool Springs was located in Williamson County, one of the richest counties in the nation, home to surgeons and music producers and chart-topping stars. It was a good place to lie low, only a twenty-minute ride from downtown Nashville.

He locked his bike in the Hyatt parking lot, and removed his helmet, thankful for a breeze in this summer heat.

Abby's upbeat voice played in his head: *Did I mention how much I love a man on a motorcycle? If that's too forward, well, fine then, shoot me.*

Killing her gave him no pleasure, especially since she too wanted peace in this world. To let her go, though, was a risk he couldn't take. She had found his place, hadn't she, even if by accident? And told him how she was talking with a Metro detective about the disappearance of Freddy C.

Serpionov invited her inside. Responded to her flirtations.

He was a man still, this was true.

He took some pride in his toned physique, yet rarely frequented bars and clubs where he could use it to his advantage. His OMON training alerted him to the predatory signals in such settings, and he feared he might lash out to protect the more susceptible of the women. By observation, he knew Natalie Flynn wasn't one of those types, while her former college roommate was a different story.

And this time he was the predator.

Serpent and scorpion.

"Abby," he had asked her, "would you like to ride with me on motorcycle?"

"Do I really even need to answer? Let's jet."

Clinging to him, she squealed around each corner as he drove deeper into the hills of Percy Warner Park, with its miles of bike routes, hiking trails, and thick foliage. He stopped along a wooded slope. Helped her off the bike.

"You are happy?" he said. "You are peaceful?"

"Hel-*looo*. Like I'd be anything but, after the day we've had."

"Yes, it is good then. You rest in peace."

She was his eighth dropped call.

Chapter Thirty-eight

Today was Natalie's first time in Pastor Teman's office. Although she had skipped her last session with Rhonda Teman, she still respected the older couple's years of service, not to mention their support of Bret Vreeland's music and ministry beyond these church walls. Places such as Haiti. And Leavenworth Prison.

"*Buenos dias,*" she said. "I'm just tagging along with Reuben."

"*Buenos dias, señorita,*" the pastor replied.

"Sweet. Didn't know you spoke Spanish."

"And I've now exhausted every word in my *Español* vocabulary. Please, I hope you know that you need no excuse, Natalie. You're always welcome here."

"You tell her, Pastor." Looking much better since the accident, Reuben shook the man's hand, and joined Natalie in the cushioned chairs across from shelves full of theology books and biographies of Christendom's brightest stars.

"I've tried telling her she needs a better self-image, but she won't listen to me."

"Well, well, you sound like a married couple already."

She stiffened. "We're only, like, a few months into this."

"The Lord sometimes works in mysterious ways. Rhonda and I, we dated for three years before calling it off entirely. A year later, we bumped into each other in a bookstore, and would you believe, the following month, we're saying our vows before God and man. She's since given me three fine children who have given me seven grandchildren."

"OK, now you're just scaring me."

"Us," Reuben agreed.

"But then, none of that's why you're here, is it?"

They shook their heads in unison.

"At least not yet." He threw them a mischievous wink.

Natalie closed her eyes, drew in a breath, and exhaled.

"He means no harm," Reuben said, nudging her.

She ventured a peek. "He's talking babies and grandkids."

"I promise, none of that's why I asked you to come here with me."

"Why, then, did you ask her to come, Mr. King?"

"Because we both care deeply about the issues

at stake with this bill. You know the one, 6336. As you're aware, Natalie's been through things that make her more receptive to the whole idea."

"Completely understandable," the pastor said.

"And I need prayer and advice so that I can make the right decision in that regard. Proverbs 8 says, 'I, Wisdom, live together with good judgment . . . Because of me, kings reign, and rulers make just laws.' "

" 'Kings reign.' I like that. We're here to rule and reign, are we not?"

"But it's the meek who'll inherit the earth," Reuben noted.

Pastor Teman folded his arms. "Reuben King, a man of the Word. Most commendable. Well, we're all on a path toward deeper understanding, I hope."

"Deeper understanding, that's what I'm after today." Reuben leaned forward. " 'This King Listens.' That was my campaign motto. I want to live up to it by hearing not only from my constituents but from God as well. My own pastor in Oak Ridge is a fine man. Our congregation's small, mostly lower middle class, and they don't take much interest in political matters unless the consequences are felt in their own pockets. Honestly, that's part of the reason I attend there. I'd have a hard time not getting caught up in political posturing at some cutting-edge, hipster church, or one with more glitz and glamour."

"Which explains why you've sought me out for prayer a time or two."

"You did extend the offer."

"Ah, yes, the Full Gospel Business Man's breakfast. Yes, I did." The pastor settled back in his desk chair. "Having been called to Nashville, the heart and capital of our state, I feel it's my duty before the Lord to care for those in positions of influence. On Sundays, we have country and Christian artists in attendance, as well as a city councilwoman and two middle school principals. We're one big family, and Father God wants to shower blessings upon His kids."

Natalie squirmed in her seat, still struggling with her own baggage attached to that male imagery. Loved Him, yes. But she was still learning to trust Him.

The pastor tapped a bronze letter opener on the desk and looked in Reuben's direction. "Mr. King, you mentioned wanting to make the right decision. Did you mean that in political or spiritual terms?"

"I'd like to think they could be the same thing."

"Wouldn't we all? Ah yes, indeed. It doesn't pay to be naïve, though."

From the corner of her eye, Natalie saw her boyfriend roll back his shoulders and lift his chin. She had bristled the same way during her last session with Rhonda Teman, and asked herself if coming here today was the best move.

Reuben was already bent beneath the weight of his upcoming decision, and to rush or goad him would be counterproductive.

His tone was firm. "I'm in my second term in office, Pastor. I may be young, but I'm far from naïve."

"Please, Representative, I meant no offense."

"During my campaign, I clearly stated where I stood on the issues, and I've never wavered. Do I get pressured by big business and pharmaceutical reps and fellow legislators? Every day. Comes with the territory. Yes, I'm aware—well aware—that there's a time for being shrewd as a serpent."

"Which I admire about you."

"Am I out of line to give this bill my support?"

"There's the real question, isn't it?"

Reuben shifted in his seat, adjusted the Kevlar under his shirt.

"I believe," the pastor said, "that God's given me some insight for you."

"I'm listening."

"We're both listening." Natalie scooted forward. "I mean, I'd like to be included in this discussion, if that's allowed."

"Of course," both men said in unison.

"Oh, uh . . . Hey, wait a sec." She peeked at her phone's caller ID, then hopped up and headed to the door. "It's my detective friend. I better take this."

• • •

The temperature was pushing a hundred as Detective Meade meandered down the incline from the university's office of the president. Trevecca Nazarene was a small yet distinguished campus, guarded by stone walls, a quiet enclave only a hundred yards from one of the seedier stretches of Murfreesboro Pike.

"Ms. Flynn." He pressed his phone to his ear. "You have a minute?"

"I ducked out of a meeting. Everything OK?"

"Do you know the whereabouts of Abigail Stark?"

"Abby? We haven't talked in a few weeks. Last thing I knew, she was trying to pull together this homeless benefit and wanted me to help."

"That's the last I heard as well. The last anyone's heard."

"*¿Que?*"

"I'm at Trevecca now," Meade said. "The president says she hasn't reported to class since last Monday, and no one's seen her on campus. She missed her volunteer Saturday at the mission, and—"

"OK, classes, I can see her skipping those. But she loves the mission."

"Has a big heart for others, from what I've seen. Big hearts have been known to land young women in trouble." He brushed the sweat from his brow. "Her credit card was swiped at Yazoo

261

last weekend, where it appears she partook of more drinks than I'd recommend. There's been no sign of her since."

Natalie eased back into the office, apologized, and found her seat. Her stomach twisted inside, but she didn't want to worry anyone. Not just yet.

Reuben reached for her hand.

"I'm fine," she assured him.

"All right." He looked straight ahead.

"Go on, Pastor. You were about to share an insight."

"That's right. Yes. It was during my morning reading that I came across this section, a little something to tuck under your hat and do with as you see fit. Here." Pastor Teman spun in his chair, hefted a large Bible from the shelf behind him, and spun back around. As gold-edged pages fell open over his hand, he lifted it with all the authoritative flair of an ancient scribe or rabbi, lending the impression that to do anything other than heed his voice was to step out of the will of Almighty God. "It's all spelled out in the first chapter of Numbers."

Natalie scrunched her eyebrows. This was unfamiliar territory for her.

"The House bill under consideration," he said, "worries some people because it leaves them feeling exposed. Perhaps their movements'll be tracked by the government or their spending habits studied by marketers. In short, they fear they'll become nothing more than another number."

"Valid concerns," Reuben said. "Don't you think?"

"Let's consider, shall we, what's written here? What're the odds I'd stumble upon this today? We see that the Lord instructs Moses to take a census of the entire community of Israel—each tribe, each family, every male old enough to go to war. Not only does he take this census, Moses also orders the people in other passages to provide inventories of all their resources and valuables."

"OK." Natalie tilted her head. "What're you saying?"

"I won't pretend that Rhonda and I never worry. We're getting on in years, and today's advanced gadgetry can be intimidating at times. I'd be the first to admit that it's like pulling teeth to introduce new technology to those firmly set in their ways."

"Tell me, Pastor," Reuben said, "would you get an embedded chip?"

"If forced upon me, no. By choice, I see no reason not to."

"Yeah." She nodded. "That's pretty much the way I see it too. I mean, we're not saying it'd be mandatory, are we? What's so wrong with a mother, for example, wanting a little peace of mind about her child's whereabouts?"

"Moses, huh?" Reuben squinted. "Hadn't ever considered that angle."

In a hushed tone, she said, "A microchip might've spared me some scars."

Reuben turned to her. "Honey?"

"It's . . . Never mind."

"In my position as a spiritual leader," the pastor interjected, "it's not my place to influence public policy-making. Quite simply, I submit to you the wisdom I find in God's Word, and the rest I leave in your good hands, Mr. King."

"So, then, you'd actually get an implant?"

"The answer seems abundantly clear. Numbering is a biblical idea."

Chapter Thirty-nine

Since their direct flight into town in July, Darcy and Bigz had set up house in her downtown luxury suite and shifted operations to Shield's regional office. With only a month remaining until the critical vote, this was crunch time.

The Nashville staff was sharp and ready to roll. In the months since the bill's initial setback, they had secured financial support and public endorsements for HB 6336 from medical companies, insurance agencies, children's advocacy groups, in-home senior-care providers, and shelters for abused women. With Nashville's massive health-care apparatus forcing the gears and wheels of statewide media outlets, the public was taking notice.

Shield was fully invested now.

The Ice Queen's reign was at stake.

She knew even as she led her troops here in Music City that her flank was exposed to some hostile board members back in Seattle. It was a risk she had to take, counting on success five weeks from now to crush any attempted takeover.

Warning came via phone from her head of marketing, Lindsey Sims.

"Do you have a moment?"

"Speak," Darcy said. "I'm working."

"When are you not?"

"I'm waiting." She saw Bigz at her door with her Diet Coke and bagel sandwich. She beckoned him in, took the food, then shooed him away.

"It's Jack Norwood, Ms. Page. Divide and conquer, that's his tactic. He's been pulling board members aside, under the guise of department evaluations, and pressuring them for pledges of loyalty in the event he takes over."

"Primitive," Darcy said. "Men and their chest-beating."

"It's working," Sims said.

"Griggs? Danby? Marevich?"

"They're not the only ones, I'm afraid."

"Fear. It's always about fear." She drank some

of her Coke. "Exactly how does Norwood think he'll accomplish this coup d'état? By intimidation, of course. It won't get him far, though. With my shares and my ex-husband's, I still own over half the company. All the board members combined can't topple me from my throne, no matter how loud Jack's chest-beating gets."

"He claims to have found a loophole in the bylaws."

"Is that so?"

"Something about dissolution of marriage between partners," Sims explained. "If one of those partners should die, the shares are no longer transferred automatically to the other partner and instead go back on the auction block, so to speak. They're not yours, in other words."

This concerned Darcy more than she let on. Of course, if the upcoming vote swung her way, she would have board support regardless.

She downed more of her drink and said, "Well, kudos to him for moving beyond jungle warfare. I happen to know, though, that he's whispered secrets to our fiercest rival in hopes of undermining my hold on the market."

"Storinka?"

"You tell him I said so, Mrs. Sims. He'll be held liable for the fallout of that mistake, and his gorilla gang will be left scratching their gorilla gourds."

"It's been near mutiny here these past few days. The chatter's disrupting work. I beg of you, please come back now so that you might sway some of the more impressionable board members. Not all have your vision. They leech on to the nearest sources of warmth and comfort."

Darcy coughed out a laugh. "Norwood's behind this phone call."

"Pardon me?"

"He put you up to this, didn't he?" She chuckled. "We're nearing our deadline, and he thinks he can pull me down by dividing my focus and energies."

"No, that's not—"

"Good-bye, Mrs. Sims. Tell Norwood his chest sounds awfully hollow from twenty-five hundred miles away."

Today, Serpionov decided, he would deliver another plot twist.

Of course, he had never intended for Abby to die. That wasn't part of his plot, and it saddened him to think of her. Did all the great Russian novelists go through this? When Tolstoy wrote *War and Peace*, did he feel like the rider on a runaway horse? When Dostoevsky penned *Crime and Punishment*, did he feel saddled to a raging bull?

Serpionov would not let go, not now. He had worked on this story long enough, woven in subplots and backstories, and it was time to give Representative King a surprise.

Nothing as violent as the C4, though.

This surprise had a different sort of power.

Using riding gloves to avoid leaving finger-prints, he gathered his work and drove his bike due north into the heart of the Capitol. He walked into the FedEx Office on the corner of Third and Broadway, where he sealed everything in an envelope addressed to the Legislative Plaza, only blocks from here. It was risky, yes, sending it from so close. But it would remind Mr. King that his watchers were near.

Still in his helmet and riding leathers, Serpionov waited until the clerk at the front counter moved to help someone in the computer area.

He quickly set the envelope on the counter with a $20 bill.

No return address. No credit card information.

He returned to his bike in the rear parking lot, threw a leg over the seat, and rode away.

When Mr. King received the delivery tomorrow, he would tear open the envelope, see the documents enclosed, and realize his secrets weren't so secret. But then, he should never have expected them to be in this land where freedom cut both ways. Most everyone's information was out there somewhere, in a file, a database, or a computer hard drive. All it took to uncover it was curiosity and perseverance.

The delivery's unspoken message would be clear:

Do what is expected, or risk your relationships and career.

Chapter Forty

Natalie scooted in a chair at a student's empty desk, gathered her curriculum, and found the school secretary at the front office.

"All done," she said. "Does it sound crazy to say that I had fun?"

"Time sheet's right there, ma'am," the stout secretary said.

"You think they'll ever get this system automated?"

"Time sheet gets the job done."

"Sure. It just seems that . . ."

Peering up at Natalie, the secretary pointed a pencil at her electric desk clock. "Time," she said. Then pointed at the clipboard on the counter. "Sheet."

Natalie signed her name and printed *3:33 p.m. Natalie Flynn.*

She headed through the front doors into the sunlight, confident she was building a good résumé for a full-time position. The K-5 kids seemed to respond to her caring classroom manner. Each one of them was precious. Were there some exasperating ones? You better believe it. Even so, most of the substitute openings she filled left her tired and satisfied, as if she had done a workout with Tuf at the Harding Place YMCA.

As she fumbled with the keys at her Civic's door, trees swayed along the perimeter of the parking lot and the chain-link fence near the soccer field rattled. For a moment, she imagined taking shots on goal, shin guards tucked into her socks, cleats digging into the turf.

Oh, to be a kid again.

She wondered how Kevin Vreeland was doing, in sixth grade now and growing taller every day. He was quite the soccer player. Had quite the leg.

She tried again with her keys, caught a hint of gray in her peripheral vision. She cocked her head to her left, saw nothing but branches waving bunches of leaves the way a cheerleader waved bright pompoms.

Get a grip, muchacha. *It's nothing.*

She dropped behind the wheel, unable to shake the sense that her actions were being marked. She locked her doors and dialed Abby. Nothing. Even with the police, university, and family members all joined in the search, Abby was still missing. A fact that flooded Natalie with her old worries and fears.

Maybe a visit to Sonic would help.

Natalie stopped in on her way home and ordered

a Cherry Limeade Slush. Three long slurps later, her anxieties still hadn't left.

"Ahhh," she cried out. "Brain freeze."

Her arrival at her house off Trousdale seemed to trip an alarm unheard by her own ears. No sooner had she pulled into the driveway than Eli rumbled in beside her in his camper-pickup, and Reuben parked behind her in his rental Mustang, provided by insurance after the destruction of his Audi A4.

"Don't I feel popular," she said.

"Here, let me help you." Now that he was done with the Kevlar, Reuben came alongside and caught the teacher's guide that tumbled from her hands.

"Lemme grab the front door," Eli offered. He was wearing his old Wranglers. "Day like today's made for some sitting 'n' sipping in the shade, if'n you two's interested in joining me. How 'bout I pour us some ice tea?"

"Sounds good," Natalie said. "Sweet for me."

"Unsweet," Reuben said.

The older man moved indoors, and Reuben stopped Natalie at the steps. She turned and looked into his eyes. Only faint scars remained from his facial wounds.

"Can I talk with you?" he said.

"Can you?"

He frowned.

"Yes," she said, "you *may* talk with me."

"I walked right into that, didn't I?"

"*Perdóneme*," she said. "I just got back from teaching a bunch of fourth graders. Normally, I try not to be a grammar guru while off school grounds."

"You're *perdónemed*."

She wrinkled her mouth. "And I thought my Spanish was sloppy."

"In all seriousness," he said, "we need to discuss a few things. I should've known this was coming. Has anyone else tried to talk to you about me?"

So, here it is. Why did I ever think this could work?

Eli Shaffokey appeared in the doorway, gray-sprinkled eyebrows arched, hands bearing glasses full of clinking ice and tea.

"That was fast," Natalie said, hoping for a way to avoid confrontation.

"Eli, I'd appreciate it if you'd give us a few minutes alone."

"Sure thing." Eli nodded at Reuben, then shuffled down the steps and completed his delivery. "Best take the drinks, though. Reckon they'll be watery 'fore ya know it. Sweet for you. Unsweet for you. And that's no judging of your characters, just what ya asked for's all."

Natalie grinned. "Thanks." She took a sip.

Reuben headed across the front lawn, dripping condensation from his glass and thumping her book against his jeans with each step. She had never seen him in this mood, and she pulled in her lower lip.

"Are you coming?" he called.

"You giving me a choice? You seem upset."

"Upset. Confused. Scared. Take your pick, Natalie."

"Can we do this later?"

"Can we? Or may we?"

"Reuben, *por favor.* Will you at least tell me what this is about?"

He pivoted in her direction, sloshing ice tea onto the grass. Despite the ten to twelve feet that separated them, his eyes pierced right through her. "The way you've been acting, the way this all came together, I need to know . . . Did you come looking specifically for me? Was I caught in your political crosshairs?"

"What kind of question is that?"

"I've been used before. Please, just answer."

"When? At the festival you mean? Yeah, OK, I made Dad a promise and went looking for you. Never, never, *never* did I expect to fall head over heels."

"It just happened, huh? And that's the first you knew of me?"

She shrank back. "I thought that's how it happened. Am I wrong?"

He looked off over her shoulder.

"Who've you been talking to?" she asked. "Will you tell me that much?"

"In Pastor Teman's office, I got the distinct impression that you were cheering him on, hoping to change my mind about this bill."

"I didn't know your mind was set one way or the other."

"You were in agreement with him, though, weren't you?"

Natalie cupped her glass, letting the chill work through her palms. "What? You want me to admit that I think microchips could be a good thing? Fine. I admit it. Have I kept that a secret between us?"

"Have you?" he said, stepping closer.

"You tell me, since you're the one acting paranoid here."

Reuben softened a little. "Look at it from my angle. Pastors are telling me I'm God's man for the hour, while others tell me I'm a tool of Satan. I'm blitzed with daily e-blasts, paper mailers, lobbyist phone calls, offers to hit the links with prominent local surgeons, promises, and even a few veiled threats from my fellow representatives. This entire 'favor factory' is in full-scale production, and right now, I'm their primary market."

"It's been a lot." Natalie nodded. "I can't even begin to imagine."

"And I watch my own car get blown to smithereens."

She squeezed her eyes shut for a moment against that imagery.

"You know," he said, "some of it's coming back, some of the memories. I thought I wanted to remember, and now I'm not so certain."

"I want to forget."

He came closer, clicked his glass against hers. "Will you tell me?"

She took a long swallow of sweet tea, her eyes on his, her nose stud refracting the rays of the sun. "Tell you what?"

"Your ten days in that hut. Will you trust me with the details?"

Nausea spread from her stomach into her chest. She touched the glass to her cheek, where its condensation left a smear. Trust him? Details? Why was she even standing here? She knew from the start that a close relationship would demand this of her, and she hated herself for getting involved in the first place—against her better judgment, against every internal warning bell. He had asked her out to pizza that first night, asked her to ride bikes around Melton Hill Lake the next day, and she could have put her foot down and called it off at any point.

Too late now, chica. *Your heart's already involved.*

"Why, Reuben? Don't you believe what happened to me?"

"Please, I'm not doubting that. Not at all. I found an archived article on the Internet, and it infuriated me to even see that sicko's face."

Natalie winced. "You went searching for the details?"

"Because I care about you."

"Do we have to do this now? Been a long day already, OK?"

"Your support of 6336 is fueled by what happened to you. I understand that it was horrible to be locked up for a week and a half, and I don't want that to ever happen to anyone, not for a minute of one hour of one day. I mean that."

"I believe you."

"You said something about scars, though. In the pastor's office."

She took another sip of tea, felt its cool liquid moisten her throat. "He whipped me," she said. "With an antenna from a car, I think, or maybe a radio. Every night, around dusk, he came by with nibbles of food and bottled water, like he was doing me this epic favor. Then he beat my legs. So there you go, in case you're curious why I wear exercise pants around you even in weather like this."

"And that's why you care so deeply about this bill?"

She gave him a curt nod.

"It's not . . ." He touched her arm. "Not for any other reason?"

She felt that swell of nausea again. Her throat constricted. She understood he was in a position that required vigilance, but what was prompting today's questioning, especially after they had grown so close these past few months?

"The scars are all the reason I need," she whispered.

He drained his own tea, and swiped a sleeve across his brow. "I've been weighing our relationship for the past few days, Natalie. I have feelings for you. You know that. I know that. For the time being, though, I think it might be best if we spend some time apart, while I—"

"No, Reuben, wait a sec." She could see it all slipping away.

"At least for this next month, while I sift through this issue's ramifications. With my legislative duties, I've been failing my insurance clients in Oak Ridge, and I owe my fellow agents for covering for me. It's too much. I can't juggle it all."

"I'm not exactly carefree over here," she said.

"I know that."

"I'm subbing two to three days a week, working twenty to thirty hours at Roast on top of that. Living with my sis can be a handful. We just buried my mom, or whatever I'm supposed to call sprinkling her ashes. Did I want her cremated? Nope, not my first choice. Here we are, though, in this big messy world, and I'm not sure who's supposed to be keeping things in order. Is that up to me, or God, or a little of both? Right now, it all feels a little overwhelming."

"Which is exactly what I'm saying. A break'll do us good."

"Really?" She sniffed. "So, I should feel over-whelmed *and* alone?"

"Boy, sounds rough when you put it that way. No, I just think there's room to grow as individuals and get through this period without harming what we have."

"*Si, señor.*" She hid behind the foreign words. "If you say so."

"Will you show me sometime, show me the scars?"

"What's it matter?"

"You matter. I want to see them, to know that they're real."

"Oh, they're real, all right," she said. "Real as hickory bark."

"Don't sell yourself short, Natalie. You drew me in with your intelligence, and your shape. And those eyes of yours? Oh boy, they melted me on the spot."

"But you want me to leave you alone for the next month?"

"I want to limit it," he said. "Allow ourselves to cool off and evaluate."

"BTW, that's a big N-O on the show-and-tell."

He shrugged and set down the empty glass. "For later, then?"

"If there is a later," she muttered. She waved once as he was leaving, and she felt that she had ruined everything.

Chapter Forty-one

High above the streets of Nashville, Shield's meeting room provided miles of vista framed by the Tennessee Tower and the First Tennessee Bank building. At the center of the frame, the state flag waved high atop the Capitol's proud cupola.

"Look there," Darcy addressed her staff. "Our target is that close."

"Uh, Ms. Page, isn't *target* too aggressive?"

Darcy saw the others lean back from this outspoken soul. She liked the power that made them quake but chose to keep them off-balance with it.

"Absolutely." She cracked a thin smile. "You make a good point. This is a gift we're offering the state, a way of empowering six million citizens like never before. It's not an invasive evil, as some claim. Pastor Teman, Nashville's own religious luminary, now stands in support, and others have joined his ranks. He tells me that even Representative King's own female interest is on our side."

At this cue, Bigz moved to the window and uncovered a digital pad.

"Many of us," she went on, "have a natural aversion to the idea of something being inserted under our skin. I'd venture some of you get the heebie-jeebies just thinking about it, don't you?"

Nervous laughter gave her the answer she expected.

"The public's now heard of the concept. That's step one. They've latched on to its many positives. Step two. Erasing their fear and revulsion is step three. In school, we all learned to grit out teeth and get our flu shots. It's now time for men, women, and children to realize how our single injection can provide a lifetime of security."

At the window, Bigz lowered the lights and entered a code into the pad.

Darcy said, "With your help, we launch our new ad campaign today."

And before her voice had faded, an icy vapor swirled through the glass, turning it into a snowy white expanse from which words materialized in indigo:

Shield Yourself . . .
Your One Shot at Protection.

Chapter Forty-two

September

This was it. This was the day. Seven years ago, at School Number One in the town of Beslan, his belief in his motherland and in his fellow man had died.

Serpionov drew the shades in his Hyatt hotel room and sat on the edge of the bed with a cigarette lighter in hand. He flicked it on and off, on and off. Watched the leaping flame cast ragged shadows against the walls.

The shadows dropped.

Tried to rise again.

Clawed at him.

Lurched.

This day and these memories were the reason he came to America, and they fueled his passion for the new story he was writing.

Flickkk-flickkk . . .

He could see the faces of the little ones through the fire, through the smoke. He heard their desperate cries, felt fingers tugging at his knees.

There were so many.

On the opening day of school, Islamic militants from Chechnya had taken hostage over 1,100 parents and children. The "freedom fighters" were armed, masked, wired with explosives, and ready to die for their cause. Chechnya wanted independence from Russia, and they believed this would send a message to Putin and those in power in the Kremlin.

Putin had never been one for prudence and patience, and after a three-day standoff, he figured he and his regime were done being shamed. It was an outrage, all of it. Such nonsense should not be tolerated.

With that decided, he ordered government forces to take back the school at all costs. Any casualties could be blamed later on the enemy.

From government positions atop nearby buildings, Shmel rockets descended on School Number One, cratering the rooftop and providing access to the hostages in the gym below.

Serpionov and fellow troops stormed the roof in OMON fatigues, helmets, and flak jackets. With a 9A-91 compact assault rifle over his shoulder, he rappelled through billows of dust. His boots hit concrete rubble. He smelled smoke and noted the orange-yellow glow of flames on his right. Scrambling forward, he scanned the area and held his rifle at the ready. He knew that government snipers were situated outside and that ground forces were converging on the building from all sides. Even the angry townspeople had armed themselves for battle, and the militants had no way of escape.

A thin shriek sounded just ahead.

Movement in the smoke.

Serpionov advanced in a crouch, coiled for action. On the ground, a boy came forward on hands and knees, fire licking at his pant leg. When he looked up and spotted Serpionov, he crawled faster and begged for help.

Farther back, a militant appeared in a black balaclava mask and green camos and yelled at the boy to come back or die.

Nyet. This, it was not the way to speak to a child.

Serpionov swung his rifle around, firing a burst aimed to cut down the militant. Instead, the boy lurched to his feet in that moment and caught two of the rounds himself. He tumbled out of sight in the swirling smoke. All around, gunshots and cries grew louder, while the inferno leaped and leered.

Serpionov blinked.

This was his job. He was only doing his job.

After the massacre, he kept his torments to himself. He wasn't the only one who had gunned down innocents under the guise of keeping the peace.

The results of that day:

1. At least 10 special forces killed.
2. 148 men and women dead.
3. 186 children gone.

This world would be a safer place, if not for the terrorists in black masks and the terrorists in power suits. Such chaos could not continue unchecked, and Serpionov decided he would finish out his commitment to OMON, and then leave behind this motherland that destroyed her young.

In 2008, he packed his bags, said good-bye to his grandmother.

And started writing a story of his own.

Flickkk-flickkk-flickkk . . .

Now, alone in the hotel room, Serpionov watched the lighter's fire rise and fall. He closed his eyes against the shadows that clawed for him along the foot of the bed and the wall. With his thumb on the flint wheel, he held the flame steady until he was certain that the circle of light would keep the dark forms at bay.

He opened his eyes, found himself bathed in a golden glow. Was this the sort of light his *babushka* spoke of? He thought for a moment that he heard her raspy voice whispering her beloved Scripture in his ear:

"God is light, and there is no darkness in Him at all."

This was foolishness, of course. She was gone now, and death was final. He knew all about death. If only more people had his grandmother's sense of peace, the boys and girls of this world could play in the streets without worries

284

of kidnappers, molesters, and masked gunmen.

Seven years ago. And this month, a new era would begin.

You will help, Mardy Flynn. It'll be hard for you to watch, but you will help.

Reuben had a choice. He could violate his self-imposed restrictions, head west on I-40, and surprise Natalie. With the next few weeks shaping up as a mad rush to the committee deadline, he wanted nothing more than to share a day with his hazel-eyed honey.

Was she ready for the truth, though?

If he expected her to ever show her scars, didn't he owe her that?

Turning east, he aimed instead for the Blue Ridge Mountains and hit speed dial. "Hi, Mom. I miss you. Do you and Dad mind if I drop by, maybe spend the night? It's a beautiful drive, and Oak Ridge isn't going anywhere."

Chapter Forty-three

Detective Meade arrived fourteen minutes after the initial report of a dead body. His first thought was of Abigail Stark. Two weeks gone by. Still missing.

With a patrol car close behind, he stopped

north of downtown's Victory Memorial Bridge, where the greenway stretched thin along the Cumberland's banks. While the officers taped off the scene, Meade interviewed the cyclist who had made the call. The man said he had found the corpse quite simply because he "needed to take a leak." He trekked off-trail in the predawn mist, where he discovered bones and decomposing tissue protruding from scraps of thick wool.

He called Metro. Said the thing looked human. Asked about a reward.

"Hate to be disrespectful," the man now repeated, "but about that reward."

"What reward?"

"You think there's any chance of it, Detective? From the relatives? I mean, with the economy being what it is, things're tight. You hear what I'm sayin'?"

Meade swatted away a pair of flies, pocketed his notebook.

"Sure'd be nice," the man said, "to get my car back up and runnin'."

"You ride by here on a regular basis?"

"Every day since my tranny went out. I cut along here on my way to work, zigzaggin' along the trails and bridges. I'm on a crew at Opry Mills Mall. Flood happened well over a year ago, and we're still puttin' things back in order. There was mud in every nook and cranny. Mold, rot, and dead fish."

Meade jutted his chin at the body. "You noticed the deceased through the bushes, is that right? What made you think the remains were human?"

A shrug. "Bigger'n most animals I know of. And the skull? Sure, we got lots of deer 'round here, but that don't look like no deer I ever seen."

Although the corpse would be examined for signs of skeletal trauma, a toxicology report could prove more difficult. Meade noted the femur. Then the humerus, an arm reaching through the bushes. Trying to swim? To grab hold of a branch? Boating mishaps and drownings were not uncommon in the Cumberland River as it snaked its way through Davidson County, and this made it a good place to dump a homicide victim. Let the elements scrub the evidence clean.

He shooed the flies again, noticed one more thing. A coincidence?

"Got any idea who it is?" the cyclist asked.

"Too early to say."

"You think it was an accident? Or somethin' worse?"

"We'll make those assessments once we have more information," Meade said, dragging a hand over his jaw and stubbled neck. "We'll do our best."

He thought of his wife and his twelve-year-old daughter, Dawna and Dawnequa. Thought of Natalie who had been held captive not far from here at the abandoned airfield, and of the

Vreelands who had survived their ordeal at the old warehouse along this same river. Thought of his own niece who'd vanished a decade ago after going to meet a man she met online.

"Either way," the cyclist said, swinging a leg over his seat, "I don't envy the relatives. But me? I'd wanna know instead of lettin' my thoughts run wild."

Meade nodded. Yes, somewhere, a mother and a father wanted answers, and he could relate to such a longing.

If only answers came that easy.

He had read articles about the 2004 Thailand tsunami, after which thousands of bloated bodies washed up on the shore. Officials gathered and catalogued the corpses, but as postmortem ID became a mounting problem, they could only hope for dental records in the absence of facial features and fingerprints. What a mess.

"We'll give it our best try," Meade told the cyclist.

"And you'll, you know, tell 'em it was me what called it in?"

"I have all your information right here." He patted his pocket, kept his expression blank.

The man gripped the handlebars. "Mighty 'preciative, Detective. You seem a no-nonsense sorta guy. I bet you'll have this figured out by dinnertime."

"Mm-hmm." Meade already had a solid guess.

● ● ●

Detective Meade couldn't clear his thoughts of that decayed body still wrapped in what was left of a wool coat. Though he had sealed the coat and logged it into the Evidence Room, he signed it out now and took it with him to Black's Espresso.

"S'up, Detective?" Aramis greeted him. "You need an evening jolt?"

"You're probably shutting things down for the night."

"No worries. Here, I'll make you something."

"That's not actually why I came." Meade lifted the sealed bag containing the weathered coat.

Aramis glanced up, his olive skin and angled features catching the beams of the overhead track lighting. He had worked through past mysteries of his own and displayed an instinct for sniffing out the truth. "Freddy C," he said. "I was afraid of this. Wasn't like the man to skip town without a word."

Meade squared his jaw. "I should've listened, should've done more."

"Hey, it's not all on you. I figured it was just his usual rambling too."

"He was found this morning along the Cumberland. By Memorial Bridge."

"Middle of Nashville? And it took this long for anyone to notice?"

"All the branches and debris, he was probably trapped underwater for weeks before washing up on the bank. Took one to the back of the head, small cal, close range, no exit wound. I have a hunch, but I'm waiting for word from Ballistics. Knowing how much you cared for him, I figured you ought to know."

Aramis touched the coat. "He stopped in just about every day."

"You, your shop, this was probably the closest he had to family."

"Yeah, he was . . . You know, I loved that old coot. Freddy C. He used to say that the *C* stood for 'crime fighter.' "

"Eyes on the street. He did help us with a case or two."

"You sure it was him? The coat could've been borrowed, even stolen."

"We'll wait for a positive ID," Meade said. "Tell me, though, in the five or six years you've known him, did you ever see him without this?"

Aramis's gaze hardened. "Hunt down his killer, Meade. Let Freddy help you solve one last crime."

Chapter Forty-four

"Hey. You. Ms. Sleepyhead."

Natalie tried to tune out her sister's voice.

"Hey." Tuf's voice grew louder. "Wakey, wakey."

"What's so important that you must get me up at . . ." She turned, peered with one eye at her alarm clock. "It's, like, seven o'clock."

"It's 7:09 a.m., if you wanna get technical. Every minute counts."

"Saturday morning."

"Well, I still gotta work later today. Things're ramping up at the warehouse, some bigwigs coming in. Like that means a flip to me."

Natalie pulled the pillow over her head. When she heard Tuf pad toward the door, she congratulated herself on a small victory for slumber-deprived teachers and coffee baristas everywhere. She snuggled deeper into the blankets, slipped back into a hazy dream.

"Do whatcha want," Tuf said. "But Grams, she's just sitting out in the living room. Drove all the way from Tuckaleechee Cove, says she's got family business that needs talked out. Yeah, you just lay there, lazy bones. See if ya don't get your butt dragged outta here the next minute or two anyway."

Grams? Oh no, what'd we eat last night? I bet the place is a disaster.

"I bet it's about Mom," Natalie said.

"Figure you're right. Won't know 'less you snap to, will we?"

"OK, OK. You sure do live up to your name."

"Try prison. For that matter, try loading dock at night and see what that'll do for ya. All cozy in your bed? Shoot, your life's a flippin' cakewalk."

Natalie couldn't resist. She rolled onto her side, let sheet and blanket slide to the floor. The haze of daylight filtering through the mini blind gave texture and dimension to the pink ridges that crisscrossed her calves and shins. She knew Tuf had seen the scarring before, while they traipsed through the nearest bathroom and allowed Eli his male domain in the smaller one by the garage, but an occasional reminder seemed justified.

"Sure, Natalie, I know you've had rough times of your own."

"Tell Grams I'll be right out."

Natalie waited for the door to close, then flopped back against the pillow. So far, this week was an exercise in self-discipline. Each morning, she wondered whether Reuben was in town, only minutes away from joining her in a park or a café. Each day, Abby's absence hammered harder at her spirits and left her gloomy in her bed, almost paralyzed. This mood affected her work at Roast and at school.

Was her friend all right? Where was the fun-loving girl who had her share of weaknesses yet cared so much for the lowly?

Where, for that matter, was God in the midst of it all?

I'm trying to hold it together here. Please, Lord, help my unbelief.

The TV was on when Natalie emerged from her bedroom. As Grams and Tuf chatted in the kitchen, she found her eyes drawn to the current ad. She had seen it before, zebras on the Serengeti and a call to "Shield Yourself," but this time that initial footage shifted to a man in a hard hat, to a female attorney, to a newborn just opening its eyes. Soothing music accompanied endorsements from medical and social service groups. The final shots returned to the zebras, a tight zoom, until only white filled the screen, serving as a backdrop for five words:

Your One Shot at Protection.

She stared at the screen, mesmerized by the vivid lettering.

"There you are, dear," Grams said from the doorway.

"Grams." She turned and gave her a hug. "Good to see you. Would've made you breakfast if I'd known you were headed this way."

"Oh my, no need for all that. I didn't want to put you out."

"What? After all the times you've taken care of us?"

"My job as your grandmother. You pass it on to your own someday."

"I'll do that."

Natalie was sincere in saying so. She wanted nothing more than a chance to raise kids of her own one day and to see them do likewise. As for getting pregnant, well, her ability to do that remained to be seen. At the rate she was going, her ovaries would be shut down and out of order by the time some guy took her hand and put a ring on it.

"She'll do it," Tuf said. "If she can hold down a boyfriend."

"Oh? I was under the impression you had a beau of your own."

Natalie shook her head. "The only bow I have is in my lower back, from all the hours standing at an espresso machine."

Tuf nudged by and sprawled across their garage-sale recliner. "His name's Reuben, right? Well, sis, if he can't see what's in front of his face, then he don't deserve you. I'm just keeping it real. What he said, all this, 'we need space' and 'we need time,' that's a buncha crud. Guys learn that in Dating 101."

"He's not like that."

"Yeah." Tuf clicked her tongue, gave a hard wink. "Right."

"You've met him. First off, he's hot, and you know it. Second, he's smart and well mannered. You'd like him, Grams. Third, he's fun to be around."

Tuf smirked. "Well, he's not around, is he?"

"Perhaps," Grams said, seating herself on the couch, hands folded in her lap, "he does need some time to decide if this is the commitment he wants."

"Nah," Tuf said. "C'mon, we all know the pattern. Guy swoops in, gets what he came for, and he's outta here."

"He. Did. *Not*. Get what he came for."

"Maybe *that's* why he's outta here."

"Shut up, Tuf."

"You and what army gonna make me?"

"Girls." Grams wore a bemused grin. "Girls, girls, girls. Considering where you've come from, the things you've been through, you really ought to appreciate what you have in each other. No need to goad with sharp words and sarcasm."

"Hear that?" Natalie said.

"Just trying to toughen you up."

"Tina. Natalie. Enough now."

Natalie settled onto the carpet, her back against the couch. Tuf's head lolled back over the recliner arm, her thorn tattoo creeping out from her shirt toward the dark roots of her hair.

"I love you both," Grams said. "Love you like my daughters. This drive from Tuckaleechee Cove wasn't for sightseeing and pleasure, you know? It's about your momma. About your father too."

Tuf's head swiveled toward Grams.

"We're listening," Natalie said. "Sorry about all that."

"Samesies," Tuf said.

"What I'm about to say, you two need to understand that it's shared in confidence. It's only fair that you know the full truth of it, now that the mystery of Janet's whereabouts has been solved. I fear for your father, though—that he'll go beyond his usual respect for justice and the laws of the land."

Natalie lifted an eyebrow and met her sister's gaze. The morning was warming up, pressing against the drawn curtains. The old rental settled on its foundation, frame and joists creaking like tired bones.

"You're both familiar," Grams said, "with the history of your hometown. Secret City it may be, but its past is not so secret now, and it's established fact that thousands of tons of mercury were leaked into the creek in Y-12's heyday."

Natalie recalled the rumors of contamination.

Sensory impairment. Liver failure. Hypertension and acute distress.

Natalie pulled her knees to her chest. "As kids," she said, "we thought we were poisoned every

296

time we had a migraine or tummy ache or new skin tag. It was like Sasquatch or vampires, the kind of stuff you only pretended was real."

"Speak for yourself," Tuf said. "Bigfoot's flippin' out there."

"You serious?"

"Girls." Grams held up a hand, fingers curled daintily. "This was a very real danger to the community and environment, and remains so to this day."

"Dad's done security for ages out at Y-12. Is he sick? Is that what—"

"I'm speaking of your mother, of what ailed her."

Tuf pulled herself up in the recliner.

"Methylmercury," Grams said, "was essential to Y-12's production of hydrogen bombs back in the fifties. I was your age then, and we knew very little about the long-term consequences of such things. Truthfully, we were more worried about the Russians back then. Wasn't till the early eighties that East Fork Poplar Creek was declared a hazard, but by then, there was nothing alive in it."

"As girls, we knew not to go near it," Natalie said.

"Yep," Tuf agreed. "Dad drilled that into our heads."

"If memory serves me, you were born between '87 and '89. By that time, the Department of

Energy was making every effort to clean up the mess. But even as of this year, they've found increasing levels of mercury in its fish population. Scientists, they say they're baffled by it. Well, there's nothing baffling about it. That water and that earth's been ruined for decades to come."

"Me? I came out just fine," Tuf said. "Don't know 'bout sis here."

"This isn't a joke. She's talking about Mom."

Grams's eyes softened. "Oh, Janet was a dear. She and your dad were both Tuckaleechee Cove kids through and through, and when they married in '84, there was rejoicing in the Flynn home. We knew Mardy'd met his match. They moved to Oak Ridge soon after, where he'd been hired on for the security job. He loved it, felt he was doing something for his country. And even though he's quite the friendly sort, keeping secrets was no chore for Mardy. His loyalties run deep."

"That's Dad," Tuf said. "Ask him the time of day, and he's all over it. Ask him 'bout something that means something? Clams up. Mouth like Fort Knox."

"He loved Janet with every bit of his being, and after she disappeared, he was never quite the same. The fact that he loved you girls as much as he did, that tells you something about the man, doesn't it? A heart that big."

Natalie had never felt prouder of her father.

Or prouder to be called his daughter.

In the recliner, Tuf leveled her gaze at her palm and picked at callused skin with her fingernails. "All a big love fest. Chillax. What about Mom?"

"Wish we knew for certain, dear."

"You done said it already, that she got that mercury crud."

The floor creaked in the kitchen, and Natalie turned to see Eli shift out of view from the kitchen. She heard the door into the garage open and close.

"Yes," Grams continued, "your father and I believe that's the truth of it. Mardy's been employed by the government all these years, and even if the work's contracted out these days, to him it's all the same. He relocated with his new bride, started a family, and bought a home downwind from one of our nation's largest security complexes. What'd it get him, this service to his country? He lost his wife to the sickness, and they denied all liability. When he pushed for details, they asked why the whole town wasn't sick. Of course, the others who were sick were asked the same thing. Mardy almost lost his job over the matter, and they later hindered his efforts to find her. Even now, after her remains had been found, they applied pressure within the sheriff's office to keep her bones from undergoing further analysis."

"We'll never know," Natalie said. "That's what you're saying?"

"Dear, we'll always know."

Tuf folded her arms. "I said my good-byes. What's done is done."

"In your father's mind, it's not. It's the principle of the thing. He watched her suffer through the symptoms—the itchy skin, the brain fog, short-term memory loss, and depression. She was a complete basket case in the days before she wandered out that door and found her calm in the woods. She was pregnant, you see? All that mercury, why, it was toxic to the growing child inside."

"What?" Natalie's throat felt thick. "And no one ever told us this?"

"She loved you both so much. When she lost your little brother, though, something snapped." Grams's voice cracked, and Natalie took hold of her hand. "I never forgave her for that. For leaving my grandbabies without their momma. But she had her reasons, she surely did. And Lord help me if I'd been the one stuck in her shoes. Poor dear was coming undone, both body and mind. The grief, the guilt—it was more than Janet could bear."

Tuf lurched to her feet. "Twenty years late, Grams, but thanks for sharing."

When Natalie reached for her, Tuf spun away and tromped outside.

Chapter Forty-five

Darcy sat at her desk, legs crossed, pale hand tracing lines on black wood as she fielded the news. So they had found the dead bum. One less mouth to feed. As far as she was concerned, the homeless were disposable souls who leeched resources from a system everyone else paid into. In various parts of the world, there had been a recent rise of demonstrations against the wealthy and their greed, and she considered it the most ludicrous of social movements.

They envied her $950,000 base pay, was that it?

How enraged would they be if they knew she hit seven figures when her company's successful quarters pushed her over bonus thresholds?

The truth was that the economic pyramid was built upon the backs of the working class, the Jiffy Lube mechanics, the Walmart checkers, the McDonald's drive-through staff. It was no wonder they gave the occasional whimper. Let them whine and write their angry blogs, but if the protesters' voices grew too loud, the middle class would get frightened.

And fear was a middle-class cancer.

This cancer never went into full remission. Each

time it flared up, it crippled consumer spending, slowed production, and killed job markets.

"Have they determined his cause of death?" she asked Serpionov.

"We're on your encrypted line?"

"Yes, yes. Do you think I'd speak of this otherwise? We're nearing our deadline, and I want to be certain this doesn't come back to bite us."

"The investigation's not over, but police say he was shot in the head."

"My, what a tragedy," she droned.

"You must cancel my lease."

"What?"

"The condo," he said. "I had to leave."

"Explain yourself."

"A girl came last week."

"You're a man. I was married to one, if you recall, and I have no interest in your gender's personal pastimes. None whatsoever."

"This girl," he said, "she was at clinic when we injected the tags."

"And she's aware of your involvement?"

"She remembered, yes. She also remembered Freddy C, the dead man, from clinic that day. Once she knew I was at this condo, I had to go."

"Is the place clean? Do you think she'll cause trouble?"

Serpionov's voice remained flat. "*Nyet*, she will not talk."

Darcy wondered how long until Music City's finest uncovered yet another homicide. "That's a plus, at least. So then, where will you go? No," she said. "I don't need to know. You should have plenty left to cover your needs."

"We also have other problem, I think."

"You're paid to deal with problems, not create them."

"I think someone else follows her and knows about the case."

Darcy stood from her desk, faced the floor-to-ceiling window. On the streets far below, Music City commuters and pedestrians were mere playthings. "You still believe there's a spy, someone working for Storinka Defense?"

"This, it's only my suspicion."

"Because of the man at the airport last December."

"Yes." The Russian lowered his voice. "But this one who follows her, it is someone else. He stays close, like shadow. And I wonder, is it you who pays him to track her?"

Darcy gave a sharp laugh. "My pockets are only so deep. Perhaps she's garnered the attention of a government spook, a media hound, an ex-boyfriend."

"He's older man, with salt-and-pepper hair. This is what you call it?"

"Salt-and-pepper, yes. Looks just like it sounds. Regardless, you're the one in possession of the case, so we have what we need. With it, she doesn't have much luck of escaping your attention, does she?"

"I must go," Serpionov said.

"One last thing. This girl in your condo, was she pretty?"

"What? No, she . . . not so much," he admitted. "She was flirt, yes."

"Very well, then. Stay in touch. Call or text. Either will do."

Darcy disconnected, mind already churning out ways to utilize this situation to her advantage. While this dead transient had not stirred much public interest, a missing college girl could come in handy, even if she did lack the beauty more likely to rivet viewers to their computers and TVs.

Fear and the media. Financial woe and politics.

They all fed off each other, and any UCLA graduate worth her degree in communications strategy knew when to capitalize.

Only two days ago, Darcy had Skyped Lindsey Sims. Together they dug up dirt on some of the Seattle protesters arrested for civil disobedience. Mrs. Sims drafted an editorial about the ones with criminal records who now dared to block businesses, scare off shoppers, and divert police from their vital roles patrolling suburbia. She funneled it to a *Post-Intelligencer* editor, who was all too happy to run it as payback for a previous favor.

Result? The public pendulum swung away from frustrations with Wall Street greed. And who was the enemy now? These tent-dwellers who lacked funds and focus and cluttered sidewalks and city parks, that's who.

Time to manipulate Tennessee news outlets on a different front.

Darcy made a call, and Mrs. Sims's bookish appearance and straight red hair filled the screen three minutes later.

"You needed me for something, Ms. Page?"

"Good work last week on the editorial."

"A joint effort, thank you."

"Tell me, who are your closest media ties here in Nashville, at the *Tennessean*? Or perhaps NewsChannel 5? That's the station down the hill from the Capitol, if you recall. Any favors we might cash in with their broadcast crew?"

Sims pursed her lips. "I always have one or two in my pocket."

"Perfect. The vote happens this month, and I know of a news item that could heighten local anxiety, if given proper rotation. Let's cash in."

Chapter Forty-six

Lunchtime. Labor Day. Diners and drinkers converged on the Gulch.

In loose black jeans and an official Kenny Britt Titans jersey, Detective Meade canvassed the streets on foot. He appreciated Forensics, Ballistics, and all that *CSI* stuff he saw on TV, even if half of it was simplified and sensationalized. But there was always a place for direct human contact and common sense.

Smile, he reminded himself.

After all, he was a thick-chested thirty-something black man standing on a street corner and handing out canary-yellow fliers.

"Here you go . . . Thank you, ma'am . . . No, it's not a drink special."

Keep smiling. Especially at the white folks.

Earlier, he had stopped in at Yazoo and spoken to bartenders, waitstaff, and clientele. He'd gone to all the neighboring establishments as well, distributing the colorful sheets with Abby's photo and description beneath the words "MISSING – HAVE YOU SEEN THIS GIRL?"

The crowds were thinning now, regrouping before they came back for a raucous evening. Metro patrols would be busy tonight.

"So what's the deal? You a cop? Her boy-friend?"

Meade studied the young man in the green felt hat, straight-legged jeans, and silk vest over an untucked shirt. "Detective Meade," he said, shaking the young man's hand. "Investigative Services."

"Chaz. I mean, I figure you're too old to be the boyfriend, but what's it my place to say? To each his own, right?"

"Have you seen her? Do you know Abby?"

"Seen her, sure. Least I think it was her."

"When was this?"

"Dude. So, she's really missing?"

"Going on sixteen days. Been all over the news, in the papers."

The young man tipped his hat at a pair of leggy brunettes passing by. They rolled their eyes, and he shrugged. "News. Sure. Listen, who reads a paper anymore? All I need to know's right here." He waggled the iPhone in his palm.

"There's news on there too."

"Kim Kardashian's marital updates? No, thanks."

Keep smiling.

"Was Abigail Stark a friend of yours, Chaz?"

"I live over there, fifth-floor condo, kickin' view. She was at the front a coupla weeks back, wondering if I knew her friend in the building. Said this dude had a foreign accent, maybe

307

Russian or Eastern European, like somebody outta one of those Bourne movies, you know?"

Meade nodded. "Good flicks."

"Flicks." Chaz grinned. "Haven't heard that in a while."

"Did you know the man she was looking for?"

"Sure, I knew the guy. Bumped into him once or twice in the elevator. 'Push button. I go fifth floor.' That sorta thing. Shoot, he's only down the hall from me. I let her in, pointed her to his door."

"You didn't ask for ID or why she wanted access?"

Chaz squinted in the sunlight. "Do I look like a detective to you? What did I care? To each his own, I always say."

"Yes, I got that. Do you know his condo number?"

"I'll take you on up there, if you want."

"Being on the side of the law, I first need to obtain a warrant."

"You really *are* a cop, aren't you?"

Natalie's thoughts were muddled, despite the rich chocolate accents of freshly ground coffee that wafted about her. At the Roast counter, she poured hot water over single-cup filters and imagined what life might have been like with a healthy mother and a little baby brother. She understood why Tuf was so conflicted, but it worried her that her sis had not come home last night.

"Here you go," Natalie said. She delivered a Nutella latte to a man in a Hands On Nashville shirt, coffee to three women having a Bible study, and a Chemex flask of fresh joe to the four guys in the wrought-iron chairs outside.

"Hey," she said. "Aren't you Eastern Block?"

A thin man with a dark, shaggy beard looked up. "We are."

"I saw you guys play at the Rutledge. Talk about an amazing show."

"Thank you. That means a lot."

"Listen, this might sound *loco*, but I have an idea. Well, it's not really my idea, more like this friend of mine's. Abby Stark. The one who's been missing."

"The girl in the news. Yeah, yeah. It's been a few weeks, hasn't it?"

Natalie swallowed. "She was my roomie back in college. Thing is, she loved volunteering at the mission, and she was pulling together this benefit concert to raise funds and awareness for the hungry. I've been thinking about it, and I want to make that happen for her. And for Freddy C, the man shot dead by the river. If she . . . you know, if she shows up again, I want her to be proud. And if not, I . . . Yeah, I want to do this for her. Does that make any sense?"

The lead singer, who was also sporting a beard, leaned forward, and his soulful eyes darkened. "Absolutely. Makes perfect sense."

"First off, I need music, need bands." She cast a glance through the window to be sure she had no one waiting at the counter inside. "I'm thinking of this one guy who's more a singer-songwriter, very heartfelt stuff. He's lost a leg, which'll connect with some of the crowd. That's just the truth. I'd also like some music with more edge, a full-on band. Of course, there's no money in it, so I—"

"Yes."

"Yes?" She gulped. "You mean, like . . ."

The four guys exchanged glances and said in one voice, "We're in."

Five hours later, Detective Meade stood in more formal clothing at the condo's door, a Metro police officer at his side. He had brought up an evidence kit from his car and had a warrant in hand, signed by a prickly judge who made it clear that she preferred her holidays with as few interruptions as possible.

"No one's seen any movement in this unit for a week or two," the property manager said. After repeated knocks without a response, she unlocked the door. "We received notice just yesterday that the lease was being broken."

"Who'd you say it's leased to?" Meade asked.

"It's under the name Darius Hammond."

"Hammond. Does that sound Russian to you?"

"Sir?"

Meade waved that off, set down the kit, and exchanged his shoes for paper slippers that hugged his ankles. Was Abby's disappearance linked in any way to Freddy C's murder? Circumstantial as it was, she had been there with him at the free clinic and might have met the same end.

The manager peered through the door. "You think there's, ohmigosh, somebody dead in there?"

"We'd already know it by now, most likely."

The officer nodded. "Once you get a whiff, you never wonder if."

"Ewww. Well, on that lovely note, I'll let y'all do your job." The manager held up her cell. "If you need anything, give me a ring. We'd appreciate it, though, if y'all keep a low profile, for the sake of our other residents."

"We'll do that."

Both men drew their side arms. Meade flicked the closest light switch with his elbow and followed the officer inside. Within sixty seconds, they had cleared the bedroom, bathroom, closets, living area, and the kitchen. The fireplace held only ashes. The furniture was minimal, nothing askew. No sign of the resident. No missing girl. No droplets on the shower curtain, and no wrinkles in the bedding.

"Cleared and clean."

"Too clean," Meade noted.

" 'Cleanliness is next to godliness,' my wife likes to say."

"I say, 'Cleanliness can also be a cover for ugliness underneath.'" Meade opened his kit on the kitchen's tiled bar and pulled out surgical gloves, a penlight, tweezers, and a clear evidence bag. "If you'd go get a statement from Chaz two doors down, I'll see what I can uncover in here."

The officer left Meade to his work. In the open living area, the windows provided a view of hills, trees, and traffic rolling along the interstate. In the late-afternoon light, vacuum treads were visible in the carpet. Perhaps they meant nothing more than someone trying to get back their full cleaning deposit.

His phone jangled in his pocket, and he fumbled for it with the gloves.

"Detective Meade."

"Hey babe."

"Oh. Hey, Dawna."

"It's Labor Day. Where are you? Or do I even have to guess?"

"I'm laboring." He shone his light along the living room baseboards.

"You forgot, didn't you? I said you'd forget, and you forgot."

Meade knew better than to ask what he'd forgotten since that would only confirm his guilt. He leaned down at the sofa, grunted to imply a man in the midst of his work, and rummaged his brain for clues to this forgotten activity, as his light searched the cushions for hair strands, nail clippings, food crumbs.

"The barbeque," he said suddenly. "At your brother's."

"That's right. He's called once already, and they're all there waiting."

"I'll meet you there, how about that? Give me a half hour."

"Which means an hour, if I know you, babe."

She was still calling him babe, and that meant his marital standing was still on safe ground. Relieved, he parted the cushions and tweezered a single dark eyebrow hair into an evidence bag. Though it might only establish the presence of the person who lived here, a case sometimes hinged on a shred of truth.

"On your way," Dawna said, "stop by Kroger and pick up a tub of potato salad. No green olives in it, though. Your daughter won't touch them."

"Sure thing. And tell Dawnequa I love her."

Forty minutes later, Detective Meade checked the time and jolted. He had not found much else in the condo, and his "babe" status would soon be in jeopardy. He sealed and logged his samples and evidence bags, then closed the kit. As he lifted it from the bar, a flash of white on the countertop snagged his attention.

Chapter Forty-seven

Serpionov coasted along the Oak Ridge Turnpike on his bike, and saw for the first time the lingering evidence of July's death zone. There in the opposing lanes, his C4 contraption had torn apart an Audi and sent a deputy to an early grave. The pavement showed signs of buckling. The woods and the undergrowth still bore blackened branches and scorched trunks. A streamer of frayed yellow police tape fluttered from a bush.

And yet Representative King had survived.

Yes, each section in this story made way for new subplots.

Serpionov twisted the throttle on his Interceptor and sped the last miles into Oak Ridge. He saw signs for the Y-12 National Security Complex. Although security had tightened since 9/11, he could join a tour of the facility if he wished.

He needed more than visual stimuli, though. He needed an insider.

"Mardy Flynn," he said, setting the kickstand as he stopped in the man's drive. "This is fine day, not so hot here in the hills."

"Hotter where you been staying, huh?" Mardy said.

Serpionov shot a look at this man who was wearing an old orange Vols cap.

"Ahh, I meant nothing by it," Mardy said. "Just shooting the breeze."

"You make contact for me?"

"Told ya I would, didn't I? Yessir, I stuck to my word. Way I see it, fella's got nothing if he don't got his reputation."

"You are good guy. You keep quiet, and we have deal."

Mardy pointed a finger. "You gotta hold up your end too."

Serpionov nodded. "Only two weeks left. Then you and me, we both get what we want, yes? You tell contact be ready. I give you time and location on morning of September 30, early, before sunrise."

"Oh, I'll be up brewing my coffee. Them's my usual hours."

Chapter Forty-eight

War Memorial Auditorium's tall stone columns and broad steps led down to the square fountains and wide expanses of Legislative Plaza. Hidden below, a maze of offices and corridors housed the state's senators and representatives.

Representative King was still driving the rental

Mustang, awaiting an insurance check due any day now. He parked in underground parking at 7:53 a.m., passed through security with a nod to the guard, and hurried down the hall.

Friday. End of another busy week.

As committee chairman, he presided over an office with two antechambers. He greeted the interns as he moved through the first, then checked his appointment calendar in the second, where his bespectacled administrative assistant, a no-nonsense woman, reminded him that his 10:15 a.m. meeting would be in the courtyard at the main library.

"Do I know this guy?" he said. "Mr. Darius Hammond."

"He says you've met before."

"What's it regarding? You know that I prefer my Fridays set aside for in-office details. Is he a lobbyist trying to sneak in a one-on-one meeting?"

"That's forbidden, sir. I'm far better at my job than that."

"Sorry," he said, resting a hand on her shoulder. "Yes, you are."

"Mr. Hammond said he works for Shield Technologies, assistant to CEO Darcy Page, and he has information for your ears only."

Reuben took a step back.

"And," she added, removing her spectacles and letting them dangle from a chain around her neck, "I ran a preliminary background check. That's been our policy since your accident, and he came up clean. Born in Memphis but now lives in Washington State. No priors. Strong educational and employment history. A stint in the military. I wouldn't have confirmed the appointment otherwise."

"Never doubted you," he said. "You're a life-saver."

Ducking into his office, Reuben realized how literal such a phrase could be. If not for that phone call two months earlier, his political career would be over, and he would be lying six feet under, while the media outlets hailed him a hero.

But he was no Gabrielle Giffords, no. The congresswoman had survived a gunshot to the head while doing a simple community event.

Now, there was a heroic public servant.

He stood, lifted his arms, drew in a breath that produced only a slight pang in his rib. Why, aside from a few foggy patches, his thoughts and memories were back to normal. He could almost hear that caller's warning all over again:

Somebody's out to kill ya. He says it ain't right that you stop kids and old folks from being watched after and helped. Says your vote can help change that.

Was it a taunting enemy? Or a well-meaning friend?

As of yet, neither Homeland Security nor the sheriff had any leads.

Reuben knew, though, that the bomber's motivation was couched within those words. While large corporations had much to gain from this bill's passage, there were also many individuals out there who believed strongly in its ability to offer protection. They had seen the ads, heard the endorsements, and believed a simple procedure could shield them and their loved ones from many dangers.

He opened the Bible on his desk. Already 8:10 a.m. The book of Proverbs was loaded with wisdom, and he wanted some straightforward advice.

Instead, he found marital commentary in Proverbs 5:18&19: "Rejoice in the wife of your youth. She is a loving doe, a graceful deer. Let her breasts satisfy you always. May you always be captivated by her love."

The words tasted bittersweet, and he thought of Natalie.

Where was she now? Was she serving coffee at the shop ten minutes south? Or was she teaching class in one of Nashville's myriad schools, going over multiplication tables, breaking up shoving matches on the playground, helping kids make Abe Lincoln stovepipe hats out of black construction paper?

He had put things on hold for fear of causing her pain, and for fear of suffering her rejection. How would she react if she learned of his secret?

• • •

Natalie worked to fill the void of Reuben's absence. Sure, he needed to focus. Why, though, had he sounded defensive, even scared? Should she be worried?

No use wallowing, chica. *Let's just hope it wasn't all in vain.*

They had now gone ten days without talking, or even texting.

So she worked. She hit Approve on all the sub openings she could find, patrolling the teacher intranet to catch them the moment they posted. She took hours at Roast, opening on the mornings the usual shift manager, Erin, needed a break. Her most important task, though, was coordinating this benefit.

On her way to the Vreelands' house, she tried calling her sis. Tuf seemed to be slipping away from her, acting erratic since their talk with Grams. She left her a message as she pulled onto Groves Park Road. The dogs barked in the backyard, announcing her presence before she could even knock.

"Natalie," Sara said, welcoming her inside. "Good to see you."

Katie squealed in delight and barged past her mother to hug Natalie's legs. Behind her, Kevin walked up with a shy grin and a greeting.

"Look at you," Natalie said, rubbing Katie's head of curls. "You're practically up to my chest now. And we won't even talk about your brother. He'll be taller than me by Christmas."

"Will not," Kevin said.

"So Daddy's really gonna sing for you?" Katie said.

"Not for *her,* silly. It's called a benefit. To help the poor."

Sara pulled her son close. "All right, let's be nice. Bret?" she called over her shoulder. Then to Natalie: "He'll be here in a minute."

"In a minute? I'm right here."

"Oh, I thought you were—"

"Putting on my leg? Yep. Guilty. Hey, Natalie's like family, so she can handle the nitty-gritty." Bret arrived with a stride that seemed almost natural. He had regained his upper body strength, and his positive attitude was on full display. "It's the upgraded deal. You like it? I've been out on tour, and this thing's much better than the first one. Good movement. Good balance."

"*Muy bueno,*" Natalie said. "I'll put you down for a dance routine."

"Hey now. Even beforehand, I couldn't dance worth beans."

"You dance with me, Daddy," Katie said.

He drew his kids to his side. "Anyone else wanna see these posters?"

Natalie unfurled the sample. "Katie, see if you can find your dad's name. Kev, why don't you tell me if you can see something hidden."

"Yes," Sara said, "you're a teacher, all right."

Against the poster's light gray background, an off-center, abstract red heart framed a black-and-white photo of two men on a bench. They stared into the camera, one serious, the other boasting a crooked yet joyous smile. It read

HEART FOR THE HUNGRY

Benefit Concert – Centennial Park

September 27, 2011 – Tuesday, 7 p.m.

All Welcome

EASTERN BLOCK – BRET VREELAND

All Proceeds Go to Nashville Rescue Mission

Natalie had picked up the posters forty-five minutes earlier from the FedEx Office outside Hickory Hollow Mall. The manager had donated two hundred 11 × 18s for placement in coffee-houses, libraries, churches, stating that he believed in what she was doing and hoped the best for missing Abby.

She hoped that too.

Meanwhile, she prepared herself for the worst, despite her optimistic front. Even second graders learned to guard their expectations in life, telling each other, "Don't get your hopes up." And each day, she sensed the shell hardening around her own heart. For the past few weeks, the media had played up the story, milking it daily, and there was still no sign of Abby. Natalie suspected this benefit for the hungry would be a final shout-out to her bighearted friend.

"Awesome." Bret wrapped his arm around Sara. "Can't wait."

"This is too easy," Katie said. "His name's right there."

Kevin nodded. "Cool. I like the cross in the background."

Chapter Forty-nine

10:05 a.m. Still ten minutes until King's appointment with Hammond. What, he wondered, did this man need to tell him?

Reuben walked down Capitol Boulevard toward Nashville's downtown library and spotted a bent woman in a head bandana and layers of dirt-encrusted shirts. He greeted her with a handshake. Her skin was dry, wrinkled. She nodded and thanked him when he pressed a cool bottled water and peanut butter granola bar into her hand. These were his standard offerings to those along this stretch.

Money? Not a chance. Food? Freely given.

In his childhood, his parents had taught him

this by example. The Bible was clear, from the Old to the New Testament, that taking care of the needy was close to God's heart. "And the book of Hebrews," his mother liked to say, "tells us we might even feed or host angels unaware. We know Abraham certainly did."

Reuben thought of the upcoming Rescue Mission benefit concert. He knew it was Natalie's labor of love, and he would be there in a show of support.

Getting to hear Bret Vreeland play would be a bonus.

He hurried through the library's soaring front lobby and made his way to the courtyard, an outdoor sanctuary right at the library's center. Despite being a few minutes early, he scanned the area for his appointment and saw only a couple by the fountain, splashing water, laughing, as well as a businesswoman sitting primly on a bench by a tree with a River Jordan novel in hand.

10:12 a.m. No sign of this Mr. Hammond.

Reuben crunched on his only other granola bar. He hummed some words from his favorite Vreeland tune, one he'd heard on the radio driving into town:

A bed for a king, amongst donkeys and straw . . . You left heaven behind, and You gave us Your all . . . I bow, I bow down, I bow down to the Servant King.

As a public servant, he found layers of meaning in that last line. He wanted to follow Christ's example and be a servant king.

No easy task, though.

Why, Reuben asked himself, had he ever concealed stuff in his past to clear his path into politics? Eventually, such things came to light. Many politicians before him had caved under scrutiny, and if he made a run at the State Senate, he would face intensified scrutiny.

Plus, what sort of man hid secrets from the woman he loved?

Forgive me, Lord. I'm so afraid of losing her.

"Representative King, we meet in person."

"Mr. Hammond?"

Reuben stood and pumped the hand of the short black man in the dark green suit and matching silk tie. He was wearing a fedora at a rakish angle, and his shirt was avocado with a black pepper pattern. The clothes would've looked ridiculous on Reuben, yet this man pulled it off.

"Mr. Hammond, we *have* met before. Refresh my memory."

"First, there's no need for formalities. I go by Bigz."

"Bigz?"

"I know, right? It's been with me since I was little. Or littler, anyway."

"And you work for Darcy Page?"

"That is correct. May we sit?"

They sat facing each other at a small table, with the sun peeking over the library roof. Bigz's green eyes shone in contrast to his smooth dark skin.

"I saw you back in February," Reuben said. "You were in the House gallery, seated next to Ms. Page."

"Good memory. But then, I'd expect a man in your position to be one sharp cat. In your case, a cat with only eight lives left."

Reuben bristled at that. "Why was it you wanted to meet?"

"Sir, I'm on your side here. I was referring to the accident in July."

"Right. I guess it *was* all over the news."

"A bomb, they say. Did they ever catch the person behind it?"

Reuben shook his head, not sure he liked this conversation's direction.

"I was there," Bigz said, "at Deputy Sevier's memorial."

"What? It was supposed to be . . . They tried to keep it private."

"I knew Chris. In fact, we attended boot camp together over at Fort Bragg. Yes, I was in the army, so please no short-people jokes. 'What are you, an army of one-half?' I've heard that more times than I can count."

"I respect our men in uniform. I wouldn't dare."

Bigz tipped his hat. "I knew I liked you."

Reuben said, "You were wearing shades at the memorial. We never spoke, but I saw you. I figured the shades were because you were in mourning."

"I was. Like I said, Chris was my friend."

"You know, I owe him my life."

"Should've never even happened," Bigz said.

"Somebody called and warned me that I was in danger. If I hadn't . . . If I'd just ignored it, the deputy would still be here."

"I wouldn't blame myself, Representative. You did the right thing, did exactly as you were supposed to do. I'm the one to blame." Bigz leaned forward, protecting his silk tie from the table's edge with his hand. "Who sent you that warning? I did. Who caused Chris Sevier's death? That would be me."

Reuben frowned, trying to reconcile this claim with his own memories. The courtyard was empty now, save for the two of them and the gurgling of the fountain. Even the birds were nowhere to be seen. This idyllic setting felt spoiled.

"No. No, wait, that doesn't fit," he said. "The man on the phone was a plainspoken guy, had a bit of an accent."

"A true patriot, but he remains anonymous as part of my deal with him."

"So, the bomb. You were behind that?" Reuben pushed back in his seat and stood, synapses sparking with ideas about this man and his employer and the warning and the audacity of this entire thing. "You arranged that explosion, is that what you're telling me? I swear to you, if I find out that—"

"Whoa there. Whoa. I'm telling you, Mr. King, that I saved your life."

"You?"

"And in the process, I lost a friend."

"Well, as I said, Mr. Hammond, I'm sorry about that part. But you need to explain this to me in plain English so that I know we're tracking together."

Bigz cast a watchful eye about the courtyard. Despite their relative solitude, he lowered his voice a notch. "In plain English? By Ms. Page's way of thinking, Tennessee is the crack in a dam that could flood the entire country with her micro-chips. And she's not the only one who stands to make or lose a monstrous amount of money here. Hospitals and clinics, private practices, insurance companies, all part of a list that's invested in this. The latest word? Pharmacies want to jump on board, offering on-site implantation."

"Assuming the bill passes."

"Which is where you come in."

"None of this is new to me." Reuben took his seat again. "It's a record that's been playing in my ears for months now. Why, it's more difficult to be objective when my arm's getting twisted. Both arms, in fact. And both legs."

"If I hadn't called in that warning, you'd be in far worse shape than that. The scheme I uncovered was meant to silence you for good."

"Who," Reuben demanded, "do you claim was behind this scheme?"

Dropping his chin, Bigz raised an eyebrow. "Darcy Page, of course."

Reuben mulled that over. While courting her company for campaign funds, he had crossed her a time or two and faced her frosty glare. She'd made it clear that she had punched his meal ticket and wanted her just desserts.

"I don't buy it. I don't think she'd go that far, Mr. Hammond."

"Bigz. Please. And if you don't think so, you don't know the Ice Queen. When her husband died, she asked how it affected the company's stock index."

"Everyone grieves in their own time."

"Not everyone grieves."

"She's shrewd, conniving, difficult, yes. But a cold-blooded killer? She's smart enough to realize such a thing could dump her in prison for the rest of her days. She's not the prison type, is she? Unless they're looking for a warden."

Bigz issued a polite chuckle.

"Prove it to me," Reuben said.

"What? Oh, that I knew about the bomb?"

Reuben waited, his arms folded on the table. He checked his watch. Almost eleven a.m. For all he knew, this man still worked for Ms. Page and was aiming to manipulate him in this less direct manner.

"I know that the bomb wasn't an IED or mine or anything like that."

"Go on."

"It was RFID based."

"Plain English, remember?"

"Radio frequency ID," Bigz said. "This tag was hidden in your car, and a remote transmitter sent the detonation signal."

Reuben's chest tightened, and a faint ache traveled through his healed rib. Though his recollections were still hazy, he knew this was a specific detail never released to the media but one the sheriff believed to be true. Hadn't investigators found a transmitter up the slope from the accident?

"Forgive me, then, Mr. Hammond. I owe you the formal name, allow me that. If what you're saying is true, you helped save my life that day."

"That was always my goal."

"I mean it," Reuben said, clasping the man's hand in both of his. "And I'm truly sorry about your friend."

"He was a dedicated law officer."

"You realize how serious your accusations are about Ms. Page? It would take a mountain of evidence to fight her and her money and prove anything."

"All I cared about," Bigz said, "was your safety."

"There's a reward, you realize, for valid leads in the investigation."

"Really? Well, take a good look at me, and you'll see I do like my things. Nice clothes. Fancy cars. Fat bankroll in my pocket. I'm leaving Shield, sir, for all the obvious reasons. But I do believe in this technology. It's the wave of the future, and when it catches hold, I'd love to know that you remember the favor I did for you, since it's always nice to have a friend in the legislature."

Reuben nodded. "Sounds like a deal to me."

Chapter Fifty

Tuf kicked off her work boots and stretched out on the couch. With her head rested on this end, her feet couldn't quite reach the other. OK, so she knew she had curves and knew how to get attention when she wanted it, but would it be a flippin' crime to have some longer legs?

"Sheesh," she said.

"You say something to me?" Natalie called from the kitchen.

Tuf didn't see any reason to answer. She ran a hand through her platinum hair, figured she needed to redo her color since it looked like cow pucky with all her roots showing through.

Like she had any money to do that.

Like she could even pay her third of this month's rent.

She swung her feet to the floor and shuffled into the kitchen, where Natalie was doing something on her phone while a sheet of chocolate chip cookies cooled on the counter. "Well, look at you, Ms. Suzy Homemaker. Gonna be just the perfect widdle wifey, aren't ya?"

"You want some?" Natalie said.

"You really made 'em?"

Still fiddling with her phone, Natalie toed the white garbage can, indicating the box from the store. "All I had to do was pop them in and turn on the stove."

"I can't pay this month."

"What?"

"Yeah."

"Just like that? End of discussion?"

Tuf leaned against the counter, arms folded. "Yeah, it is what it is, OK? Thought you oughta know, since no warning'd just be rude."

"Not paying is rude."

"They cut my hours. So sue me."

"Our agreement was splitting it three ways. Mr. Faranzmehr's already cut us a lot of slack, but we can't take advantage of that. Please, Tuf. I mean, this is bad timing. The worst. You realize I have over $30,000 in debt? Yeah, and we have all this stuff that's gone on with Mom and Dad and Grams, and I can't stop thinking about my friend out there somewhere, and I'm in the middle of pulling together this benefit. And as if that's not enough, I'm working every second I can at the shop and subbing." She lifted her phone. "What do you think I was just doing? Signing up for another opening."

"OK, so *you* got all the problems. Good to know."

"That's not what I mean. It's just, I can't . . . It can't all be on me."

"Eli. He pays his part, don't he?"

"Yeah. Because he honors his word." Natalie slid her phone onto the counter and massaged her lower back with both hands. "Go in and talk to your manager, Tuf. Tell them you need more time on the clock. I mean, you bust your buns on that loading dock, right? They don't want to lose—"

"I got canned."

"What? When?"

"What's it matter?"

"We owe rent in, like, ten days."

"Why d'ya think I'm telling ya now? Sheesh, sis. Chillax. And it was two nights ago, if ya gotta know so awful bad. Me and Grant, one of the drivers, they caught us out smoking, like on our flippin' break time, so it's not like it was even hurting our work. I'll find something else. You watch."

"My phone," Natalie said. "You see a confirmation e-mail yet?"

Tuf read from the screen. "Metro Nashville Schools."

"So what were you smoking? Please tell me it wasn't weed."

"This is my problem, not yours, OK? All this stuff 'bout Mom, it's got me where I can hardly think to do my job. You, maybe you's just fine with it all, but my head's like a hand grenade. I just . . . I needed something to take the edge off."

Natalie turned away, hands still pressed against her back.

"Oh, that's how it is? Just turn your back on the bad apple?"

"Whatever, Tuf."

"Listen. You and Eli, you and Reuben, y'all have your happy life." Tuf marched into the living room, shoved her feet into her boots. "Me, I'm outta here."

Benefit posters look great. C ya there.

With this first text from Reuben since the embargo on their relationship, Natalie flopped onto her bed and stared at the lush magnolia tree outside her window. Tuf was gone. Staying at some friend's place, she said. With things rushing toward a breaking point, Natalie's own stress levels were high.

But the text? This was nice.

She texted back: Thx. TTYL.

Just enough to leave him wanting more.

She floated her thumb over her lips, those same lips Reuben had kissed for the first time beneath the flowering magnolia in Centennial Park. In five—no, six days, she'd be there in the park again coordinating the benefit. Maybe between her dartings to and fro, she would find a way to rekindle the fire.

Those undeniable, unreliable sparks.

At her small desk by the door, Natalie ran down a checklist for the benefit. Would she ever pull this together on time? Metro Parks and Recreation had cut her a special rate for the band shell, because of the event's charitable nature. She had enlisted dozens of volunteers from the mission. The college group at the church had distributed the posters far and wide. When the actual evening arrived, would five people show, or five hundred? She didn't have Abby's effervescent people skills that drew others in so quickly. Would donors respond to her efforts or turn away without opening their wallets?

Stop, you dingbat. This isn't about you.

This was about the hungry and the neglected.

There was one other motive behind the event as well, which only she and Detective Meade knew. They planned to scan the crowd for RFID tags and find at least one or two who had been at that clinic with Abby and Freddy C.

Chapter Fifty-one

What truths would his findings at the condo uncover?

While Detective Meade awaited results from the crime lab, he huddled at his desk in Investigative Services and pulled his black jacket tighter against the AC that blasted through the building. Were they warding off muggy weather here? Or storing dead bodies? If he didn't know better, he would think he was in the autopsy room at the medical examiner's office.

He logged into state and federal records, typed in the name of the person on the condo's lease: Darius Hammond.

Mr. Hammond was a Memphis-born African American. He had served in the army, done basic at Fort Bragg. His service record had some gaps, but this wasn't unusual from the military. He wasn't a big guy, and it was possible he'd served in military intelligence. He'd gone on to earn a college degree. Had no priors. Only three moving violations—two in Tennessee, one in Washington State where he now resided. At age twenty-nine, he looked to be a respectable single man with a profitable career ahead. His current employer, Shield Technologies.

Did he work at the regional office here in Nashville? Was that why he had the condo? Why had the man with the foreign accent been there?

Meade leaned back, wondering how all this tied into the mystery of a missing girl. On his desk, a framed photo of Dawnequa smiled at him. Dee, as most called her, had caramel eyes offset by milk-chocolate skin and high cheekbones. He couldn't imagine the horror of anything happening to his daughter. Couldn't imagine the horrible things he might do in return to anyone who dared touch or harm his baby girl or his wife.

Every day, Meade fought to uphold the laws of the land.

Every day, he also watched deviants and defendants slip through the system's cracks on technicalities and legal loopholes.

God help me if anything ever happened to my babe or my baby.

Sergeant Evans poked his head into Meade's office. "Got a minute?"

The sergeant rode a desk over in Ballistics, but poked his nose into other departments at will. By Meade's observation, the man meant no harm. He wasn't like others who stirred interdepartmental rivalries and pried for details that later leaked to the media "from unnamed sources." No, Evans was a people person, plain and simple, and he couldn't sit long in a solitary desk chair.

"Just as you suspected, Detective." Evans

slapped down a folder. "There, take a look. The lab'll e-mail you the files, but I figured I'd bring the hard copies over myself. Give you the first chance at seeing what we've learned."

Detective Meade grunted, opened the cover.

"You see it there?" Evans propped himself against a cabinet, badge flashing on his belt, tie riding high enough to fail any modern fashion standards. "Your sniffer was on the money. You find this Q-tip pressed down between some counter tiles and think it smells like mineral spirits. Well, you were right."

"Do we know the brand yet?"

"Lab's working on a full chemical breakdown. Once they have that, they'll compare its composition to all registered brands, see if they can match one up."

"Find a brand that sells in only one region, and it might tell us where this guy's disappeared to. Of course," Meade added, "Abby's my main concern."

"I realize she's been gone for some time now, but the person living in that condo's gone too. You ever consider the possibility that they ran off together, maybe some lovers' escapade?"

"Considered lots of things, Sergeant. Meanwhile, we still don't know where she is. I tried getting a subpoena so I could look at security footage from the condo, but I was told the whole thing's too circumstantial at this point. I have no direct link between Abby's disappearance and the two homicides."

"That's true. We don't even know that a crime's been committed."

Meade gave another grunt.

"So we don't have a body. Not yet. And we don't have a motive, unless you think this girl heard something incriminating from the homeless guy before he bought the farm. You know what we do have, Detective? We have the weapon."

"The smears on the Q-tip," Meade said.

"Carbon residue, that's right. And what's that mean? Here's what it means to me." Evans smoothed his tie between two fingers, flapping the end like a tongue. "Means this guy—this Russian, Romanian, Rastafarian, whatever—was cleaning and oiling a gun."

"Rastafarians are pacifists, I believe."

Evans let go of his tie. "No law against cleaning a firearm, or owning one, or carrying one. But it does raise eyebrows when there's already been rare Russian ammo involved in two homicides within a twelve-month period."

The detective raised an eyebrow of his own.

"Your dead guy by the river," Evans explained. "The bullet matched. You were on the money with that hunch as well."

"We ran his prints and got a hit. His name was Frederick Chipps," Meade said. "Freddy grew up in Chicago, did janitorial work in the schools there. He moved in this direction and spent the last years of his life in Nashville."

"Good to have that settled, I guess."

Meade pulled two bottles of Dr Pepper from his mini fridge, handed one to his fellow policeman. Meade glugged the cold liquid till his eyes watered from the carbonation. He wished he had paid more heed to Freddy's suspicions, yet even looking back through the written statement, he found very few specifics.

Sergeant Evans wiped his mouth. "Man, that's good."

"So this bullet? You say it's the same caliber as the airport shooting?"

"Same caliber, same riflings." The sergeant thumped the file on Meade's desk, his casual demeanor giving way to an obvious interest in the subject. "It's all there in the report. This 5.45 × 18mm ammo is used in dart guns. Oh, the look on your face. No, not real dart guns. Can you imagine if that were the . . . No, I'm speaking of the OTs-23 Drotik handgun. In Russian, *drotik* means 'dart.' "

"If you say so. Still tracking so far."

"The Drotik's small, easy to conceal, and got to be pretty popular back in the day, with KGB uppity-ups and military officials. It's never been available on this side of the ocean, not legally, but Wolf Performance sold ammo for it."

"For a weapon that isn't available?"

"Couldn't begin to tell you why."

"Do we know which stores still distribute the cartridges?"

"None that I know of." Evans leaned back against the cabinet, a bit deflated. "If the stuff's still trading hands, I'd guess it's through private parties."

Meade rubbed his chin. "That doesn't help me pin down our shooter."

"Between you and me, I don't think we'll find this girl alive."

"There's the irony, huh? Until we have a body, I can't get the subpoena to go looking for details to help me find her."

"The convoluted legal system. Don't act surprised."

"Even if you're right," Meade said, "I'm not giving up on her. She deserves that much, I think. And I'm giving it my best shot."

Sergeant Evans took another swig of Dr Pepper. "What do you think about those ads? 'Your One Shot at Protection.' That's some nifty stuff, huh? I don't know that I'd want them poking some chip into my own arm. But if my kids weren't all grown, yeah, I'd want that peace of mind."

"My twelve-year-old hates needles."

"It'd be your call, not hers."

Meade huffed. "You don't know my twelve-year-old."

Dee was still smiling at him from the photo.

Now there was a mystery, the way such a fun-loving child could have such a hard head. He insisted that it was from Dawna, of course. Dawna insisted it was from him.

Perhaps, in the process, they both proved the other right.

Evans crunched his empty can, dropped it into the recycling bin. "They're on to something with this 6336 thing. I say, give us cops some help for once. Why should we always be the ones with our hands tied by legalities?"

"Mm-hmm." Meade felt much too cynical for his age.

"Take this Abby girl," the sergeant said. "If she'd been chipped, wouldn't matter. Dead or alive, we'd know where she was by now."

"If the good guys know, the bad guys might also."

"Least it'd make it a fair fight."

Chapter Fifty-two

The mind was a funny thing, wasn't it?

Two months earlier, a mind-rattling blast had left Reuben King cut, broken, and concussed in a bed at Methodist Medical of Oak Ridge. His first conscious thoughts contained only wispy memories of the event, as though looking through the wrong end of a spyglass at a pirate's ship cloaked in fog.

Now, however, things were growing clearer each day.

While the fog still brushed over certain sections, his mind had turned that spyglass around and brought most of the day's events into startling clarity. Yes, many of his initial symptoms were physical, but some seemed psychological. The human psyche had that ability to block out traumatic events until body and emotions were prepared to bear the weight.

Since the accident, he had taken the alternate route to and from Nashville. Today, though, he decided it was time to visit the site.

He was on the turnpike, rounding the bend.

There was the sign for Novus Drive.

And the charred roadside.

The death zone.

Though it was true that he needed to face his fears, his real motive was more tangible. Maybe, just maybe, he would recall something related to the caller, the warning, the bomber himself.

Last week, Mr. Darius Hammond, a.k.a. Bigz, claimed that he was the one who blew the warning whistle, risking his job as Darcy Page's right-hand man to protect a representative of his birth state. Reuben believed it. Or most of it. He had even called the Anderson County sheriff to share the information.

"An interesting lead," the sheriff said.

"A lead? He practically wrote out a confession."

"He didn't claim that he was the bomber, did he?"

"No, he said that—"

"He painted himself as the hero, that's what he did, Representative. If he's so heroic, why'd he wait till now to tell us?"

"He's humble?"

"Did he seem humble?"

"No," Reuben admitted.

"No," the sheriff said. "Instead, he pointed fingers at another party that wasn't even present to offer a defense. He provided no evidence, and expressed some possible bitterness that has made him want to move on from that company. I know you're trying to help us, Representative King, but disgruntled employees are unreliable whistle-blowers, especially when they come running forward without being asked. Heckuva story, but the whole thing smells fishy."

"What about the RFID element? How'd he know that?"

"Lucky guess, maybe. Or could be that it seemed the most plausible way of connecting a technologies company to the attack."

"So that's it?" Reuben said. "You don't think there's anything to it?"

"Afraid not, but we'll add it to our list of leads." The sheriff switched to a lighter tone. "We've even had one caller who was after the reward, and his theory was that Y-12 left a few mini bombs lying around during World War II, like those stories in the news where some farmer digs up an unexploded rocket in his cornfield."

"Thanks for your help, Sheriff."

"Anytime. You take care."

A quarter mile past Novus Drive, Reuben brought his car to a halt along the roadside. Just ahead, the pavement shimmered in the sunlight, still sprinkled with fine bits of glass and metal glued down by the explosion's fireball.

He remembered this spot.

And the Audi purring along in front of him.

Panic rose in his chest and shoved its fist into his throat, making it difficult to breathe. The harder he fought, the tighter his air passages constricted. He believed for a split second that an explosion would reoccur here and incinerate him in this very seat. Just like it had done to Deputy Sevier.

Enough of this, Reuben. Slow breaths. Easy.

Then he was in the ambulance, his entire body in pain.

He hadn't remembered this part before.

They were racing him into ER, voices all around, electronic beeps, and bright lights. He was on fire. Tiny flames of pain licked his cheeks and brow. A tree trunk seemed planted across his chest.

The sheriff, there in his uniform.

Then Natalie, in a sweater, skirt, and leggings.

Don't let go of the spyglass, Reuben. You're close to something important here. Listen up.

Natalie had tears in her eyes. She gave him a kiss.

She was talking: *My dad says he heard sirens . . . found out you'd been in an accident . . . thought you were dead . . . afraid to even turn on the news . . .*

Reuben passed beneath tulip poplars and parked within view of a rusted red tractor. This was his territory, District 33, and he didn't have much difficulty finding where Mardy Flynn lived in a town the size of Oak Ridge.

Secret City or not.

Reuben knew from his chats with Natalie that this was the home in which she and her sister had been raised. He imagined her dashing around the corner of the house in a game of tag, kicking her soccer ball against the side of the garage, picking flowers from the small beds on either side of the front steps.

Let it go, he told himself.

Natalie didn't need him and his baggage. She deserved better.

In his rearview, he watched an old Bronco rumble up the drive. So as not to startle the other man, Reuben stepped out and waited for him to kill the engine. He needed to do this face-to-face, needed to look the man in the eye.

"Howdy," Mardy said as he hopped down from the Bronco.

"Mr. Flynn. I'm Reuben King."

"Yes sir, I know your name. Met ya at the festival and seen your posters 'round about town and whatnot. You're the fella's been seeing my daughter."

"She, uh, told you that?"

"Been coupla weeks since we talked, but she speaks mighty highly of ya."

"Thank you. Actually, I should doubly thank you, Mr. Flynn."

Mardy lowered his chin and glanced at Reuben from under hooded brows. "Can't say that I know whatcha mean, sir." His gaze shifted toward the drive, and he took a step back toward his house.

"It's a good thing," Reuben said. "If I'm not mistaken, you called my number back in July to issue me a warning. Why, you spared me an early grave."

"Where'd ya go and get a notion like that?"

"A bomb obliterated my car. On the turnpike. And before the news was even out, you knew I'd been involved in the accident."

Mardy frowned. "How could I know a thing like that?"

"Because you were waiting to see if the bomb went off when you said it would, hoping I'd heeded your message. And even with your voice

346

muffled, I heard you used words like *fella*. You're the one who called me from that library."

"If I did, what of it?"

"Why didn't you just say who you were from the start?"

The older man's jaw muscles flexed beneath his sideburns.

"Do you know who the bomber was, Mr. Flynn? Did he threaten you too?"

Mardy's frown flattened, and his muscles relaxed. "Yep," he said. "Yep, that's about the way it went, sir. Best if don't say a dang thing more."

"But you do know who it was, don't you? We need to catch this guy."

"Don't know his name, where he lives. Don't know nothing about him."

"Did you ever talk to a short black guy, last name Hammond?"

"Nope, there weren't no black fella. He . . . Listen, Mr. King, I don't think ya need to worry 'bout him trying to kill ya no more. If I talk to the police, they's gonna question me, but I have nothing to say. I warned you, and you're alive, aren't ya? Standing right here. Heck, that's all the reward I need."

"Thank you. If you don't mind, though, I had something else in mind."

In Her Hands

"They reckon they got it all figured now, don't they?"

"Oh, you sound bitter."

"Well, it's just not right. When my girl comes 'round to seeing things the way I'm a-looking at 'em, well then, she'll wish she paid more attention."

"You can only do so much, you know? You're given a responsibility to watch after her, nudge her toward what's right and away from what's going to hurt her. You can't force her steps, though. She may be your girl, but it's only in a limited capacity. They grow up. That's part of the process. They learn, good and bad. Oh, do they learn."

"Learn the hard way, more like."

"That's up to each one. Why, look at Tina. She's walked a tough road, if you'll pardon the pun, because of her own choices. I'm not saying those choices were easy, they never are, but she's reached the crossroads and still made more than one poor decision. Does that make you love her any less?"

"Reckon not."

"And me neither. I love both those girls with my

whole heart. Why else would I tell you to keep watch over them? They're more precious to me than anything."

"Seems to me, Tina's mostly going backwards again."

"She's made strides. I still believe she can conquer her past."

"S'pose it's Natalie that's got me worried now. I'll do just like you told me and put the choice in her hands. That's what you said, am I wrong?"

"In her hands. Yes."

"So you must have some notion one way or 'nother what she's gonna do."

"A notion. A good notion."

"Well, she best think it through, or I'll have a right mess to clean."

Chapter Fifty-three

September 27

If attendees at the Heart for the Hungry benefit wanted to enjoy cool drinks, freely donated clothes, and live outdoor music, they had to face the handheld scanner.

Natalie served as coordinator.

Detective Meade was the enforcer.

All they needed was one fish in this net, and then maybe they would better understand the link between the murders and the disappearance.

"Here they come," Meade said. "All the media frenzy about Abby and her volunteer work, it's just helped our cause. I figure we'll have a good turnout."

Filled with men and women from the Rescue Mission, buses lumbered into the parking area. A Tuesday evening escape from downtown was appealing. The sun gilded the treetops in gold, and the lawns and the lake of Centennial Park lolled in the cloying heat. According to the detective, these grounds had once been Freddy C's daytime territory.

Only one section of the large park was allotted for the concert. Toting helium-filled balloons on strings, waist-high cones stretched plastic taut around the perimeter, with the band shell closing off the front of the rectangle. There was enough room for five to six hundred people, as well as tables of bottled water and juice, pamphlets on helping the area's needy, and tubs of clothing.

Volunteers wore official red-and-gray T-shirts and ID lanyards. They manned the tables and tubs, ran sound and electric cords, and guarded the exits.

"This will be their point of entry," Natalie said. "They stop here first, go through security, and get a heart stamped on their hands. After that, they're free to come and go through any of the five points."

"You done this before?" Meade said.

"For fifth and sixth graders."

"Well then, you have all the experience you need. Take my word for it."

"Got kids?"

"How'd you guess?"

She pointed. "You're up, Detective. Start waving your scanner."

"You first," he said. "Lead by example."

The handheld device was similar to ones Natalie had seen used by clerks taking inventory at any Walmart, Target, or Kroger. The detective had explained to her that it functioned much like the antitheft poles shoppers passed each day and barely noticed. It sent a radio signal that searched for flattened copper antennae within RFID tags.

The copper coil charged the tag just long enough to awaken the encoded chip and fire its data back at the scanner.

Scanners were limited, though. When a store clerk took inventory, the handheld's nose sniffed out only a small window or missed contact altogether.

"The implants are typically placed in the back of the upper arm," Meade told her. "If any of our mission friends got injected with microchips, that's probably where we'll find them."

Natalie held out her arms as the detective ran the scanner back and forth. Across the grass, she saw church vans pulling in with youth groups and college-age kids. Beside her, the scanner wasn't doing anything.

"What's it supposed to do?"

"Squeal," he said. "At least, that's what some call it."

"It didn't squeal."

"We're not done." He checked her legs and torso as well.

"Still didn't squeal."

"Guess you're good to go."

"Stamp me. I have to go talk to the sound crew."

"Here," he said. "Have a heart."

Natalie examined her hand, nodded, and faced the oncoming throng. She gestured them toward the small blue canopy and the waiting detective. "You saw how it's done," she said. "Step on up, then head in toward the band shell. Eastern Block takes the stage in ten minutes."

And boy, did they ever take the stage.

Reuben knew a few Eastern Block tunes from Lightning 100 FM, but the live experience took it to another level. The four-man band melded classic rock guitar flavors, signature vocals, and the textured crunch and rhythm of modern alternative. As the music simmered and swelled, he stood twenty feet from the stage, loving every minute along with the head-bobbing crowd. And he knew Bret Vreeland came next, with a mellower vibe that was every bit as powerful.

When the set was over, Reuben went to find Natalie. She would be too busy to notice a text. "Looking for the event coordinator," he told a volunteer.

"Back by the security area."

Natalie was handing over two $20 bills, sending out a search party for more ice. "Be back ASAP. And bring my change and receipt," she instructed.

She turned, almost bumped into him. "Hey, honey," he said.

"Honey? Really?" She swept hair from her face. "I have stuff to do."

"Do you think we'll have a chance to talk later?"

"Ohh, so we can talk now? That's allowed?"

"I suppose I deserve that."

She softened. "Your timing's just bad. Tonight,

any talking's out of the question, unless you want to wait around till eleven or so for me and the teardown crew. I mean, you're certainly more than welcome, *muchacho*."

"You know, I've missed your goofy Spanish."

She planted a hand on her hip. "Good to see you too."

"Thursday, Natalie, I'd like to take you to Chaffin's Barn. They do this casual but top-notch dinner theater. I want you to be my date."

"I thought we . . . You really want to do this? Risk hurting each other?"

"I can't promise we won't, but I'd like the chance to lay everything out there, with full honesty, and see if we can make this work. Not during the theater part, of course. Afterwards, I suppose."

"Trying to get me to spill my secrets, huh?"

"No." His eyes stayed on hers. "Other way around, actually."

"What time, Mr. King?"

"I'd pick you up at your place at five thirty."

"OK." She nodded. "Yeah, I'd like that."

"I also wanted to let you know—"

"Sorry, Reuben, but I have, like, a million things going on at this moment."

"It's your dad," he said. "Mardy's going to be here tonight."

Her eyes widened. "That's, uh, kind of random. I mean, that's great news, but I didn't expect him to come all this way in that old Bronco of his."

Skeweee-skeweee . . .

Natalie stopped. "What was that? Did you hear squealing?"

"You're not running a greased-pig contest, are you?"

"Funny. Very funny."

"That might work at the Secret City Festival, but not here in more cosmopolitan Nashville." Past her shoulder, past her thick brown hair, Reuben spotted a gleaming dark blue vehicle trolling for a spot in the parking lot. He grinned. "Speaking of your dad, I do believe he's just arrived."

Natalie swiveled her head, raised an eyebrow, and cast a look back at Reuben. "What's he doing in a brand-new truck?"

"A 2011 Ford Ranger, four-by-four, with all the extras."

"How do you . . . What's this about?"

"It was a gift to him."

"That's his?"

"Go ask him. Would've done more if I could have."

"OK, back up. Back up. You're not talking sense, Reuben."

"He's the one who called to warn me. He's the one who saved my life. He didn't want all the attention, didn't want the publicity. This was the best I could do with the insurance money I received from the accident. He deserves it."

"My dad's the one?" Natalie tilted her head. "That's . . . that's epic."

"Don't act so surprised. Considering his job at Y-12, I knew he was a patriotic guy, and something American-made seemed like the obvious choice."

Natalie met her father with a hug at the edge of the parking lot. He patted her back and told her how he didn't deserve such a fine gift from Mr. King, and how proud he was of her work with this benefit concert.

"You done good, Duckie."

"Sounds like that goes both ways. You're a hero."

Skeweee . . .

"Nah," he said. "It weren't nothing but a phone call."

Skeweee-skeweee . . .

She gave him another hug. "Enjoy the show, Dad. Got to run."

"You go on. Don't let me keep ya."

With that, Natalie darted across the grass toward the blue security canopy, where newcomers were still being scanned. Detective Meade caught her eye and pointed out a thin-haired man in mismatched tennis shoes.

"Over five hundred people," he said, "and this is our second squealer. The first, she's a woman I've seen about town for years. Sweet thing, but not all there. It's impossible to get a coherent sentence from her. This guy, he's been at the mission off and on since last year, admits he was at the clinic with Abby that day, but won't tell me anything else. Law officers aren't always their favorite people."

"You're sure it was a chip that set it off?"

"Check it out for yourself."

Natalie took the scanner, stepped toward the forlorn man, and moved the device along his arm. When it reached his triceps, it emitted an electronic squeal and flashed information on the digital panel:

Jake Blevins, male, age 38
ST-1-13-1799-2256

"Jake?" she said. "Is that your name?" When he looked up, she met his eyes. "I want to help you. I was a friend of Abby's. She was there with you at the clinic that day, wasn't she?"

"You knew Abby, ma'am?"

"She was my roommate back in college."

"All of us, we liked her. If somebody took her, that's not right."

"Agreed. Could you tell me about that clinic?"

Jake scratched at his thin hair. "I don't want any trouble, ma'am."

"If you know something," Detective Meade interjected, "and you fail to share it, you could be charged with obstruction of justice, Mr. Blevins."

Natalie shot the detective a glare. "I've got this." She waited until he retreated a few steps. "Thing is, Jake, I didn't go to all the effort of setting out these cold drinks and clean shoes and clothes just to cause you grief. That'd be silly. You hear what I'm saying? All I want is to find my friend."

"Is it true, about something in my arm?"

"A tracking device."

"Didn't know it was there." He shrugged. "I thought they were giving us some kind of shot. My arm had a knot for a day or two, figured that was normal. But my head, my stomach—nothing felt right afterwards. Same with the others. We figured they might've done some experiment on us, with chemical weapons or something." He lowered his voice. "The CIA, they do that sort of thing, you know? Look it up on the Internet. We knew better. Should've never gone along with it. And that clinic, those doctors—the next day, they were gone."

Meade muttered in Natalie's ear.

"Can you tell me this, Jake?" she said. "Was there somebody Russian there that day? Some guy with an accent?"

"Sure. Not real tall, but strong arms, big chest. That the one you mean?"

"If I got my hands on a video of him, do you think you'd be able to point him out?" Meade said.

Jake looked to Natalie. "Would it help you find Abby?"

"That's the hope," she said.

"Sure, ma'am. Could give it a try."

"That'd be much appreciated, Mr. Blevins," Meade said.

"Come on, Jake. I bet you're thirsty, and we have lots of shoes to choose from. The best part? Bret Vreeland's about to play. You'll love it. Guaranteed."

"This thing." He rubbed his arm. "Think I'm going to die?"

"No, the chips aren't dangerous. They're actually meant to protect you."

Chapter Fifty-four

Was this coincidence? Serpionov doubted it. He scooted his desk chair forward in his Hyatt Place room. The Shield case was open before him. He touched two fingers to the screen, zoomed the satellite image to a three-mile square in Nashville's West End, and confirmed that three of the circles he was monitoring had converged at Centennial Park, two of them within feet of each other.

The first: *Natalie Flynn, tagged last September.*

The second: *Jake Blevins, tagged back in February.*

Serpionov gazed out the window at the burnt-orange sun slipping behind the hills west of Cool Springs. In less than seventy-two hours, not far north of here, the Health and Human Resources Committee would meet at Legislative Plaza, room 16. This was public information, available online.

If Mr. King and his people approved the bill, Serpionov would carry out his demonstration for Mardy Flynn and the contact. The sacrifice would be made, the transaction completed, and the world would be a safer place.

If the committee rejected the bill, the demonstration would be canceled, the potential industry of human microchipping would be crippled, and he would start destroying any evidence of his involvement.

Either way, Natalie Flynn would die.

On the TV beside him, the "Shield Yourself" commercial filled the screen. Ms. Page had gambled everything, buying ad slots before the bill's passage, trying to sway public opinion and pressure the politicians to "represent."

Bah. Did people not see the irony in her imagery?

In the wild, zebras stayed safest when in a pack, all their stripes blending their individual shapes into one large mass. A lion's strategy, then, was to divide and conquer. It was the only way. Yes, whether on the savannah or in the supermarket, predators fared far better when they singled out their prey.

Even in his official role at tonight's benefit, Detective Meade figured he could stare ahead stone-faced and hum along to his favorite songs. No one would know. Meanwhile, he had already placed a call to the morgue, where he knew an assistant to the medical examiner. Despite the job's grisly requirements, she still had kind eyes above thin, almost-purple lips. He hoped to hear back from her soon.

From the cones and plastic along the perimeter, he watched Bret Vreeland walk onto the band shell's stage amid loud cheers. Bret propped himself on a tall stool, pulled the mic stand closer, and, without preamble, sang a cappella:

We have crooked hearts, we have broken
    souls,
We want love to fill us, but we're full of
    holes . . .

With one strum of a chord, he launched into the song. And the crowd was hooked. Meade nodded, proud to know the man on that stage. He admired him both as a person and as a musician.

Perhaps saving Bret's life had bonded the two of them like that.

Perhaps Meade still felt guilty that he hadn't arrived sooner and saved Bret's leg, before the showdown at the old Storinka Defense warehouse.

> We have twisted bodies, we have darkened minds,
> We want love to cleanse us, but we're still looking to find . . .
> What we need, we do not know, what we know is that we need,
> What we're crying out to say is that we're crying to be whole.

Meade knew "Whole" from Bret's album. It was the title track and the latest single. He hummed along, caught up in the song's building layers.

"Dude, I'm reporting you. This is a clear dereliction of duty."

The detective turned. "Aramis."

"Closed up shop and got here soon as I could."

" 'Least it's only a few blocks."

"I brought you something." Aramis wiggled his eyebrows. He wore fashion jeans, a wide belt, and a T-shirt under a button-down shirt. "I know it's a little late for a Hair Curler, but what about a snickerdoodle?" He slipped over a small bag. "Think you can handle the sugar rush while on duty?"

"Guess we'll find out."

The moon was above the trees now, a celestial

spotlight upon the Parthenon building across the park. The music carried over the lawns, and streamers of lights gave the benefit an enchanted feel.

On stage, Bret was finishing "Whole":

What we need, we do not know, what we
    know is that we need,
What we're crying out to say is that we're
    crying to be whole . . .
Crying to be whole, crying out, we're crying
    out . . .
Oh, God, please come and make us whole.

By the last refrain, Detective Meade's snicker-doodle was gone.

"You're a monster," Aramis said over the applause of the crowd.

A short, shapely form approached them. As she stepped into the lights, the detective saw she had platinum hair, hints of a tattoo along her shirt collar, and a face structure similar to Natalie's. If Natalie was the casual and collected version, this girl was the more raw and volatile one.

"Hey," she said. "Don't mean to interrupt y'all, but I'm looking for my sis."

Meade said, "You a Flynn, by any chance?"

"Tina. Just call me Tuf."

"T and F. Tuf." Aramis nodded, eyes latching on to her. "I like it."

"Guys. You're so flippin' predictable."

"Ahh. So you are tough," he said. "Or at least you pretend to be."

"And who asked you?" She turned to Meade. "She anywhere close?"

"I'm Aramis." Aramis extended his hand. "Aramis Black."

"And I'm not interested."

"Who asked you?" he said, eyes twinkling.

"Can I get an answer 'bout my sis? I need to talk to her."

"She's very busy at the moment," Meade said. "She's the event coordinator, and—"

"Well, I'm her sister."

"You said that already," Aramis noted. "And I'm the owner of Black's Espresso, just down the street on Elliston Place. Next drink's on me."

"If I'm gonna drink, and not saying I am, it'll be harder stuff than that."

Meade and Aramis exchanged a glance, and said together, "Hair Curler."

"What's a Hair Curler?"

"Only one way to find out," Aramis said. "I open up at 5:30 a.m."

Natalie appeared from the concert area. "Tina? You're here too?"

As Natalie and Tuf moved out of earshot to talk, Detective Meade's phone buzzed. He checked the number, saw it was the assistant from the ME's office.

● ● ●

Natalie hadn't seen her sister in days. She hated the way their last encounter had ended, but couldn't allow money woes and drug troubles to enter the house. It would strain their landlord's patience as well as their sisterly relationship.

"Who's the guy?" she said, trying to keep things light.

"The detective?" Tuf said.

"The other one, dingbat. Did he come with you?"

"Just met him. Aramis. He thinks he's all that."

"Uh, from here?" Natalie grinned. "Yeah, I'd say he's pretty hot."

"He's . . . Can we drop it? I came to give you rent money, OK?" Tuf extracted an envelope from her pocket, shoved it toward Natalie. "Take it."

"Where'd you get this?"

"Rent's due Friday, right? Couldn't just leave ya hanging, could I?"

Natalie peeked into the thick offering, realized it was mostly $5 and $10 bills. "How much is this?" she said.

"Hundred and eighty."

"¿Que?" She took a calming breath. "Tuf, that's, like, less than half."

"A hundred and eighty more than nothing. Sheesh, I'm trying here."

"You should've tried saying no to a few tokes."

"Forget you," Tuf growled. "You think I need this crud from you? No. Don't even touch me. You want your cushy little life? Well, have at it. All yours."

"Wait a sec."

"I. Said. Hands. Off."

Natalie watched her sister shove past Aramis and vanish once more.

Chapter Fifty-five

September 28

No use staring in the rearview mirror. Best to focus straight ahead.

Detective Meade strapped on his shoulder holster, chambered a round, and slipped his firearm into place. He covered it with a windbreaker—something light enough to breathe in this late-summer heat yet bulky enough to conceal his weapon—and grabbed a microwave breakfast bagel on his way out the door.

So the RFID tags were real, with the homeless used as guinea pigs.

If only he had listened to Freddy C's ramblings, he might have—

Enough. Straight ahead.

Dawna was gone, dropping their daughter off at school. He left the empty house locked, peeled off West End Avenue, and stopped at Black's Espresso for his morning jolt. There was a rare lull at the coffee establishment, with no line at the counter. Must be that all the Vanderbilt students were already in their classes.

"Great night last night, huh?"

"Missed half of it," Aramis said. "But yeah, good times."

"Tuf was a little firecracker, wasn't she?"

Aramis grinned.

"Think she'll ever stop in?" Meade asked.

"She'll wait a week or so, to make a point. But she'll be here."

Meade accepted his drink and switched topics. Nearly six years as friends, and his trust in Aramis was as strong as ever. "The morgue's checking into it," he confided.

"Whaddya think they'll find?"

"I believe Freddy's going to help us solve this thing."

Aramis pulled up his sleeves, tattoos vivid on his forearms, and braced himself against the counter. "You think he had one of those implants in his arm?"

"I'd bet my pension on it."

Darcy Page gathered her regional team in the impressive front lobby of the Nashville high-rise and gave them the news: They were all laid off. Here's your measly severance package. Here's your pat on the back. Thanks for busting your hump the past six months, but it's time to consolidate.

"For the time being," she later told Bigz, "you're safe."

"*Indispensable* is the word."

"Don't think you're above it all."

"Woman," he said, reclining on the bed. "I know your secrets."

"Get out of my room, Mr. Hammond."

"And go where? We've shared this space since shifting operations here."

"Saturday," Darcy said, "we head back to Seattle. It's true, you know? I'm consolidating. Consolidating power. Resources. Personnel. And dealing with the mutineers, namely Jack Norwood and his band of merry men."

"Our strategy's worked," Bigz said. "I think this bill will pass."

"I'm optimistic, but cautiously so."

Darcy thought about Natalie. Ignorant Natalie. The girl had no idea she had been tagged a year ago by Magnus, a rogue operator. Darcy had since used her as she saw fit, and her worth would be revealed forty-eight hours from now.

Let Natalie learn to live with those consequences.

Assuming, of course, the Russian had no other plans for her.

"Optimistic?" Bigz said. "And yet you've just

cut the legs out from under the southeast regional office. I didn't think you'd go through with it."

"You convinced me. The last thing we need is old-timers flapping their gums about how we went about making this happen. If 6336 fails, I've done my hatchet work in advance. If it succeeds, I hire a new team, new salespeople and support, and we hit the ground running. Start fresh. Stay hungry."

"You're cold. You just stiff-armed nearly two hundred employees."

"What's that tell you, Mr. Hammond?"

"That the Ice Queen cometh."

"The Ice Queen cometh. So don't get too comfortable over there."

"Never," he said. "I know better than that."

Chapter Fifty-six

September 29

Detective Meade's first significant call of the day came at 8:55 a.m., from Greta Slayton at the county morgue. He listened to the ME's assistant, imagining her purplish lips barely moving, snipping sentences into palatable portions.

"Received a verbal from the examiner," she said. "We have no need for scanners here, but I made minor incisions. Peeled back tissue and muscle layers. Checked for possible subdermal implantations in the triceps of Mr. Frederick Chipps. Examined both arms. Found no bioglass tags, capsules, devices, or microchips."

Meade rested his head in his hand, eyes focused on the top of his desk.

"Wish I could tell you otherwise, Reggie."

Few knew his first name, and fewer still used it in conversation. Meade and Greta went back over a decade, to the case of his own niece lured away by an Internet predator. To this day, it remained unsolved.

Not for much longer, though. Not if he and Aramis had their way.

"What about the legs?" Meade said. "Or the hips?"

"There are certain protocols. You know this well. Dignity for the dead, as well as respect for those who mourn. I'll need a directive from my boss to do any additional exploration."

"No, Greta, that's all right," he said. "I was just so convinced."

"Anything else?"

"Thanks for the quick response."

"I only do it because you send me Christmas baskets."

"Gifts," he clarified. "Not bribes."

"Let's hope we won't have to talk again till then. And come Christmas, think nuts. Cashew, almonds, macadamia. Nuts. Can't get enough of them."

"Nuts," he said. "For one of the most sane people I know."

Natalie wiped down the counter, swept up the grounds from the floor, and readied things for the next wave of Roast Inc. customers. Tomorrow she would be subbing, while today she was a coffee barista. Earlier in the week, she had been an event coordinator, helping raise over $48,000 for the hungry and homeless.

What, she wondered, would she be a year from now?

Yes, OK. She wanted to be a wife at some point.

And her yearning to be a mom rose from somewhere even deeper, rooted in the loss of her own mother, in the what-ifs and might-have-beens.

Watch it, chica. *Don't get ahead of yourself.*

Her thoughts wandered from her rent to Tuf's irresponsibility to Dad's actions that had saved Reuben's life. In the morning, the committee would vote on the bill. And, if all went as hoped, it would mean a less stressful future.

What about Abby, though? Was it already too late?

The door chime turned Natalie's attention to an older gentleman with alert gray eyes and salt-and-pepper hair. Every time she slowed down long enough to take notice, he seemed to be somewhere close.

"Eli," she said. "You're done at the church?"

"Hmm. My work, it's not ever done."

"Did you get paid, though?"

"Brought ya the cash, so's we can settle with Mr. Faranzmehr."

"Tuf's so infuriating. I can't believe she bailed on us and stiffed us for the rest of her rent money. I'm sorry. I mean, I know it's on me for even letting her into the house, trusting that she'd really changed. Yeah right."

Eli's bushy brows rose. "She's family. You did whatcha had to."

"We're still over two hundred short."

"Nosiree." He patted his pocket. "Reckon I got us covered. And what fun's a date if'n your nerves is a-jangling. No, tonight you oughta enjoy yourself."

"Seriously, Eli? That is amazing. You don't even know."

"This mean you'll gimme a coffee? Or I gotta stand here and beg?"

Detective Meade's second significant call came at 11:18 a.m.

He stared at his Caller ID: Greta Slayton. "Again?" he said.

"Just got word here in the office, Reggie. Your missing girl, Ms. Abigail Stark. Pretty ripe. Advanced decomposition. Found by a horseback rider deep in Percy Warner Park."

"Mm-hmm." Meade cracked his neck. "So she's been IDed?"

"They have a unit there now. Scene's being taped off. Clothes are an exact match of descriptions from the last day she was seen. Hair's blonde. She's not a thin girl, so that's also a match. First responders reported one small cranial wound. Small-caliber gunshot, at first guess."

Another 5.45 × 18mm round? Three deaths from the same Drotik gun?

"Why don't I know about this already?" he said.

"Got called in less than an hour ago, direct to the medical examiner. She issued a temporary media blackout to protect the integrity of the scene."

"Thanks, Greta. That's twice in one day."

Armed with this latest knowledge, Detective Meade resubmitted his request for, and received, the subpoena for condo security footage dated August 18 through 24. Although the property management team was compliant, he sensed their reticence. No one wanted to believe that a homicidal killer was on their doorstep, riding in their elevator, living a few floors up.

"I do hope," the manager said, "that y'all will keep the news channels from raising a ruckus. We're proud of this building and our fine occupants."

The reticence, it seemed, was driven by mostly corporate interests.

Meade received the footage on DVD just before 6:30 p.m. He spent the next three hours studying various clips of Abby entering the building with Chaz. Knocking at the door down the hall. Meeting the man in that unit. Later departing with him in the elevator. He wasn't tall, but he had solid arms and a barrel chest above thin hips. His hair was cropped, cheekbones hard beneath a cool stare.

The detective scanned and enhanced the image, and then sent it in an e-blast to every police station, post office, and hotel within a fifty-mile radius.

Someone out there had to recognize this killer with the Russian accent.

Chapter Fifty-seven

All the clues were coming into focus.

Time now to see how they pieced together.

Writer's Block was an original murder mystery, presented by a professional troupe of actors at Chaffin's Barn. Located on Highway 100, on the city's westernmost edge, the sprawling red barn housed one of the nation's oldest privately owned dinner theaters, and Natalie was impressed at the quality of food and production.

"Act 3 will begin in two minutes."

Natalie and Reuben finished their last trip through the buffet and hurried back into the theater area. Between acts, they had exchanged light conversation. Yet certain things remained unspoken between them. Hadn't Reuben promised he would be fully honest tonight?

Not that Natalie even wanted to go there.

Why ruin everything, chica? *You should at least wait till after tomorrow.*

She gazed over dessert into his piercing blue eyes. It was a perfect evening—perfect weather, perfect setting. Why risk throwing it all away? The truth might be more than either of them was ready for, decimating any chances that this relationship would last.

"Thirty seconds."

The lights dimmed, and the stage descended from the ceiling to reveal a man and a woman alone in a room. As the final act unfolded, the actors peeled back layers of love and hate, of murder, ambition, and betrayal.

Once the cast had taken a final bow, Reuben introduced Natalie to the owners, John and Janie Chaffin. Natalie told them she loved the play's plot twists and red herrings. John Chaffin nodded. Janie smiled. They both studied her as though judging her merit on the arm of one of their state's esteemed officials.

John clapped Reuben on the back. "Thanks for coming, Representative. We had quite a crowd here tonight—couple of corporate bigwigs, a minister, a local author and his wife. Even a hockey player from the Nashville Predators. Mingle if you'd like. Feel free."

"Actually," Reuben said, "Natalie and I wanted to watch the sunset."

"You'll find a good view of it out these doors," Janie said. "We'll let you two enjoy a romantic evening."

Reuben offered his arm to Natalie, and she moved alongside him.

"Don't forget," John added. "Vote wisely tomorrow."

Set atop a rise, the barn's perimeter featured small trees, ponds, and flowers for those who wished to enjoy them after the show. As most people departed, Reuben and Natalie joined hands and found a secluded area in the glow of the dying sun. They settled next to each other on a bench, within view of the black 2008 Camry he had bought as his replacement car.

"Still can't believe you gave my dad a truck."

"Doesn't it seem like it means something, the fact he saved my life and I'm the one falling in love with his daughter?"

"Reuben, I . . . I don't want to hurt you."

"Am I wrong? Don't you have similar feelings for me?"

"That's what worries me. We've grown so close so fast."

"And that's a negative?"

She squinted into the setting sun.

"I want to come clean with you, Natalie. Full disclosure."

"No, it's fine," she said. "We can do that later. You have your big meeting in the morning, and I don't want to keep you up. Have you even decided yet?"

"That's all I've thought about." He squeezed her hand. "Almost all."

"Well, you already know what I think. It seems even more obvious after what happened to Freddy. And Abby. And . . ."

He squeezed tighter. "And to you?"

She nodded.

"Can I see them?" he whispered. "Am I allowed to even ask?"

She knew what he meant, and it sent heat coursing through her limbs, crackling at her temples. She wanted to stand and walk away. Never see him again. Never take that chance. She didn't deserve his love or affection, and this was no time for prying her heart open and letting him peek inside.

I want to trust You, Lord. But look at me.

Her and her deceitful little heart.

Reuben's voice was tender. "It's part of you, part of your past and who you are. Natalie, if I'm going to love you, I want to love all of you."

She pressed her eyes shut. The sun's glow

seeped through her closed lids, rich golden honey oozing through her thoughts.

"Please, honey."

Honey . . .

Eyes still shut, she nodded. She wanted this more than anything, and for that very reason, it terrified her. "They're ugly," she said, her voice hoarse.

"That's all right. Life's not always pretty."

"Believe me," she said. "I know."

"Are you sure, Natalie? I know it's not even fair of me to—"

"*Por favor.*" She held a finger to her lips and stared straight ahead. She swallowed, then lifted one foot up onto the bench. She tugged on her pant cuff till it reached her knee and her scars were in view. She hooked her finger into her sock and pulled it down. "There," she said.

Reuben touched her shin first.

And she flinched.

"Does it hurt?"

She shook her head. "Shhh, *corazon.*"

With his warm hands inching down her shin to her ankles, she closed her eyes again. He slid two fingers along either side of her Achilles tendon, as though counting the ridges, counting the rings in a fallen tree trunk. In her mind she was aged and decrepit, marred and imperfect. And he was the artisan finding the beauty within, buffing it out, bringing rich hues and shapes into the light.

His fingertips feathered the tops of her feet, then curled around to her calf muscle until his entire palm cupped the skin. He moved in a slow circular motion, massaging, soothing, apologizing, and asking for forgiveness for the evil that had been done.

She felt the request in his touch, and she answered by lifting her other leg. With both knees pulled to her chest, she felt vulnerable on the bench.

A statue propped there in the evening light.

And coming back to life.

"You're beautiful," Reuben said.

She dragged her lip between her teeth.

"I hate that anyone's ever hurt you, Natalie. Until recently, it seems like I've been so blind. I've made my decision, though. I'm voting yes on 6336. I don't want anyone to suffer unnecessarily. If there's any way, any way at all, that you could've been spared what that man did to you, God forbid I would be the one to stand in the way."

She gave him a nod. "Thank you. That makes me happy."

"I know it was never the Lord's desire for you to go through this. You're so precious to me, and I can't even imagine how precious you are to . . ."

When his voice caught, she looked and saw tears in his eyes.

"I'm sorry," he said, "but I . . . we need to talk before we go any further."

"Listen, Reuben, there's something I need to tell you too."

He withdrew his hands. "Honey, I didn't mean to hurt you or deceive you. Please know that's true. But this is something I should've divulged long ago."

Reuben King's chest was ready to blow apart. He loved this lady before him so much more than he ever thought possible. Caressing her legs, her scars was the most spiritual and sensual thing he'd ever shared with a woman. She had trusted him. Surrendered to him.

And now I'm going to lose it all.

"I don't deserve you," he said.

She stared at him.

"You've been owed the truth from the beginning."

She eased her pant legs down. "What're you talking about?"

"The more time that's gone by, Natalie, the harder it's been for me to tell you. I've lived with this for six years, trying to keep it buried, mainly because of what it might do to my political aspirations. I realize now that I could've survived the fallout, but I didn't know how to deal with it then. And the fact that I hid it only makes me appear guiltier."

Natalie was still as stone on the bench.

"Remember tonight's play," he said, "how we thought the husband and the wife were ready to kill each other?"

She didn't move.

"Well, that's what . . . It was something along those lines with my wife."

Natalie's chin snapped toward him. "Your wife?"

He nodded.

"You're married?"

"Was. Yes."

"When? How long ago? Where's she now?"

"I was twenty-two, and I—"

"We've dated these past few months and you never thought to mention this? Not even *once?*" Natalie stormed away from the bench, paced the dirt. "Is she around, like, where you still see each other? Do you have any kids? OMG. I've saved myself, thinking you might be the one. And you were *married?*"

"Ex-wife." He clenched his jaw. "No kids."

"OK. Keep talking."

"And she's not around."

"Go on."

"She was murdered."

Natalie swung around to face him. Tears spilled down her cheeks, and her voice quivered. "What happened, Reuben? You tell me what happened, or so help me . . ."

"We were young. Probably too young. We'd

moved to Charlotte, where she was finishing med school. I caught her one night in our bed with my best friend. This was only a few months after our wedding, and I went ballistic. No, please hold on," he said as Natalie recoiled from him. He reached for her, but she swatted his hands aside. "You have to believe I didn't do anything to hurt her. I admit, I was furious that night. That much is true. I screamed at her, threw stuff, but I never laid a hand on her or harmed a hair on her head."

"You said she was murdered."

"With my gun."

"Reuben!"

"It was my friend who grabbed it. He knew where I kept my stuff, and he pulled it from my nightstand, my own gun, and shot her as she was crawling toward me and vowing it was all a big mistake. He shot at me too, but I . . . I shouldn't have left her lying there, Natalie. What was I supposed to do? She was dead. Killed instantly. I would've charged him because at that point, I hardly cared if I died, and I sure as heck wanted him to. But I knew that thing was fully loaded, a semiautomatic. I dove into the hallway and ran."

The evening shadows thickened, with only thin fingers of sunlight reaching through the leaves, circling bright red drops of paint on the western barn wall.

"The cops came," Reuben said. "My friend was gone."

"And they blamed you?"

"He was never found. Vanished, just like that. I was taken into custody. Held without bail for eight days. When they released me, they didn't apologize, simply told me I was free to go. For weeks, detectives called and stopped by to question me, treating me with utter disdain. I'm sure they thought I was guilty and they'd get me to snap."

"But you were never indicted, right?"

"To some people, that didn't matter. They were convinced I'd made up this alibi to save my own skin, even though no one could explain why my friend was gone. Thanks to my parents' money and a high-powered attorney, all charges were dropped, and the scandal was swept away as quickly and quietly as possible. I moved back to Oak Ridge soon after, and that's when I got my start in politics."

"You should've told me, Reuben."

"I know." He stared off down the slope. "I didn't mean to hide it so long."

"Well, if you're innocent, you have nothing to—"

"See?" he said. "Right there. *If.* 'If you're innocent.' That's what I have to deal with. That's why it's almost easier to keep it buried."

"Your wife, did you love her?"

"At the time, I thought it was going to be for life."

Natalie stepped closer.

He said, "Guess you just never know, do you?"

She shifted her weight, brushed her hair back from her face.

"If you hate me," he said, "I completely understand. You'd be justified. If you need time to think, or if you need to talk to Pastor Teman and his wife, or whatever, I'm not going to push. I hope there's still a way to make this work between us, though. My feelings for you, they're real. Completely real."

"I don't want to hurt you either, Reuben."

"What? How could you? No, you've been nothing but—"

"I've kept something from you too."

His vision blurred, and his thoughts turned hazy. "Something from me?"

She plopped onto the bench beside him. "My turn," she said.

Natalie meant to reciprocate honesty with honesty. She felt Reuben's hip against hers, firm and warm, and realized how much she cared for this man.

All or nothing, Natalie. Here goes.

Before she had uttered a word, however, a trio of figures approached them from the front corner of Chaffin's Barn.

"Hello," Darcy Page called out. "What a splendid show, huh?"

Pastor Teman and his wife followed in her wake.

"Ms. Page?" Reuben said. "What're you doing here?"

"We were also there in the theater, the three of us, for a night out."

"All right. Well, meet Natalie Flynn. She's a—"

"Reuben, please," Darcy said. "She and I, we already know each other."

"I didn't know." He looked to Natalie. "Had no idea."

Chapter Fifty-eight

Serpionov spun in the darkness, his flashlight's beam revealing his handiwork. The laptop and the webcam both powered off for now. The two pillowcases, the zip ties waiting to be used as restraints. The gas cans. Although cicadas sang a shrill chorus outside these walls, there were very few sounds from within.

He nodded. Yes, this should work. He envisioned his plan unfolding, coming to completion tomorrow morning:

1. Natalie Flynn would be his captive.
2. Mardy Flynn would be en route with the contact.
3. Serpionov himself would go miles south, to prove the technology's effectiveness from a distance.

4. And in conclusion, he would make the final sacrifice.

After that, woe to those who haunted the dreams of the innocent. They would become the targets, always wondering if they were the next to die.

For you, babushka. *I hope it makes you proud.*

Like many of his countrymen, Serpionov had no instruction in the religious writings that once intoxicated his grandparents and great-grandparents. He loved his grandmother, yes. Endured her nagging while under her roof. But her fairy tales? *Nyet.* Those weren't relevant in a world of suicide bombers and power-drunk dictators.

Beslan was no bedtime tale.

That child lurching to his feet was no happy ending.

Did the God in your Scriptures understand sacrifice? To protect others, was He willing to pay the price?

Serpionov turned off his flashlight, stalked outside through the tall grass, and left behind the sweating metal walls of the abandoned Quonset hut.

Detective Meade settled into his family room chair, feet up on that thingy his wife called an ottoman. In her mind, fancy names turned common items into fancy things. Not in his. If he could put his feet on it, there was nothing fancy about it.

Funny how such little stuff could become a distraction.

What he really wanted to know was the where-abouts of a man who fired Russian ammo for a "dart" gun. Three people were dead. Nothing funny there.

"I hope you're hungry," Dawna called from the kitchen.

"Mm-hmm. Where's Dawnequa?"

"At a friend's. Told them to have her back by nine, since it's a school night, but that means you and I have the house to ourselves for a while."

"What's she doing over there?" he said. "Do we know this friend?"

"Relax, Reggie. Dee's a smart girl. They're just watching *The Notebook*."

"Never heard of it. Is that a video?"

"Video? No, babe. We call them DVDs these days, remember?"

Grinning, he channel-surfed with the volume on mute. Sure, he knew they were DVDs, but why should he update his terminology every six months to keep up with the times? He had enough hamster wheels to keep spinning as it was.

"You hear what I said?" Dawna poked her head through the kitchen doorway. "We have the house to ourselves, and aren't you off work tomorrow?"

Today's casework was still heavy on his mind,

but at least some loose ends had been tied off. Abby had been found, and Freddy's body searched. It was interesting, though, that Abby was seen leaving a condo leased by a Shield employee. Shield Technologies had a lot to gain by the passage of a certain bill.

You're off work. You hear that, Detective? You're—

He tried again.

You hear that, Reggie? Don't even think about that office junk.

"House is ours?" he said aloud. "Mmm, you know, I like the sound of that."

Dawna sauntered forward, hips swaying, big brown eyes zeroed in on him. With exaggerated motions, she pulled his phone from his jacket, powered it off, and set it on the end table. He felt unarmed. Out of the loop. All of that faded, though, as she placed a hand on his chest and planted her lips on his.

Chapter Fifty-nine

Natalie swallowed hard. Reuben was beside her on the bench, studying her in the darkness, while Darcy stood before her as casual as could be. Natalie jolted to her feet to avoid the eyes of the man she loved.

The man she had deceived.

"Yeah," she said. "I mean, it's not like I know Darcy real well, but we met through the Temans. After a Sunday service, I think it was."

"Actually, I first heard of Natalie through the prayer chain."

That surprised Natalie.

"Not that I'm in the chain," Darcy added. "But word gets around. When I learned of the turmoil this young lady endured as a captive . . . Well, I suppose my heart went out to her. And I won't deny, she seemed a perfect candidate for our company's technology. Her 'Shot at Protection.' "

"You've given her an implant?" Reuben said.

"I've done nothing of the sort."

"No implants here," Natalie agreed. "Meade scanned me at the benefit."

"And until new laws pave the way, I'm not authorized to go that far, am I, Representative?" Darcy arched a penciled brow. "I only wish she *were* Shielded."

"Well, that may soon be an option. I still have some concerns, but nothing insurmountable. I don't want her, or others like her, to suffer without reason."

"Pleased to hear it, Mr. King." Pastor Teman stepped closer, his wife at his side. "When Darcy brought us out tonight, who would've guessed we'd find you here? Why, it seems preordained. How about joining us for some coffee and final prayer at the Belle Meade Starbucks?"

"Coffee sounds good." He looked to Natalie. "What do you say?"

She shrugged, a little uncomfortable with this scenario. Preordained? Like this was God's hand at work? She suspected it wasn't as benign as that.

"Actually, if Natalie's tired, I could give her a ride home," Darcy said.

"I'd still like some time with my date," Reuben reacted. "I simply thought, in light of the breaking news . . ."

"*¿Que?*" Natalie frowned. "What news?"

Rhonda Teman filled the silence. "Oh, honey, we're so sorry. We heard it only moments after the show, on our phones. It seems your friend from Trevecca's finally been found."

"Found." Her heart dropped. "What's that mean?"

"Not far from here, in Percy Warner Park. A gunshot is what they say."

"Abby. As in, Abigail Stark? No. Please, no."

"Our condolences, Natalie. It's truly heart-breaking."

She felt something tweak deep within. Since her mother's memorial, she had done her best to restrain this anger, this fear and resentment. She'd moved on, looked ahead. Stopped shaking her fist at the heavens. In this one moment, though, the dam gave way, and all those old feelings came flooding back.

"Condolences," she said in a flat tone. "What's that even mean?"

"Such things are difficult," Rhonda said. "But we have to trust—"

"Trust. Right. Trust God, since He's up there doing *nothing*."

Reuben reached for her hand.

She jerked away. "Trust. Oh, right. Since *you* can tell me all about that."

Pastor Teman said, "Careful, Natalie, lest cruelty becomes a substitute for your pain."

"*I'm* cruel? Did I shoot her? Did I leave her in the park? Did I ask to raise my own sister while my mother was lying dead in some park too, rotting away for years until someone found her? Yeah, I'm the cruel one. No, I'm *angry.* I'm ticked *off!* Where's God in all this, huh? A million light-years away, just watching, wishing He could do something? That does *not* work for me." Natalie spun toward Darcy. "Would you *please* take me home? I am so over this."

With Natalie buckled into the BMW's passenger seat, Darcy headed east on Old Hickory Boulevard. They passed through the lower end of Percy Warner, where stone fences and lines of trees stood as black sentinels on the park's rolling hills. Somewhere up in there, a corpse had been discovered.

Darcy accelerated, moving toward Franklin Pike.

Still not a word from her passenger. She seemed

to be a fried circuit board, a tripped breaker, no longer able to conduct feelings.

Darcy was pleased with the way things had transpired. The original plan had involved the Temans coaxing Reuben into last-minute prayers, while she pulled Natalie aside for an update on her boyfriend's state of mind. Instead, Reuben had stated his decision for all to hear. Yes, Representative King was getting ready to hand Darcy the keys to the technological kingdom.

Good-bye, Jack Norwood. So long, Storinka Defense Systems.

Eyes fixed out the window, Natalie spoke in monotone. "I did it."

"You certainly did."

"I used him."

"And once the vote's confirmed tomorrow, you'll receive your $32,000. No more loans. No more debt. I'll never contact you again, never call or text. You'll be free to pursue a career and a relationship without your financial burden."

The BMW hummed north on Franklin and turned east onto Harding Place. The traffic was light this Thursday evening. They were passed by a Metro patrol car, and then Darcy steered onto Trousdale. Only a few more blocks to go.

"Will this bill actually protect children, Ms. Page?"

"Shielded like never before. I believe whole-heartedly in our product."

"I should've told him." Natalie had an elbow on the windowsill, her knee bouncing up and down. "I mean, I never knew that he'd fall in love with me."

"Don't second-guess it, Natalie. What you did was similar to the job of any paid lobbyist, and they're perfectly legal. Watch most any advertising, and you'll see how emotions are used to impact decisions in the brain. Here, you were that emotional connection. Two small-town kids, single and attractive, in politics and education. There's no science to such things, but it seemed a good gamble."

"A $32,000 gamble."

"Precisely. And you helped him reach an informed decision."

Chapter Sixty

With the Shield remote unit in hand, Serpionov had a small yet clear view of Natalie's coordinates. The red circle slid along the amber grid, following the mapped line of Trousdale Drive.

Four blocks away. Three.

The kickstand was down, and his motorcycle was hidden by these corner shrubs a few houses from Natalie's rental. Her sister lived there too, but he hadn't seen her for days. Eli, now he was another story. This older man came and went on an erratic schedule, seeming to have undeclared plans of his own.

One block away.

Dressed in his black-and-red riding leathers, Serpionov watched Darcy's BMW glide around the corner and into the drive behind the faded-blue Civic. Natalie exited, trudged zombie-like to her door, and let herself in. The porch light came on, and the BMW left the same way it came.

He trotted across the street to Natalie's door and knocked. She would assume her ride had returned for a last word or a forgotten item.

As expected, the door swung open.

"Natalie," he said.

She tried to slam it shut, but with his boot shoved into the gap, the wooden panel bounced back into her face. She grunted, her nose gushing blood. He stepped inside, fended off her watery-eyed blows, and snaked his right arm around her throat. Cranking it tight with his left, he cut off the carotid artery and the oxygen flow to the brain. Within fifteen seconds, she was out.

An immobilized patient was much easier to tranquilize. With her arms and legs zip-tied around his neck and torso, he carried her limp body to the motorcycle and drove her north to their destination. To other motorists, she must have looked like a woman hanging on for dear life.

Blackness. No, not completely. Blackness pricked by faint light.

Natalie blinked.

Something covered her face.

Her nose throbbed, her jaw felt loose, and her front tooth was chipped. She inhaled, and the air passing over the damaged enamel made her wince.

What happened?

She recalled a door opening, then flying back at her face.

Impact.

Stars exploding.

Arms twining, tightening.

Serpent coils.

Then—

Nothingness.

She tried to assess this situation. Her wrists were bound by thin sharp plastic, and her ankles seemed to be in the same predicament. She was huddled on a hard floor, a metal wall at her back. She was gagged and couldn't breathe right, not with this material that cut into the corners of her lips and twisted around the back of her head. When she flexed her mouth to loosen the material or dislodge it, the cloth yanked at the hairs on the back of her neck.

Where am I?

Through the head covering, which she guessed

to be a pillowcase, she detected scents of grass and her own sweat. Of old oil stains and gasoline.

Sounds of moving water. The Cumberland.

And then she knew.

She *knew.*

The hut.

This realization broadsided her with all the force of a fighter's fist. Panic tore at her, and she wanted to scream. But she had learned a year ago how ineffective that was while one was gagged. When she tried to tear herself free, it only tightened the plastic bonds and further cut off her blood flow.

Who's behind this?

Not Magnus. She had seen him die with her own eyes.

What do they want?

Maybe it had to do with Reuben and 6336. Someone had tried to kill him on that turnpike, so maybe now they'd decided to kill her instead. Or hold her hostage and try to force him into a favorable decision.

That seemed ludicrous. Certifiably *loco.* The moment he proved that he had been threatened, blackmailed, or coerced, the results would be nullified and a later vote recast. Darcy Page had already employed Natalie for more subtle methods of influence, and her plan had succeeded.

Thanks to my deceit.

Natalie wanted to die. Just leave her be.

She couldn't face the idea of another ten days of torture in this place. Was God teaching her some sort of lesson? Slapping her down for her doubts and questions? If this was supposed to give her clarity, it was failing to do so. If anything, it seemed to confirm His lack of interest in her piddly life.

"Natalie Flynn."

She recoiled from the sound.

"It's almost midnight, yes? Soon, it is one year from day you were prisoner." The male voice sounded Russian. "It is fitting, I think. This month I have anniversary also, from day I'm in Beslan and watch boys and girls die."

She didn't mean to whimper, and she was ashamed that her reaction came more from her own terror than from his description of what he had seen.

"Don't be afraid," he said. "I want to save children."

She had no idea what he was talking about.

"I need you," he said. "Through you, I'll show military contractor new weapon against terror, you understand? U.S. government, it buys from other countries—France, Italy, Spain, England. Also from Storinka Defense Systems, started by a Ukrainian man who came to this country years ago."

She knew of it. Magnus had died in the lot outside a Storinka warehouse, and Storinka

Defense made the news when it lost contracts with the Pentagon.

What did any of this have to do with her, though? Did he work for Storinka? So long as he kept talking, she might get a better picture of what this was all about and her chances of survival.

"My grandmother, it'll make her happy when I help Ukrainian company. It is your country," he said, "that kills terrorists. Even when no one else helps, America fights these people. But the rats, they still hide in holes. So you'll help me, Natalie. What if we show we can find rats in any hole? Anywhere on earth? It is nice thought, I think. We'll make them all live in fear."

OK. Right. Some Russian guy wants to join the war on terror.

She tasted dried blood around the gag. She coughed, choked on her own saliva. Coughed harder.

"You will not yell?" he said.

She shook her head.

"I take off gag for you, for one minute only."

The sweet rush of air filled her mouth and lungs. It cleared her head, even while pinpointing the chipped tooth. She would need a dentist to look at it, like she could afford one. From previous experience in this place, she knew she was a half mile from any house, maybe farther. Screaming for a second or two would serve no purpose.

"Thank . . . you."

The pillowcase was still in place, but as her pupils dilated, she made out a thick form before her.

"Last year," the form said, "Magnus, he brought you here. He didn't do what our boss tells him, and he hurt you. Now you're part of my plot. It is pity that you die, but this final sacrifice will save others. It makes a better story, yes? Very Russian, with drama and tragedy."

"A sacrifice to save others? Sorry, that's an old story."

"This, it is my story."

"Not very original. God did this one already. In the Bible."

"If it's from Scriptures of my *babushka*, it's only false promises."

"False promises," Natalie spat out. "Yeah, I'm starting to wonder."

But she wasn't about to haul out her list of complaints again, since that only made her sound pathetic. Who needed another whiner around? Everyone's troubles were unique. Yeah, yeah. And in the end, that was what made them all so very much the same.

"What is this sacrifice story?" the Russian asked.

"Seriously?"

"I do not know of it."

She adjusted herself on the ground, tried to keep circulation flowing. "Well, humans had messed things up on earth," she said. "They were

399

dying of sickness and sin, completely hopeless. So God sends His Son, Jesus, to walk on the earth and die in their place. A substitute. He was the final sacrifice."

"Yes." The form nodded. "This is noble plan."

"The whole thing was supposed to bring peace. I mean, Jesus was even called the Prince of Peace. Look around, though. Am I wrong? Seems to me like things've gone way off-track."

"Peace. This is what I want."

"Good luck in this lifetime."

"Minute is over."

She begged for a minute more, but the material snapped tight around her head again, prying apart her lips so that her tongue was forced back against the roof of her mouth. She rolled onto her side, and the floor dug into her hip bones. The plastic ties were thick—like those that the police used for quick restraint—and she found she couldn't move more than six inches from the metal wall.

"*Do svidanya*, Natalie Flynn. You and me, together we will make this a better story."

She yelled through the gag, kicked her feet.

The far door scraped open and shut.

The hut fell silent once more.

And this is Your beautiful plan, God? My mother and friends are taken from me, and I end up back in this hellhole? What sort of story is this?

Her tears ran hot and bitter beneath the pillowcase.

Chapter Sixty-one

September 30

It was 6:48 a.m., and Detective Meade feared for Natalie's life. He had enjoyed last evening with his wife, even managed to turn off his phone, but his scalp prickled as he listened to a message from Greta Slayton.

It seemed the ME's office had agreed to find her a scanner.

And it seemed Freddy C was a squealer, after all.

This had nothing to do with Natalie, not directly, yet Meade's daily job involved gathering odd-shaped pieces of data and fitting them together until the entire puzzle became clear.

Could it be possible?

Could she have been targeted since this time last year?

He remembered that day when Natalie had vanished from East Nashville's Sip Café, and recalled her condition ten days later when she stumbled out to freedom. She had suffered neglect and abuse, and he was one of those who jotted down her litany of aches and pains in a report.

He had also searched out that metal hut at the overgrown airfield, joined by a team of others who combed the scene for clues to the perpetrator's identity.

There had been chains. A five-gallon waste bucket. A cloth gag.

All these corroborated Ms. Flynn's descriptions of her ordeal, and he felt sobered further by the blood spatter that marked her location against a girder.

There was one bit of evidence, though, that had baffled him.

Composite resin.

Just a dab on the floor.

At the time, he'd decided that it was there from the days when the airfield was still in use, from some fuselage repair on a single-prop plane. After Greta's call, he had an entirely different theory.

No two ways about it, he told himself now. *We've got to find Natalie.*

Mardy Flynn loved his girls, yessir. He never meant for any grief to come to them, but he figured he sure enough was to blame for moving their momma to this town. He'd signed up to serve his country at the Y-12 National Security Complex. And in the end, Janet died as a result of the area's high mercury levels.

Why some people were affected and others weren't, that he couldn't explain. He could tell you, though, that the same dang military contractor responsible for his wife's death still had contracts at Y-12, despite repeated scandals, investigations, and cover-ups.

That, he knew, just weren't right. Not far as he was concerned.

Mardy had been cautious during his initial conversations with the Russian fella, but the man was a defector who told horror stories of massacred schoolchildren and showed off high-tech toys. Mardy's suspicions, however, were put fully to rest after that warning that saved the life of Representative King.

"So you'll make contact for me, yes?" said the Russian. "These men and women, these contractors who come every day to Y-12, they trust you. To talk to them, this is not strange from you. You can arrange it, I think."

"Sure 'nuff," he said. "That's something I can do."

Mardy's asking price: *$75,000.*

His finder's fee for a potential multimillion-dollar contract.

Of course, the money wasn't for him. After the grief that he had caused his family, he figured he oughta help Natalie get done with her college debts, and help Tina get a degree of her own.

This was it. This morning he was bringing along the contact from Storinka Defense Systems, the man now beside him in his new Ford Ranger. As a military contractor, Storinka Defense was eager to bump aside other contractors and climb back into bed with the Pentagon. They just needed the right enticement.

A way of killing a specific person, even from halfway round the globe?

A way of targeting terrorists without accidentally killing off a whole goat-herding family or desert wedding party?

Yessir, that was the kinda tool that could do the trick.

Detective Meade tried Natalie's cell phone first, tried Roast next. When neither of those worked, he dialed Reuben King at 7:05 a.m.

"You caught me on my way out," Reuben said. "I'll have this turned off for the next couple of hours while in committee."

"I'm looking for Natalie. Any ideas where I might find her?"

"She should be home. We went to Chaffin's Barn last night, but things got a little heated afterwards, and the news of Abby's death really upset her. Darcy Page, of all people, was also at the show and ended up driving Natalie home."

"If you have Ms. Page's number, I'd appreciate it."

Again, that Shield Technologies link.

Meade had seen Ms. Page's recent interview on NewsChannel 5. She was an advocate of House Bill 6336 and spoke with zeal about offering average citizens above-average security. But how did any of it connect to Natalie?

He called the woman's number, kept his tone nonthreatening.

"Yes, of course," Darcy told him. "I dropped her off, oh, perhaps ten ten, ten fifteen, at her place off Trousdale."

"Mm-hmm. Well, no one's seen or spoken to her since."

"Have you checked the house? Not to cast a bad light on her, being that she's young, but she wasn't in too chipper a mood when I left her. Perhaps she's still sleeping off a few drinks."

Meade journeyed south on I-65 to Harding, made his way to the Trousdale address. At 7:17 a.m., he pulled in behind a Civic and an old camper-pickup.

"Detective," Eli said from the front steps.

"Morning, Eli." They had met a few times in recent years, and Meade appreciated the work this gentleman did at the Temans' church. "How're you?"

"Up'n about."

"That's Natalie's vehicle there, isn't it?"

"Our collection of ole beaters. Quite the sight, eh?"

In his line of work, Meade took note of inconsistencies in a person's words and body language. He noticed, for example, that Eli's casual grin didn't match up with his gray-eyed vigilance. Meade said, "That pickup costs you a bundle in gas, I bet."

"Oh, I got other ways of getting 'round."

"Listen, I'm worried about Natalie. Is she here? May I speak with her?"

"Come on in."

Just that easy?

The older man held open the screen door, gestured down a hall. "I came in late last night, but there's not been a peep from her room since. Go on, knock if you like. That girl, she's always been a hard sleeper, but at least when she comes 'round, she's not too awful mean. Now her sister, that's a whole 'nother story."

"You know them pretty well, I take it."

"Feel responsible for 'em, sure. You coming in?"

The weight in Meade's shoulder holster gave him the assurance to proceed. He stepped inside, past a collection of shoes at the door.

"Cup of coffee, Detective? It's no trouble."

"Let's see if she's here first."

This entire situation felt awkward as Meade announced his presence, called out Natalie's name, and knocked at the appropriate door. No answer. He tried again, louder. Still nothing. Was she simply safe in her bed, fast sleep?

After a third and fourth attempt, he took his cue from Eli's nod and tested the handle. "Ms. Flynn?" he said. "Natalie?"

But the room was empty, the bed made.

"Not there?" Eli said. "So what's all this fuss over anyway?"

"Heard some news earlier that leads me to believe she's in danger."

"Danger?" The older man's eyebrows lifted, forming a single solid line. "Well, you're not the only one worried 'bout her. For some time now, it's seemed to me she was getting herself wrapped up in trouble, just walking right on into it."

"That so?" Meade sensed an opportunity for more information.

"C'mon," Eli urged. "Coffee's hot. Almost seven thirty, and I'm sure ya got stuff to do, so I won't keep you long. Why dontcha sit, have a cup, and tell me whatcha know? First sign I see of her, 'course I'll be sure to pass the word along."

Chapter Sixty-two

Through the long night, Natalie dozed off only a few times. Her bones felt brittle, her muscles sore. Her temples pounded. She stomped her feet to fight off the tingling in her extremities. Lost in her pillowcase shroud, she shivered through the predawn hours, then thawed as the sun's first rays broke through the line of dusty windows at the top of the hut.

It seemed she was reliving the same horror from a year ago.

Why was this happening? Who would bring her back to this spot?

What did the man want from her? A sacrifice?

She shuddered to even think what that meant.

Was there some lesson to be learned? Or was this entire experience a coincidence, just one more event on a meaningless timeline?

Last evening's events played through her thoughts. While she was still upset at Reuben for withholding such important information, she understood his fears. She had concealed things for similar reasons, hadn't she?

Abby's death was a bigger blow. Although Natalie's anger and grief still hovered, she felt minor relief in having answers at last. It was horrible to think of her friend dead, but it was better than not knowing.

Was it fair of Natalie to blame this on God?

Was He the one who put the gun to a college girl's head?

The notion was ludicrous, and yet He hadn't stopped the violence, had He? If such things continued to occur, how could Natalie trust Him to ever intervene? What was the formula, if any? When and how? Why and why not?

She gritted her teeth. Decided to shrug off the bad and list some of the good things of the last year.

The Vreelands.

She loved their family. They had all survived quite an ordeal, hadn't they? They'd welcomed her into their home. Let her borrow their car, share their food.

Eli Shaffokey.

He had given her rides in his camper-pickup. With his help, she now had a house to live in, someplace close to her work.

Mr. Faranzmehr.

He'd extended grace periods with their rent.

Grams, dear Grams.

She was a family pillar, and the early graduation gift had helped Natalie get a car. The Civic was a reliable little vehicle, even if the paintwork was a joke.

Her job as a teacher.

She had made it through college, earned her degree, and landed a position, even if temporary, in the local school system. She loved working with the elementary school kids and hoped for a full-time position soon.

Her position at Roast.

Sure was nice to have a job so close to where she lived and with such good coworkers.

Tuf and Dad.

Through the good and the bad, they were family. Each of them shouldered parts of the load, and it was as important as ever that they cling to each other.

And of course, Reuben King.

Cramped and aching, Natalie found some solace in the memories of his tenderness on the bench last night. He had also spilled his own secrets, taking a huge risk, and he deserved much better than her petty responses. It was true that she had targeted him at the festival, even while question-ing if she should go through with the plan. All she'd really wanted was to pay off her loans, protect the helpless, and get her dad off her back for the night.

Falling in love.

That was where it all went wildly, wonderfully wrong. The meeting of their eyes kindled sparks that still burned.

And last night, in her pain, she had tried to douse them.

Tuf knew she had messed up, with her pot-smoking and attitude and lack of rent money. Sure, she had pulled together a hundred and eighty bucks, which was a lot of paper. Sure, Natalie could have shown a little more appreciation. In the end, though, it was Tuf's fault for putting her sis in this situation.

See here, I'm taking responsibility. Taking care of my own bizness.

Which meant she still owed $220 on the rent.

Tuf had it all figured out. At 7:40 a.m., with cash in her pocket, she had a guy friend drop her off at the elementary school, where she waited in the parking lot for her sister's Civic to pull in. Tuf remembered seeing the confirmation e-mail showing that on this date, at this school, at this time, Ms. Natalie Flynn would sub for the second-grade class.

7:47 a.m. No sign of Natalie.

Now you're running late, sis. Where are ya?

Tuf called her sister's cell and got nothing.

7:55 a.m.

Still nothing.

She joined the flow of elementary kiddos and let them carry her through the school doors. She veered off into the front office, where a spindly man in a green sweater vest greeted her and asked how he might be of assistance.

"It's my sis," Tuf said. "She's s'posed to be here today."

"And what grade is she?"

"Grade? Nah, she's your sub. Ms. Flynn. Dontcha got a schedule?"

"She's on the schedule, yes. And she's late."

"Why d'ya think I'm standing here? Have you heard from her?"

"No, ma'am. Have you?"

She spun back through the doors and scanned the parked cars. This was not like her older sis. Late for supper, well, that was one thing. Late for covering a class, that was a big-time sin for a teacher.

She called her friend. "I need ya back here. We'll run by the house, see if she's there. I don't think she's changed out the locks on me. Least I hope not."

At 8:13 a.m., the Monte Carlo rolled into the lot and Tuf hopped in.

Twenty miles south, at the Hyatt in Cool Springs, Serpionov sat at this post. It was 8:14 a.m. His room shades were drawn, and he was ready to conclude this story.

"The contact is with you, Mardy?" Serpionov asked into the phone as he checked the hallway through the peephole. "You're driving this direction now?"

"You betcha. I s'pose we're not more than an hour out."

"Go direct to place I told you. *Pozhaluista*, do not delay."

"Hey now, wouldn't wanna get myself pulled over, would I? We'll be there, dontcha worry. I'll park outta view like you said, and I'll call when we's just about there. This demonstration, you're sure he's gonna be impressed?"

Serpionov moved back to his desk, touched the screen on the open case, and watched the oblong window appear:

Natalie Flynn, female, age 24
ST-1-12-1799-4328

On the laptop beside the case, wireless Internet allowed him to view a feed from the hut, where Natalie was crouched against the wall.

"Yes," he said, "you'll both see with own eyes. Webcam in hut lets me know when you are there. This demonstration, you can't stop or start it since only I can activate the tag. When this is over, I'll deliver the control case to him, and he will pay. Easier with no paperwork, I think. He has money with him now?"

"Yessir," Mardy said. "He's got it here, done handcuffed it to his arm. Croutons! A half a million dollars. Well, long's I get my $75,000, we won't have no troubles. I'm a man of my word."

Serpionov watched daylight creep into the hut in the live feed, its fingers tugging at Natalie's feet, clawing up her legs.

He said, "Tell this man with you, be ready for good demonstration. All RFID implants have protective gel inside, but this is special tag that holds special gel. When I enter the code, a signal to coil activates heat primer, builds pressure in seconds, and cracks the bioglass. When this happens, drops of ricin, very poisonous, spill out and kill person. Over quick, but very painful."

"You don't mean that we . . . Is it a live person we'll be seeing?"

"Small sacrifice. It is good, I think."

"I don't want no part of—"

"But you do want weapons against terrorists,

yes? With this, an agent can put tag in person's drink to be swallowed. Or CIA doctor, undercover in Afghan clinic, he injects warlord with implant. It can sit for hours or years, but can still kill from thousands of miles away. These butchers, now they'll know what terror is. No place to run or hide. But we must see that it works, yes?"

"Nah, you listen here. I won't be part of nobody getting killed today."

"Then this money, you will not get paid. Then the contractor that causes your wife to die, they will stay in business at Y-12, and nothing changes. This is what you want, Mardy? *Nyet.* I think sacrifice is worth it."

"Nah, what's wrong is wrong, and I'm not gonna—"

"You will go. It's your daughter, Mardy. Natalie is one in hut."

"My girl? What, you're saying *my* girl's the sacrifice?"

"If you send police, she will die. You must not be foolish."

"*You* best not be foolish!" Mardy roared. "If you so much as—"

Serpionov disconnected the call, confident his delivery boy and the military contractor would arrive at the hut sooner than scheduled.

On the laptop, he watched Natalie shift herself into the sunlight the way a flower sought warmth and life. A year ago, she had been tagged in this very spot—not by Serpionov but by Magnus, in his act of rogue experimentation.

I'm sorry, Natalie. This plot, it was the one that unfolded for me.

By killing the man at the airport, Serpionov had learned of Storinka Defense's interest in this new technology. It seemed Shield's rivals were using corporate espionage to steal information. With his own interests at stake, he shifted allegiances from corporate-minded Darcy Page to military-oriented Storinka.

He checked the time. 8:25 a.m.

In the next hour, this would be over.

Of course, loose ends couldn't be left hanging. That's why he had placed a special detonator and extra RFID tag that only he knew about. Once the sacrifice was complete, and once the contact had made his hasty exit, the second half of the timed sequence would ensure a fiery end to the evidence.

Chapter Sixty-three

The Health and Human Resource Committee met behind closed doors in room 16, at 8:30 a.m., on this last Friday in September. With Representative King serving as chairman, they were twenty members strong.

Today's agenda was simple.

As enacted, HB 6336 authorizes hospitals and health care facilities to implant children and patients with FDA-approved microchip technology, for their safeguarding, upon the notarized request of a parent, legal guardian, caregiver, and/or licensed medical practitioner.

For months they had straddled the fence on this, ever since their chairman's stunning opposition in front of the assembly last February. A few had even called for Reuben to step down, while most admired his caution in this matter. Nobody questioned his objectivity, though. And today, his word carried the most weight.

Reuben stood before the nineteen others, removed and folded his jacket over the back of his seat, and thus signaled that work was about to get done. He thought of Natalie and her scars, of the protection this bill might offer.

Would she ever forgive him?

At the moment, he couldn't think about that.

"This is it," he said. "We all know how much attention this bill's received in the media, particularly in light of the recent homicides here in the Capital. I'm sure I'm not the only one who's been bombarded with e-mails, letters, and phone calls. Lobbyists, businesspeople, pastors, even some in the music industry have tossed in their two cents on the issue. If we vote this down today, we keep things as they are, and no one will blame us. If, however, we approve it, we won't stop there. We'll push it straight through the assembly to the governor's desk. If that happens, our names will be linked forever to this historic decision. No more excuses. No more delays. An hour from now, I want us to take our final vote."

Chapter Sixty-four

Mardy gripped the steering wheel of his new Ford Ranger, tendons twanging along his forearms as he drove past Percy Priest Dam toward the skyline of downtown Nashville. It was just past eight-thirty, and the traffic here was thicker. At the rate they were going, he figured he would be pulling up near that old airfield a half hour from now.

He tried Natalie's number. No answer. He told himself this was a joke, that his Duckie couldn't be stuck in some hut just waiting to be killed where she sat.

But that Russian fella, he wasn't the joking sort.

What fool mess have ya got her into now? Mardy asked himself.

He racked his brain for options, but the time frame was short and the Russian held all the cards, didn't he? From wherever the man was sitting right now, he could end a life simply by sending a signal with a few taps at his little keyboard.

Sounded awfully good when it was them terrorists being targeted.

Not so good now that Natalie was in the sights.

"Whatcha think?" Mardy said. "You think it actually works?"

Beside him, the contact from Storinka Defense Systems didn't seem to give a care, just cradled that dang briefcase full of money in his lap.

"I'm talking to you, sir. It's my girl's life on the line."

"I hear you," the man said. "And yes, I'm sure it works. I've seen its other applications in fine form, and have every reason to believe a military-grade option is just as effective. If not, I've burned all my bridges with nowhere left to go."

"Me, I dunno 'bout no bridges. Just help me save my girl."

"Do you know who I am?" the man said.

"Mr. Hammond, with Storinka Defense. You drove past my booth a coupla times, so I oughta know your name."

"Storinka Defense wants back into the fold, that's right. And with my military background, I've helped them open that door. They'll be a player again."

"Could be. I dunno."

"Of course, if Darcy Page knew any of this, she'd fire me."

"That woman that works at Shield?"

"Now you see what I mean about burning bridges. Five years I've been there for her, and does she notice? Not really. It's all about her kingdom, built on the backs of those doing all the work. I'd love to see her face when she realizes what I've snatched from beneath her icy nose."

Mardy was no stranger to stories of corporate espionage. Right now, though, not one word of it mattered to him. The interstate was taking them closer to East Nashville. To his girl.

"Mr. Hammond, you can have your weapon," he said. "Even keep my part of the money. Just please, tell the Russian we don't want no demonstration. Not a live one. Tell him ya don't want no part in it."

"But I do."

"You—"

Mardy stopped, realizing the man had a gun aimed at him.

"Keep driving," Hammond said. "Driving this truck that should've been mine. That's right. I went to Mr. King, gave him the impression that Darcy Page was behind the bombing of his car. An attempt to discredit her and her company, and to shift blame. Did he buy it, though? I thought so, but when it came time to hand out a reward, you ended up with a new truck. Go figure."

"You want it? Go on, then. It's yours. I'll sign over the title."

"Not a Ford man," Hammond said.

"Just help me call off this demonstration. That's all I'm asking, OK?"

"You think I don't want to see that this weapon works? I'm investing $500,000 of Storinka's money. That's on me. My rise to the top. And of course, *I'm* not going to set up a demonstration on a live human. That would be wrong."

"It *is* wrong. Croutons in a bucket, you fool! My daughter's life is at stake."

"I didn't put the chip there. I'm not pushing the buttons."

"*Call* him! Or see if I don't drive off the road and kill the both of us."

"Sure." Hammond shrugged. "And leave your girl without her dad?"

Tuf's key still worked. Barging into the Trousdale rental at 8:39 a.m., she almost tripped over the shoes by the door as she called out her sister's name. The Civic was parked in the driveway, but there was no answer.

"Sis, where are you? Natalie?"

The place was empty.

A phone rang. Rang again.

Tuf followed the sound, thinking it strange that someone had left the house without it. She found Natalie's cell peeking out from a tennis shoe by the front door. Like she'd just dropped it there by accident. Speaking of accidents, was that a drop of blood on the shoe's toe? Sure looked like it from here.

The phone was still ringing.

"Yeah, whatcha want?" Tuf barked into it.

"Tina? Whatcha doing with Sis's phone? Is she there with you?"

"Hey, Dad. Nope, I'm trying to find her. You know, maybe she canceled everything for that meeting her boyfriend's part of."

"Tuf, listen. Are you OK? Tell me you're OK."

"I'm OK."

"Good. You stay put. Don't have time to feed ya details, but Sis, she's in a mess, and I don't want nothing happening to you. You hear what I'm saying?"

"Sure, Dad. Whatever."

She meant it too, but then she got to scrolling through Natalie's texts and missed calls. Wasn't it every little sister's job to nose around in her big sister's stuff? Came with the territory, right? Her attention was nabbed by a text from Darcy Page. Wasn't she the one all over the news of late? What was she doing acting all chummy with Natalie?

The text was a few days old. Friday's almost here. Friendly yet firm, don't forget. Don't let boyfriend off the hook.

Tuf changed her mind about staying put. She dashed back out to her friend in the Monte Carlo and told him to get her downtown "right quick."

●●●

Detective Meade broke free from the downtown traffic, caught Ellington Parkway to Hart Lane, and bumped into the lot of the Medical Examiner's Office. He parked his unmarked sedan with government plates, noted the time on the dash.

8:44 a.m.

Perhaps his hurry was wasted. But Natalie Flynn was nowhere to be found, and that had an ominous sound to it against the backdrop of yesterday's discovery at Percy Warner.

Meade was barely through the front doors when Greta Slayton greeted him and handed over a hard plastic case.

"Much appreciated," he said.

"Sign your life away." She held up a clipboard. "The scanner? Nearly $400. If you lose it, the ME will not be happy. The batteries aren't fresh, but they're good enough for government work."

"Thanks, Greta. Might be a waste of time, but I'm going with a hunch."

"Tsk-tsk." She wagged a finger. "Detectives only do that in books. In real life, they go by facts."

"Even facts get misinterpreted. It's the truth that I'm after."

A grin spread across her purple lips.

He never could tell if the purple was natural, painted on, or a result of working in cold rooms.

Fact: They were purple. Truth: He wasn't about to ask.

"Anyway," he said, "it's someone else's hunch, not mine. Tell me, what'd you find out about the tag's manufacturer?"

"The components come from three different companies, and they're assembled by Shield Technologies. I could be reaching here, but the tag has the capacity to be used as a weapon. In fact, one of the companies was responsible back in World War II for mass-producing poison gas."

"Poison gas."

"The stuff Hitler used to kill Jews."

The very thought sickened Meade. And infuriated him.

He thanked her again, and returned to the lot where Eli's camper-pickup was now parked amid a settling cloud of exhaust. The detective coughed, passed the case through Eli's window. "There're instructions in there. Just be careful with it. And let's hope our theories are wrong, huh?"

"Reckon I feel the same. Best thing to do is find her."

The detective held up a hand, pulled his phone from his pocket. He had a message stating that a Hyatt Place desk clerk in Cool Springs believed she had seen the man from the e-blast pics. And yes, he had a strong accent. Today was the last day this man was booked in room 422.

"Have to run, Eli. Try looking for Natalie in all of her usual spots."

In the hut's warmth and stillness, Natalie pushed back the panic crowding her thoughts. She was hot with this pillowcase on her head. She was hungry. She had to pee. Her entire body was stiff from a night of trying to get comfortable.

She recalled her own words to her captor:

"The Prince of Peace . . . Good luck in this lifetime."

This world could sure use some peace, on that she and her captor agreed. She also realized how immature it was to blame God for the actions of humans, since everyone had to accept their own responsibility. Heck, she dealt with that sort of childish blame every time she taught a class of third graders.

OK, fine.

She got that.

Where, though, was the peace in a world of kidnappers and rapists and terrorists? When did the Prince of Peace step in? Was there ever a time He intervened, or was humanity basically on its own while on this planet? "But hey," people said, "keep that chin up, least you have heaven to look forward to."

A great reward, sure. A nice exit plan.

But right now, Abby's death was an immediate horror for family and friends, a senseless crime.

And Natalie and Tuf knew the reality of living a lifetime without a mother. Children and spouses were facing abuse at this very moment across this one state alone.

How do You watch it all and do nothing?

If Natalie were God, able to see all that went on, she would be in a rage.

Ready to scream her lungs out. To lash out.

WHERE WERE YOU?

Her own cry in the Oak Ridge Forest.

Natalie rolled her shoulders, stretched her neck. She didn't want to be a bitter person. She really didn't. The first time she had watched *Anne of Avonlea* with some college girlfriends, she'd vowed never to become like that tight-laced schoolteacher who was poisoned with resentment and regret.

And here I am, twenty-five next month, and already clinging to stuff.

Branches creaked in the breeze outside, and birds chirped back and forth, oblivious to her situation.

A year ago, she had been in this same space and known only bits and pieces about the Bible and a relationship with God. She huddled here feeling abandoned and utterly alone, some of the emotions she'd faced since girlhood.

In the months after stumbling to freedom, she'd studied and memorized Scripture with the Vreelands. What was that section in Matthew 10?

"Don't be afraid of those who want to kill you . . . Not even a sparrow, worth half a penny, can fall to the ground without your Father knowing it. And the very hairs on your head are all numbered."

These verses should be a comfort, shouldn't they?

The birds outside continued chirping.

But all she could think of was Abby, left to rot just like Natalie's mother in the woods. They'd both fallen to the ground, hadn't they?

And the Heavenly Father knew it.

You knew it, and You didn't send anyone to help.

Shrouded in the pillowcase, Natalie became aware of every pebble digging into her skin, every hair pinched by the gag, each dry spot on her lips. Her jaw ached. Her teeth hurt. Her stomach twisted. The entire world seemed to collapse upon this one square yard in which she was trapped, and she didn't feel any sense of God's presence within or without.

She was alone, wasn't she?

Based on the Russian's farewell last night, she knew her captor wasn't coming back. Maybe that was his "plot," as he called it: to leave her here to rot like the others.

Natalie squeezed her hands and tried to pull them from the zip ties, but this cinched the plastic a notch tighter and cut at the skin on her wrist bones. She tried to shake free of the pillowcase. She moved her feet along the floor, hoping to find some metal or glass shard she could use to saw through her bindings.

Nothing. *Nothing.* NOTHING.

Then she heard it. A large engine rumbling toward her direction.

Chapter Sixty-five

Mardy followed the directions on his phone, curling from I-40 onto I-24 and down an off-ramp into East Nashville. His Ford Ranger sure took the ruts in this road a whole lot better than his old Bronco, and he sped along Shelby Avenue.

"Slow it down," Hammond said from the passenger seat.

"Looks to me, I'm the one driving."

"And I'm holding a loaded Beretta."

Mardy cast a glance at the black fella, whose hand was all too comfortable round that pistol grip. Hammond was dressed in a reddish brown suit over a shirt the color of a pumpkin. With those clothes, looked like he was fixin' to be in some fall parade.

"It's my girl." Mardy checked his screen, turned onto Eastland. "The thought of her trapped all over again, I'm telling ya, it's not right."

"Then don't get pulled over. Or is that your hope, that maybe you can sneak a message to a cop. Listen, that aw-shucks mentality doesn't fool me. I know it doesn't take a genius to work a security booth, but Y-12 doesn't exactly let idiots wander around either. Both hands on the wheel. Keep to the speed limit, and I'll feed you the directions."

"Yessir. We're looking for Shadow Lane."

9:06 a.m. Just about there.

Rosebank swung them round toward Airpark Drive, and it hit Mardy then where they were headed. He had never been to the site where Natalie was held prisoner last year, and she had never wanted to go back, but the reports listed it as Cornelia Fort Airpark.

Was this the same place? What fool game was going on here?

"Make sure to park it a few blocks away," Hammond said. "A walk'll do us good."

The door scraped open, a horrible sound that flooded Natalie with memories of Magnus and his nightly visits with the antenna. She cowered, even more terrified by the fact that she couldn't see who it was this time.

Steps, shuffling closer. Labored breathing.

She stiffened.

"Natalie?"

That voice . . .

What is he doing here?

"Shhh, now. I'm gonna need ya to stay still."

The gag came loose. Next, the pillowcase was lifted from her matted hair and left wet strands clinging to her nose and lips. She blinked, pupils adjusting to the daylight that spilled across this side of the hut. It was almost blinding. The dusty air, the smell of gasoline, the musty grass scent—it all swirled about her.

She had herself a rescuer, and that made her smile. "Eli? I don't know how you found me. Guess you can tell me later, but let's get out of here."

"Not so fast." Thick brows hooded his eyes as he set down a tool bag.

"Least cut me loose. I can barely move, and my legs're fast asleep."

"Got a lil' something needs doing first."

"What? Really?" She worked saliva into her dry mouth. "Your tool bag there. I'm sure you have a knife in it, don't you? Just cut me loose."

"Shhh, Natalie. Be still."

"You're not helping me get out of here?"

"I might need for ya to be held down, case it gets too painful."

Dread rose in her now. She had misjudged Magnus last year, and never even suspected Reuben's secret past. Heck, she didn't know all the deceits in her own heart. So what had she missed about Eli? Her thoughts skipped from one time to another to another when she had caught him watching her, or listening in on her conversations, or tagging along behind her. Each time the questions arose, she had brushed them aside. He was her friend, right? Her housemate. Nobody to fear.

But now . . . What didn't she know about sweet gray-eyed Eli?

"OK," she said, trying to keep her tone light. "Least tell me what you're doing. You can do that much, right?"

The older man squatted beside her, brushed the hair out of her face with one hand, and turned her chin away with the other.

"Hello?"

"I've gotta hurry," he said, avoiding her gaze. "But this might take a bit."

She watched him lift a handheld device from his bag, noticed it was similar to the one she and the detective had used at the benefit concert earlier in the week. Eli held down the Power button, and she saw the LCD display light up.

"Just gotta check," he said. "Just a hunch of mine, that's all."

"That I have an implanted chip or something?" When he nodded, she said, "Nope, I was cleared already. Listen, we don't—"

"Hold still."

Instead of letting the device sniff along her arms or legs, he pointed it toward her mouth, which didn't make any sense. Didn't he know how to operate the thing? All you had to do was—

Skeweee, skeweee . . .

" 'Natalie Flynn,' " he read off the display. "Oh, not good." He had her chin in his hand again, fingers hooked into her mouth. He pried it open, peered in with a Maglite from his bag. "Yep, must be that one there. Clear on near the back."

"Eees eennma tooff?"

"Reckon so. That's how they done it with Freddy C."

With her head angled away by his work-toughened hand, she spotted the thin glow of a laptop about fifteen feet away, open on top of a big oil barrel, with the eye of a webcam pointed her way. She didn't know what was going on with this talk of Freddy and her tooth, but she had to say something.

"Uh, Eli? Over there. Looks like we're being watched."

He turned on one knee. Squinted through dusty sunbeams. In a movement quicker than she knew he was even capable of, he dropped his stuff into the tool bag and shimmied away with it toward the hut's darkest corner.

Seconds later, the door on the other side screeched open again.

It was 9:09 a.m., and the cleaning staff was moving room by room up the corridor. The faint vibrations of a vacuum hummed through the flooring. There was chatter and light laughter.

And every bit of it gnawed at his nerves.

Serpionov pushed away from the desk and his electronica, marched over to the door, and slipped the DO NOT DISTURB sign over the outer doorknob to discourage any interruptions. He still had nearly two hours until checkout.

More than enough time.

Soon he would hear from Mardy and the Storinka Defense contact. They would wade through the grass to the hut, watch the demonstration, and then he and the contact would meet elsewhere to exchange the funds and the Shield case.

For Serpionov, this was less about the money and more about the chance to get advanced antiterrorist weaponry into the hands of a military willing to use it. He didn't care how it filtered through Y-12, so long as the Americans could strike fear into the enemies of peace. In the process, Storinka Defense Systems would benefit as the contractor, thus rebuilding their reputation.

And you, babushka, *you'll have reason to be proud of Ukrainian roots.*

It was almost time.

He used the toilet, washed his hands, and grabbed a bottle of water from the mini fridge. On his way back to the desk, he detoured for a peek through the shades at the day and its activity in the parking lot below.

Cars swung beneath the hotel entryway,

followed by airport shuttle vans and personal SUVs. Then a clean, unremarkable vehicle raced into the lot from the street. As it moved past his fourth-story window, he saw that it bore government plates such as those used by diplomats or unmarked police cars.

This car, it was probably nothing.

Nevertheless, Serpionov reclosed the shade, double-checked the locks and chain on the door, and opened his cell phone with its small-caliber barrels. He had three rounds left, three 5.45 × 18mm rounds. It would have to be enough.

As he stalked back to the laptop and the black case, he dialed Mardy Flynn's number to see if they had arrived.

Chapter Sixty-six

"Dad?"

"That you, Duckie? You all right?"

Natalie didn't know how her dad had found her, but relief swelled through her. The man behind her father, a short black man, remained on the far edge of the daylight. From where she sat, only his legs and his polished shoes were clearly visible. She was still bound, still unable to move, but she had her vision and voice.

Eli's presence on the far end of the Quonset hut

was obscured even more by the swirling curtain of light than by the darkness. He wasn't saying anything, which implied he wanted to stay hidden.

Was he working with her enemy?

Should she alert her father to his presence while she had the chance?

"Dad, please just get me out of here. I'm going to pee myself, and I'm starved, and I have no idea when the guy who attacked me is coming back."

Her dad started toward her.

"Whoa there, Mr. Flynn," the other man told him. "I dare you to move any closer to your daughter. I know I don't look very intimidating, but I spent seven years in the army and my aim is good. At this distance, my Beretta'd knock you down like an elephant gun."

Natalie's mind was now spinning. Somehow she seemed to be at the center of this. She tried not to look in Eli's direction, though he appeared to be her best option for help. His detection of a tag in her tooth worried her. When had it been put there? She hadn't even been to a dentist in a long year or two.

A cell phone rang.

"Should I get that, Mr. Hammond?" Mardy said. "The number, it's his."

His? Whose?

"Turn around where I can see you," Hammond said. "Slowly. Now answer it."

• • •

At 9:14 a.m., Serpionov studied the laptop's webcam and pressed his phone to his ear. "You didn't call," he said. "Why is it you don't call?"

"Sir, we done just got through the door."

"A minute or two is not 'just got through the door.' I see you've already taken gag and cover from your daughter's face." Serpionov scolded himself for wasting those two or three minutes to secure the room, relieve himself, and check the parking lot.

"Please," Mardy Flynn said. "I don't want no trouble. All I ask's that you don't hurt my girl."

"But she is sacrifice."

"What you're talking 'bout's against the law, and I can't abide by that."

"Bah. Sometimes it's necessary, yes, violence to stop violence? If nobody fights Hitler, we would all march goose step today and wear swastikas."

"This is America. And me, I'm proud of that fact."

"You do not study history? Perhaps you should learn lesson about how U.S. military experimented with biological warfare. Is it surprise that military contractor wants to see this weapon work, even if one girl dies? *Nyet.* Only a surprise to fools too weak to fight the bullies of the world. America is not weak, though. This is why I come here to find solution. To make way for better future, yes?"

"Listen, you wanna talk 'bout fighting the bad guys, I'm gung-ho. I want that same thing. But my girl, she don't deserve none of what you got planned."

Serpionov knew his grandmother would also disapprove, but even her God of Scripture knew He had to make a sacrifice. His very own son. It was hard enough to sacrifice yourself, but to sacrifice someone you loved—this was deep courage. This was a God he could admire.

His grandmother's words: *Your name is already inscribed upon the palm of God's hand . . . God hears and He whispers your name.*

Serpionov liked such sentiments.

Whispers, though, would not drown out the Beslan shrieks in his ears.

On the live feed, the view was hazy. He told Mr. Flynn, "You and contact, please move toward camera. I want everyone in picture for demonstration."

He heard the instructions being passed along, and also heard movement in the corridor outside his hotel room. Was the unmarked car sending up an officer? Or was it—?

The squeak of a cart and the giggles of the cleaning staff filled in the picture for him. He took precautions anyway, arming his weapon with the code.

"Yes," he said into the phone. "Yes, this is good."

On the screen, the forms were visible in the

hut's wavering light, and a dark face materialized, one belonging to Darcy Page's assistant and rumored lover.

"Bigz?" Serpionov grinned at this revelation. "He is contact?"

"Sir?"

"Tell Mr. Hammond hello for me."

So this explained the corporate leak at Shield Technologies. The man killed last December in airport parking was probably sent by Mr. Hammond to snatch the case from under Ms. Page's nose. Instead, Serpionov succeeded where that man failed and, in the end, circled the case back to her rival anyway. This, it now made sense. Yes, of course, it all fit.

Another twist for his story's plot.

"Actually, Mr. Flynn, let me speak to Hammond."

A pause. "Hello?"

"Bigz, so it is you. This is good, I think. We are proud partners."

"And you are de Russian. Your fame precedes you."

"*Spasibo*." He flushed with pleasure. "Thank you. Now, are you ready for me to demonstrate weapon's ability? I think first you need make sure Mr. Flynn doesn't try to be hero. Tie him close to Natalie. It is best that you send him on journey along with his daughter, or he'll be trouble for us later, I think. She will die when I send signal to RFID tag embedded in her tooth. It'll be sad story, but with tragic beauty, yes?"

Again, there was movement outside the door.

"Tie Mardy up," Serpionov said. "And be ready."

"Consider it done."

At 9:16 a.m., Detective Meade entered the hallway, fourth floor of the Hyatt Plaza, in Cool Springs. He'd arrived minutes earlier, pulse throbbing in his neck after the ninety-mile-per-hour race from Ellington Parkway in the north to this bedroom community south of Greater Nashville. The desk clerk stated that she was 99 percent certain the man in the e-blast photo was Stepan Serpionov in room 422.

Serpionov. So that was his name.

Meade knew he should wait for backup. He also knew this man was very likely responsible for three homicides in the past nine months.

Well, don't be his fourth.

Everything in Meade's training told him it was a poor choice to proceed, but proceed he did. He had his Glock drawn, a round chambered, with fourteen more in the clip. His badge was in hand, and he waved it at the woman just arriving in the elevator. She let the doors close.

A cleaning cart sat alone at the far end of the hall.

There was the door. Room 422.

Natalie still wasn't sure who to trust. Was Eli involved in this? What did he carry in that tool

438

bag? And why was her father entangled in all of it?

She did realize, though, that it all centered on her.

How? She had no clue. The tag in her tooth?

She ran her tongue along her back molars, feeling for anything different. She remembered the pain in her teeth a year earlier, the soreness in her entire jaw. She had attributed it to being clobbered from behind while being captured, but she'd also been passed out for a significant gap of time afterward.

And that left room for other possibilities.

Natalie saw Magnus's confident smile, almost a smirk, and thought again of his parting words: *What is our word? Shouldn't be hard to forget . . . Keep those antennae up.*

Had he planted one of these RFID tags on her?

Radio frequency ID.

Antennae.

She had seen pictures of the flattened copper coils, the antennae at the core of each tag's performance. Was it that obvious? Was it even possible? Had he popped out an old filling in her mouth and refilled it with that composite resin that was so popular these days, letting it harden over an encoded tag?

It would certainly explain how he had managed to monitor her whereabouts all those months, even while she lived with the Vreelands.

Her eyes slid toward the shadows in the far corner. Eli said that Freddy C had also had an implant in a tooth. Probably given to him at that clinic. It seemed this had tipped off Detective Meade, who passed the word along. She still wasn't sure what Eli meant to do with such info, though.

"Move." The short black man had zip-tied her father's hands and feet. He frog-marched him toward a spot along the wall. "Sit here," he said.

Mardy stood ramrod straight, until his knees were swept with a sudden kick, and he landed on the hard floor. His stare was flint-hard and proud as he turned toward her. "I'm sorry," he said. And then his eyes softened as they moved to the wall beside her. "You . . . you never told me 'bout that."

She turned and saw her faded words, still scratched into the metal:

Always your girl, Dad — Duckie

"That was just in case," she said. "Only if the worst were to happen."

"Let's hope that's not right now."

Detective Meade knocked. "Metro Police."

Nothing.

"Metro Police. We'd like a word with you, Mr. Serpionov."

Still not a sound.

440

Aiming his heel at the portion just below the door handle, Meade struck the DO NOT DISTURB tag with three-quarter force. He stepped back, delivered a harder kick that splintered wood, ruined the key-card slider, and probably merited an official wrist-slap for acting without authorization.

He thought of Freddy C.

Of Abby.

The third kick snapped the chain from its slide and blew the door inward. Weapon braced with both hands, the detective moved forward in a crouch. He spotted an open laptop, and a slender black case with a glowing amber grid.

The desk chair had been pushed back and left empty.

As far as Darcy Page was concerned, the meeting and the vote were formalities. With Pastor Teman beside her, she waited in the seating area on the lower level at Legislative Plaza, positioned to catch movement from the rooms in either direction. On the wall across from her, the clock said 9:21 a.m.

She had managed quite a feat to reach this point. While some consumer groups protested the use of RFID tags in grocery stores and malls, the average consumer didn't know or care. But wide-scale human microchipping? Now that was an entirely different challenge.

All a matter of marketing. Of perception. And that was her forte.

Product: Secured Human Identification, Encrypted Lifetime Device.

Price: $180, varying between hospitals and private clinics.

Placement: In clinics, hospitals, and insurance facilities statewide.

Promotion: "Shield Yourself" materials and "Your Shot at Protection" TV ads.

People: Whether dead (Abby) or alive (Natalie and Pastor Teman), people were key to stirring proper fears and dispelling unhealthy ones. The padding of feet yanked Darcy out of her self-congratulatory trance. She glanced up and spotted a short, platinum-haired woman scurrying down the hall. The movement alerted a female security guard in the nearby screening area.

"Ma'am, please no running. *Ma'am.*"

Darcy and the pastor exchanged a glance, then followed the young woman at a brisk walk. They watched her burst through the doors of room 16, where twenty committee members reacted with cries of fear and confrontation.

"Reuben!" the girl called out, her breath ragged. "It's me, Tuf. I need to . . . Don't touch me, people! Tell 'em it's OK, Reuben. Thank you. So the thing is, this is all wrong. This vote's got strings being pulled every which way, and now 'cause of all that, your dear Natalie's missing."

Chapter Sixty-seven

His girl, his baby girl. She'd gone on without her momma, done the best she could and got herself a college degree. Just didn't seem right to have it end like this.

Mardy stared at those words on the wall again.

She had been here. Ready to die.

And she'd thought of him.

No way he was going to let it end now without a fight. If they aimed to kill her anyhow, well then, he would keep it interesting. That was what that Russian fella wanted, wasn't it? A story that kept your interest.

Fifteen feet away, Mr. Hammond stood by the webcam with Mardy's cell in his hand. He was asking what the delay was and how long he would have to wait. A delay? That there was the best news all day, and there was no more waiting left, not for a man who wanted to protect his daughter.

Mardy knew he couldn't break free of these doggone zip ties. He'd used them himself in training classes and seen how tough they were. What he could do was cause a commotion. Cause a stink. Sure, he could do that. He saw gas cans lined up along the far wall. That would be good for a distraction, if he could light a fire. But he didn't have no lighter, and he would be shot by the time he got that far.

Best thing was straight ahead.

He braced his back against the wall, got his feet up under him, and worked his body halfway up. With all his strength coiled in his thighs, he exploded forward in great leaping hops, aiming for Mr. Hammond in his reddish brown suit and pumpkin shirt and that phone still pushed against his ear as he waited.

Hammond pivoted toward him. "What're you doing?" he barked. "I warned you not to move."

Up came the Beretta.

"Dad," Natalie cried. "Watch out!"

Detective Meade found Serpionov reclined on the hotel's king-sized bed, casual as could be. The man had a phone to his ear, and he nodded as though it was commonplace for him to ignore doors being kicked in and police invading his room.

"Mr. Serpionov."

"*Pozhaluista*," the man said, covering the mouthpiece with a wide hand. "This call is important, yes?"

Detective Meade admired his cool and bravado. Was this all a mistake?

He scanned the room and catalogued its contents in two sweeps, the bed, the dresser, the Gideon Bible opened on the far nightstand, the computer items on the desk, dress shoes placed side by side near the table. The TV was on but muted, and the alarm clock said it was 9:23 a.m. The shades were drawn. He had already cleared the bathroom and the vanity area, as well as the entry closet.

No signs of a Drotik gun.

Easy to conceal, remember? Perhaps in a drawer. Under the pillow.

"Just me and you, huh?" he said to the thick-chested Russian, keeping his Glock at the ready. The man's physique was that of someone fresh out of the military. "Go on and end the call so I can ask you some questions."

Serpionov kept talking.

"Sir."

"Don't worry," he said to the other person. "Delay will be short, I think."

With hands zip-tied and attached to the metal girder, Natalie didn't have the freedom of movement afforded her father, so she had remained motionless as he inched up the wall only a few feet from her. She had no clue what he had in mind, and the other man was on the phone, still unaware of Mardy's actions.

In that moment before her dad took action, her attention shifted to the far corner. Draped from the windows above, the curtain of light shimmered gold and bright, but she saw a flash of movement on the other side of it, a form slicing through shadow.

She had known Eli for a number of years now, and never known him to draw attention to himself. In fact, most people looked right past him. When he worked, he did so methodically. When he talked, he didn't rush.

Never had she seen him move so quickly.

And her dad, with hands tied behind his back and feet strapped together at the ankles, moved quickly too. Bounding. Like a man in a sack race. It would have been comical, if not for the dread she felt.

The other man lifted his gun.

"Dad. Watch out!"

From the darkness, Eli Shaffokey charged into the frame of sunlight, head lowered, legs driving. He threw both arms around the man with the weapon, caught him in the side, and drove him into the oil barrel. The gun fired, its barrel licking the air with a brief flame, and the two men landed, rolled, wrestled for control. Beside them, the barrel wobbled, and the webcam tumbled onto the laptop's keyboard.

Eli pinned the man's right hand, but the other hand whipped across his cheek and sprayed blood. In the split second that Eli weakened, the gun came back into view.

When Mr. Hammond first pointed the Beretta at Mardy, Mardy figured sure enough, he was a dead man. Never once did he expect to see that older fella, salt-and-pepper hair, come flying into the picture from outta nowhere. Never once.

Still hopping forward, Mardy watched the two men tussle.

Watched the gun come back into view.

He arrived with a final bound. He dove for the firearm, headfirst, nothing to stop his fall, what with his hands still behind his back. His shoulder caught Hammond's arm midair, deflecting his aim so that a round fired and pinged off metal somewhere.

It was the last sound Mardy heard before his exposed skull cracked into the concrete floor, which left him unconscious atop small and wiry Mr. Hammond.

Detective Meade realized that Serpionov was playing him for a fool. While Meade had destroyed the hotel door, the Russian had carried on with his business from the comfort of large pillows and soft lamplight. Never bothered to answer the door. Never bothered to announce himself.

Cool as a cucumber, yes. But hardly typical behavior.

"Did you kill Abigail Stark?" he asked the man.

"Abby? She is flirty girl, I think."

"And Freddy C? Did you put that tag in his tooth?"

"I look like dentist?" Serpionov smiled. "I am like you, a police officer."

"No, you're not like me."

"Special unit. OMON. Do you know of this?"

"I do not." Meade's Glock was steady in his hand. "Was Freddy's tag poisoned? Isn't that the sort of thing you Russians are good at?"

"I love my motherland, but it is sad day in Moscow. We need change."

"Was it poisoned? Is that why he felt delusional?"

"He was delusional man." Serpionov shrugged. "*Nyet*. He had toothache, so it was chance to put implant in, what do you call it, his feeling? Or is it *filling?*"

"What about Natalie? You know where she is?"

Another shrug.

Meade made a quarter turn, eyes scanning the room again, focusing this time on the live feed playing on the laptop ten feet away. The feed looked like it was on its side, a blur of darkness and light, movement and shadow. Then the screen cleared so that a woman was distinctly visible, curled against a wall.

What sort of sick, demented—?

"Natalie," he said aloud.

Beside him, the Russian stretched out his phone. "Here, would you like to use? You can call for help, yes?"

Natalie had never seen Eli like this before. Leaving her father passed out on the floor, he

448

turned the gun on the man who had fired the shot and strung him to the oil barrel with baling wire from his tool bag.

"You can't stop it from happening," the man mocked.

Stop what? Natalie wondered, drawing her knees up to her chest.

"It's already set. It is what it is, old man. Accept it."

Eli stalked back over to him, shoved a rag into his mouth.

"What's he talking about?" Natalie said.

Kneeling beside her, Eli set down his bag and searched her eyes. "Do you trust me?" he asked.

"*¿Que?*"

"Don't reckon there's much time for explaining." He produced the scanner again, verified the presence of the tag in her mouth. "Yep, still there."

"Just cut me loose. We'll deal with the implant later."

"There's no later. Wherever ya go, that thing'll know it."

"OK. Fine. That Russian guy could be coming back any second, though, so let's just get *out* of this place."

A determined look darkened Eli's gray eyes. She wasn't sure how to read this expression on a man who had been nothing but kind and respect-ful to her over the course of their friendship. It frightened her.

"Eli?"

"Way I figure," he said, "I gotta yank that tooth."

"What're you . . . Have you gone *loco*?"

He spread a towel on the ground beside her, withdrew items from the bag, and laid them out. A small plastic tube. A bottle of water and a container of ibuprofen. The Maglite. Soft-jawed pliers. A ball-peen hammer. He nodded, clenched his jaw, and faced her again.

"This is in*sane,*" she said, trying to scoot away. "No! Undo my hands."

"Best if you don't fight me." He lifted the tube. "This here's an over-the-counter oral anesthetic. I just rub it in, and it'll soak down to the roots. Thing of it is, a good minute's gotta pass before it starts to work. If I'm gonna use it, it's gotta be now." He removed the cap, touched a finger to her lips. "Whatcha say?"

She bit at him. "Get away!"

He sat back, his eyes sad and his mouth down-turned.

"That's your only way to help?" she spat at him. "By hurting me? No, thank you. You know, that's the way it seems to go. God up there, arms folded, just watching us go through all sorts of horrible things. Is He too powerless to do anything? Or is it some sort of game to Him? I guess it's all right for murderers and rapists to run around doing whatever they want. Or for mothers to wander off and abandon their children. Whatever. What a joke."

"Shhh," Eli said. "No, Natalie. D'ya think I wanna hurt ya? No, I'm trying to help. Sometimes, see, sometimes pain's only so you don't have to face something worse. I need ya to trust me here. Will ya do that?"

"By letting you rip a tooth out of my head?"

"By helping you live. You got a choice, simple as that."

"No! Simple enough?"

"That thing in your mouth, it didn't just wander in on its own. Figure Magnus musta put it there last year. He tracked ya with it, and it's still got its antenna. It's still able to get orders, even from way off. Whatcha think you're here for now? And the others? Seems to me you're in a heap of trouble."

"Exactly." She cussed at him. "Get. Me. *Out*. Of here."

"I *wanna* get you outta here. Alive. Not in some body bag."

Her confusion and rage melted into desperation. She shook her head as moisture pooled in her eyes. She knew he was right, that Magnus had put the tag in her mouth. She knew there was some larger scheme behind her imprisonment here, a year to the day after her last point of capture.

Across from her, the man tied to the barrel was smirking. An eager look on his face. Anticipatory.

What had he said earlier? *It is what it is . . . Accept it.*

"Please, Natalie."

She peered into the eyes of Eli Shaffokey. She saw genuine love and concern, saw a man who hated the thought of what he was about to do but was willing to be hated, to be spat upon, and cursed if it could save her life.

"Will ya trust me?" he said. "Please, can ya do that?"

Biting her lip, she nodded. "OK," she said. "OK, let's do it."

Chapter Sixty-eight

Instinct took over.

The moment Detective Meade saw that offered phone, saw it aimed at his chest, he knew he had encountered a weapon small enough to match those $5.45 \times 18mm$ rounds. He'd read reports of such things confiscated in Eastern Europe a few years back, and a man had been murdered with such a phone in St. Petersburg, Florida, in 2004.

A dart gun?

No, this was a cell gun.

All this flashed through his head, and he dove for cover at the foot of the bed as Serpionov fired the first shot.

The weapon's bark was nothing compared to a Desert Eagle or a .45 Magnum, but it sounded vicious enough in this small space. On the opposite wall, the mirror over the dresser exploded into glittering shards.

Meade rolled onto his back, Glock held in both hands and pointed toward the bed. He waited for the Russian to show his face. At this angle, though, he could only see the pools of light thrown onto the ceiling by the nightstand lamps.

"You are fast," Serpionov said. "Or did I hit you?"

Meade honed in on the voice. He thought of lifting himself with his abs, just enough to peek over the mattress edge, and firing off a few shots that would pin the Russian back against the wall. From this awkward position, though, he might miss and cause collateral damage in the next room over.

Could he deal with the guilt of harming an innocent bystander?

He had already lost Freddy by not paying more attention.

"Your Glock," Serpionov said, "it is deadly weapon. So, it's a showdown, like in Old West. You have advantage, I think."

"What've you done to Natalie? Where is she?"

"I want to help people, same as you. Natalie is only one person."

One thing Meade knew for sure, he was open game if he stayed down here, and he had no idea how many rounds that cell phone had left.

Rolling onto his stomach, he nudged up lengthwise against the bedframe, lifted himself on his toes and free hand, and rocketed toward the hotel corridor in a low sprint. Two more rounds from the cell phone tore into the wall as he grabbed the splintered doorframe and swung around out of view of the room.

A three-inch sliver of wood had lanced the skin between his thumb and second finger. He groaned and pulled it out. Wiped the blood on his pant leg.

"You're free to go, Detective. *Do svidanya.*"

Meade moved back down the hall so that he wouldn't be vulnerable to a bullet through the wall. He wasn't so sure this weapon packed that much punch, but it was best not to risk it.

"If you leave, though, you'll miss the end of my story."

"What story, Serpionov?"

"Tragedy. Sacrifice. In the end, the world is safer."

As the man talked, Meade fished for his own cell. He would wait out here for backup, rather than being the one trapped in a room four floors up. He said, "So, tell me, is that what the laptop's for? You're writing your story there, with Natalie? What's your setting, huh?"

The mattress squeaked. Feet settled onto the hotel room floor.

"Come look. You know the place, I think."

Know the place? What?

"Natalie was there before. Magnus doomed her with special prototype in her tooth. It is only one, very dangerous. He let her go, but this time she'll die."

That was it.

Detective Meade knew he was being baited, but this man had killed before, and Meade couldn't let Natalie in that live camera feed become a victim to this man's twisted plot. He put his finger around the trigger, inched toward the doorway, and prepared to rush the hotel room.

Natalie had sat in a dentist chair before, received shots of local anesthetic, and felt her gums and lips go numb. She had survived. *No hay problema.*

But this was different, wasn't it?

Her entire body shook as fear and adrenaline shot through her, and she understood now why Eli had left her in constraints.

"Gotta open for me," he said. He had the black tube ready.

She spotted the gleam of light on the pliers, and her mouth clamped shut.

"Natalie, your messing round's just gonna make it worse. C'mon now, we don't got time."

"It's going to hurt, isn't it?"

"Reckon so."

She closed her eyes. "I'm scared."

"I'm trying to help you." He gripped her arm with a sudden intensity that caused her eyes to pop open again. "Ya put this off, you're gonna die. And it'll be a whole lot worse than any of what I gotta do."

"Why am I the one who ended up with this tag in my mouth?"

"Ya gonna ask questions or lemme deal with the problem?"

He was right. Of course he was right.

Modern technology had allowed mankind to play God, to know when a sparrow fell from the sky, to keep track of every hair on a person's head. It didn't act on its own, though. It simply responded to its commands and programs. The only way to fully trust such technology was to trust the one in control of it.

Who was in control here?

Lord, I've tried doing things on my own understanding, and I keep getting tripped up. I want You to have control. I trust You. I do. Please, help my unbelief.

"Do it *now*, Eli. Don't let me fight you. Do it *quick* and get it over with."

She tilted her head back and opened as wide as she could.

Without a word, he reached in with the soft-jawed pliers and applied them to the second-to-last molar on her lower right jaw.

"Paaaynekeeler," she said. Her tongue felt swollen.

"Too late for that."

"Whaaa?"

He had tears in his eyes. "Ya done took too long."

Her palms broke out in a sweat, and her knees rattled against each other. With no way to move her hands or feet, the pent-up energy quivered along her spine and through her shoulders. *OMG. Is this really happening?*

The pliers grabbed hold of the tooth and wiggled.

The pressure increased.

And then it was more than pressure. It was suffering. It was torture. Her entire jaw was caught in a clamp that twisted and cranked, until she thought the bone itself would dislodge from her skull. The pain drew black across her vision, and electricity seemed to spark and crackle along her nerves.

God, please!

He repositioned himself, with a knee against her sternum, and wiggled the pliers again, back and forth, back and forth. At first nothing seemed to happen, and then the roots started to give. Just a little. The same way she'd worked her baby teeth loose as a kid, wiggling, wiggling, until they seemed to just hang there.

Eli adjusted the pliers so that one end touched

the inside edge of the molar. He reached for the hammer.

"Nnaawh!"

He pounded it against the handle of the pliers.

"Aaarghhhhhh!"

Tears rolled down Eli's cheeks, as though he was crying for her, as though her pain was his own intensified.

He pounded the hammer again.

Craaaccck!

The pliers latched back on, and through her tears and the agony, she saw Eli grip the silver handles with both hands, plant his knee and elbow, and prepare himself for one mighty backward heave. She had chosen this path. She wasn't going to fight it now. She closed her eyes and prepared for the worst.

Lord, I TRUST YOU! *You work all things together for my good.*

Serpionov was out of bullets. Standing over the desk, he let his fingers play over the keys and enter the digits for the activation sequence.

The detective swung into his peripheral vision. "Get away from that," he shouted. "Or I swear, I'll shoot."

Serpionov reached for the Enter key.

And never even heard the gunshot that tore through the side of his skull. Never felt the key that was depressed by his falling head. Never saw the results of his handiwork on the screen.

Natalie screamed as the molar broke free from its socket in a spray of saliva and blood. The raw nerve in her lower jaw was a snake's fang hooked into her entire body and injecting pain, *pain,* PAIN beyond anything she knew possible.

Was this her big victory moment? Or a senseless exercise?

She wanted to die.

Dear God, I WANT *to trust you, but it hurts! Oh God,* IT HURTS!

Eli's pliers gripped the tooth. Through a pool of tears, she saw it there, off-white and dripping red. She was still bound and helpless, but by her own act of surrender. She quivered and wondered if this torment in her jaw was worth it.

The signal shot from the slender black Shield case, linking through the wireless network and cell provider to circling satellites, which bounced and triangulated that data around the planet, through ether and ozone, seeking for RFID tags that would respond. Traveling thousands of miles per second, the signal zeroed in on a field of limestone along a river, where tall grass and trees encircled a hut that contained a young woman whose tooth hid a bioglass tag and chip encoded with the label ST-1-12-1799-4328.

•••

Two seconds later, the tooth emitted a thin sharp crack, and clear liquid oozed through fissures in the dental composite.

It dripped from Eli's pliers. Struck the floor, bubbling and hissing.

Venom secretions from a serpent that had failed to reach its mark.

Chapter Sixty-nine

Eli severed her bonds with a razor knife from his tool bag. He propped her up, gave her a drink of bottled water, told her to rinse her mouth but not to swish, and to spit it out. He opened a capsule of Advil.

"Should help fight the pain," he said. "And the swelling."

Eyes closed, she washed down the pills. Her entire head was wrapped in fiery anguish, and her limbs felt limp, her thoughts woozy. She followed instructions without argument. Simply did as she was told. He pushed a wad of gauze back into the toothless gap, told her to bite down gently and hold it there.

Behind them, Mardy groaned and rolled onto his knees. He cradled his head and looked toward Natalie. He frowned. Blinked. Widened his eyes.

"S'OK, Dad," she mumbled.

"Mr. Flynn, why don't you get her outta here," Eli said. "Me, I'm gonna gather up my things and these bits of evidence. Nobody'd believe us otherwise."

Mardy stumbled, made it to his feet. He wrapped his arm around his daughter, and together they tottered out the door. Natalie winced with each movement, dragging her feet. The tall grass brushed her elbows. Birds chattered in the trees, seemingly without a care in the world. It was a beautiful day.

Natalie stopped and glanced back over her shoulder.

"Ya need to go slower, Duckie? Fine by me."

"Is Eli coming?"

"He's—"

A deep concussive sound like one hard bang on a bass drum shook the ground beneath their feet. The hut's walls bulged, and the glass panes exploded as gasoline and airplane fuel detonated, flaring red and hot and angry, flattening grass, and knocking father and daughter onto their backs. As Natalie tried to regain her breath, billows of gray-black smoke rose into the sky.

Chapter Seventy

October 10

On a Monday, in a wood-paneled, windowless room on the lower level of Legislative Plaza, the Health and Human Resources Committee reconvened. Reuben King had arranged for Detective Meade and Natalie Flynn to share all that had occurred ten days prior along the banks of the Cumberland River.

This was a closed meeting, and it looked to be a long morning. Before it was over, the future of House Bill 6336 would be decided.

Aye or nay.

Metro police officers guarded the doors. Sealed bottles of water waited on the tables, as well as freshly brewed coffee delivered by Black's Espresso.

The Metro detective gave his own account of the scheme used to coerce Representative King into supporting the bill under consideration. He described the violent tactics carried out against a number of individuals, resulting in multiple deaths and in a final conflagration during the early morning hours last Friday. Some of the guilty parties had already paid with their lives for their actions. Others were still free, and more arrests were sure to follow.

Despite a swollen right jaw, Natalie detailed her own knowledge of the event, confessing her involvement in the scheme, based on her belief that this bill could shield the small, the elderly, the helpless. She explained how, instead, her life had almost been sacrificed by the very use of such "lifesaving" technology.

"What I thought could be good has so much potential for evil," she said.

After the committee members had thanked her and expressed their sympathies, Meade and Natalie headed down the corridor to wait.

As chairman, Reuben tried his best to remain detached. He read the proposed bill aloud to his fellow legislators and said simply, "In an age of individualism, I believe that we need more community. I move that we strike this bill and craft one more suitable for the times in which we live."

The meeting was adjourned. From her chair in the sitting area near the bottom of the escalators, Natalie watched Reuben come down the hallway wearing an expression of weary relief. Creased black slacks showed off his long legs, and a tailored jacket draped his shoulders and white collared shirt. His chest pushed against a tie the same color as his eyes.

Almost twenty-nine years old now, he had a noble jaw and a solid nose framed by healthy black hair. Despite his youth, Natalie caught a sudden glimpse of him as a fifty-year-old man.

He would be just as handsome then.

Maybe more so.

"I'm headed over to discuss our decision with the governor," he told her. "Will you walk with me?"

She followed him through security into the Motlow Tunnel. A cocoon of polished limestone and fluorescent glare, the tunnel stretched beneath Charlotte Avenue and facilitated foot traffic between the Legislative Plaza and the State Capitol, where the governor's office was situated.

"So, what'd you decide?" she asked. "Or is it a secret?"

"I wanted to ask you the same thing."

"Huh?"

"You and me. Us."

She bit her lip. "I want *us* to work."

"Me too, Natalie. I'll do everything in my power to make sure that we do, but I need to know you're willing to take that risk along with me."

"Yes," she said, lips tingling. "I want to take that risk."

They reached the elevators at the end, and Reuben reached for her hand. His touch was warm, firm, slightly rough. And everything about it seemed right.

"Next week," he said, "up on the Plaza, we have the Southern Festival of Books. What's not to like? Authors, books, readers—all of it within a stone's throw from my office. So what do you say, honey? Will you go on a date with me?"

She leaned into him. "Absolutely, Mr. King."

Detective Meade watched the report on News-Channel 5 at four p.m. He nodded in satisfaction, ran a hand over his short hair. Then his thoughts turned to the new side project he was partnering on with Aramis. He'd had enough for one day. There would always be more work ahead, but this evening, he just wanted to share a quiet meal at home with Dawna and Dee.

Before things got wild and wooly again.

His phone rang, and he answered. "What now?"

It was an investigative clerk. "I'm looking at recent case files, combing through them for inconsistencies and loose ends. I'm reading over the data concerning a structure fire and explosion that resulted in two deaths along the Cumberland, at the old Cornelia Fort airfield north of the CSX train trestles."

"September 30th?"

"Yes, Detective. Only a week and a half ago."

"Go on," Meade said.

"In compiling and comparing accounts, fire marshals understood that two bodies would be recovered, Darius Hammond and Eli Shaffokey. After thorough searches of the scene and rubble, they found only one."

"What? How'd you find this out?"

"A clerical error perhaps, but it's all here in the file."

"Which one?"

"Sir?"

"Missing. Which one?"

"Eli Shaffokey. Mr. Hammond was identified, but there's no evidence of this other man. He's a vapor. I find nothing under that name—no courthouse records, no vehicle registration. Nothing. Not even a hit on Google."

"But he did janitorial work at Pastor Teman's church. They would've had him fill out a W4 for tax purposes."

"Already checked into it. Everything indicates he was paid in cash. Either way, Detective, Mr. Shaffokey's nowhere to be found."

In Her Ears

"I hated seeing my girl like that. Hated every minute of it."

"Oh, we never like to see our kids in pain. We want what's easy for them, what's fun and pleasant. That's not the way this world works, though."

"Not since way back when, I s'pose."

"Not since way back when, that's right."

"Got messed up from the get-go."

"And who gets blamed for all that happened as a result? Kids, it seems, find it easiest to blame their parents. It's been that way with each of my own. You love them, give them every opportunity to succeed, show them support, and let them grow. Yet if something goes wrong, who gets the brunt of it? Who gets yelled at and cursed? Why, at that point you keep loving them anyway. That's when love often speaks the loudest, in the midst of trial and temptation."

"I done the best I knew how. She oughta know that, dontcha think?"

"You did good."

"Was a close thing, though. Thought for certain I's gonna lose her."

"And look at her now, healing so quickly already."

"Figure she'll blame me on down the road?"

"For what?"

"All that she went through."

"It was out of your control. You did all you could."

"Reckon so."

"Your words'll stick by her, always there in her ears. She won't forget."

"S'pose that's good enough, eh?"

"Mind you, there'll come a day when you can't stop the inevitable. Tough as it is, you can't save them from everything, can you? That time, it comes for each and every one. But even then, perfect love casts out fear. Even then."

Chapter Seventy-one

March 2012

On the eighth day of the month, Governor Haslam signed House Bill 7374 into law, regulating the use of microchips in humans and thus protecting the homeless, the mentally challenged, the bedridden, and those who were too young to comprehend the ramifications of an encrypted lifetime device. Yes, technology had its benefits, but clear minds would keep it from running amok.

Representative Reuben King addressed the 2012 General Assembly and declared this a bipartisan victory, a triumph for the citizens of Tennessee.

Later, awash in the rich history of the State Library, he stood at the base of its spiral staircase and shook hands with his fellow committee members, other supporters, and even a few begrudging political foes. He received promises of support in the future, should he seek election in the Senate, and a few hints at favors that might be expected in return.

Oh, the joys of this vital process. So easy to become entangled in the churning machinery and grinding gears.

Yet democracy rolled along.

As the crowd thinned, the rich colors of the library's carpet, shelves, and vaulted ceiling came alive in the late-afternoon light. For the first time all day Reuben wasn't speaking or being spoken to, and he reveled in the moment.

Recent reports stated that Storinka Defense Systems was no longer a viable entity, its operations suspended indefinitely while under federal investigation. Shield Technologies was rebounding in the stock market under its new CEO, Jack Norwood, due in part to its modern RFID applications in home appliances. Darcy Page faced charges of extortion and conspiracy.

Meanwhile, the Nashville Rescue Mission filled beds and mouths in record numbers, in a city that attracted the needy with its moderate climate, friendly reputation, and volunteers willing to serve so generously.

"Representative King?"

He zeroed in on the person before him, a broad-shouldered man who stood slightly off-kilter on his artificial leg. "Bret Vreeland, you're looking good."

"Didn't think you'd remember my name. I'm impressed."

"Of course. I have all of your songs in my iPod."

"Wow." Bret nodded. "OK, I appreciate that. I was in the gallery during the assembly, heard every word. Took me a while getting down those narrow stairs afterwards, but here I stand. My wife and I, we're glad to have a man of integrity representing us and our kids. I'd like to think there are more like you around."

"Believe me, I couldn't do this alone," Reuben said.

"Sorry you got some shaky advice from the Temans. I want to believe the best about them, but we had a face-to-face with the pastor—Natalie, my wife, and I—and let him know we'd be looking for a church family where money's not polluting the way things're done. Listen, I won't keep ya. Here's something Sara put together, a coupla comments she thought you'd appreciate."

Reuben waited till Bret was gone, and then opened the note and read:

Today is Purim. On this date, the 14th day of Adar according to the Hebrew calendar, Jews celebrate Esther's success in working with the king to save her people from Haman's schemes. As they read the story aloud, the crowds drown out Haman's name with jeers and hisses.

Thanks to both you and Natalie for drowning out that same potential for evil in our state.

Reuben's thoughts leaped from the bombing of his Audi and his time in a hospital bed to that horrible hut, where his girlfriend escaped death by mere seconds, and where two men perished in the flames.

Liberty always came at a cost.

Give me liberty or give me death.

It was a truth that pulsed within the Constitution and the Declaration of Independence, and it was the heartbeat of this great land. As far as Reuben was concerned, the day that truth stopped beating was the day this country died.

The legislative chambers and corridors of power were almost empty, simmering in the sun's glow that spilled like honey through the western windows and arches.

"We have the place to ourselves," Reuben said.

"Security closes the doors in a few minutes, don't they? I guess we'd better call it a day."

"The day's not over yet, Natalie." He reached for her hand. "What happened in there earlier," he said, "the passing of this measure, it marks a turning point in our state's history, perhaps even in the decision-making process of our entire country."

"You did good."

"No matter what happens, we can't live in fear. The Lord is our shield."

"I want to believe that for myself, Reuben. It's just sometimes, I guess, I still wonder why He doesn't step in and do more."

"He's given some of that responsibility and power to us."

She nodded. "To you as a politician, especially."

"Not just to me," he said. "To you too. You're my Esther, you know that? Without you, I might've been convinced that the good of this technology outweighed the bad. In your own, uh, roundabout way, you convinced me just how dangerous it could be. In the wrong hands, it can be a nightmare."

"Well, I'm glad the nightmare's over."

"This one is. And if another comes along next month, next year, next decade, I hope that you and I can face it together."

Her heart skipped. "Together?"

At the foot of the spiral stairs, beneath the watching medallions of famed statesmen, writers, and poets, he knelt in the waning light. Still holding her hand, he said, "On such a momentous day, I still have a question to ask. Natalie Flynn, will you marry me? Will you please be my wife?"

"Your second wife, you mean?"

"My only wife."

She blinked, blinked again, sure that her eyeliner and mascara would run, but not worried either way. "*Si, corazon*," she breathed. "Yes."

Chapter Seventy-two

July

Natalie King applied makeup in front of the bathroom mirror. She felt like a little girl again back in her childhood home, with the butterfly stickers and the water-stained sink.

From childhood to adulthood and now back to Oak Ridge.

Talk about full circle, chica.

Despite its checkered past, the town was committed to healthy living. Efforts in that regard had been redoubled by the Department of Environment and Conservation. And this was Reuben and Natalie's town. This was where their memories had been born and would be born again.

A year after meeting, after a whirlwind romance and courtship, Natalie and Reuben had tied the knot in June and honeymooned along the sunny beaches in Destin, Florida. Now they were settling into their new home. From here, it was a ten-minute drive to her dad's place. He had found a new job as a salesman at American-Built Auto Sales. Her grandma wasn't far away in Tuckaleechee Cove. And Tuf was Tuf, working as a fitness instructor at the YMCA and taking classes at Nashville State. The cat who always managed to land on her feet.

Natalie and Reuben's place was a two-story, three-bedroom, and two-bath, set in a cul-de-sac on the quieter end of a subdivision. It boasted a two-car garage and a fenced backyard large enough for a toolshed and a small pool.

She loved being a wife, even if Reuben was more "guy-ish" than she had been prepared for by growing up with a sister. Those differences weren't all bad, of course. Some were pretty incredible.

The Kings were local figureheads, heralded by some, targeted by others. They took a few basic precautions, in light of all they'd been through.

They exercised their right to bear arms.

This address was unlisted.

There was no name on the mailbox out front.

Regardless, Natalie and Reuben jogged daily along these sidewalks and often stopped to chat with their neighbors. Even in exercise, Reuben was on the campaign trail. He genuinely cared about his constituents and the policies that affected their lives, and hardly a day went by when he wasn't working for them.

His goal? A run at the State Senate a year from now.

While he didn't believe that politics should be the territory of churches, he did believe that individual Christians should serve in politics.

Weren't all followers of Christ called to serve in their workplace as unto the Lord?

Reuben's workplace was in the legislature, and he would do his best. He chose an appropriate verse and hung it on a plaque beside his office desk:

For the king trusts in the Lord.
The unfailing love of the Most High will keep him from stumbling.

—Psalm 21:7

"You close to being ready in there?" Reuben called from the hall, his baritone voice bouncing off the hardwood floors.

Natalie dropped her arms. "News flash, Mr. King. I'm running late."

"That's not news," he said. "Just kidding. It's a social function, a bunch of palm-greasing and back-slapping. We'll be fine. Plus, we're the talk of the town, you know? The young representative and the hot schoolteacher."

Natalie had been hired at local Willow Brook Elementary, the very school she and her sis once attended. Considering the last year, it was strange how things circled back around. Calm amidst the chaos. The new school year started next month, and she was armed with lesson plans, projects, and field trips.

"Hot?" She tilted her head, put on an earring. "Who's saying that?"

"I am. I've seen your rain dance, remember?"

"That was for your eyes only, *corazon*."

"Don't worry," he said. "Being a politician, I know how to keep a secret. Anyway, nobody's going to die if we arrive two seconds late."

"Uh, Reuben?"

He looked her way through the open door.

She met his eyes in the mirror's reflection and slipped on the other earring. "I'm a . . . a little later than that."

His gaze turned quizzical.

"That's right," she said. "I'm, like, at least two weeks late."

"Two weeks?"

She emerged from the bathroom in a red dinner gown that hugged her hips and waist. In her hand was a white plastic object. "See for yourself. You know, for such an intelligent guy, it's amazing how dense you can be at times."

"You're—"

"Pregnant, *si*. I am with child. So much for the doctor's worries, huh? Looks like you, Representative King, are going to be a daddy."

With a whoop, he swept her up in his arms and spun around, then set her down gently. "Sorry. You don't think that I . . . That didn't hurt our baby, did it?"

"I'm sure it's OK. And I know you'll be a great dad. Better play it safe, though," she added with a smile, "and pamper us every chance you can get."

"Am I allowed to touch? I don't want to hurt you or—"

"Touch away," she said. "Our baby's in there, already growing. I bet I'll be able to squeeze into my skinny jeans a few more months, but will you still love me when I start bulging? I'm warning you, this belly's going to get epic."

"Bring it," he said, gesturing. "Honey, bring on the epicness."

"That's not even a word."

"Epicocity?"

She slapped his arm.

"Well, not to push," he said, "but *andale, andale.* We really should *vamonos.*" He pulled on a long black overcoat, buttoned it over his jacket and tie.

"I'll have to be careful tonight. No steep steps. No alcohol."

"I won't let you out of my sight."

"*Muy bueno.*" She stepped into her heels, adjusted the straps, and then stood and rested her arms on his shoulders. "But it's not all on you, is it?"

"It's not," he agreed. "We have someone good watching over us."

"Yep, and that's all I need to know. Let's go."

In Her Heart

"You reckon she suspects?"

"Bits and pieces."

"Seems she'd find a measure of comfort if'n she did."

"Oh, in her heart, she senses it. I've written of it in my letters, and she's read how she might, on any given day, rub shoulders with angels unaware."

"Poor thing, she thinks I'm dead and gone."

"To her, you are. Eli's gone, and you'll never again appear in that form."

"She thinks I done burned up in that fire."

"A bit of irony for you, since you're one of the unfallen. Fire won't ever be your eternal destination. Those ones who did rebel are much smaller in number, and because of them, the veil remains in place for the time being."

"Too bad, eh? Just think of the stories I could tell my girl."

"*My* girl, to be precise. I love her more than life. Remember, understanding comes to those who have the eyes to see and ears to hear. Best that she seeks it out on her own. I never leave my children without guidance or hope, and there's something to be said for mystery and wonder."

"For heaven's sakes, I cooked her grits."

"You sure did."

"Drove her 'round in my camper."

"Safest driver in town."

"Did a fair share of dental work."

"All right, all right. This isn't a job interview."

"Just sayin'."

"She's still your girl to guard. You've watched over her throughout her life and never overridden her power of choice. I know there are some who view free will as a curse, but it's actually a gift, a chance to partner with me in this dance."

"Well then, with your permission, reckon I best get back to dancing."

Acknowledgments

Jonathan Clements (Wheelhouse Literary Group)—for your perseverance and faithfulness. You add a human touch to an often-heartless process.

Art Ayris and Steve Blount (Kingstone Media Group)—for your patience and belief. After I missed my deadline, you could've changed the title to *Two Months Late*. I'm so glad that you didn't, and I look forward to working on more books together.

Mona Gambetta (Mona Roman Advertising)—for working with me to find images and colors that capture the feel of my books. You've dressed up my babies nicely.

Liz Calledo and Melissa Penaflor (Bluepen Publishing Solutions)—for editing these words with an eye for detail, when my own eyes had gone blurry and bloodshot.

Carolyn Rose Wilson (wife of twenty-one years)—for joining me on autumn walks and in times of desperate prayer, for loving and believing in me even when visible evidence suggested it was time I set my writing aside. You're my babe!

Cassie and Jackie Wilson (daughters)—for maturing as young women, for showing responsibility, positive attitudes, and a desire to keep looking forward. May you keep your eyes open to see God's goodness and His purposes for you.

Shaun Wilson (brother)—for regular phone calls, insights, and advice. I look forward to our next adventure, wherever it may lead, and I'll never forget your birthday gifts to me. I see them every single day.

Matt and Heidi Messner (brother-in-law and sister)—for your persistence in pursuing your callings and gifts. I still can't believe we were in Alaska together. I wonder where we'll go next.

Mark Wilson (father)—for being a great dad and friend. Looking back, I remember learning from you how to laugh, love, and so much more.

Deborah Mart (mother-in-law)—for clinging to hope, even when circumstances seem grim. You've poured out your life to us in so many ways over the years.

Barbara Guise (grandmother)—for your love and generosity. We miss Grandpa. You're an anchor in our family, and I'm so thankful for you.

Elizabeth Daniels (sister-in-law)—for explaining to me the educational system and the teacher's life. You're the closest person I know to a Natalie Flynn. You rock!

Sean Savacool (family friend)—for continued friendship, even though the parameters have changed. Congrats on your growing success with Eastern Block, and on the upcoming marriage to Jillian!

Louis and Jamie White Harrison (family friends)—for sharing my love of sports, food, music, and books. You're the epitome of hospitality, and we're blessed to have you as neighbors. Go, Preds!

Kyle Saylors and Erica Lane Saylors (family friends)—for including us on some of your road trips. We have such a great time with you two, whether it's in serious or humorous moments. We're cheering for you in film and music.

Vaughn Forbes (family friend)—for believing all these years, and for investing in my writing through coffee, cash, and prayers. You've helped us over more than one hump.

Ted Dekker, Steven James, Kevin Kaiser, Robert Liparulo, and Tosca Lee (friends and authors)—for including me in a great weekend at the Ragged Edge, and for personal encouragement and admonishment at points along the journey.

River Jordan (friend and author)—for your passion and diligence. You've given your readers prayers and miracles, saints and messengers, and even a little gin. What treats! And hey, Owen's not a bad guy, either.

Matt Bronleewe, Kevin Kaiser, and Chris Well (The Council of Four)—I'm oldest but far from wisest. Thanks for allowing me to let down my hair, gray hairs and all.

Ray Blackston, Ninie Hammon, and Doug Peterson (friends and authors)—for crafting honest and powerful stories. I'm honored to be in the same fold.

Joe Keleher (friend and author)—for chats about life, faith, books, and travel. Thanks also for details regarding teaching and mercury poisoning.

Representative Glen Casada (Tennessee House of Representatives)—for providing insights into the process over a cup of hot coffee. This book's errors are my own.

Erin, Brad, and Lesa at Roast Inc. (coffee retailers)—for pouring some of the best java around. Thanks for letting me include your great shop in the story.

Kimberly Robertson (reader)—for timely words regarding the underbelly of the political monster, and of the motives that often dirty its toes.

The 77s, The Black Keys, The Classic Crime, Coldplay, Eastern Block, Chris Sligh, Smiletron, and Switchfoot—for searing and soothing my eardrums, while I stared at the screen into the long hours of the night.

Friends and fans (you know who you are)—for reading, reviewing, and promoting my books. Your e-mails mean a lot. Your prayers are appreciated. And I hope we meet again in my next novel, if not at an actual book event.

Father God—for watching over us and keeping an eye upon the sparrows.

Jesus the Son—for giving perfect love that casts out all fear.

The Holy Spirit—for providing unity and the power of a sound mind.

About the Author

Eric Wilson is the author of eleven previous novels, including *1 Step Away*, *The Best of Evil*, and the *New York Times* best-selling *Fireproof*. He isn't presently fitted with a microchip, at least not as far as he knows.

Center Point Large Print
600 Brooks Road / PO Box 1
Thorndike ME 04986-0001 USA

(207) 568-3717

US & Canada:
1 800 929-9108
www.centerpointlargeprint.com

82 JUL 1 7 2014
41 DEC 1 7 2014
15 JAN 2 0 2015
48 FEB 0 9 2015
60 MAR 1 0 2015
12 APR 2 8 2015
122 MAY 1 8 2015
17 JUN 2 2015
82 SEP 1 0 2015

33 OCT 0 1 2015
127 MAY 1 2 2016
42 MAY 2 7 2016
82 NOV 1 7 2016
82 SEP 6 2018
82 MAR - 5 20
13 MAR - 2 202
82 JUN 2 3 202
130 JUL 1 8 202